NOT BROKEN *JUST BENT*

NOT BROKEN JUST BENT

by Amanda Graham

CONSCIOUS CARE PUBLISHING PTY LTD

Not Broken Just Bent

First Published 2015 by: Conscious Care Publishing Pty Ltd
PO Box 776, Rockingham, WA 6968, Australia
Phone: (61+) 1300 814 115
www.consciouscarepublishing.com

First Edition printed December 2015.

Conscious Care Publishing publishes in a variety of print and electronic format and by print-on-demand. Some material included with standard print versions of this book may not be included in e-books or in print-on-demand. If this book refers to media such as a CD or DVD that is not included in the version you purchased, you may download this material at www.consciouscarepublishing.com

National Library of Australia Cataloguing-in-Publication entry:
Author: Graham, Amanda 1967 -
Not Broken Just Bent / by Amanda Graham
ISBN 9780987409782 (Paperback), 9780987409706 (Hardback), 9780987409799 (Digital)
Graham, Amanda 1967 -
Hope Connolly, Freedom Images, Cover Image.
Rocky Hudson, Editor

Printed by Lightning Source
Typeset & cover design by Conscious Care Publishing Pty Ltd

ISBN: 978-0-9874097-8-2

To Carl Nield.
You weren't just my cousin,
you were my mate and
I miss you every day.

BEN | 1

Knock, knock. "Richo, you ready? Taxi's here."

"Yeah mate," I say as I open my door and join Davo, Kiwi and Rabbit and we walk outside and get into the taxi waiting to take us to The Pub. This is the first week of a fourteen week course in Perth and our first night out. I have to admit I'm ready to have a few drinks and let loose because this week has been brutal and by all accounts it's going to get worse, a lot worse.

"So who's going to get laid tonight?" laughs Rabbit.

I just laugh along with the guys and listen to them bragging about what they are going to do tonight with any willing woman. It doesn't take long before the taxi is pulling up outside The Pub. The Pub is smallish inside but the beer garden is a decent size and because it's February the weather is great, so we grab a few beers and sit down at one of the benches near the bar. It's a great spot because we can get drinks quickly and we have a good view of everyone as they walk by us.

"Fuck me drunk, will ya look at the tits on that one," sighs Kiwi. "What I wouldn't do to have my face buried in between those lovelies."

I look to my right and I see a woman with long blonde hair, a tiny waist and the longest legs I have ever seen; she is wearing white shorts and a red tank top. Her top is so small that if she leans forward her tits will definitely fall out. Note to self, keep a watchful eye on that one as the night progresses.

Not long after we get there the band starts up, they do covers and I have to say they're pretty good. People are dancing on the dance floor inside and anywhere they like in the beer garden, which again is good for me because I have a great viewing spot and the majority of the dancers are women.

It's my shout so I line up at the bar. I'm in my own world when I hear two women in front of me arguing. Normally I steer clear of women when they argue because they can become raving bitches — I should know I have two sisters — but one of the women is so damned funny I can't help but listen.

"Did your dress come with that scowl or did you have to pay extra?" the funny one says to the other.

"What's your problem?"

"The problem is that you spilt your drink over my friend, ruined her top and didn't apologise."

"And?"

"And you need to apologise."

She leans towards the funny one, looks around her and mumbles, "Sorry."

"Now that wasn't so hard, was it? But don't worry we won't ask for you to replace the ruined top because the way you dress you look like an escapee from Whore Island. Have a nice night," she says, smiling, as she turns and guides her friend toward The Pub. The other woman just stands there with her mouth wide open and I can't help the roar of laughter that is coming from me.

After a few more rounds we decide to go inside and watch the band. I survey the dance floor and notice the funny girl from the bar is dancing, she has her back to me, she's a good dancer and has all the moves to go with that smart arse attitude. I stand there watching her for a while, then it looks like she has bumped into someone by accident, they look at each other, smile and mouth 'sorry' and she shuffles to her left, giving me a view of her dance partner. It's as if time stands still, the woman she is dancing with has the most beautiful smile that lights up her whole face, and she dances with such confidence and it looks like she doesn't care who is watching. She has deep red hair and a body to die for, curvy with a decent set of tits that bounce when she moves. I can feel my dick stirring in my jeans and I can't take my eyes off her.

I feel a soft hand on my right arm and as I turn my head I notice the girl with the tiny red top smiling up at me. "Hi, I'm Jenna, you wanna dance?"

Normally she's my type, but at the moment I can't keep my eyes off the curvy red head on the dance floor. I know I'm a good looking man, six foot two, with brown hair and eyes, and a good body as a result of my daily gym workouts. My tattoos seem to really turn on the opposite sex, so I'm no stranger to female attention.

I smile back at her. "Sorry, not tonight ,but I'm sure Kiwi would love to dance with you." I turn to Kiwi. "Jenna this is Kiwi, Kiwi this is Jenna." I guide Jenna to Kiwi's side and then resume my position and go back to watching the curvy red head.

A short time later I feel an elbow in my ribs.

"Richo, it's not like you to sit back and watch for this long, if you see something you like you usually go after it," says Davo.

"I will when I'm good and ready," I say as I take another swig of my beer. I try to catch the red head's eye but either she doesn't notice me or she's ignoring me. I finish my beer, hand Davo the empty bottle and decide to make my move. As I step onto the dance floor the band starts playing Bruno Mars' *Locked Out of Heaven*, a great song with an amazing up tempo beat. I start to make my way over to where the red head is dancing, but the floor is packed and I'm finding it hard to get to her. After a little while I find myself behind her and I just stop and stare; she moves so sexily, I forget to breathe. I shake my head as I come back to the here and now and gently place my hands on her hips. I can feel her body tense but then quickly relax. I take this as a good sign so I move my body closer to hers and start to move with her. I feel her start to turn around and I'm a little concerned until I see that she is smiling up at me. She is more beautiful up close and I'm lost in her eyes, they're a deep brown with flecks of gold and it's like they are looking right into my soul. She slowly runs her hand up my abs to my chest, the whole time not breaking eye contact. She grabs my shirt and I think she is going to pull me in for a kiss when I feel this sharp pain in my groin and I buckle forward as I fall to the floor and land in the foetal position cradling my burning balls. I seriously doubt I will ever be able to father children after the kneeing I just received. I can hear myself let out a small scream but it's a few octaves higher than it normally would be. I can hear gasps of shock and laughter all around me as I try to calm myself down enough to stand up and get the fuck out of here. After what seems a lifetime I sit up and look at her and I really wish I hadn't because I don't think I have ever seen a woman so angry in all my life.

2 | CARLY

"Don't you ever fuckin' touch me without an invitation!" I yell at the douchebag that was grinding into me. Who does he think he is? Doesn't anyone say hello anymore? I grab Nicole and walk to the bar to get a drink. When we get to the bar I turn around to see some guys around him laughing and trying to help him up. Nicole is my best friend and has been since day one of high school. I turn to her. "What the fuck?"

"Chica, that was hilarious, I could see him circling you like a shark, trying really hard to get to you, but I never thought he'd just grind on in there without saying hello or even at the very least making eye contact first," she laughs.

That guy really picked the wrong girl tonight: I have personal space issues and my father taught me how to defend myself, and clearly I learnt well because my harasser was a big guy, definitely over six foot, with a solid build, and he went down like a bag of shit. The old saying must be correct, the bigger they are the harder they fall.

Nicole and I walk to the back of the beer garden for a bit of fresh air and so I can calm down. We turn our backs to the crowd because a lot of them are staring and more than likely talking about what I just did. There is a small fence that we lean on and try to figure what just happened.

"Seriously, Nicole, why did he think that was ok? I'm so fuckin' angry right now I could scream." I take a long drink of my cider. Before he touched me I had a nice buzz from the cider but now I have sobered up and I'm not a happy bunny.

"Try not to let it ruin your night. Let's have a few more drinks and then get back on that dance floor, the band is awesome and I want to shake my groove thing some more," laughs Nicole.

We lean against the fence having a laugh, then we are interrupted. "Nicole, it's great to see you again."

"Is there a full moon tonight?" mumbles Nicole. "What do you want Tom?" Nicole turns to face Tom Holden.

Nicole had a one night stand with Tom about three months ago, and she pretty much regretted it the moment they got back to her house. From what Nicole said, Tom bigged himself up, saying he would be the best lover she would ever be with, and he hoped she had taken her vitamins because he could go all night. She said he was a great kisser, so she thought she was in for a treat. They got into her room and he stripped his clothes off quickly, leaving Nicole just standing there while he settled on her bed and told her to hurry up. She took off her clothes and when she climbed on the bed he tried to push her head down so she could give him a blow job and when she told him maybe later he wasn't too happy. They kissed for a little longer with general groping but nothing to get her too wet. She was about to call it a night when Tom put on a condom, climbed on top of her, and without warning thrust inside her. Nicole said because she wasn't very wet it hurt a bit, but she was hoping it would get better. Unfortunately she never got the chance to find out. Less than a minute after he first thrust into her he was done. Tom rolled off Nicole, blew out a breath and said with a smile, *'Babe that was amazing. Give me five minutes and you can give me that blow job.'* Nicole got up off the bed, threw his clothes at him and told him to get out. After he tried to talk her around he finally gave up and called for a taxi.

"Babe don't be like that. We had an amazing time, and I for one would like a repeat." Tom says this with a smirk that I believe he thinks is sexy, but it makes him look like a creep.

Nicole's face is white with rage. "You have to be fucking kidding me. You and I remember that night very differently. You weren't happy when I wouldn't give you a blow job, there was next to no foreplay and you were a Captain-Come-Quick, you blew your load within a minute of penetration."

"I think you have me confused with someone else. It was an awesome night."

"I could agree with you but then we'd both be wrong. Tom, it's never gunna happen so see ya later," says Nicole as she turns her back on him.   Luckily Tom takes the hint and leaves. We stand there in silence for a while, then Nicole says, "I've had enough. Are you ready to go?"

"Yeah come on lets go."

Nicole and I grab a taxi and go back to her place. Even though

I live with my parents I have my own room at Nicole's in case I pick up a guy. It would be bad form to take someone back to my parents' house; I'd have to try to be quiet while doing my thing, and then get him out before my dad woke, or heaven forbid do the walk of shame in the morning.

We get comfy on Nicole's lounge and engage in our usual debrief of the night's activities, we burst into laughter that quickly turns into hysterics. Just as we are settling down I hear my mobile go off.

I stop abruptly and look at the time, it is 2.15 am, and nothing good comes of a call at that time of the morning. As I grab my phone I don't recognise the number. Panic sinks in as I press the answer button."H..he..hello."

"Is this Carly?"

I nod unable to speak.

"Hello, are you there? Is this Carly?"

I weakly reply, 'Yes.' I can't stop shaking, I hold out my hand for Nicole and she takes it immediately and then pries the phone out of my other hand.

"Hello this is Nicole, Carly's friend. I have you on speaker, how can I help you?"

"Were you out with Carly tonight?"

"Yes I was, why?" Nicole asks with a curious look.

"It's about an incident that took place on the dance floor tonight."

I see red and start yelling, "If you're calling to say that you're coming to arrest me for defending myself against that douche that had his hands all over me you have another think coming. If he intends to press charges then so do I."

"No, that's not what this call is about."

"What the fuck is going on, who are you and how did you get my number?"

"George gave my mate your number."

My heart stops. "H..how do you kno..know George?"

"I don't, he was at the pub and gave your number to one of my mates."

"Why would he do that?"

"Because I am the guy from the dance floor"

"If you're after an apology, you'll be waiting a long time!" I yell.

"I'm not."

"Then what do you want, dickhead?"

"Ben."

"What?"

"My name is Ben."

"I don't give a toss what your name is, what do you want?"

"I would like to get to know you."

"You can't be serious. You got to know my knee on a very personal level tonight. How'd that work out for ya?"

He coughs. "I have to admit that it hurts like a Mother but no other girl has stood up to me like that before and even though my balls feel like they are in my throat I can't stop thinking about you."

"That will pass."

He laughs. "You're so feisty"

"Hanging up now." I press end, turn my phone on silent and throw it on the lounge. Nicole and I just stand there staring at each other dumbfounded by what had just happened.

Nicole utters the words that I have been silently saying, "Fucking George."

I go my room, change into my tank top and boxers, grab my iPod and headphones and press play. *Super Massive Blackhole* by MUSE thumps into my ears. Not exactly the type of music to go to sleep to but I doubt I will be getting much sleep tonight anyway. I collapse on my bed and keep saying over and over, "What the fuck!"

As predicted, I didn't sleep very well. In the morning I walk out into the kitchen and Nicole has just boiled the kettle, she holds up a cup and I nod, she hands me a cup of tea as she sits next to me. "You look like shit."

"Cheers Nicole, I love you too."

She just laughs and asks me what my plans are for the day.

"I have my game of softball at 1 pm. Do you fancy catching a movie tonight? I just want to relax and not have to think."

"Yeah sounds good to me, let me know what time."

I finish my tea and go to my room to get changed. I have a few clothes, shoes and toiletries at Nicole's so I don't have to wear last night's clothes. I hug Nicole goodbye and then get in my car to go home.

As I turn down my street I can see *HIS* car in the driveway. I grip the steering wheel and drive slowly, trying unsuccessfully to calm down. I throw open the front door, storm past my mum, chanting, "Fucking

George." I wrench his bedroom door open and yell, "What the fuck? Why did you give that arsehole my number?" George jerks his head up off the pillow, smirks, rolls onto his side and leans his head on his elbow. By this time my mum is standing next to me.

"Why?"

"Coz I saw you knee him in the balls and I thought he didn't deserve it. I was hoping he would press charges and I would be extremely happy to assist him with that little venture. It would be my absolute pleasure. I would definitely be a witness for him if it went to trial."

"I can't believe we are related, you have done nothing but make my life a living hell. JUST. LEAVE. ME. ALONE!" I scream.

I storm to my room, slam the door shut, fall on the bed and proceed to break down. How could my own brother do that to me? The biggest mistake I ever made was being born. The day I was born our dad brought George to the hospital to see Mum and meet me, his new baby sister. Mum was holding me when dad and George entered the room, she called out to George to give her a cuddle but he refused and just stood in the doorway behind Dad. Mum asked Dad to take me and then got out of bed and crouched in front of George, pulling him into her arms. George turned his head in my direction and said, "Why did you have to have her, everything was fine til she came along." I was only 2 hours old, I didn't stand a chance.

There is a knock at my door "P..pp..please go away M..M..Mum," I say.

She doesn't listen, she never does. Mum sits down on the edge of my bed and asks what happened. I explain the night in detail to her, knowing full well George would have made me out to be in the wrong. I don't know why I'm surprised but she tells me that she thinks I overreacted and I had no business kneeing that guy like that. Typical. I just look at her with disbelief. She's OK with a random guy grinding into me? WTF? I seem to be saying that a lot lately. It looks like she has taken George's word over mine, again.

I spend the morning calming down and after lunch get ready for my game. I can take all of my aggression out on the ball. I'm warming up with my team and having a laugh with a few of them when I look up and notice a guy standing next to the net behind home plate staring in my direction. I'm too far away to make out his features so I go back to what I'm doing, but every time I look up he seems to be staring at me and smiling. When we run in to start the game he's gone so I think nothing of it. We take the field first and they get in two runs. I am fourth at bat and we have loaded bases. There is a reason I bat where I do, I usually hit at least one home run per game. The first two pitches are balls, and this really pisses me off because before I got up to bat her pitching was fairly straight down the middle. Unfortunately pitchers on the opposing teams try to walk me instead of letting me hit the ball. I get it, but really, it is so damned frustrating. The third pitch is a strike, finally, I've got my eye in now. Just as she is winding up to send in the fourth pitch this voice comes out of nowhere, "Come on Carly, smash it." I turn to look because I vaguely know that voice but I can't see where it is coming from. Whoosh, "Strike two." Shit I need to concentrate. My coach yells at me to get my head in the game. The next pitch is straight through the middle, I swing at the ball and it goes flying over the right fielder's head. Even though I'm right-handed I have positioned my feet and swung just a little late. The opposition wasn't expecting it. Home run with loaded bases, just what the doctor ordered. As I round third base the coach waves me home, and when I touch home base my team members are there to slap my hand and pat me on the back. As I reach for my drink another hand reaches for it at the same time. I start to straighten up and apologise because I think I have picked up the wrong one, and that's when I see his face. It's the guy from the pub.

"What are you doing here?"

"I heard softball was played here every Saturday and decided to check it out, imagine my luck when I saw you. By the way, awesome home run."

"Um, thanks."

"Nelson are we keeping you from something? Your team is waiting for you."

"Carly Nelson, good to know," he says with a smirk.

"I'm not interested, please leave and by the way, lose my number."

I run past coach on the way to the field. "Thanks for giving that arsehole my surname."

He doesn't leave and my game is not the same anymore, he really gets under my skin and has distracted me. By the end of the game he and coach seem to be best buddies and coach even invites him for a drink in the club house. Shoot me, just shoot me now. I try to sit as far away from him as I can, but he always finds a way to sit next to me. In the end I have had enough of playing musical chairs, I get up and say goodbye to my team, grab my gear and walk out to the parking lot.

As I get to my car there is a hand on my shoulder. I swing around, "Didn't you get the message last night or are you a bit simple? I don't like to be touched so take your hand off me this second or I will do more damage to your balls."

"I just wanted to talk to you and apologise for my behaviour last night. I was pretty drunk last night and I don't know why I didn't talk to you first. For what it's worth, I am sorry."

"Fine, whatever. I have to go now."

"Can I take you out to dinner some time?"

"Are you high? What makes you think that I want to go out with you? I am struggling being in your presence at the moment. Goodbye."

"Ben."

"What?"

"My name is Ben."

"Seriously, I don't care what your name is." I put my gear in the boot and then get into my car. I look up and he is smiling and waving at me. He must have been dropped on his head or something as a baby. I laugh as I drive away.

I call Nicole when I get home and we decide on a movie and time for tonight. I jump in the shower, wash my hair and get ready. I am pleased we are having a quiet night because I can wear comfy clothes and flat shoes, my feet are going to love me.

We buy our tickets, drinks and food and settle in our seats near the middle of the cinema. Nicole and I sit there chatting away as the cinema starts to fill up. We are in our own world, not taking too much notice of the other patrons, when I hear a voice behind me. I shake my head. "You have to be fucking kidding me." I turn around and there he is with a few other guys that I vaguely recognised from last night. "Either you are stalking me or you have planted a tracking devise on me somewhere."

"Carly, what a coincidence," he says with a huge smile.

"You really are a slow learner if you think I am going to believe that you just happened to be at the same movie that we are at."

"Ben."

"Seriously, do you have Tourette's? Why do you keep saying your name?" I say as his mates laugh.

"Because when you think of me I want you to know my name. And Carly, you will think of me," he says with a wink.

"Someone thinks very highly of himself and honey, you're not all that. I think I am going to have to talk to you like you are a five-year-old because that's the only way I am going to get through to you. You and I are *NEVER* going to happen, I don't know any other way to get it to sink in."

"Oh we will," he says with another wink.

"I think you need to see a doctor coz not only do you have Tourette's, you have a problem with your eye, it keeps twitching and makes you look simple."

"She's got you there, Richo," his mates laugh.

Just then the lights dim and the previews start. Thank god for that, I turn to the screen and try to watch the movie. It's not easy because I can feel his presence behind me. The movie finishes and we get up and walk out as quickly as possible, but we aren't quick enough. He is there just outside the only exit with his mates. I turn to Nicole and just shrug.

Nicole looks at me and says, "Carly he's pretty cute and seems really into you. I know he did a stupid thing last night, but he has apologised and asked if he could take you out to dinner. Don't you think you could just ease up on him a little?"

I glance over and take my first real look at him. He looks about 6 foot tall, brownish short hair, clean shaven, neatly dressed, tattoos and very good looking, but this has to be a windup because I am an average looking girl. I am 5 feet 6, brownish/reddish hair, hazel eyes and a bit chubby. Not what a guy that looks like him usually goes for. No, it has to be a bet or something and he can't win because I keep turning him down, that has to be it. I shake my head at Nicole and whisper, "Not gunna happen."

"You have to let it go sometime, it's been 18 months, Carls. When are you going to start living again and believing you deserve to be happy?"

"I'm not ready, I lost myself once and I will not let that happen again. He controlled everything I did, said or wore, and that fucker fed me up so he thought no other guy would be interested in me. He didn't believe me when I said that he was the only one that I loved and wanted. I know I was never skinny but I was happy with my body, then that all changed. I understand that was his insecurities that he projected onto me, but I was too young and naïve to do anything about it."

"I doubt Shaun would have been able to treat you like that if you weren't already beaten down by George. You expected Shaun to protect you and be there for you. He was just as bad as George, honey. George physically beat you and Shaun emotionally beat you, you couldn't escape," Nicole says with a sad look.

"That's why I am better off on my own with random hook-ups, no expectations, just a mutual need that is met and we don't have to see each other again."

"It's just sad that's all."

"It is what it is. Come on, let's go and please don't engage in a conversation with him. Say goodbye if you have to, but don't strike up a conversation."

"Ben, his name is Ben."

"Not you too. OK, Ben. Please don't strike up a conversation with Ben. There, are you happy?" I say as I roll my eyes.

We walk outside. Just about everyone has gone but unfortunately Ben and co. are still here. We walk past them and he jogs to catch up to us. I hug Nicole goodbye. As his mates walk her to her car I watch to make sure she is ok; there are three of them and only one of her and it makes me feel a bit uneasy. I watch her get into her car and start to drive away. I turn to my car and he says, "They were just making sure she got to her car safely, they are good guys and wouldn't hurt a fly."

"Well I don't know them, or you, so excuse me if I'm a little cautious."

"We could rectify that, let me take you out for dinner, coffee, anything, I just want to get to know you."

"Not gunna happen."

"Are you a lesbian?"

I open my car door and swing around to face him, poking my finger in his chest. "And that there is one of the reasons you're an arrogant, obnoxious, son of a bitch. You think coz I won't go out with you that I am a lesbian. Could you be any more conceited?"

He puts his hands up as a sign of surrender "Sorry, sorry, you're right, I must have Tourettes, it just came out."

"I don't want this," I say, moving my hand between him and me, "it's not going to happen."

Just as I get the last word out he grabs my shoulders and crashes his mouth down onto mine. I try to pull away but he has a firm hold. I can't knee him because he has conveniently positioned himself on the other side of my car door. It looks like he learnt something after all. I finally get myself free, I am speechless, and I have to say that doesn't happen often. He just stands there grinning.

"Arsehole," is all I manage to say. I get in my car and slam the door shut. He just stands there smiling as I drive away. How the hell did that happen? I thought I made myself very clear and Ben just ignores everything I say and kisses me anyway. Holy shit, I just used his name. When did he become Ben and not him?

I toss and turn all night, I can't stop thinking about that kiss. My alarm wakes me up at 7am. I groan as I roll out of bed and make my way to the bathroom. I lock the door and make sure the water temperature is just right before I step under the shower. As I start to wash my body my thoughts drift back to the kiss. I feel butterflies in my stomach, I haven't felt like this for such a long time and I have to admit it scares me. I start to wash my hair and try to forget about Ben. There you go, I'm using his name again.

I am one of those lucky people who love their job. I have worked as a beautician in a busy salon for the last 3 years. I am booked up every day and I love my clients.

My day is going great, I'm having a fantastic time with my clients and the music is pumping through the salon. My stomach is telling me it's nearly lunch time and I have one more client booked in before I can take a break. I check that my room is set up for my next client, then my colleague Megan appears at the door. I look up and ask if my client is here and Megan tells me no, she called to cancel, but that there is someone out the front who would like to see me. I follow her out to see a woman holding a beautiful bouquet of yellow and orange flowers. I smile and ask if I can help her.

"Are you Carly Nelson?" she asks.

I nod and she passes me the bouquet. I ask who they are from and she says there is a card, and with that she smiles and says goodbye. I open the card and can't believe my eyes. The flowers are from Ben. This is getting weird. How does he know where I work? I'm starting to get worried now and believe that he might be stalking me.

At the end of the day I go out the back and get the flowers while Megan locks up the salon. On the drive home I keep looking at them, they smell beautiful and I don't know if it was chance or he knew somehow, but yellow and orange are my favourite colours. I have a feeling he knew because most girls like red or pink. So I'm pretty sure someone is feeding Ben information about me and I think I know who it is. Fuckin' George.

I pick up my bag and the flowers and start to walk inside. My neighbour calls out to say hello and as I return his wave my phone rings. I answer it without checking the number.

"Good afternoon, Carly. How was your day?"

I pull the phone from my ear to take a look at the number, it's blocked.

"Who is this?"

"Do you like the flowers?"

I sighed, "Yes, I do, they are beautiful, but this has to stop, it's gotten really creepy. I'm going to ask you a question and I would appreciate the truth."

"Of course."

"How did you know I played softball, that I would be at the movies, and where I work?"

"Ummmmm, I spoke to George and he told me. When he gave my mate your number the other night he said he was your brother and if I needed to ask him anything that I was to call him anytime, so I did and he has been letting me know things about you because you won't give me the time of day."

"WHAT. DID. HE. SAY. ABOUT. ME?" I yell.

"Wow what has gotten you so angry?"

"JUST. TELL. ME."

"Wow, calm down. All he told me was where you play softball, the movie, where you work and what gym you belong to, that's all. What has gotten you so angry?"

"Not that it's any of your business, but George and I hate each other and he has no right feeding you information about me." I can feel the tears start to well up. When is George going to just leave me alone and let me live my life in peace? I can feel the frustration build and with that I start to cry. I hate that about me: whenever I get frustrated I cry and then I get angry with myself for crying and generally cry harder, I'm such a sook.

I hear a voice in my ear, "Carly are you ok, I didn't intend to make you cry, I'm sorry."

I didn't realise I was still on the phone and had it to my ear when I had my mini meltdown. I manage to say that it's not really his fault and apologised for crying.

"There's no need to apologise. Listen Carly, I know you keep pushing me away, but as I said I would really like a chance to get to know you. Just agree to have a meal with me and then if you don't want to see me again I will leave you alone."

"I am a just average girl, there's nothing special about me at all, so why are you so persistent?"

"Carly, you are really selling yourself short, I don't know if anyone has told you that you are anything but average. You have a beautiful smile that lights up your whole face, amazing hazel eyes and the most infectious laugh that just makes me smile when I think of it. You are sarcastic, quick-witted and you really know how to put me in my place and I have to admit that is a huge turn on for me. As I have said before, you're feisty and not a pushover. I would just like a chance to get to know you, please give me that."

"Fine," I sigh.

"Great, I'll be there in an hour."

"Whoa, hang on a minute, what do you mean you'll be here in an hour?"

"You just agreed to have a meal with me and I am coming to get you tonight because I think if we make it another night you will find a reason to cancel on me and I'm not giving you that chance."

I think about it and he is probably right. "OK, I'll give you my address."

"No need."

"What do you mean no need?"

"Ummmmm, I err, sorry, George told me that too."

"Whatever, I'll be ready in an hour." And with that I end the phone call.

I walk inside, give Mum and Dad a kiss hello and let them know I won't be home for dinner. Mum goes to say something but Dad shoots her that look that says just leave it. I smile at my dad, silently thanking him and then go into my room and put my flowers on my bedside table. I lock the bathroom door and start taking my makeup off. I look like shit, my mascara has run because I've been crying. I get in the shower to wash the day away. I get out and re-apply my makeup and go into my room to decide what to wear. I can't, so I call Nicole.

"Hey Chica, how was your day?"

"A bit weird, I got flowers delivered to me at work today and they are my favourite colours too."

"Oooohhhhh who sent you flowers?"

"Ben, and I agreed we would go out to dinner together tonight.

Apparently George has been feeding him information about me which, as you can imagine, has pissed me right off."

"Well Carls, I am pleased you have decided to take a chance and go out on a real date. What you going to wear?"

"Well that's the main reason I called you. I don't want to give him the wrong impression and get glammed up but I don't want to dress down so much that I look like a slob. What do you think I should wear?"

"Carly, you look great in anything; your hair and makeup are always perfect and he obviously likes you, so I doubt you could go wrong. What about jeans, your purple top and a small heel? That's casual enough for a casual dinner."

"Nicole, you're a star. I'll call you later and let you know how tonight goes."

"You're very welcome hun, enjoy and try to let your guard down, I think he might surprise you. Luv ya, bye."

I put the phone on my bed and plug my iPod into its dock. I scroll down my playlists and find just what I'm looking for. OneRepublic - Counting Stars. I press play and start to sing to myself as I get ready. My taste in music is varied and has always played a massive part in my life, I go to concerts and see pub bands all the time. I know my bedroom with its books and music were my saviour growing up, it was the only safe place I could go to escape George. For some reason, no matter how bad things got, he never entered my room, though as soon as I set foot out into the hallway I was fair game.

George use to hit me when my parents were out or just in another part of the house. He always hit me where no one could see, he is sly like that. Throughout my teenage years I wore jeans and t-shirts because I used to have bruises all over my back, upper arms, stomach and legs. George said if I ever told anyone he would kill me, and I believed him, so I never told a soul, I was so ashamed. When I met Shaun I was seventeen, I felt I had someone I could confide in. He was sympathetic to begin with, but in the end used it to his advantage and sucked the life out of me because I was weak and broken.

A knock on my door brings me back to the present. I open the door and my dad is standing there. "Ratbag, there is a young man here to take you out for dinner."

I love my dad and especially his nickname for me. We have a great relationship and I am such a lucky girl. I hug him, kiss his cheek and say that I will be there in a minute.

I take one last look, reapply my lip gloss and then walk out into the lounge. Ben stands up as soon as I as I enter the room. He smiles at me. This is the first time I have really looked at him close up. He is wearing jeans, a light blue button up shirt and runners. He has light brown eyes and dimples. OH MY GOD I love dimples. If he wears glasses too then I won't have a chance; I love a guy who wears nice glasses, I find them sexy and such a turn on.

Ben opens the passenger door of his car for me and I frown at him. "What's that look for?" he asks.

"A guy has never opened a car door for me before. Come to think of it, no guy has ever opened any door for me before."

"Well I'm glad I could be the first to do that for you," he says with a huge smile. There they are again, those dimples.

We drive the first few minutes in awkward silence until I ask where we are going for dinner.

"I thought we could go a great seafood place I heard about. It's by the sea and I have booked a table outside because it's a nice night."

"Yeah, sounds good." I'm not the biggest seafood lover but there are a few things that I like.

We reach the restaurant. I go to open my door but Ben stops me and asks me to wait. He races around to my side and opens my door for me. "Really this isn't ne..ne..necessary. I'm sorry but it's m..making me a little u…un..uncomfortable." Shit I'm stuttering, this is the last thing I want.

"That isn't my intention. You see my dad always instilled into me that you open doors for women, but if it makes you uncomfortable I will try to stop."

"Thank you, I re..really appreciate it, s..s..sorry."

"No need to apologise, it's fine. Come on, I hear the food here is amazing, some of the guys I'm on course with came here the other night and they have done nothing but rave about it."

"On course?"

"Yeah, I'm in the Navy and I'm in Perth on a 14 week course."

"Oh ok, so how long have you been here for?"

"Well today was the start of my second week, so how lucky am I that I met you when I did."

I sigh, "Ben please don't g..g..get ahead of yourself, I..I..I agreed to a meal that's all and o..o..only because you sent me flowers. I'm s..s.. sorry to be rude but I have to be hon..honest with you. I hate being l..lied to and the last thing I want to do is gi..give you false hope."

"That's ok, I have broad shoulders, I can handle the truth, but I intend to have changed your mind before I drop you back home tonight."

"Don't count on it," I say with a shrug.

We walk up to the door of the restaurant and Ben opens the door for me with a wink. I just shake my head and walk inside. The guy behind the counter greets us and asks if we have a booking. Ben says yes, he has a booking for two under the name Richardson.

"This way, please," the waiter says as he leads us onto the patio, where it looks like we are the only diners tonight. The view is beautiful, Australia really has a breathtaking coastline.

Ben pulls my seat out, I roll my eyes and sit down. The waiter takes our drinks order and leaves us alone to our awkward silence and the sound of the sea rolling in. Ben leans forward. "Tell me about you, Carly, I want to know everything."

"Not much to say — I'm 20, live at home, play softball and I'm a beautician."

"I already knew all of that except your age. There must be something else."

"No, that pretty much covers it."

"You're not making it easy for me are you? OK, let's try this, what music do you like?"

"I like all types, I like certain bands, but I am also open to songs from artists I generally don't follow."

"Such as?"

"I like *Firestarter* by The Prodigy, *Loose Yourself* by Eminem and, I can't believe I am actually admitting this, but I like One Directions *Story of My Life*. And if you ever mention that to anyone I will deny I ever said it," I smile.

The waiter brings us our drinks, cider for me and beer for Ben. He asks if we are ready to order and Ben asks for a little more time. As the waiter leaves us Ben leans forward and gently asks, "Carly, who did a number on you?"

I snap my head around and I can feel my eyes filling up, this is why I don't date and why I just have random hook-ups. I am so fuckin' stupid agreeing to go to dinner with him. Ben takes my hand and I wrench it back like I'd just touched an open flame.

He lowers his head. "I'm sorry, Carly. I forgot you don't like to be touched, I can see that my question has upset you and that's the last thing I want to do. I know I said I want to know everything about you, but if you don't want to talk about yourself that's ok, I respect that. Can we please start over again?"

I stand up and excuse myself, stating that I need to take a minute and I will be right back. I go to the bathroom and lean my head against the mirror. What was I thinking going out for a meal with him? This is just too hard, I have to get out of here.

I walk back to the table and Ben stands when he sees me. "I'm s.. so..sorry Ben, but I..I..I can't do this, ca..can you please take me h…h… home?"

Ben just nods and we walk to the counter to pay for our drinks. I try to hand him some money for my drink but he lightly pushes my hand away, stating that he has invited me so therefore he pays.

I walk to the car with my head down.

"Carly it's pretty obvious that something heavy has happened in your life and if you don't want to talk about it I'm cool with that, but I really don't want to take you home yet. The beach is just there can we sit and talk, we can talk about anything or just sit there in silence, it's up to you, but I'm not ready to give up on this yet."

I lift my head up as a tear rolls down my cheek. I wipe it away and just nod. We make our way to the beach and sit on the soft sand watching the waves roll in and the cormorants diving for fish. We sit there in silence watching the sun set, I can feel myself start to relax, the beach is so calming. When I need to talk to my dad in private this is where we go, I have his full attention and he helps me talk through my problems.

Once the sun has set I turn to Ben. "Sorry, I h..ha..have really ruined the n..n..night for you."

"How could it be ruined? I'm spending time with you and that's all I wanted. How about you ask me some questions. I promise to answer anything"

"OK. Tell me about your family."

"There's my mum, Lucy, my dad James, my older sister Piper, her husband Justin and my niece Chelsea who's 4, then there's Darcy, Damon and my youngest sister Kelsey."

"Are you all close?"

"Yeah we get on great, we have family BBQs once a month and I try to talk to one of them at least every other day."

A pang of jealously hits me. "You're very lucky. Where did you grow up?"

"Born and raised in Wollongong New South Wales and my family still live in and around there."

"AFL or NRL?"

"NRL, St George Illawarra."

"I support Melbourne Storm."

Ben tilts his head and smiles. "WOW you just offered something up, that's a start."

"It's nothing earth-shattering, it's just a rugby team. So why did you join the Navy?"

"I have always loved the sea and wanted to travel the world, so why not combine the two? I joined just out of High School and have never regretted that decision."

"I hate the sea. Actually it's what's in the water that I'm afraid of. I'm petrified of sharks so I don't go swimming in the sea. I don't go in their water, they don't come on my land."

"You don't go swimming at all?"

"I don't swim in the sea but I do swim in pools. I'm actually not a bad swimmer I just don't want to get eaten while I do it."

He just smiles and shakes his head. "OK, next question."

"Favourite movie."

"Oh that's a hard one coz there are a few I like. The Fast and Furious movies, Lord of the Rings, Avatar, Thor and the X-Men franchise."

"Looking over that lot there is a bit of a theme going on, you like your super heroes and fast cars. But I have to say I agree with X-Men, Hugh Jackman is hot as all hell. Even tho he is twice my age, I could look at him all day," I say with a grin. "Favourite band?"

"Again that's a hard one."

"OK top five."

"Foo Fighters, Kings of Leon, Eskimo Joe, MUSE and Justin Timberlake."

"WOW that's quite a group, I like all of them plus a few more"

"Like who?"

"One Republic, Pink and Birds of Tokyo. I have heard that they are all touring later this year, Nicole and I are planning on going. I love live music, it's so raw and electric and I get so lost in it. I believe it's such an honour to be at a live gig." I lean back onto my elbows, cross my feet and stare out to sea. I look over at Ben and realised he is staring at me.

"What?"

"You were so passionate just then talking about those bands, your whole face lit up and I could see them through your eyes, it was amazing. Carly, can I ask you something?"

I lower my head and whisper "Please don't sp..spoil this Ben."

"OK, I'm sorry, no pressure. Ask me another question."

I keep quiet for a while just listening to the sounds of the ocean and I turn to look at Ben. He is staring out to sea deep in thought. "I'm s..so..sorry I've been a b..b..buzz kill. We can call it a n..night if you like?"

"Carly, it's fine. I'm enjoying myself."

I raise an eyebrow at him

"No really, I'm having a good time and I'm not ready to have this date finish yet. Carly, I like you and I want to see you again even if it is just as friends. I am happy to take anything I can get as long as I get to spend time with you."

"Ben there's no point in us starting anything, you live in Sydney and will be gone in 3 months, it's pointless."

"So you are thinking about it."

"What?"

"You're thinking about giving us a go because you haven't said no."

"Ben I'm da…d..damaged..."

He tries to interrupt but I stop him. I try to calm my breathing. "I have huge issues t..that go right back to my early ch..childhood and more recently with my ex. I am no g..good for you. I am moody, sna.. snappy, and opinionated, I..I..I don't let people in or make friends easily and y..y..you have probably noticed that I st..stu..stutter and have quite a temper."

"I don't know what has happened in your past but I hope that one day you will trust me enough to tell me. I will never let you down or betray you, I just want the chance to get to know you. If you are willing we can go at your speed and you can call the shots, please just give me a go, give us a go."

"Can I think about it? It's not a yes, but it's also not a no."

"Of course you can. While you are thinking about it, is it ok if we stay in contact? Like texting, phone calls and going out."

I look at him "I'm ok with all three as long as when we go out we are in a group and not just the two of us. I will bring Nicole and you can bring the guys, that is the only way this will happen."

"Deal, that was easier than I thought," he laughs.

He's got a nice laugh. I just hope I am not making a big mistake. "Ben, do you wear glasses?"

"That's a random question," he chuckles, "I do throughout the day but when I go out at night I put in contacts. Why is that?"

"No reason." I am so screwed.

Ben stands up and asks if I'm hungry. I nod my head and he holds out his hands to help me to my feet, I accept them and as we head back to the car he still has a hold of my right hand. The awkwardness between Ben and I has seemed to have disappeared. He opens the car door for me and then asks what I fancy eating. I explain that there is a good burger place a few streets away.

Because it is a Monday night and also fairly late we pretty much have the place to ourselves. Once we get our meals we sit down at the bench and eat while watching the world go by. I am pleasantly surprised at how relaxed I'm feeling in Ben's company. We chat away about nothing important, laugh at the drunk man having a conversation with himself and try not to listen to a woman having very loud conversation on her mobile phone.

I turn to Ben and say, "If you had one question you could ask me what would it be?"

He sits there and thinks for a while, my heart is thumping and I become angry with myself because I think I have just opened Pandora's Box. He turns in his seat to look at me and asks me to do the same. We sit there, knees touching, my heart is pounding in my chest and I am looking anywhere but at him. Ben reaches out with his right hand and puts one finger under my chin. "Please look at me." Once my eyes are fixed on his he begins to speak. "My question is – are you happy?"

I take my time answering. "For the most part, yes. There are aspects of my life that I'm not happy with, but there is nothing I can do about that, it's out of my control. I love my parents, Nicole and my job, so yeah, for the most part I'm happy."

Ben picks up my left hand and gently kisses the back of it. "I'm pleased."

We sit there for a few minutes just absorbing what has happened. Ben stands up and asks if I am ready to go home, I nod and we head for the car. The conversation is easier on the way home and I have to admit that I'm a little sad that the night had come to an end. We pull into my drive and the place is dark. Mum and Dad always go to bed early and hopefully George is either out or in bed, fingers crossed. Ben gets out the car and races around to my side before I have a chance to put a foot on the driveway.

"Seriously dude, you have to stop that, it's freaking me out."

"Sorry Carly, it's just habit and how I was brought up," Ben laughs.

"I know it's just you and most other girls would love it. You never know, one day I might be able to explain to you how it makes me feel. Anyway, it's time I went inside. Thank you for tonight, I know things didn't go as you planned them, and again I am very sorry for that."

"No apology necessary, I wanted to spend time with you and that's exactly what I got and I hope we can do it again soon."

With that I start to walk to my front door, I turn to say goodbye to Ben and he is right behind me. "Don't tell me, you were taught to walk the girl to her front door." He simply nods and gives me the broadest smile I think I have ever seen. We reach the door and I put my key in the lock, I twist my body around to say goodbye and Ben leans in to kiss me on the cheek. It takes me by surprise, I don't say anything I just walk inside and shut the door.

Thankfully George isn't home but Dad is in the kitchen getting a drink. I walk up to him and give him a cuddle. "Dad, I'm s..sc..scared." I don't have to explain, he knows what I mean.

"Ratbag, your mum and I spent a few minutes in Ben's company tonight and we both got a good feeling off him. In my line of work I can spot a liar and a dirt bag in a heartbeat and that young man is very genuine. Just give him a go, I think you will be pleasantly surprised."

I kiss Dad goodnight and then go to bed. I replay the night over and over in my head and I have a feeling that I'm not going to get much sleep again.

3 | BEN

For the next few days I'm so busy in class and also with all the home-work I have to do. This course is kicking my arse. Carly and I send text messages back and forth and she starts to open up a little bit and tells me a few things about herself. She has a quirky sense of humour and we spend the time on the phone laughing at each other's stories. Mine are about my family and my life in the Navy and Carly's all involve Nicole, nothing about her family. One day I hope she will open up to me.

Fridays we finish early so I jump in my hire car and head to Carly's salon, hopefully to take her for a late lunch. I wear my Navy whites on purpose because I know women love a man in uniform and I fill mine out very nicely.

I walk into the salon but I can't see Carly. There's a girl behind the counter that is eye fucking me. I smile to myself when I walk up to her. "Hi is Carly here?" I ask.

"She is but she's booked out. I'm Megan and I'll be more than happy to help you out," she says with a smile.

"Thanks for the offer but I would like to see Carly if that's ok? Can you tell her that Ben is here?"

"So *you're* Ben," Megan says with a wink. "Wait here and I'll go get her."

I take a look around the salon as I wait for Carly. It's a small space, on one wall there's a glass case containing jewellery and products, and a variety of posters that explain the different treatments offered line the walls that lead to the rooms. It's neat and clean with white shiny tiles, there is music pumping and it has a good atmosphere. I hear a gasp behind me and without turning around I know Carly's there.

As I begin to turn around I hear Megan whisper to Carly, "Close your mouth you're drooling."

I knew there and then it was a good idea to wear my uniform. Because it's summer I am wearing my perfectly pressed whites. As I face Carly I see that she is looking at me in a way she hasn't before, and I know I am finally breaking down her barriers. Hopefully that means our relationship can be more than it is at the moment.

"Ummm hi. Are you here for some waxing or maybe a piercing?" laughs Carly.

I can feel myself getting hard just being near her, hearing her voice and that laugh. I feel like a horny teenager. "No, I finish early on a Friday and I was hoping to have a late lunch with you, if that's ok?"

"I have one more client and then I have a break. Megan, are you ok if I go to lunch then?"

"Actually you're free for lunch now coz your last client called to reschedule, so go and enjoy this handsome man and I will see you back here in about thirty minutes," smirks Megan.

Carly goes out the back to grab her bag and then we walk the short distance to the food court. We talk about our day as I make sure that I give Carly her personal space. We are only a few feet away from the salon when I notice Carly tense up.

"Are you ok?" I ask as we walk.

"Yes. Why wouldn't I be?" she replies in a short sharp manner.

I touch her arm to stop her. "Carly, what's going on?"

"I don't know what you mean," she says as she looks anywhere but at me.

"Look at me please," I say as I wait for Carly to turn her head towards me. "Tell me what just happened."

"It's embarrassing."

"Tell me," I smile.

"This has never happened to me before, and as I said it's embarrassing."

"You can tell me, I won't laugh. I promise."

"Ok. Here goes. As we were walking I noticed a few girls look your way and they did a double take and I have to say it pissed me off. I wanted to punch them in the throat," Carly says as she shuffles her feet nervously.

I stand there taking in her words and my heart is beating rapidly. "You're jealous."

"I am not, don't be ridiculous," pouts Carly.

"Oh yes you are," I say, putting my hand on her arm so that she looks up at me, "and it makes me so damned happy."

Carly bumps my shoulder as she starts to walk away. I catch up to her and we walk the rest of the way in silence.

Carly grabs a chicken and salad wrap and I have pizza, we find a table and just as I am about to take my first bite I hear her say, "Oh my fucking god are you trying to kill me?"

"What?"

"Ummmm nothing, how's your lunch?"

"Carly don't change the subject, what's wrong?"

She starts to fidget. "Nothing's wrong, it's all g..good."

"No something's wrong, please tell me."

"I..I..I can't believe that I am g..going to tell you this it's s..so embarrassing."

"You can tell me anything, no judgement here."

She takes a deep breath. "Well ok, you wanted to know. I errrr …ummmm…I have a thing for guys with glasses, it's a real turn on for me and you have just put your glasses on," Carly blushes.

"Ahhhhhhhhhhhh so that's why you asked me if I wore glasses, good to know, GOOD. TO. KNOW," I smile. I put my slice down. "Carly, please look at me." I wait for her to look up. "I will make a point of wearing my glasses more often around you now that I know," I say as I place my hand on hers and give it a squeeze. She seems to relax a little and doesn't move her hand away. Carly's skin is so soft, it feels amazing underneath my hand. No girl has ever gotten under my skin the way Carly has. I feel like a horny teenager every time I'm around her. We talk and laugh through lunch, but unfortunately Carly's lunch break is over too soon and she has to go back to work. I get up and pull Carly's chair out for her, knowing it will make her laugh and she doesn't disappoint.

"You just did that to get a reaction out of me," she laughs.

"It was worth it to make you laugh," I smile as I take her hand in mine, thrilled she doesn't pull away.

We reach the salon and I pull Carly in for a hug. I'm pleasantly surprised when she actually hugs me back, this is progress.

CARLY | 4

For the next month we speak and text daily, and Ben comes to my house once a week for a home cooked meal. I'm a terrible cook but luckily my mum is a wiz in the kitchen. Sometimes it is a bit awkward because George is there. George puts on an act when Ben is around but luckily Ben sees right through it. Even though he doesn't know what the deal is between George and me, he knows that I hate George and that is enough for him. Ben gets on really well with my parents and the conversation flows freely every time he comes around.

On the weekends, as promised, we go out as a group. Nicole and I take the job of tour guide very seriously and every Sunday we have a new touristy thing to show the guys. Our favourite outing is in Fremantle. We take the guys to Fremantle Jail (which was operational until 1991), Freo Markets and E Shed Markets, we see the Sea Shepherd docked in Fremantle Port and get to meet a few of the crew and then we go for a few drinks and a meal at The Sail and Anchor Pub.

Ben and I notice that Nicole is getting very comfortable with Davo, and they have gone out with each other a few times apart from the group. I don't know his real name because they all use nicknames. Ben is Richo, then there is Davo, Rabbit and Kiwi.

"So what's the deal with you and Davo?" I ask Nicole as we wait for the guys to bring back the drinks.

"We're just having a bit of fun, seeing where it goes."

"From where I'm standing I can see that you quite like him."

"I do like him but I'm trying not to get too carried away. We live in different states so this can't be a long term thing."

"As long as you're comfortable with the situation then I guess it's ok."

Just then the guys come back to the table with our drinks, Ben sits next to me and Davo next to Nicole.

"This has been a great day," says Rabbit. "Nicole and Carly you have been the best tour guides, I doubt I would have seen this much of WA if you hadn't taken us under your wings."

"It's been a lot of fun for us too, Rabbit," Nicole says as she tips her cider towards him.

"Kiwi, are you still seeing, and I use that word loosely, Jenna?" I ask.

"Carly, she has a body to die for and is amazing in the sack, but she's as dumb as a box of rocks. There is no conversation and she just agrees with everything I say."

"Isn't that every guy's dream?" I laugh.

"In theory, but it can never last, there has to be some kind of interaction other than sex."

Nicole snorts and chokes on her drink, "Oh my god Kiwi, you sound like a girl."

"No I don't, Nicole, it's just that I need more if it's going to go the distance."

Just then the buzzer on our table alerts us that our meals are ready. Ben, Rabbit and myself go to the counter to get them.

"Who knew Kiwi was so deep," I say as we reach the counter.

"He couldn't believe his luck when he met her, he was like a dog in heat, but obviously he's not that happy with the situation. I think it's a case of be careful what you wish for," says Ben.

"Is that something that worries you?" I say to Ben.

Ben smiles at me knowing full well what I mean. "Not at all, bring it on."

After we finish our meals we decide to head back because we all have work in the morning and it's getting late. Ben's driving today so I sit in the front with him while the rest are in the back. We drop Nicole and Davo off at Nicole's and then Ben makes his way to my house. I say goodbye to Kiwi and Rabbit as Ben opens my door.

We walk to my front door in silence and Ben waits for me to put the key in before he speaks, "I have really enjoyed today, thank you, Carly."

"Yeah, it's been great," I say as I turn to face him. "You still coming round on Tuesday for dinner?"

"Yeah I'm looking forward to it."

"I have to admit my mum is a great cook."

"That's not the only reason Carly, I'm looking forward to seeing you again," Ben says as he leans in and kisses my cheek.

"Night Carly."

"Night Ben." I say as I watch him walk to the car and then drive away.

5 | BEN

On Tuesday I go around to Carly's place for dinner but I'm a little nervous. I want to ask Carly something but I'm not sure how she's going to react. Three times during the night I try to ask her but every time I chicken out.

Carly pulls me to the side. "Ben, what's going on?"

"Nothing, why?"

"Don't bullshit me, there's s..something up because y...you're not yourself tonight and you won't l..l..look at me. If you want to fin.. finish what's going on here just tell m..me."

My head jerks up. I have played this all wrong tonight, I keep chickening out because I'm nervous and scared she will say no. "No, you've got it all wrong Carly."

"Then w..what is it coz you are making m..me very uncomfortable."

"I'm sorry, Carly, that's the last thing I want to do. It's just that it's my birthday on Saturday and I would just like to spend the day with just you and not the whole group. I know you said we could only go out as a group but I would just like that day to be with you and I... I know it's selfish, but..."

Carly cuts me off, "Of course I'll spend the d..day with just you, birthdays are v..very special, and I am honoured you chose me to spend the day w..with. What do you want to do?"

"Leave all the planning up to me. Just be ready at 11 am," I say with a huge smile. I can't believe I nearly stuffed that up, thank god she took it the right way and said yes. I'll wait a few days before I mention the Skype session with my family.

"OK, you have to give me more than that, what do you want me to wear, and bring?"

"Just wear flat shoes and comfortable clothes coz we will be doing a bit of walking. Oh and bring a jumper in case it gets cold later."

I hate spending birthdays away from my family but I think this one will be a good one. I hope I can make a breakthrough with Carly and she will let me in, that would make the day perfect.

On Friday night everyone goes to Carly's house to watch a movie and have a few drinks. Luckily they have two living areas so we get a room to ourselves. During the movie Carly bumps my arm and points to Nicole and Davo. Nicole is leaning on Davo and he has his arm around her gently rubbing his hand up and down her side, and every now and then he turns his head to kiss her forehead. As I turn my attention back to the movie I feel Carly's hand gently touch mine, my heart skips a beat. Without taking my eyes off the movie I slowly entwine our fingers. I can see out of the corner of my eye that Carly is smiling. We hold hands throughout the whole movie while I trace circles on her skin with my thumb. It feels good to be able to touch her without her pulling her hand away.

Nicole is driving us back to base tonight but I need to have a private word with Carly before we go. I stand and ask Carly to come to the kitchen with me. "I'm really looking forward to tomorrow, Carly, but there is something that I would like to run by you now because you might need time to think about it before you answer. You see, because I'm not home for my birthday, my whole family will be at my parents' house and they want to Skype with me so it's like we are all together. It will be during our date tomorrow and I just wanted to know if you're ok with that."

"Of course that's ok, you didn't have to ask. I'll just go do something while you are talking to them so you have some privacy. No problem at all."

"Carly, you don't understand. I have told all my family about you and I would like you to be involved, if you are ok with that?"

Carly crosses her arms across her chest and becomes very defensive. "What have you told them about me?"

I take a breath before I answer because I don't want to get her anymore upset. "All I have told them is that I have made a few new friends and that we have been spending a bit of time together, that's all, I promise. To be honest I don't know much about you so there isn't a lot to tell."

Carly looks at the floor. "I'm sor..sorry I overreacted," she whispers.

"It's ok Carly, it really is. Don't answer me now just think about it overnight and we can talk more about it tomorrow if you like. I'd better get moving coz it looks like they are waiting for me."

Just as I'm about to walk away Carly throws her arms around my neck and hugs me. "I'm s..sorry," she whispers.

I place one hand on Carly's lower back and with the other hand I cradle her head and hold her close to my body. "Shhhhhh there's no need for an apology, it's ok." After a while we pull apart and I lean in to kiss Carly on the cheek goodbye.

CARLY | 6

Ben comes to pick me up at 11 am, he looks great in khaki shorts, white t-shirt and runners. I hug him hello and wish him a happy birthday. I give him a card and a small present. I have to admit I feel awkward about giving him a present because I haven't bought a guy anything for such a long time and I don't really know him well. Ben thanks me and asks if it is ok to wait until later to open them. I nod, and Ben says goodbye to my mum as he grabs my hand and walks me to the car. He opens my door and with a smile he says, "You look beautiful, Carly." I start to blush and look at the ground, and he touches my shoulder. "One day you will be able to accept a compliment."

The day is wonderful. We go to the Fremantle Museum and Arts Centre. It was built by convicts and opened in 1864 as a lunatic asylum. It's a beautiful building and is thought to be haunted. I have been there quite a few times before but it was great to see it through Ben's eyes. We have a late lunch and a much needed drink at a café. It's mid-March but still quite warm during the day, even though we are nearing the end of the first month of autumn.

We go back to the car and Ben drives off towards Perth. I ask him what is next but he just smiles and says," You'll see."

The traffic is horrendous so it takes a lot longer to get to Perth than it normally would, but that's ok because I am having a great day with Ben, the conversation flows and there is a lot of laughter. We drive to Kings Park and Ben pulls the car into the first available parking spot. He looks at me. "Make sure you grab your jumper," he says, "because we are going to be here for a while and I would hate for you to get cold."

We take a walk through the botanical gardens and look at the plaques of fallen diggers from the first and second world wars down the Honour Avenues. The plaques are placed at the bottom of trees lining the streets in Kings Park. It was quite an emotional walk because some of the fallen where younger than me when they died. The newest memorial is for the people killed and injured in the Bali bombings on October 12th 2002, and I hope the families and friends of the victims are happy with the memorial. Finally we have our photo taken by the huge Karri log; it is estimated that it was 363 years old when it fell in 1958 and it weighs 110 tonnes. Everyone in Western Australia knows about the Karri log and most people have a photo with the log in the background. It's an icon.

It is getting late, and Ben asks if I would walk to the car with him because he needs to get something. As we get to his car he opens the boot and pulls out an esky, a rug and his lap top. "I thought we could have a picnic as we watch the sunset." We find a spot on the grass overlooking the Swan River and Perth City, Ben lays the rug down and asks me to sit. We have about forty-five minutes before the sun starts to set. Ben turns to me. "Carly, have you thought about joining me when I Skype my family?" he asks.

"I have and I…I'm really n…ner…nervous about it. What if we have n…nothing to talk about, what if th…they don't like me and y..you waste the time you have with them be..because of me."

"Carly, my family will love you, and trust me not one of them are ever lost for words so I doubt you will even get a word in," Ben laughs.

I smile at his comment. "OK," I say.

"OK?"

I nod, and Ben grabs his mobile and sends his sister a text to let her know that he is setting everything up. He receives a text back that they are all waiting at his parents' house. I start to fidget and Ben places his hand on my arm and gives me a reassuring smile. Then all of a sudden the screen comes to life and there they are. I can't stop this, it's really happening.

They all start talking at once and Ben roars with laughter. "One at a time please," he says. His family laugh and it's infectious, you can feel the love radiate through the screen, as they laugh and take the piss out of Ben and each other. I just sit back and watch them all interact with one another; they genuinely love each other and I become very envious. I don't care if George doesn't love me, all I want him to do is like me but that is never going to happen. After a while a gorgeous blue-eyed little girl gets right up in front of the monitor and when she starts to talk the others quieten down.

"I miss you Uncle Ben," she says.

"I miss you too Chelsea, have you been a good girl for Mummy and Daddy?"

She nods. "Brandon's a very naughty boy, Uncle Ben, he pushed me over and made me cry so my teacher put him on the naughty stool."

"What did you do to him?"

"Nuffin."

"Chelsea you know your nose will grow if you tell a fib, what did you do to Brandon?"

"He said I smelled like poo so I pinched him."

"Did you tell the teacher you pinched Brandon?"

"No Brandon did."

"So did you get sent to the naughty stool too?"

Chelsea looks away sheepishly "No."

"Why not Chelsea?"

"I really love you Uncle Ben," she says, batting her eye lashes.

I try hard to stifle my laugh.

"And I really love you too Chelsea but why didn't you go to the naughty stool?"

"My teacher asked me if I pinched Brandon and I said no."

"Chelsea why did you lie to your teacher?"

"Coz silly I didn't want to go to the naughty stool and miss out on story time."

That did me in, I roll to my side away from Ben laughing my arse off. This kid has something about her and for a four-year-old her speech is really good. I motion to Ben that I will give him some time to talk to his family in private and walk to the War Memorial.

As I stand there looking over the city I become very emotional. Why can't my family be like Ben's? I'm close to my dad but even though I hate George I really wish it had turned out differently. I can feel the tears falling down my face just as Ben reaches my side. He looks at me with confusion.

"Your f..family are lov...lovely."

"Carly, why are you crying."

"Y..you are all so close and lo..love each other, that comes across l..loud and clear and Chelsea is ad...adorable, I just wish I had that."

Ben puts his arms around and me pulls me close. "It's George's loss." Ben holds me tight as I break down, he doesn't say a word just holds me and I melt into him. He is giving me hope that I can let someone in and it's not as scary as I think it is.

I notice it is starting to get dark. We stand there in each other's arms watching a beautiful orange and red sunset. Once the sun has gone down Ben grabs my hand and walks me to the rug and pulls out a bottle of wine, glasses, the food, the card and present I had bought him. Ben hands me a plate of food and a glass of wine, we clink our glasses and I wish him a happy birthday. I become nervous when he starts to open the card and present I bought him, it was just something small for him to remember his time in Perth.

Ben turns to me with a huge grin. "I love it."

"It's nothing mu..much."

"Carly, this is perfect, I love history and just glancing through this book I can see that we have visited quite a few of these places and there are many more to explore. Thank you so much."

We eat our meal while taking in the breathtaking view of Perth City at night. I notice they have multi-coloured lights at the bottom of the massive trees lining the roads leading into Kings Park and it sets quite a romantic mood. The weather starts to get a bit chilly so I put on my jumper and lay on my back looking at the stars. Everything about this moment in time feels right, I've had a wonderful day with an amazing guy who is so kind and patient and wants to share his birthday with me. I take a deep breath and turn my head to face Ben. "Can I…I tell you about m..me?"

Ben looks down at me. "Carly, if you want to tell me about you I am more than happy to listen, but please don't feel any pressure."

"I don't, it's ju..just that when I start I..I doubt you will want to see me ag..again."

Ben lays down on his side with his hand supporting his head. "Nothing you could tell me could make me not want to see you again."

"Well we will see, bu..but you have to promise me th..that the only time you interrupt me is when you can't l..listen anymore."

"I promise."

I start to shake so I sit up and turn my body to face him, Ben does the same. I take a deep breath and try to calm myself down because I don't want to stutter. Once I start I can't stop, and the whole time Ben sits there looking at my face while I explain what George has done to me.

"It started the day I was born. George hated the intrusion to his perfect family of three and he would have nothing to do with me when we were young children. When I started primary school he was ahead of me by three years, and he use to hunt me down in the playground and throw rocks, sticks and anything else he could get his hands on at me. When I was about seven years old I left early one Saturday morning to go play at my friend's house. Dad was at work, Mum and George were still asleep. I got home late that afternoon and Mum grabbed me by the arm and smacked me hard. I thought I had stayed out too late but when she yelled at me that I could have burnt the house down I was really confused. When George heard me leave in the morning he'd thrown a lit match into the paper bin next to the front room curtain. As you can imagine, the curtain caught alight, George went running into Mum shouting fire, she put the fire out and when she asked George how it happened he said he didn't know, he said he just woke up and smelt smoke then found the curtain on fire. He did add, however, that just before he smelt the smoke I had left the house.

"When I was about nine the physical abuse started. I came home from school one day and George was there with his mates in the pool. Mum and Dad where out. It was a hot day so I changed into my bathers and went outside to go for a swim. I hadn't even put my foot in the water before George came charging out of the pool and grabbed me by the arm and said if I took one more step towards the pool he would drown me. I turned to walk away because I knew it was no use arguing. George twisted my arm behind my back and punched me in the side. I doubled over in pain and started to cry, which was the worst thing I could have done. George got furious and started to hit me over and over, saying he would really give me something to cry about. A car pulled into our drive, and George let me go and told me to go to my room and never tell my parents about what had happened or he would kill me.

"The abuse continued throughout the years at varying degrees. He always hit me where my clothing would cover up the bruises. I was too scared and ashamed to tell anyone what was happening to me. I didn't have friends over because George was a loose cannon and I was never sure what he would do next. I withdrew within myself, spending most of my time in my room either reading or playing music. I wouldn't look at anyone in the face when they spoke to me and I developed a stutter.

"When I was seventeen years old I met Shaun and I thought he was my saviour, that he would protect me from George. To begin with it seemed that was the case. But slowly Shaun started to tell me what to wear, what to eat, what I could watch on TV, where I could go, who I could talk to, and even the books I could read. I lost my identity.

"When I was eighteen and a half Shaun was out of town with work, so I asked Nicole to come over for the night. Mum and Dad were visiting friends and George wasn't home, and I felt free for the first time in such a long time. Nicole and I were dancing and singing to one of the music channels when the front door slammed open. George stumbled through the front door and I could tell that he was drunk. Nicole and I quickly sat down and didn't look or speak to him. George stormed towards me and yelled, 'What are you looking at?' I just looked down and prayed that he'd get bored and would leave me alone, but that's not what happened. George came at me with so much rage in his eyes, I knew right then he was going to kill me. I had to act and fight for my life. When George got close enough I pulled my knees tightly into my chest and kicked him in the stomach as hard as I could in the hope that he would go through the lounge window, unfortunately the coffee table got in the way and he toppled over it and landed with a thud on the other side.

I sat there unable to move. 'RUN!' Nicole yelled. 'Carly move, get the fuck out of here!'

"I jumped up and made a run for the kitchen but I was too slow. I felt a kick at the back of my knees and I fell hard onto the tiles. George started to kick me in the ribs and it seemed to go on forever, all I could hear was Nicole screaming and my bones cracking, the pain was unbearable and I started losing consciousness. I thought, this is the day I'm going to die, he's finally going to make good on all those threats over the years. The last thing I remember was hands tightening around my throat and then it went black.

"I woke to searing pain throughout my body, Nicole and my mum were crying and Dad had George by the throat up against the wall. I couldn't understand why my head and face were wet. All I wanted was a shower. I tried to get up but I couldn't. Nicole told me not to move because the Police and an ambulance were on the way. I muttered, 'No Police, I just want a shower.'

"I must have passed out, because I woke in an ambulance with a paramedic taking my blood pressure. We stopped, the rear doors opened and Mum was there waiting for me. I spent all night in the emergency department with the doctors and nurses doing numerous tests on me. The Police came to get my statement but I refused to press charges, I was so embarrassed and ashamed and somehow thought it was my fault. My parents, the doctors and nurses tried to get me to change my mind, but I refused and shut down. In the early hours of the morning I was admitted. I had three broken ribs, a broken nose, a dislocated left shoulder, a fractured left eye socket, a deep gash to my forehead, chipped teeth and five broken fingers, which the Doctor explained to me were probably defensive wounds. I looked in the mirror and I didn't recognise the girl staring back, my face was so swollen.

"I stayed in hospital for two weeks. Shaun returned home four days after my attack. He came to the hospital and asked me to explain what had happened. Once I had finished he stood up and informed me that I had antagonised George and got what I deserved. I sat there dumbfounded, I felt like I was in the twilight zone. The next thing I know I carefully got out of my bed, shuffled to the door, turned to Shaun and told him to get out. Shaun looked me in the eyes and smirked, 'I'll leave for now so you can come to your senses but I will be back in the morning.'

"Don't bother, we are over, I want you out of my life.

"Carly don't be stupid, you are nothing without me.'

"That's what you would like me to think, and I have to admit up until today you managed that perfectly well, but I don't love you, in fact I despise you. Get the fuck out and never contact me again.'

"Shaun moved towards me and I put up my hand to stop him. 'I'm serious Shaun, we are over. NEVER. EVER. CONTACT. ME. AGAIN. DO. I. MAKE. MYSELF. CLEAR?' He walked past me without saying another word.

While I was in hospital George was thrown out of home. I don't know or care where he went.

"Due to the attack I had to take an extended leave of absence from my job, but thankfully they were very understanding and kept my job open for me. My ribs took a long time to heal and the nightmares really took their toll. I was afraid to be in my home alone, so Mum and Dad took it in turns to always be there with me.

"After a while I started to get my life back and I made myself a promise that I would be no-one's victim ever again, either physically or emotionally. I swore I would never have another boyfriend because all they do is use me. I was going to call the shots from now on. I would hook up with random guys and never see them again, perfect plan. That's how it has been for the last two years."

I had been looking at Ben the whole way through but I wasn't seeing him. I took a huge breath and focused on his face. Ben was crying, crying for me and for the pain I had suffered. I lean over and wipe his tears away. "I'm so s…sorry I didn't mean to up..upset you, especially on your birthday."

"Carly, you are the most amazing girl I have ever met. You told me that you were broken and damaged. You're not, you're so brave and strong to come back from all of that. Is it ok if I ask you a few questions?"

I nod my head.

"How come George is living at home?"

I calm myself. "He lost his job and couldn't afford the rent so he convinced Mum that he had changed and she let him back in. Dad was livid, he didn't want George back in the home and anywhere near me, but as usual Mum felt sorry for him. It caused a lot of problems between my folks, and Dad would only talk to him when he had to."

"Do you still have the nightmares?"

"I do. It happens if I have a hard time with George, but most of the time it's just every now and then."

"Other than the nightmares do you have any lasting physical effects from that night?"

"I have developed migraines, and I used to have panic attacks though they seem to be under control now. And as you would have noticed, I stutter when I'm upset. My fingers ache and are very painful especially in winter which makes my job harder, but it is what it is. I'm alive," I say with a shrug.

"What made you decide to tell me?"

"I saw how close and loving your family is and how you wanted me to be a part of that. You could have quite easily Skyped before you picked me up or asked for a bit of privacy to talk to them while we were out, but you included me and your family were so nice and welcoming. I didn't get that with Shaun. I met his mum once and she did nothing but look down her nose at me. I knew nothing about Shaun's life, his mum was the only relative I met, I have no idea what he did for work, or anything about his friends, siblings etc. I was never allowed to ask him any personal questions. He'd pick me up and we would go to his home, eat and watch a movie or a TV show that he picked."

"Fuck, what a prick."

"Yeah that's one word for him," I laugh.

"Have you seen him since the hospital?"

"No. I think he has moved on to his next victim because he has left me alone. I feel very sorry for her, no one deserves to be treated badly, I know that now."

"Thank you for trusting me enough to tell me about your life, I fully understand why you freaked out the night we met, I was such a dick. You will never know how sorry I am about that."

"You weren't to know. Besides you got off quite lightly. After the attack my dad made sure I took self-defence classes," I laugh.

"WOW you really amaze me, you're not bitter or angry."

"I told you I won't ever be the victim again and if I hold onto what happened that means it owns me, and I won't let that happen."

I'm exhausted. I had held that inside me for so long. I flop down on the rug, look up at the sky and take a few deep breaths to calm my rapid heartbeat. I start to have a panic attack. Oh my god, what have I done, I have given him the power to hurt me, I am such an idiot, such a fuckin' idiot.

Ben rolls onto his side and pulls me close, he cuddles me from behind. "It's ok Carly, I will never hurt you, I'm not like them and you're safe with me."

I don't know how long we lay like that but I know it was long time after my panic attack had finished. Ben was right, I feel safe with him, especially in his arms. I decide to give this, whatever this is, a chance. I slowly roll over to face Ben and nuzzle into his neck, he smells amazing. It's now or never.

I start to feather kisses on his neck. I feel Ben's body stiffen, then his arms hold me tighter and he lifts his neck so I can have easier access, our breathing starts to speed up and I can feel his chest rise and fall rapidly. I slowly kiss my way up his neck while Ben runs his hands up and down my back. He lets out a low moan when I kiss his chin and make my way to his mouth.

I stop and we look into each other's eyes for a few seconds, silently making sure the other person is ok with what was about to happen. I nod and a huge smile breaks out over Ben's face.

He places a hand behind my head and guides my mouth to his. Ben's lips are soft and he kisses me gently at first but then the built up sexual tension takes over and our kissing becomes more intense. Ben rolls me onto my back, places his left knee between my legs and presses himself into me, it feels amazing, it feels so right. I have never been kissed like this before and my whole body tingles and comes alive. What is happening?

After a while Ben leans up, smiling. "You are amazing, I have waited such a long time to do that and it was so worth the wait."

I blush and turn my head away from him. He pulls me back to face him. "Please don't hide from me, I mean every word. I wish you could see yourself through my eyes."

We lie in each other's arms kissing and talking, we are in our own little world and it's a magical place. We sit up and look around us and notice we are alone, I check my watch and it is just past midnight, time has flown.

"I don't want this date to end but we can't stay here," I say. "Would you like to stay at my place tonight?"

Ben looks like I'd just told him he had won Lotto.

"I mean to sleep, you can stay in my bed with me but nothing is going to happen, just sleeping."

"Are you sure your parents will be ok with this?"

"They will be fine with it, they like you and they trust me. I will just send them a text to let them know and that way there will be no little surprises in the morning."

"Ok then, what are we waiting for?" Ben says as he gets to his feet.

"Eager much?" I laugh.

We pack up our things and make our way to Ben's car. I send Mum a text informing her of my house guest and was surprised when I got one back immediately. I start to laugh and Ben asks what was so funny. "My mum's response to you staying overnight is, and I quote, *ABOUT BLOODY TIME XX*."

The drive home is quick, which makes me smile, Ben holds my hand the whole way home. We pull into the driveway. "Carly, are you sure about this?"

A cold shiver runs through me, I put my head down and I pull my hand from his. "If y..you would rather g..go back to the base th..that's ok."

"Carly, you need to stop doubting me. Trust me when I say that I *REALLY* want to stay with you tonight, but I want to make sure you are ready for this. I know we are just sleeping in the same bed but I also know this is a massive deal for you and for me too, I don't want you to feel pressured."

"Ben I am s..sure but can we have some gr..ground rules?"

"Of course."

"Do you ha..have anything to sl..sleep in?"

"I wear boxers, is that ok?"

I take a moment to calm my breathing. "Yeah that's fine. I need to put all my cards on the table so there is no confusion. We will be clothed, there can be kissing and cuddling but defiantly no sex. Is that ok with you?"

"Carly, I just want to be with you in any way possible, if this is how you want things to go then I am happy with it," he says with a smile.

OH MY GOD those dimples are going to be the death of me. I put my hand on the door handle. "Are you ready?"

"More than ready."

Ben holds my hand from the car to the front door, as I start to open it with my key George's car pulls into the driveway. I can feel myself tense up and Ben holds my hand a bit tighter, I look at him and he is clenching his jaw. I know he is thinking about what I had told him earlier. I lean into Ben and say, "Please no..not tonight."

"If he touches you or says one wrong thing to or about you I will kill him."

"Let's just ig..ignore him, he's not w..worth it, besides we have had a mostly wu..wonderful day and I just want that to con..continue."

"Carly, today has been one of the best days of my life, I got to share my birthday with you and my family and as predicted they loved you. How could this not be a wonderful day?"

I smile and lean in to give him a quick kiss on the lips. We walk inside and just as we are walking through the kitchen George calls out to Ben.

"Hey Ben, you wanna have a drink with me, I could give you the inside scoop to my little sister, the stories I could tell you," he says with an evil sneer.

I tighten my hold on Ben's hand, and keep walking, chanting softly, *"Nearly there, nearly there."*

Ben looks at me like he wants to kill George.

I mouth, *"He's not worth it."*

Ben just shakes his head and we walk into my room and shut the door. Ben sits on my bed with his fists clenched either side of him, his breathing is fast and he is looking at the floor. I sit next to him and give him time to calm down. After sometime I notice his hands start to relax and his breathing slowing. I put my hand over his fist and start to massage his hand.

Ben lifts his head and looks at me. "I have never wanted to beat the shit out of anyone before, I don't know how you can live in the same house as him after what he did to you. I just want to beat him to a pulp, I want him to beg for your forgiveness and for him to say how wrong he was for all the torment and terror he gave you."

"It'll nev..never happen, he thinks he is in the ri..right and I am in the wrong, that I am m..my parents' favourite child and sp..spoilt. I think it all boils d..down to jealousy and that has m..made him very bitter and twisted. Anyway, I d..don't want to talk or think of h..him anymore. Let's go to bed."

I grab my tank top and boxers and head for the bathroom. When I get back into my room Ben is sitting there on my bed just in his boxers. HOLY SHIT his body is amazing, it's toned, nicely tanned and he has tattoos down both arms and down his side that disappear into his boxers. I hope I get the chance to get up close and personal with that one day.

"I didn't know what side you preferred so I waited for you."

His voice snaps me out of my thoughts. "Either is fine."

Ben holds his hand out for me, I walk towards him and he leads me to the bed, pulls the covers back and lets me get in first. As I crawl over to my side Ben grabs my hip and it stops me in my tracks.

"You have a tattoo," he says.

I feel Ben's fingers trace the tattoo on my right shoulder blade, it is a yellow frangipani with the script – I'M FREE. "I got it a few months after my recovery, I believe it was the end to that chapter in my life."

"I'm free?"

"I got away from Shaun," I say with a smile

"It's beautiful, just like you," Ben says as he kisses my tattoo.

I roll over to turn out the lamp and then turn back to find Ben's arms waiting for me, I snuggle into him, enjoying having him hold me in my bed. I just hope this isn't too good to be true.

We spend the next couple of hours kissing and talking. I try to stifle my yawn but Ben notices. "It's time for some sleep I think, turn around so that I can cuddle into you."

I just lay there.

"What's wrong?"

"Ummmm…I..I have never had a g..guy hold me to go to sleep."

"Never?"

"No," I say, embarrassed. I am realising more and more how fucked up my relationship with Shaun was. Even though Shaun and I had slept in the same bed there was no touching or cuddling, he had his side and apparently I had mine and I was never to cross over onto his side unless I was invited and that was never.

Ben looks at me with a puzzled look.

"Shaun was the only relationship I had and we only touched when he said we could. I have had hook ups but it was just sex and nothing else. When we were finished I asked them to leave."

"WOW... Carly, I would like to hold you while we go to sleep. Are you ok with that?"

"Yeah I think I'd like that," I say with a smile.

I roll over and Ben pulls me back into his body. I lay my head on his pillow and he places his right arm around my waist. Ben moves my hair out of the way and plants kisses on my neck while he presses my body against his. I can feel his erection in my lower back, and I just smile to myself and relax into him.

"Good night Carly."

"Good night Ben. Thank you for today, it was wonderful."

"It sure was."

7 | BEN

It takes me a while to wake up this morning, I had the deepest sleep I can ever remember having and the most wonderful dream. When I open my eyes I see Carly is fast asleep with her head resting on my left shoulder, her arm is across my stomach and her left leg between my legs. I lay there for a while just listening to her breathing and watching her sleep. It feels so natural having Carly asleep in my arms. I know I only kissed her for the first time last night but I know she's the one for me. I've never felt like this about a girl before. I've had my fair share of girl-friends and sexual partners but Carly is special and different. She starts to stir and I pull her in closer. I lean down to kiss her forehead. "Good morning Beautiful, how did you sleep?"

"Well, and you?" Carly yawns.

"I had the most wonderful dream." I smile as I kiss her forehead again.

All of a sudden Carly stiffens in my arms and starts to pull away. "I'm so sorry."

"What are you sorry for?" I say as I hold her close.

"About lean..leaning on you, I didn't kn..know I was doing it."

"Carly it's fine, in fact it's more than fine. I have been awake for a while now and I liked that I woke with you cuddled up to me."

"This is s..so new to m..me."

"I know it is but please trust me when I say I like it," I say with a smile. Just then my stomach starts to growl.

Carly lifts her head and looks at the clock. "It's 10.30am are you hungry?"

I raise my eyebrows up and down and smirk. Carly slaps my stomach. "I mean are you hungry for food?"

"Ohhhhh I see what you mean," I say with a grin. "Yes I'm hungry. Do you want to go out for breakfast or stay in?"

"I can cook bacon and eggs for us if you like, I have to admit it's the only thing I can cook well."

"That sounds great, do you want a hand?"

"No it's ok, but you can talk to me while I cook."

As Carly cooks our breakfast I set the table and make small talk with Carly's dad Andrew, he's a lot like my dad, easy to talk to and loves his children.

In the middle of a conversation we hear a crash near the stove and when I look I see Carly crumpled on the floor struggling to breathe. Andrew and I reach her at the same time and I position myself behind Carly on the floor. I gather her in my arms and gently rock her back and forth while whispering in her ear that she will be ok and that I have her. The attack lasts about five minutes. Once Carly is feeling better I loosen my arms and help her to her feet.

"Do you know why this happened?" Andrew asks Carly.

Carly just shakes her head but I watch the unspoken words between Andrew and Carly and I suspect that she knows why it happened. I don't ask questions because if she wanted me to know she would have told me.

We eat breakfast and then decide to spend the day at the beach because luckily the weather is still in the high twenties.

Carly calls Nicole and I'm not surprised to find out that Davo is there, they agree to meet us at the beach. We find a great spot and wait for them to arrive. Carly lays down on her towel and I can't help myself, I kneel between her legs and lay on top of her but making sure I support my weight so I don't crush her. I run my hand down her cheek and then lean in to kiss her. I can't get enough of her, it's more than a physical thing. She has an amazing mind, a fantastic sense of humour, is great to talk to and she really listens when I talk to her about any subject. She is perfect for me. We have been kissing for a few minutes when we hear a wolf whistle, Carly starts to laugh, I shake my head and say, "Nicole."

I get up and help Carly to her feet. Nicole smiles at us before giving Carly a hug hello and I shake Davo's hand. We decide to go in the water, I take off my t-shirt and throw it onto the towels. I can see that Carly looks a little hesitant and I give her space so she can take her time. I'm standing behind her as she slowly peels off her t-shirt and slides her shorts down her legs. She just stands there and I can see her body is tense. Oh my god she looks amazing; she's wearing a blue and black one piece that accentuates her curves, and fuck me it takes my breath away. She is my walking wet dream. Before I get a complete hard on I race up behind her, pick her up and run into the water. Carly squeals as we fall, it's so cold. I grab Carly's hand and start to swim out into the deeper water. She yanks her hand out of mine and says "There is no fucking way that I am going any further, I told you I am afraid of sharks and the deepest I will go is up to my waist."

"Come on Carly, I will keep you safe."

"I appreciate the thought but you can't save me from a big arse shark so I am happy to stay here while you go for a swim."

"Hey Davo, do you want to swim out to the pontoon?"

"I'll race ya," yells Davo.

We get up onto the pontoon and sit there catching our breath. "How's everything going with you and Nicole?" I ask Davo.

"Yeah good, we're just having fun nothing serious. Not like you and Carly," he laughs.

"I can't tell you how she has managed it but she has really gotten under my skin."

"You're not used to women telling you no. You're used to them coming onto you. I have never seen you work this hard for a woman before."

"Yeah I know but I'm happy I persevered because she is so worth it," I sigh. "So you and Nicole. Not going anywhere?"

"Nahhh we both know the score. Don't get me wrong she's a great girl, funny, so sarcastic and a wildcat in the sack but it'll never be a long term thing."

"Fair enough. You ready to go back?" I ask as I stand. Davo nods and we dive in the water and make our way back to the girls.

CARLY | 8

After we finish our meals Nicole and I excuse ourselves and go to the toilets.

Nicole nudges me, "Spill, I want all the details."

"Nicole, I'm screwed, I really like him but it's going to go no-where. I live in Perth and he lives in Sydney and he is leaving shortly. I can't allow myself to let my guard down fully and have the possibility of getting hurt again."

"Carly, I need to tell you something. Ben has talked to Ryan about you."

"Who's Ryan?"

"Davo, his real name is Ryan Davies…anyway… Ryan and Ben have been mates for a few years and he has seen Ben with other girls. Ryan said that Ben has had girlfriends but nothing too serious. Ryan was there the night he met you and Ben has done nothing but talk about you since that night. Carly, according to Ryan, Ben is in love with you."

"Don't be stupid, I only met him five weeks ago. How the hell could he be in love with me?" I scoff.

"How do you feel about him?"

"I told you I really like him but I'm scared."

"Tell me, how do you feel when you're with him?"

"I get butterflies in my stomach when he touches me and my knees go weak when he kisses me. Yesterday he asked me to stay with him when he Skyped his family. Nicole, they were so welcoming I was very envious. They seem so nice and they are all close to each other and his niece Chelsea she is so damn cute and hilarious.

"Ben stayed the night with me last night," I said, and Nicole raised her eyebrows. "Not like that. He had on his boxers and I had on mine plus a tank top. We kissed and cuddled and it felt wonderful falling asleep and waking in his arms, I have never had that before. But I had a panic attack this morning thinking over everything."

"Was Ben there?"

"He was amazing, Nicole. He sat behind me on the floor and just held me until it was over. He never asked any questions he was just making sure I was ok. I'm not use to being treated this way. Is he too good to be true?"

"I don't think so, Carly. From what I have seen he is a solid guy, he treats you very well and he's put a smile on your face. That's good enough for me. I think you're in love with him too."

I ignored Nicole's comment. "I told him about George and Shaun."

"What? Everything?"

"Pretty much."

"How did he react?"

"He was very upset and angry. When we got home last night George was there and I had to ask Ben not to do anything. I know it really affected him, but I don't want my problems to become his problems."

"Can you just promise me one thing?" I nod. "Please continue to let him in, I know telling him about your history is a huge deal and from what you said he took it well and treated you the same afterwards if not better. I'm telling you he is in love with you and you know you're in love with him, it's written all over your face. You deserve to be happy and I believe Ben's the guy for the job."

I stand there thinking about what Nicole has just said to me. Ben does make me happy, I feel safe when I'm with him. He listens to me when I talk, and I mean he really listens, like my opinion matters. He's kind and very thoughtful, I get tingles when he kisses and holds me, and I'm going to miss him when he has to leave. That last thought made my heart drop. Am I in love with Ben? I couldn't be, could I? I thought I was in love with Shaun but I now know that he manipulated me into thinking I loved him.

After a few minutes I turn to Nicole. "You're right," I say with a tear in my eye.

"I know I am, Chica, and I am so happy for you. It's about time you got yourself a great guy," she says, hugging me.

After a while we go back to the table and Ben smiles the most beautiful smile at me. "Everything ok?" he asks as I sit down.

"All good," I say as I squeeze his hand that is resting on his thigh.

Ben and Davo tells us stories about their time at sea and about each other, some of the stories are hilarious and I can't remember laughing so much ever in my life. It feels good, I feel normal, I can't remember feeling this relaxed before. I look over at Ben and he is laughing at something Davo said, and it hits me like a tonne of bricks, I love him, I really do. What am I going to do when he leaves? Because he will, he has to go back to Sydney. Just then the DJ starts up. Ben stands as he holds his hand out to me. "Dance with me, Beautiful."

I smile and I place my hand in his as he leads us to the dance floor. Just Give Me a Reason by Pink and Nate Ruess starts as we hit the floor. Ben places my arms around his neck as he puts his arms around my waist and holds me close. I'm blown away when he leans his head down and starts singing to me. His voice is soft and low so only I can hear. *'Right from the start you were a thief you stole my heart and I your willing victim.'* I feel we are the only two people in the room as I get lost in the moment. We dance as he continues to sing to me, halfway through the song Ben leans back and lifts my chin up so I'm looking him in the eyes and then he sings *'You're not broken just bent and we can learn to love* again.'

We stop dancing and just look into each other's eyes. Time stands still. "Would you like to stay the night with me again?" I ask breathlessly.

"There's nowhere I'd rather be," Ben replies with a smile.

We go back to the table and say our goodbyes. Nicole and Davo just laugh at us, we can't get out of there quick enough. Nicole mouths *'call me'* just as Ben grabs my hand and leads me to the car.

We are silent on the way back to my house, Ben rests his hand on my thigh and gently squeezes it every now and then. We reach my house and my heart skips a beat, not out of the usual fear but out of excitement; I am excited to experience what is about to happen. I can't believe how easily Ben has wormed his way into my heart, I have been shut down for so long I didn't think it was possible.

When we walk inside Mum is in the lounge watching TV. I know it is rude, but we wave and say goodnight as we make our way to my bedroom. I shut the door. "Do you mind if I have a shower," I say, "because I have sand in places it has no right being."

Ben smiles and kisses me. "Take your time."

I grab my boxers and tank top and make my way to the bathroom. I make sure I lock the door before I start to undress. The water is hot and it feels great, I wash my hair and take my time washing my body using my frangipani body wash, it smells beautiful. I dry my hair and get dressed before I go back into the bedroom. Ben is sitting on the end of my bed watching TV, he gets up, kisses me and asks where the spare towels are. Then he heads to the bathroom so he can shower.

I'm sitting in bed reading when Ben enters the room. I look up and he is wearing boxers and a t-shirt. He gives me a sexy smile and then slowly lifts his t-shirt over his head, my mouth gapes open, his body is perfect. I put my book down on the bedside table and turn to face him. Ben crawls up my body and starts to kiss the exposed skin on my arms all the way up to my collarbone, and I let out a small moan which seems to spur him on. Ben sucks my bottom lip into his mouth and gently bites down, a tingling feeling shoots to my inner thighs and I start to breathe heavily. He looks into my eyes and whispers, "You're not broken just bent." And then his lips comes crashing down on mine, our hands are exploring each other and it feels so good, I can feel my nipples harden against the fabric of my top and I realise I'm wet between my legs. Ben moves the doona aside and positions himself over me, I can feel his erection and I start to rub up against him. Our kissing becomes more frantic, then all of a sudden Ben leaps off the bed.

"Carly, we have to stop otherwise I won't be able to help myself," he says panting heavily.

"Wh..what if I don't want you to st..stop?"

"What are you saying?"

"I think you k..know."

"Carly I need to hear you say the words so there is no confusion."

"Ben, I want you t..to make love to me," I say as I sit up.

"Are you sure? I mean, are you really sure?"

"Yes, I have n..never had a guy make love to m..me before and I want you to be my first, bu..but I have to let you know I am very in... inexperienced in a lot of things. I hope I don't dis…disappoint you."

Ben sits down next to me on the bed so we are face to face. "You could never disappoint me, I love you Carly, I know it's very early on, but I can't hold it in anymore. I'm not expecting you to say anything back but I just need you to know. If you decide that you want to wait I am fine with that, there is no pressure at all."

I take a bit of time taking in what he has just told me. "I do want you but you are going to have to be patient with me. I know this is probably not the right time to tell you this but Shaun was very mechanical in bed, there was hardly any kissing and fore play didn't exist when it came to me. He wouldn't touch me because he said it was dirty and he didn't like having my bodily fluids on him; however he said it was ok for me to go down on him because he never came in my mouth. Sex was always in the same position, missionary, with a condom and with the lights off. I have never had an orgasm from a guy; even with the hook ups it was pretty much wham bam but I have to say that's how I wanted it."

Ben sits there for a while "Well then I will have to make this a night you'll never forget. I intend to take my time exploring every inch of your beautiful body and make you come so hard you'll be screaming my name."

"Don't you think you're putting yourself under a lot of pressure? Also I don't want my mum to hear us," I say with a cheeky grin.

"Well you had better be quiet then sweetheart," Ben says with a wink.

"Ben, in all seriousness, you have my h..heart in your hands, please don't hurt m..me."

He holds my face in his hands and looks me right in the eyes. "I will never hurt you, ever."

Ben dims the lights so there is a lovely soft glow, climbing onto the bed, he kisses me and then starts to undress me like he is unwrapping a present, he does it so slowly and carefully, looking into my eyes the whole time. When I'm completely naked he leans in and kisses down my neck to my breasts, then takes a nipple in his mouth while his finger and thumb gently pinch the other. I arch my back because the sensation is amazing and my heart beat increases. Ben kisses his way back up to my ear, nips at my lobe and says, "You are perfect."

I run my hands down Ben's sides, feeling every muscle. His body is tight and feels fantastic against mine. My hands move around to his back and I slowly run my nails up and down, I can feel Ben shiver with my touch. We kiss like our lives depend on it. My hands move lower and I can feel the material of his boxers; my hands are continuing their path south when Ben stops me.   "You will always come first," he smiles. Ben kisses his way down my body and stops at my hip, where he sucks and nibbles, then he starts moving down my left leg, kissing and nibbling every couple of centimetres. It feels so good, my body feels so alive and sensitive. Ben stops at my feet and slowly massages my left foot, hitting the right pressure points as he gazes into my eyes. He starts kissing my instep and then all of a sudden he sucks on my big toe. My body convulses as a delicious feeling shoots to my groin and I moan his name. I feel Ben smile against my skin. "That won't be the last time you're moaning my name tonight," he whispers. He reaches for my other foot, massaging it and sucking my toe. Holy fuck I have never felt anything so weirdly wonderful before. Next he slowly kisses and nibbles up my right leg and stops at my hip. He stays there for a while slowly kissing from one hip, across my stomach to the other hip and back again, then looks up at me and silently asks if it is ok for him to keep going. I bite down on my bottom lip and nod. He makes his way to the centre of my stomach and as he kisses his way down his eyes never leave mine. As he gets lower he begins to smile. My toes curl and my body jerks with the first stroke of his tongue, I have never felt such an intense sensation before, I feel so alive. Ben begins to slowly tease me by softly blowing warm air in-between kisses; he knows where and when to touch my body and I love it. He starts to lick my outer lips, then he slowly spreads them and flicks his tongue. My body feels like it has received an electric shock, I have no control as my body convulses with each stroke.

"Oh my god, Carly, you taste amazing and you're so responsive, I can't get enough of you."

Ben controls the tempo as my body rises and falls with the expertise of his tongue and mouth. He slowly licks my clit and then takes it in his mouth and sucks it gently, all of a sudden Ben started to hum. HOLY FUCK BEN, I think as my body starts to shudder and he wraps his arms around the back of my thighs, holds them apart as I come. Ben laps up all my juices, kisses his way up my body and lays down next to me allowing me to slowly come down from my high.

"That was…ummmm….fuck….oh…my…god," I babble unable to string a sentence together.

Ben starts to laugh. "I couldn't have said it better myself, but that is only round one. Get your breath back, I have more of you to explore and all night to do it in." He slowly strokes my arm as my breathing begins to slow down.

I stretch my body, not able to put in words how I feel; I just know I like it, I really like it. I roll towards Ben and start to kiss him, I can taste myself on his lips and I have to admit it turns me on. Our kissing becomes more passionate. I push him onto his back and I straddle him, I can feel his erection underneath me. He plays with my nipples as we kiss, I grab his hands and hold them against the mattress above his head, and I kneel between his legs and kiss my way down his chest to his happy trail. I lower myself so my face is level with his erection, and my heart skips a beat as he lifts his hips so I can remove his boxers; I pull them down slowly and his erection springs free. "WOW now that's impressive," I say as I remove the boxers from his legs and throw them on the floor.

"I aim to please," he says with a sexy smirk.

I wrap my hand around the base of his cock and he lets out a low growl. I lift his cock and run my tongue from base to tip a few times. I can feel his body reacting to what I'm doing, so I lick him like a lollipop for a while then, without warning, I cover my teeth with my lips and take as much of him as I can into my mouth.

Ben's hips jerk forward and he grabs a handful of my hair. "Babe that feels so fuckin' good," he groans.

I smile and start to move my head up and down, applying just the right amount of suction. I make sure his cock is covered in my saliva as I move my fist up and down twisting my wrist as it reaches the head and then flicking the head with my tongue.

I can feel Ben's body tense as he pulls my mouth away from him. "Carly, I won't last long if you continue to do that, besides, it's still your turn."

In a blink of an eye he grabs my arms, and pulls me up and over his chest so I am riding his face; he parts me with one hand and places a finger inside me while he laps and sucks on my clit. I can feel another orgasm building. He puts a second finger inside me and slightly curls it until he hits the right spot. My body shudders as I come long and hard, I ride Ben's fingers and mouth until I collapse on the bed.

I point to the top draw. "Condoms," I manage to say.

Ben opens the draw and pulls out the box, he removes one and rips it open and places the condom on his very erect cock. "You told me you have only been in the missionary position. Would you like to try another position or stick with missionary?"

"Can we try another position?..If that's ok with you?" I say shyly.

"Babe, we will do whatever you want, just name it."

"Well I would like it if you sat up and I straddled you; I would like to be able to kiss, touch and look at you. Are you ok with that?"

"I am more than ok with it, Beautiful."

Ben shuffles his way up the bed and leans against the bed head. He holds out his hand and I crawl towards him. I lean down and give his cock a quick kiss before I straddle him. He places his cock against my pussy and then he stops. I look at him with a puzzled expression. He puts both hands on my face, looks me in the eyes and says, "Are you certain you are ready for this? Please don't feel obliged to continue."

With those words ringing in my ears I push my hips forward and Ben slowly sinks into me. It takes my breath away as he deliciously stretches me. My previous partners haven't been as big as Ben so it takes a little while to get used to. We stay still just looking at each other, enjoying this feeling, and then I start to move; I look down to watch Ben going in and out of me and I become more turned on. Ben grabs my hips and starts to move us quicker and we let out a few cries of *'oh god'* and *'you feel amazing.'* Ben grabs my hips harder and I know he is close, so I start to thrust a bit faster, suddenly Ben moans, "Carly, I'm gunna come." His body tenses up, he lets out a few groans and then collapses into my arms.

This has been the most mind blowing night of my life, I can't believe how happy I feel right now and it's all thanks to this gorgeous guy who is still inside me. I kiss the top of his shoulder, and he places his arms around my waist and pulls me as tight as he can into him.

"Carly, do you know how happy you have made me? You are truly an amazing girl and as for worrying about not being experienced enough, you need to seriously get rid of those thoughts, you have nothing to worry about."

We stay like that for a while, just enjoying the closeness.

"I hate to move," Ben says, "but I have to get rid of this condom. You get comfy in bed and I'll be back in a minute. Please don't get dressed I want to hold you while you sleep with nothing coming between us."

I turn out the lamp as Ben settles back in bed. I move to the middle where he is waiting for me with open arms. Exhaustion takes over quickly and we fall into a deep sleep.

I wake with a start, it is still dark and there is something moving between my legs. I grab the sheets and my body arches and shudders with an unexpected orgasm. Ben kisses his way up my body to my mouth, "Good morning, Beautiful."

I turn on the lamp "What a way to wake up. I want you in me, now," I growl.

"I was hoping you would say that." Ben looks down, my eyes follow his, and I laugh because he already has a condom on. "I put it on while I was enjoying your body."

I laugh. "You are a multi tasker, good to know. Now come here and make love to me."

"With pleasure." Ben climbs up my body, runs a hand down my left thigh to my knee, places his hand behind my knee and lifts up my leg to place my ankle on his shoulder, and then he enters me.

It takes my breath away and I grab his shoulders as he pumps into my body. "Faster..Ben please…holy shit…the angle…it's…fucking amazing…don't…don't stop," I pant. Ben places my other ankle on his right shoulder and wraps his arms around my thighs, his thrusts go faster and deeper, and just as I'm about to come he nibbles on the instep of my left foot and that sends me crashing over the edge, a few more thrusts and Ben collapses on top of me as he lets my legs go and nestles between my thighs. I hold onto him and slowly kiss the top of his head. Tears start to roll down my cheeks, I have never been this happy before and it scares me. I try to wipe the tears away before Ben see them but I'm not quick enough.

Ben lifts his head and gives me a confused look.

"They are happy tears, I promise. I'm just scared that's all."

He pulls out of me, places the condom in a tissue and puts it in the bin, then he lays on his side and pulls me into him. "Can you tell me what you are scared of?"

I take a deep breath, it's now or never. "Being hurt em..emotionally, you leaving, never feeling this h..happy again and being too scared to tell you that I lu..love you too." Ben just lays there not saying a word. Oh shit I have really fucked this up, why did I have to open my big fucking mouth, George and Shaun are right, I'm such a loser, I'm nothing, why did I think that someone as great and as hot as Ben could actually have feelings for me? I'm stupid, so stupid, SO FUCKIN' STUPID. I started to get up off the bed.

Ben grabs my hand. "Where are you going?"

"I am g..going to leave before I..I make more of a fool of my.. myself. I'm sorry, I obviously read this wr..wrong. Please excuse me I need to take a sh..shower."

Ben jumps up off the bed and blocks the door. "Carly, talk to me, what just happened?"

"N..n..nothing, it's not im..important," I whisper with my head down.

Ben grabs my face in his hands and lifts my head. I feel so stupid that I shake my head and close my eyes as tears stream down my cheeks. "Ben pl..please don't make me do this."

"Carly, you opened up to me again, told me you had never been this happy, and that you're scared of me leaving, and then you said the most wonderful thing — I'm just hoping I didn't imagine it. Did you say that you love me?"

I can't say anything, I just stand there wishing the ground will open up and swallow me.

"Carly, please tell me I heard right. Do you love me?" I just nod. "I need to hear the words," he says.

I swallow and then whisper, "I love you."

Ben's mouth crashes down on mine and he swings me around so my back is pressed up against my wall. He kisses me with so much passion it's overwhelming. His knee separates my legs as he presses his body into mine. "Put your leg around my waist," Ben growls as he grabs my bum and lifts me like I weigh nothing, he presses his body into mine and I wrap both my legs around his waist. I can feel his erection rubbing between my legs and it feels so good, as I reach down and grab his hard cock, Ben sucks in a breath. I position him to enter me and without warning he thrusts forward hard and pounds into me, the pace is carnal and frantic. He chants over and over, "I love you, I love you." He starts to shudder and just holds me.

My head jerks up. "We didn't use protection."

"Babe, I'm clean, I haven't had sex for about six months and I had a routine test three months ago and it all came back clear."

"I was tested four months ago and it was clear, I have only had one partner since then and we used protection, plus I have had the rod put in my arm so no unwanted guests will arrive in nine months."

Ben pulls out and walks me to the bed. We lay down on our sides facing each other. "I have to admit I have always used a condom and that was the first time without one, and oh my God that felt fuckin' amazing, Carly." Ben moves his hands to my face. "So you love me?"

"Yes I do," I say with a smile. "Can you tell me why you went quiet when I told you?"

"I just couldn't believe you said you love me and I wanted to ask you to repeat it. I was scared I misheard."

"Why do you make me look in your eyes when you talk to me?" I ask.

"I hold your face and look deep into your eyes so you can see that I am telling the truth. I will never lie to you, I will always tell you the truth whether it is good, bad or ugly."

"I'm happy with that, I just hope there is more good than bad and ugly."

"Me too. Carly, I want us more than I have ever wanted anything in my life. I don't want this to be a casual thing, I am serious about you and I want you and I to be exclusive. How do you feel about that?"

"Ben I'm a moody cow, do you think you are ready for that?" I giggle.

"Bring it on, I want to know all of you."

I start to laugh. "Be careful what you wish for."

The alarm sounds for Ben to get ready for work. Luckily I have a late start so I can have a lay in. He showers, we eat breakfast together and then he has to go. I walk him to the door and he pulls me in for a goodbye kiss that makes me weak at the knees.

"Can we go out for a meal tonight?" he asks.

"I'd love that," I say with a huge smile. I watch him drive off and I go back to bed.

I lay down on Ben's side, wow look at me, Ben has a side, in my bed. I get up and start jumping up and down on my bed like a child. I am so happy I want to scream out how happy I am so everyone knows. I lie back down on Ben's side and smell his pillow, it smells amazing. I close my eyes and I can imagine him here with me.

I grab my mobile and call Nicole. "It's about bloody time you called me," she says. "How did last night go? And I want all the details."

"Nicole, words don't do it justice. Ben is a wonderful and a very, very generous lover. We didn't fuck, we made love. At times it was slow and steady and other times it was hot and carnal. No guy has ever made me feel this alive and loved before."

"Loved, did you say loved?"

"When we got home he told me he loved me and I told him I loved him this morning. I know it's very early on, but Nicole, it felt right to tell him, I can't stop smiling."

"Honey I am so happy for you. When are you seeing him next?"

"Tonight he is taking me out for dinner. He asked if we could be exclusive and I said yes."

"That's fantastic news. He's a good guy. Anyway, I have to get ready for work. Luv ya Chica."

"Luv you too, have a good one."

I have a shower and get ready for work, Dad has already left and Mum is still asleep. I couldn't care less where George is because no one can wipe this smile off my face today. My day is busy and it goes fast, but I start to get butterflies as it gets close to finishing time. We lock up and as I'm walking to my car Ben phones.

"Hey Beautiful, how was your day?"

"It was great. How was yours?"

"Better now that I am talking to you. Are you still up for a meal out tonight?"

"Definitely, what time do you want me to be ready?"

"I have booked the restaurant for seven. Does that work for you?"

"Yeah I'll be ready, see you later." I hang up the phone just as I get to my car. I can't wipe the grin off my face. On the way home I play my music loud, it is a Kings of Leon kind of day, *Sex on Fire* blasting from my car and I dance in my seat and sing along.

When I get home no one is there. I lock the front door and go into my room to decide what I'm going to wear. Once I have made my choice I go for a shower. Even though I'm alone I still lock the door, probably out of habit. I've just about finished when I hear loud knocking on the door, it's George. "I'm nearly finished."

"Get the fuck out here bitch."

His voice doesn't sound right, he sounds drunk, oh fuck, my heart starts beating hard in my chest. I don't have my phone in here with me and no one else is in the house. I start to shake, thinking about the last time he was drunk; that's when he nearly killed me, I am so scared I am unable to move. He bangs on the door again and I jump. "Ben will be here soon so just leave me alone."

"You fucking slut I heard the two of you last night, you're a bitch in heat and you will screw anything with a pulse. GET.OUT.HERE. NOW or I am coming in."

"George just calm down, I will be out in a minute." I have no intention of opening that door. I leave the shower running, quickly put my work clothes back on and quietly make my way to the bathroom window, I slowly open it and start to climb onto the vanity, I'm halfway out the window when hands grab me and pull me with a thud to the ground. I scream, look up and see George leaning over me with a smirk on his face.

"You think you are so fucking clever, I will always be one step ahead of you. You're a stupid, fat, ugly cow."

I start to scream for help, I'm not sure if anyone is home yet, what time it is, or if the neighbours can hear me but I have to do something. George yells at me to shut the fuck up and then punches me in the face. I think I get knocked out because all of a sudden I am being pulled by the hair in the back yard and I'm spitting out blood. I start to scream again as loud as I can. George yells at me to shut up and kicks me in the ribs. I roll into a ball and try to protect myself as best I can. George continues to kick me as I scream.

I hear bodies thumping together and George is yelling for someone to get off him. I try to move my head and get to my feet but I can't do either. I hear a woman's voice. "Ma'am can you hear me?" I just hold up my hand and someone touches it. "Ma'am I'm Constable Smyth, an ambulance is on the way so please stay still. Is there someone I can call for you?"

I manage to say Ben's name and tell her that my phone is in the bedroom. As soon as the paramedics arrive Constable Smyth leaves my side to call Ben. As I am being looked at by them I can hear Constable Smyth talking.

"No it's not Carly," she says. "My name is Police Constable Smyth and there has been an incident. Can you please give me Carly's address and describe her to me." There is silence, I assume Ben is answering her questions. "Can you please tell me your relationship with Carly." More silence. Constable Smyth says, "Please hold on for a moment." Then she covers the mouth piece and asks me, "Is Ben your boyfriend?" I nod. "Are you ok for me to inform him what has happened here?" I nod again.

Constable Smyth proceeds to tell Ben what she knows and that I am going to be taken to the hospital soon, and that he should meet me there.   When she hangs up I say, "Dad."

Constable Smyth nods, scrolls through my contacts and calls my dad. Again I can only hear Constable Smyth's side of the conversation. "No Sir, it's not Carly, I'm Police Constable Smyth and there has been an incident at your home involving Carly and a young man." Silence. "Yes Sir, we have him in custody and Carly will be on her way to the hospital shortly." Silence. "I will tell her, thank you Sir."

"Carly your dad, mum and Ben will meet you at the hospital. You're safe now, your attacker is in the back of the Police car and he can't hurt you anymore," she says with a sympathetic smile. She must see domestic violence cases all the time.

"Carly, my name is Martin and this is Steve. We are just going to lift you onto the gurney, this might hurt a bit but we will try to be as gentle as possible."

I try to brace myself but as soon as the Paramedics move me pain shoots through my body and I let out a howl. I'm placed in the back of the ambulance and rushed to the nearest hospital. Ben is waiting there for me when the doors of the ambulance open and my parents arrive as they are wheeling me into the emergency department.

Ben and my parents are asked to wait in the E.D. waiting room while they get me settled in. My blood pressure is taken and I am hooked up to a few monitors, blood and urine samples are taken and I am sent for an ultrasound and X-ray to see if there is any internal damage from the kicking that George gave me. When I'm settled back in the E.D. Ben and my folks are allowed in.

The curtain parts, I can't look at them, I am so ashamed. I hear a gasp and my mother starts to cry. I assume I look as bad as I feel. My mum and dad stand one side and Ben stands the other side of my bed. No one speaks, I look up at Ben, I can see that he has been crying and there is so much pain on his face. I can't continue to look at him because I know I am the cause of his pain.

Ben places his hand in mine and lean in to kiss my forehead. "I am so sorry I wasn't there for you, sweetheart. I will never ever let you down again." I can feel his tears fall on my skin.

The Doctor comes in and says, "Carly, there are two Police Officers out in the waiting room, and if you are up to it they would like to talk to you."

"Can you please give me a minute?" I mumble.

The doctor exits the cubicle. I feel three sets of eyes on me. I motion to my dad and he comes closer. He kisses my forehead. "Ratbag you have to press charges this time, this can't continue."

"I c..can't." I whisper.

My dad put's his head down, "Carly, he deserves to have the book thrown at him for what he did to you, it has to stop, please press charges."

"But wh..what about your j..job, I don't want th..things to be awkward for you."

"Carly, if he serves time, and I am praying he will, I will make sure that he is sent to another prison. He won't come to the prison I work at, and besides, I will talk to my Superintendent to make doubly sure."

I take a shaky breath. "Ok, ask the officers t..to come in, but.. please don't be angry w..with me, I would like only B..Ben here with me. What I'm about t…to tell them isn't pr..pretty, and no matter how y… you feel at the m…moment, he is still your s..son."

My dad nods, grabs my mum's hand and leads her towards the waiting room. Constable Smyth and her partner enter the cubicle.

"Your Dad said it was ok to come in. Carly and Ben, this is Constable Bruce Hadden and I'm Kate Smyth. I believe you are ready to give a statement."

I look at Ben, and he places my hand in his and gives it a gentle squeeze. I turn back to the Officers and say I'm ready. "In your own words, can you please tell me what happened?"

I go through what happened, at times Ben squeezes my hand harder, shakes his head or looks away trying to calm himself down. When I have finished Constable Smyth asks me if I want to press charges, and I say I do. Ben looks relieved. I also ask if I can get a restraining order against George, and Constable Smyth said she will make the phone call for the VRO (Violence Restraining Order) when she gets back to the Police Station. I ask if they are going to let George go and Constable Smyth said not for a while, they are going to petition that he stay in custody until it goes to trial, but just in case she will apply for the VRO.

They say that they will be in touch and leave. When we are alone Ben moves the chair so it is facing me, he is still holding my hand and looks like he is struggling with what to say. I start to hyperventilate and the monitors go off. Ben jumps up and sits behind me, holding me gently and whispering in my ear how much he loves me. The nurses come rushing in and Ben explains that I'm having a panic attack, so they turn down the volume of the heart monitor and leave me in Ben's care. My whole body shakes, it hurts to breath or to move and it hurts having Ben's body and arms around me, but I don't want him to let me go. We just sit like that not saying a word. I don't know what to say and either Ben feels the same or he is being respectful.

A short while later they admit me and move me to a private room. My parents say goodnight and tell me that they will come and see me in the morning. After a bit of persuasion they allow Ben to stay the night on the lazy boy chair in my room because I'm too scared to be alone. Once the Nurse has completed her rounds Ben climbs in bed behind me and gently holds me until I go to sleep. It seems like I have only been asleep for a few minutes when I feel Ben pull me closer and speak softly to me. I'm covered in sweat, I've had a nightmare and Ben woke me from it. I cry in his arms for a long time. It's the only place I feel safe.

I'm discharged from Hospital after a few days. My ultrasound showed no major internal damage. The X-ray shows George has damaged the ribs he broke last time, but it looks like I was able to protect myself better during this attack and there are no new injuries, thank god for small mercies.

Due to my injuries I am unable to work for a while and my boss has to let me go. I plead my case but she said that this has happened in the past, and even though she is sympathetic to my situation she can't keep my job open. I am gutted, I love my job, my clients and work mates. "Fucking George w..wins again, he always ru..ruins my life," I cry as Ben holds me.

I rest through the day while Ben is at work and at night he takes good care of me, cooking me dinner and watching TV or movies with me. And when I'm up to it we go for walks on the beach. Ben has basically moved in and my parents are ok with that. I don't know or care where George is. Because of the restraining order he has to stay away from our home. The court date is set for later in the year, and I just want it over and done with.

BEN | 9

My final week arrives and as I say goodbye to Carly that Monday morning I ask, "Are you up for going out for a meal tonight?"

She raises her eyebrows at me. "Ben, the last two times we have planned to go out for a meal have not gone well. I'm not sure if I want to tempt fate."

"Please let's try, I just want to take my beautiful girlfriend out for a lovely meal."

"Ben I am a h..hot mess and I'm not sure I am com..comfortable going out in public, plus there is still some bruising and sw..swelling on my face."

"Carly, you are the most beautiful girl I have ever seen, I love you and I would really like for us to relax and enjoy a wonderful meal in a nice restaurant. Don't decide now, I will call you at lunch time and you can tell me what you think," I say as I kiss her goodbye and drive to work.

I pull into the car park just as Rabbit is walking up the path. "Morning mate, how's Carly?" The morning after the attack I turned up to class emotionally and physically spent, having been with Carly in the hospital all night. Because we are a small class word got around about the attack and everyone has been concerned about Carly.

"Mornin' Rab's. Physically she's healing well, but mentally and emotionally it's a struggle for her. She's having nightmares most nights and she's withdrawn into herself, so getting her to go out in public is hard. Anyway, I have asked her to go to dinner with me tonight and she'll give me her answer at lunch time," I say with a shrug.

Rabbit puts his hand on my shoulder. "She's a cool chick and from what you've told me she's tough, she'll get through this," he says as we make our way to the classroom.

The morning goes slowly and I'm unable to keep my mind off Carly. I can't believe how lucky I am that I found her. I know the circumstances weren't good but I have really loved living with her, coming home to her every night and waking up with her in my arms every morning. She's my future and I just have to find a way to make that happen.

At lunch time I call Carly. "Hey babe, how's it going?"

"Not too bad. How's your morning been?"

"Alright I guess. Anyway, how about tonight?"

"Yeah ok. I'd love to go out to dinner with you."

I can hear the smile in Carly's voice. "WOW. I'm so happy about that. I'll book the restaurant and I'll see you when I get home. I love you."

"I love you too Ben."

As I hang up the phone I stand there for a minute. I'm so proud of her, she sounds different than she did when I left this morning. Lighter maybe? I don't care what it is, I just know it makes me happy.

On my way home I pick up some flowers for Carly and as I drive into the driveway I see her open the front door and stand waiting for me. She smiles as I make my way to her, I walk into her open arms and she kisses me like there's no tomorrow. "I've missed you," she whispers into my mouth.

"I've missed you too, Beautiful," I say as I pull her in a little tighter, but not so much that I'll hurt her.

"Are those for me?" Carly asks, looking over my shoulder at the flowers.

"Yes they are, because we are going out on a date and I wanted you to have these before we left."

"They are beautiful. Thank you," she says as she kisses me and leads me to our room. I notice the room has had a major clean up and that the curtains and window are open. They have been closed since the attack. "I've decided I won't be a victim," Carly says quietly behind me. "I can't let him win."

I turn around and gather her in my arms. "I'm so fuckin' proud of you," I say as I rest my forehead against hers.

Carly gets a vase as I get out of my uniform. I'm just putting my jeans on as she walks back into the room with the flowers. She places them on her chest of drawers and rearranges them as she starts to speak. "As you can see, I cleaned up a bit, changed the sheets and opened the window. I forgot how much I missed the fresh air in our room. I don't know how you put up with me."

I love the fact that she called it our room. Rightly or wrongly, that's how I see it. "There was nothing to put up with, I wanted to be with you and that was what you needed."

"I applied for a few jobs today," she says happily.

For some reason I wasn't prepared for that. I knew she was upset about losing her job and that she would one day look for another, but I didn't think today was the day she would do it. I know it's selfish of me, but I like coming home and having Carly waiting for me.

After a while I make my way to the shower. I'm still upset that Carly is looking for a job. I love that fact that she's independent but I miss her when I can't see her. Jesus Christ, I need to get a grip. I look down to make sure I haven't grown a vagina in the last two hours. I finish my shower and walk into our room in just my towel. Carly is dressed in a mid-thigh black skirt with a pink blouse and is putting on her makeup.

She just stands there staring at me with a small brush held up to her lips. "See something you like?" I say raising my eyebrows. That seems to startle her out of her thoughts

"Oh you know I do," she says with a smile.

"It's great to see you smile again, I have really missed that."

"Well you will be seeing it a lot from now on. My life is back in my hands, no more victim."

"That's my girl," I say as I sweep her up into my arms to kiss her.

We arrive at the restaurant and I open the door for her. She doesn't fight me on this anymore, so it looks like she has gotten used to it. We are shown to our table and order our drinks. Carly has a coke because she's still on medication from the attack and I order a beer. I reach for her hand and we just sit there talking as if we don't have a care in the world. We order our food and enjoy each other's company. Halfway through our meal I put down my knife and fork and reach for her hand again. "Carly, there is something I would like to discuss with you."

"Of course, what's up?"

"You know that Friday is my last day on course and that I am supposed to fly back to Sydney on Saturday... Well, I spoke to my Chief at H.M.A.S Kuttabul in Sydney and he has approved three weeks leave for me. Would you be ok if I spent those three weeks with you? We could go down south to Margaret River for a week or up north to Monkey Mia, it's up to you. What do you think?"

A huge smile beams across her face. "That would be wonderful, I don't care where we go as long as I'm with you. I love you Ben. I know I don't say it very often but I do."

"I know you do. Don't get me wrong, I love hearing you say you say it, but I do understand that you're not as comfortable as I am when it comes to you telling me how you feel. Hopefully one day you will be, but if that doesn't happen it's still ok. When we get home we will check out both places on the laptop and get somewhere booked."

"Sounds like a plan."

We finish our meal and drinks and then make our way to the car. I hold Carly's hand as usual, I love the connection, skin on skin. We get to the car and I press her up against the door and kiss her passionately. I have missed this, since the attack we had been more restrained with each other due to Carly's injuries.

Carly pulls away. "We need to go home, now."

"Are you ok, did I hurt you?" I ask worriedly.

"Honey, you didn't hurt me, just the opposite. I want you and I want you now. So we need to get a move on and get home so I can have my wicked way with you."

"Fuck, Carly, you're killing me," I laugh.

I open the door for her and then race around to my side. Luckily we only live about 10 minutes away from the restaurant. We race inside waving to Andrew and Kathy on our way to our bedroom. We close the bedroom door behind us, I grab Carly around the waist and kiss her as I walk her backwards to the bed. The backs of Carly's knees hit the bed and I gently lay her down. I crawl up her beautiful body and continue to kiss her. After a while she asks me to stand up. I go to take off my glasses and she stops me. "Let me take them off," she says with a grin.

Carly kneels down and removes my shoes and then works her way up my body. She kisses me while she slowly undoes the buttons on my shirt one by one. My breathing becomes shallow, especially when she kisses her way down my neck to my chest then to my right nipple, she flicks it with her tongue and I let out a hiss. She moves to my left nipple and takes it in her mouth and lightly bites it. "Fuuuuuucccccck-kkkkk," I moan. I can feel Carly smile against my skin as she works her way down my stomach. She kisses, nips and sucks her way down to my jeans. She runs her nails up and down my chest and stomach as she kisses all around my snail trail. I am so turned on right now and my cock is so hard I'm surprised it hasn't broken the zip on my jeans. Carly kneels on the carpet and starts to undo my jeans.

I place my hands on either side of her face, as she looks up at me I say, "I love you so much, Carly."

Carly smiles. "I'm about to show you how much I love you." She slowly slides my jeans down my legs and throws them in the corner. As she kisses her way back up my legs she looks me in the eyes until she's facing my erection. She leans forward and kisses me through my boxers. I can feel her lips and breath and I let out a low growl. I can feel my body twitch. She places her hands on my hips and runs her thumbs under the waistband until she can feel the base of my cock. Carly starts to remove my boxers and my rock hard cock springs free. She places her hand at the base and slowly takes me in her mouth. She sucks and flicks her tongue until my body is at her mercy.

I reach down and grab a handful of Carly's hair and start to control the pace. "That's it babe….just like that….oh god….Carly….fuuuc-ccckk," I pant.

It feels so fuckin' good but after a while I'm going to have to stop her because I can feel my orgasm build and I'm not going to last much longer if she keeps going. "Carly, you need to stop, I'm about to come," I moan. She grabs my hips and quickens her pace. I try to pull her away but she won't stop. It's too late, I've tried but I can't stop it and I come in her mouth. My heart's thumping in my chest. That's the best blow job I have ever had in my life. I let go of Carly's hair and she releases her grip on my hips.

"Well that was a first for me," she says with a sly smile on her face.

I lean down and help Carly to her feet. My mouth crashes down on hers "You never cease to amaze me, and now it's your turn." I pick Carly up and she lets out a squeal as I place her in the middle of the bed. I go to take off my glasses and she stops me.

"Please leave them on. Let me take them off you."

"Your wish is my command," I say as I leave them on and proceed to undress Carly. I don't take my time and I'm little rougher than usual, but I find that it's turning her on. I can smell her arousal as I get to her underwear, they are very wet and I can't wait to be inside her. After I remove all her clothes I make my way to the bottom of the bed and kneel on the floor. I grab her ankles and pull her down the bed. She squeals with surprise and excitement. I place her legs over my shoulders and spread her thighs wide. Carly looks at me with so much love and lust as I lean my head in between her thighs, licking, sucking and nibbling her into an overwhelming orgasm. She comes so hard and long, she has to beg me to stop because she can't take anymore.

Once Carly comes back down to earth she says, "You know how we are both clean, and I have the rod and we are exclusive, would it be ok if we didn't use protection? I'd love to feel all of you with no barrier."

I have been inside her once without a condom and that was heaven and I'm not sure I could go back to using them, so thank god Carly feels the same. "Babe, I would love nothing more," I say as I get up off the floor and make my way to the bed. I sit in the middle of the bed as Carly regains the use of her limbs again and joins me. Carly pushes me onto my back, removes my glasses and straddles me. I grasp my cock with one hand and place my other hand on Carly's hip. I position my cock at her entrance and I pull her down onto me. I feel a shiver go through my body as I grab her hips and start to control the pace. As we find our rhythm I start to tease her clit with my thumb and finger, I flick and pinch it until her body is shuddering and coming around my cock. Carly lets out a muffled scream into my shoulder as I feel her body relax into mine. A few more thrusts and I'm moaning her name as my own orgasm explodes inside her.

"I love you so much Ben, thank you for finding me," Carly pants.

We just lay there for a while looking at each other and enjoying the moment.

Before we go to sleep we book a week in Margaret River.

CARLY | 10

Ben finishes his course on the Friday, all the guys pass and a night out is planned for them at my local pub. Nicole, myself and a few other girls were invited to the meal and drinks afterwards. Ben and I pick up Davo and Nicole. I am the driver for the night so they can enjoy a drink and let their hair down. Rabbit and Kiwi are also there and it is great seeing them again; it has been a while and they seem a little uncomfortable around me. I figure that they know about the attack. I lean towards Ben and whisper in his ear, "Who knows about the attack?"

He takes a deep breath. "Everyone, I was a mess after what happened and because we are a small class word got around." I'm speechless. I just look at him. "Carly, everyone is very sorry for what happened to you, no one is judging you and they are all happy that you are on the road to recovery."

"Yu..you could have warned m..me," I stutter.

"I did think about telling you but I didn't think you would come if you knew."

"Ok f..fair point, but in future pl..please tell me so I'm not bli.. blindsided."

Ben kisses my hand. "I promise."

We have a great night, the meal is lovely and the banter around the table is fun, it makes me forget for a while what has happened. Later in the night the place gets packed, and we dance while the DJ plays. It's wonderful just letting loose and enjoying a night out with Ben and friends. I feel like I don't have a care in the world. I say good bye to Rabbit and Kiwi because they are flying back to their bases in the morning. It takes me a while to get Davo and Nicole in the car because they are so drunk, it is like one step forward and three steps back, they are so damned funny. We drop them off at Nicole's and I drive Ben and me home.

We pull into the drive and Ben stumbles out of the car and he races around to the driver's side to open the door for me, I laugh and hold his hand as I exit the car. "You are such a gentleman," I laugh.

"That's because you bring out the best in me, Carly, and I only want the best for you."

I kiss him and we walk inside. Ben tries to be quiet but it seems the quieter he tries the louder he becomes. He announces that he is starving so we go to the kitchen to make him a toasted sandwich, he sits at the counter while he watches me prepare his food. I look up at him and he has a stupid grin plastered on his face. "What's that look for?" I ask.

"Carly do you realise how happy you make me?"

"Yeah I'm a real barrel of laughs," I scoff turning back to the toaster.

I feel his arms wrap around my waist and turn me around.

Ben places his hands on my face and looks me in the eyes. "Carly, you are the strongest woman I have ever met; I don't mean in physical strength I mean in here." He places his hand over my heart. "I love you more than I have ever loved anyone, you make me so happy and I couldn't believe my luck when you told me you loved me too. I don't want to go back to Sydney on my own, please come with me, I hate the thought of leaving you. I know you would be leaving your family and friends behind but we wouldn't be on our own coz we have my family there and they love you."

"Ben they don't know me."

"They know we love each other and that's enough for them."

"Ben you're drunk."

"So? Everything I have said has been the truth and I will repeat it when I'm sober. Just please think about it."

I just smile and pass him his toasted sandwich while I drink a glass of milk. We go to bed and I have to help Ben undress because he is too drunk and seriously uncoordinated, he is a funny drunk but I doubt he will remember our conversation tomorrow. I get him settled in bed, he faces away from me and I cuddle into his back with my arm around his waist.

"Thank you for loving me and taking care of me," Ben whispers.

"Always." And with that we go to sleep.

Ben is hung over and extremely delicate the next morning. I

bring him some toast and a coffee in bed, the poor darling is really un-well. We just have a lazy day, Ben sleeps off and on and finally feels human again by dinner time. We pack our things later that night because we are leaving for Margaret River in the morning.

Ben lays on the bed and holds his hand out to me "Come lay with me Beautiful I want to talk to you."

We lay face to face and he runs the back of his hand down the side of my face, it is so sensual and loving, I feel so safe with Ben and he makes me happy. I'm beginning to think that maybe, just maybe I deserve to be happy and hopefully that includes Ben.

"I want to apologise for getting so drunk last night but thank you for taking such good care of me."

"There is nothing to apologise for, you're a cute drunk and as for taking care of you that is my pleasure."

"I know I said a few things to you last night and I just wanted to talk to you about it." I nod. Ben grabs my face and looks me in the eyes "Carly, I am serious about you moving to Sydney to come and live with me. I don't want to live without you or do the long distance thing, I love you and my future is with you. I am posted to Kuttabul for the next twelve to eighteen months. We can get a place in Sydney, I would love to get a dog, you can get to know my family and I know they will treat you like one of their own, though I have to admit I'm not sure if that's a good or a bad thing because they are full on," he laughs. "You don't have to decide right away just promise me you will think about it."

"I will seriously think about it and as soon as I have come to a decision one way or the other I promise you will be the first to know. You have to understand this is a huge thing for me, not just the moving but actually living together. What if we don't get along? What if we have very different views as to where and how we live? You say your family love me but what if you're wr..wrong and they only tol…tolerate me? What if we d..don't like the same br..breed of dog?" I can feel my heart rate increase and I'm becoming dizzy.

Ben pulls me to him, kisses my face and repeatedly tells me he loves me, that this will pass and I'm going to be ok. Luckily for me Ben always realises when I am having a panic attack and he knows just what to do.

Once the attack had passed Ben start's to speak. "Do you feel ok now?"

"I'm so sorry, I have no control over them, at times I get so overwhelmed and overthink things and that's when they tend to happen. Thank you for taking care of me."

"I will always take care of you. Babe, when did they start? And have you thought about seeing a counsellor?"

"I actually don't remember when they started, I can never remember a time when I didn't have them. I have thought about seeing someone but I don't want to talk about it to a stranger and I'd really like to put all of it behind me."

"Ok, I respect your decision. Can I address some of the things you said?" I nod and smile. "No one knows if they can live together until they try and we will be the same, we will figure it out, we will both decide on where we are going to live, please don't worry about my family, they are thrilled that I have found someone that I am crazy about. My concern is not that they won't love you, it's that they will love you too much and try to monopolise your time and I won't get a look in. And as for the dog, what kind of dog do you like?"

"I like big dogs especially Rottweilers, they are good for protection, how do you feel about that breed?"

"Yeah, I'm cool with Rotties, they are good looking dogs and I agree good for protection so if I'm not there I know you will be ok. Please think about what we have talked about and when you are ready, give me your answer. You ready to get some sleep?" Ben asks with a yawn.

"Yeah it's getting late, thank you for listening to me. I promise I will seriously think about moving with you and if I have any questions or concerns I will ask you. Good night honey, I love you," I say as I kiss him goodnight.

"I love you too, sweet dreams."

I don't sleep very well, all I can think about is what Ben asked me, I toss and turn so much that I wake him. I feel Ben's arms reach out for me and drag me across the bed to him. He kisses the back of my neck as he cuddles me from behind. I can feel his erection press into my lower back. I shuffle back a bit more and rub myself against him, he lets out a soft moan, places his hand around my breast and plays with my nipple until it becomes hard.

"Babe, roll over."

I do as he asks and he makes love to me.

We wake a little later in the morning than we would usually do. Ben is on leave and I'm unemployed. I'm not happy about being fired but at least I get to spend extra time with Ben. No matter what I decide to do I have to find a job. I love what I do and besides, being a lady of leisure is so damned boring.

We get to our chalet late in the afternoon. It is situated two streets back from the main street in Margaret River. It has an outdoor spa easily large enough for four people which is secluded under our patio, a self-contained kitchen, a main bathroom, and two bedrooms. The master bedroom has a massive king size bed and a beautiful en-suite with his and hers sinks and a shower built for two, which I know will be put to good use over this week. There is a pond just a few feet away from our chalet that has a family of ducks living in it. The gardens are beautiful, filled with mainly native plants, and there are also hiking tracks not too far away.

We decide to go for a walk into town and get a few supplies for the week, we are eating in tonight because we are a little tired from the long drive. We go to the local butcher and buy some juicy steaks, to the baker to get crusty bread and to the grocery store to get some veggies to make a salad.   Throughout the week we visit wineries and the local breweries, walk along the beach, go for a few hikes, visit the chocolate factory a few times and sample the local food at the many amazing restaurants in town. It is so relaxing and just what we both need.

We make good use of the spa and shower, and the bed is so big I need a GPS to find Ben. It's wonderful doing what we want when we want and being as loud as we want, I feel free. I know if I move to Sydney our lives won't be exactly like this because work and life will get in the way, but if it could be like this fifty percent of the time I would be a very happy girl. I know in my heart I am swaying towards moving with him, but I would still like a little more time before I make that final decision.

The week goes by quickly and we are sad to leave. On the drive home I get a call from two salons that want me to go in for an interview later in the week. Ben becomes very quiet and we drive in silence for a while. When we make our first stop I sit down next to him on the bench. "Honey I'm just keeping my options open, I haven't made a decision one way or the other and if I decide to move I can always decline the job if it's offered to me." He seems to settle down a bit but I can tell it concerns him.

For the rest of the week we just hang out, going to the movies and out to lunch and dinner. On Thursday I have my two interviews. One is at a salon in Fremantle and the other is in Claremont. Both are lovely salons, well established and the staff seemed happy. Both owners tell me that they will call me on Monday to let me know if I have been successful or not.

On Saturday afternoon Ben asks me to pack an overnight bag because he is taking me somewhere special for the night. He also asks me to bring a dress because he is taking me out to dinner in a nice restaurant. We drive to Perth and he pulls up at Crown Casino. Ben has booked a beautiful room at Crown Metropol and has organised a couple's massage for us. We get a glass of champagne on arrival and I feel very special. The massage is amazing and I'm so relaxed.

En route back to our room Ben says we need to do a little detour, and he walks me to the hair salon and tells the stylist who I am and that I have an appointment. He kisses me and says that he will see me back at the room, then walks away smiling and very proud of himself.

I can't believe how lucky I am that I have him in my life. I sit in the chair and the stylist is talking to me but I don't take notice of what she is saying, I feel a tear run down my face. I realised there and then that I don't want to live without Ben; he loves me, and treats me like I am the most precious thing in his life, so why haven't I told him yes? I'm such a fool. I start to get out of the chair to go after him but the stylist convinces me to stay. She asks me to describe the dress that I am wearing tonight and she puts my hair up. I usually don't wear it that way but I have to say I am happy with the result. Just as she is finishing another stylist asks me to follow her. As we enter the back room I realise she is the makeup artist and she is there to do my makeup. I explain to her that I usually do it and I don't need her, but thank her anyway, and she informs me that Ben has left strict instructions that I am to be pampered and must not lift a finger. I reluctantly sit in the chair. I have to say that she did a good job — I will only have to fix two things but she doesn't need to know that.

I walk back to the room and I realise that I don't have a key card to open the door, so I knock, hoping that Ben is inside. I hear noise in the room and then the door opened. *OH MY GOD* Ben is standing there in a charcoal suit with a black shirt and tie; fuck he looks hot, I'm speechless. Ben smiles, takes my hand and walks me into the room, where I see a beautiful arrangement of yellow and orange flowers next to my side of the bed. I regain the power of speech and manage to say, "You look amazing and the flowers are beautiful. Thank you for arranging my hair and makeup for me, it's a lovely thought."

"It's my pleasure and you look beautiful. Would you please change into your dress because I would like to see the complete picture."

I grab my dress and go into the bathroom to touch up my make-up and get changed. My dress is an off-the-shoulder style in crimson that sits just above my knees, and I have matching crimson four inch heels. I have had the dress for quite some time but I have never had anywhere special enough to wear it, until tonight.

I take one last look in the mirror and I'm satisfied with what I see. I open the bathroom door and walk into the bedroom. Ben is sat on the bed but gets up as I walk in, he stands there staring at me with the broadest smile I have ever seen. "Carly, you take my breath away. You are so beautiful and I am one very lucky man to have you as my girlfriend." I blush and put my head down. "No, no, no, please don't hide from me. I hope one day soon you will be able to accept my compliments, I will make it my life's mission." I laugh and smile at him.

"I have a booked us a table at a restaurant that has been recommended by a friend of mine. So if you are ready? ...we will make our way down."

"Ben, before we go can I please talk to you about something?" He looks worried. "I have been thinking a lot about you asking me to move to Sydney to be with you. Thank you so much for not putting any pressure on me and allowing me to make this decision on my own and in my own time. As I was sat in the chair about to get my hair done I got my answer." Ben starts to nibble at his finger nails as he waits. "Ben, I don't want to have a long distance relationship with you, my life is empty without you in it; I want to see, hold, kiss, talk to and make love to you every day. I would love nothing more than to move to Sydney to be with you."

Ben races to me, pulls me into his arms, picks me up and spins me around while kissing the shit out of me. "Carly, you have made me so happy." He puts me down, puts his hands on my face and looks me in the eyes "I promise that I will always love and protect you and I will never let you down." We stand there kissing for a while until Ben pulls away. "Babe if we don't leave this room now we will never leave." I smile and excuse myself to fix my hair and makeup.

We walk down to the restaurant arm in arm, I feel like I'm floating on a cloud at the moment and I couldn't be happier. Ben holds my hand between courses and he smiles the whole time, it's so cute. We decide to go to the gaming floor and play a few hands of black jack. I have never played before, so Ben starts to teach me. He gets me my own coloured chips, they are yellow and he gets dark blue. I win a few hands but I lose all my money in the end; Ben on the other hand does really well, he just keeps winning hand after hand and soon enough there is a huge pile of chips in front of him. "What do you think I should do Beautiful? Should I keep playing or cash in my chips?"

"I have no clue, I lost all my chips so I obviously have no idea what I am doing. Honey you have been doing great without my help so you decide."

"You are next to me and that in itself is enough," Ben says as he kisses me. "How about I cash in and we make good use of that huge bed in our room?"

"I love how you think," I say with a wink.

Ben cashes in his chips at the cashier. I nearly pass out because he has won twelve thousand eight hundred dollars. "We will put that towards things for our new home," he says proudly.

"This is your money so you should spend it on something for yourself."

"Carly, our new life together is something for me. This is our money now, what's mine is yours."

"Is it ok if we talk about this upstairs in private?"

Ben entwines his fingers with mine and we walk back to the room. He opens the door for me and we sit on the bed facing each other. "What would you like to talk about?"

"You said earlier that your winnings is our money, and what's yours is mine. That is a beautiful thought but it is very one-sided. I don't bring much to this relationship and I don't want you or anyone to think that I am taking advantage of you. I don't have a job right now and very little savings in the bank, and besides, I like to pay my way."

"Have you finished?" I say that I have. "OK, I love you and you love me, we are in an exclusive relationship and we are going to move in with each other, so in my eyes what's mine is yours and what's yours is mine, we share everything. When you get to Sydney and get settled you'll look for a job if you want to and if you don't want to that's ok because I make a pretty good living and I am happy to support us both. The Navy will subsidise the rent so we don't have to pay the full amount, I already have a car that I own, and as for taking advantage of me, you can do that any time you want," he says smiling and raising his eyebrows.

I slap his arm and laugh. "You have a one track mind Ben Richardson and I have to say I am very happy you do. Now let me get you out of that suit and make love to you."

"Anything for you, Beautiful." Ben slowly undoes his tie and then places it around my waist and pulls me to him. We kiss as we undress each other and make love on the bed, against the wall and in the shower. By the time we finally decide to go to sleep my body is deliciously sore and we are exhausted.

We skip breakfast and make our way back to my place. I have to call the salons and withdraw my applications; we also have a lot of things to organise for my move to Sydney. We decide not to tell my parents just yet because we want to make sure that we can do what we want to; there is no need to say anything until it is all organised. By Wednesday of that week Ben has identified me as his next of kin and officially stated that we are in a de facto relationship. We look at Navy homes via the internet, and after a virtual tour of about nine of them, we decide on a two bedroom, bathroom plus en-suite unit with a small back yard. The kitchen, bathroom and en-suite have been recently renovated and there are bare floor boards throughout the home. It's about ten minutes' drive from Ben's base. I fall in love with it and that's good enough for Ben.

Two days later Ben is informed that the unit is ours but it won't be ready for another month, so that means that Ben will be in Sydney for three weeks until I can get there, which sucks. We realise there is nothing we can do about it so we decide to go and look at furniture. We go to the big stores that are Australia-wide and make sure that what we were going to buy is available in Sydney and that they can hold it in the Sydney store until we move into our new home. We have the dimensions of every room so we know the furniture and white goods we buy will fit.

Our bedroom is big enough for a king-size bed and we both are very happy about that. We buy beautiful linen for the bed, towels that match the bathrooms, bedside tables with matching chests of drawers, very comfortable lounge chairs in a neutral colour, a stand-alone fridge and freezer, a small dining table with four chairs, a washing machine and a clothes dryer. I choose the dinnerware, cutlery, glasses, pots and pans etc. because Ben is not interested in that kind of thing. The last thing we look at is a TV and DVD player, which I let Ben choose because I can see he is in heaven and I really don't care what we get, I only care that they are easy to operate.

After a full and exhausting day of shopping we decide it is time to tell our parents. I'm pretty sure my parents will be happy for me because they like and trust Ben, but I don't think they will be happy that I'm moving across to the other side of Australia. However, I don't know Ben's family and I'm scared how they might react; Ben assures me that they will be happy but I'm not so sure. He organises a Skype session with his parents for later today and I am shitting myself; if this doesn't go well then it will make life very difficult for us.

For the Skype session we go to the park down the road from my house because we want privacy. The screen comes to life at the arranged time and Ben's parents meet us with a huge smile. Lucy and James talk excitedly about Ben coming home, especially because Chelsea will be turning five in a months' time.

Ben holds my hand. "Mum, Dad, there is something that Carly and I would like to tell you. You know that we have been seeing a lot of each other... well, things are serious between us and I have asked Carly to move to Sydney to live with me and she has said yes."

"Is she pregnant?" We hear a male's voice and it isn't James. Lucy and James look to their left with a frown and shake their heads.

"What, it's a valid question, they haven't known each other long."

"Damon, is that you?" Ben asks.

"Yes and the rest of the family are here too," Damon laughs.

All of a sudden Ben's siblings appear in front of the screen with sheepish looks on their faces.

"Well I suppose this saves on phone calls, but you could have told us you were all there. This was supposed to be a private conversation with Mum and Dad, I should have known." Ben looks at me and mouths 'sorry', I just shrug my shoulders and smile.

The questions start to come thick and fast. "Is Carly pregnant, are you getting married, where are you going to live, when are you coming back?"

"Hold on a minute, one question at a time. No Carly is not pregnant, and we are not getting married, well not just yet anyway," he says with a wink. "We have found a place close to the base and I will be back next week, but Carly won't be coming over for about four weeks after me because the house isn't ready yet. So are there any other questions?"

"Uncle Ben, Uncle Ben."

"Hello Chelsea, you look pretty, do you have a question?"

"Uncle Ben and Aunty Carly will you be at my birthday party?"

My head whips around to Ben with my mouth open, Chelsea has just called me Aunty Carly, she has only seen me once on Ben's birthday and she has only spoken to him. Ben squeezes my hand tighter and smiles a huge smile that shows his dimples. He motions to the screen and I start to talk. "I would love to come to your birthday party Chelsea, if that's ok with you?"

"Yay. Do you know how old I'm gunna be?"

"No I don't, how old will you be?"

"I'm gunna be five and I go to big School soon. Mummy and Nanny got my clothes for big School and they are red and... Mummy, what's the other colour?" I can hear a female voice and I assume it is Piper's. "Mummy says it's black."

"I bet you look like a big girl in your uniform."

"Nanny and Poppy say I look beautiful." She grins.

"If your Nanny and Poppy say that it must be true." I reply.

"Aunty Carly, Mummy has a baby in her tummy."

Ben straightens up and yells "WHAT?"

Piper comes closer to the screen. "Thanks blabber mouth," Piper says as she kisses Chelsea on the top of her head. "Surprise. We found out a few weeks back and we have just got past the three month mark. We wanted to get into the second trimester before we told anyone. I'm due late November."

"Congratulations you guys, that's wonderful news. I can't wait to meet my new nephew or niece, I'm so happy for you." Ben beams.

Ben and his family speak for a while longer. I join in on the conversation at times but mainly sit back and listen. We say our goodbyes and the screen goes black.

"That was crazy," I laugh. "Talk about put us on the spot. Chelsea is adorable and how exciting you get to be an uncle again."

"Yes, and you get to be an aunty again. How cool is it that Chelsea called you Aunty?"

"Did you put her up to that?"

"I swear on Chelsea's life I didn't. It's official, you are a part of my crazy family," Ben says laughing.

We pack up Ben's laptop and make our way to my house. We have decided to take my parents out for a meal so we can tell them. We get ready and make our way to my family's favourite Chinese restaurant. We order our drinks and ask for a minute to look at the menu. Ben is nervous and starts to fidget with his napkin and shirt collar. I place my hand on his thigh and give it a reassuring squeeze.

"Ben, you look very nervous, do you have something you want to tell Kath and myself?" my dad asks.

Ben shifts in his seat. "Andrew, you know that Carly and I have been spending a lot of time together, and I need to tell you that I am crazy about your daughter, I love her."

"That's obvious to us that you love Carly," says Dad.

"I have to fly back to my base this weekend and I have asked Carly to move to Sydney to be with me, and she has said yes." Ben takes a deep breath and waits for Mum and Dad to say something.

"This is not a total surprise to us. Kath and I talked about the possibility of this happening when Carly started seeing a lot of you. I'm assuming you know what you are doing. You seem to be a stand-up guy and you treat Carly very well, but I need to let you know that if you hurt her in any way, shape or form I will hunt you down and make you wish you'd never been born."

"Andrew, Kathy, I promise you I will never hurt Carly, or lie to her or let her down. She has been through enough hurt in her life and all I want to do is make her happy and I promise you I will make that my life's mission."

Dad looks at me, holds his hand out. "Ratbag, is this what you want?"

I place my hand in his. "More than anything. I love Ben like I never thought I could love anyone. He makes me so happy and I don't want to be apart from him."

"So when will you be leaving?" Mum asked.

"Ben has to go back on the Sunday and I will be following in a few weeks. We have found a place and we went furniture shopping today and it will all be waiting in Sydney for us when our place becomes vacant. We Skyped with Ben's family earlier, so everyone is on the same page. "

"Carly, I don't want to be a downer but what about the court case?" Dad asks.

"Ben and I have spoken about it and we will fly back when it goes to trial. We don't want George to know where I am." I look straight at Mum and say, "Can you promise me he won't find out where I am?"

My mum lowers her head and says, "I promise I won't tell him." I hope this is one promise she will keep. Only time will tell.

We enjoy a nice meal and the conversation flows freely. When we get home I call Nicole and arrange to meet her for lunch tomorrow.

I'm nervous as I get ready for my lunch date with Nicole. I am happy about my relationship and the new life we are planning but I don't want to leave Nicole behind; this is going to be one of the hardest things I have had to do. I know that might sound crazy considering what I went through with George and Shaun, but she has been there with me the whole way through, never judging me, always sticking up for me and trying to protect me when she could. I get ready, kiss Ben goodbye and drive to the café on the beach front. Nicole is already there sitting at a table outside. It is a little chilly but nice.

Nicole squeals when she sees me, she jumps up hugging and kissing me. "I've missed seeing that cheeky face, I have hardly seen you hun, how you been?"

"I'm good, actually I'm better than good, I'm great," I say with a goofy grin. "There's no easy way to say this, but Ben has asked me to move to Sydney with him and I have agreed to go. Nicole, I love him so much and I can't imagine my life without him, please be happy with me."

"I know you love each other but, moving to Sydney to be with Ben on your own? Do you think you are really ready for that? Do you think your relationship will hold up?"

"Yes of course I do, Nicole. I never thought I could be this happy. Shit I never thought I deserved to be happy but Ben changed all that; he treats me like I'm the most precious thing in the world, he loves me in spite of what I have been through and he's there for me when things get too much, holding me, never judging me... How did I get so lucky?"

"Chica, that's good enough for me, I have never seen you this happy and you do deserve to be happy. I am going to really miss you bitch," she says with a laugh.

We have a wonderful long lunch, talking about everyone and everything. It hits me all of a sudden that I am leaving and I start to cry. "Hun I'm really going to miss you. No one gets me the way you do."

"You don't leave for a few weeks, so we will have to make the most of the time we have. Besides, I will come to visit you, often; you can't get rid of me that easily bitch," Nicole says as she hugs me hard.

I drive home to Ben, he hugs and kisses me as I walk in the door and it feels amazing. We have a quiet dinner and decide to watch movies in bed. Well, that was the plan, I don't think we watch more than ten minutes of the first movie before Ben pounces and I surrender willingly.

11 | BEN

Friday night we go to the pub and invite Nicole to come with us. We want her to be with us and see us as a couple. I go to the bar to get us some drinks and we stand there talking for a while. I ask Nicole what is happening with her and Davo.

"Ryan has gone back to Darwin. We have talked and texted a few times, but what can we do we live so far apart? If it's meant to happen it'll happen."

After a few more drinks Nicole and Carly hit the dance floor, they're having a great time just like when I first saw them. I watch them laugh, hug and dance their arses off. I love watching Carly enjoy life; after everything that she has gone through she deserves to be happy. I can't believe this beautiful, wonderful, sexy woman loves me, I'm so fuckin' lucky. After a while I notice a few guys eyeing up the girls so I make my way onto the dance floor. I move in behind Carly and place my hands on her hips as she leans back and pushes her arse into my groin and rubs up against me. We dance like that for the rest of the song.

A few guys asked Nicole to dance and she is happy to do that but if they want to buy her a drink or get her number she politely refuses. One guy won't take no for an answer and tries to get handsy with her. She is patting his hands away but he is very persistent. I go to help a few times but Nicole motions that she's ok. Finally she has had enough, looks at me and mouths *'HELP'*. I tap the guy on the shoulder, lean in and tell him that Nicole's boyfriend is away training for a cage fighting match at the moment, and he won't be overly happy that another man has had his hands on his woman. The guy leans back and holds his hands up in surrender, turns to Nicole and says sorry and then walks away.

"What did you say to him?" asks Carly.

"I might have told him that Nicole's boyfriend is away training for a cage fighting match."

"You are a genius." Carly laughs as she kisses me.

The three of us continue drinking and dancing until closing time, we have had a great time. The taxi drops Nicole off first and then we make our way home. I pay the driver and then help Carly out my side of the car. She stumbles and falls into my arms and we land on the lawn laughing our arses off. We lay on the lawn kissing and groping.

Carly is kissing my neck and making her way south.

"Babe we need to take this inside otherwise we'll get done for indecent exposure," I laugh. I help Carly to her feet and we stumble inside. We try to be quiet but I know we aren't successful when Andrew comes out of his bedroom.   "Had a good night have we?" Andrew says with a smile.

"Andrew, we have had a great night. Do you know how much I love your daughter?" I say as I kiss Carly's hand. "Thank you for bringing her into the world."

"Well son I didn't do it on my own but I will pass on your thanks to Kath," laughs Andrew. "Now how about you go to bed and sleep it off."

Carly hugs Andrew and then she takes my hand as we stumble down the hall to our room. I pounce as soon as Carly shuts the bedroom door behind us. "Do you know how sexy you are?" I whisper in her ear.

"You're drunk that's why you're talking shit." Carly giggles as she looks at the floor.

I shake my head. "Carly, look at me please." I wait for her to lift her eyes. "You are the most beautiful, sexy and funny woman I have ever met. I feel like I'm a horny teenager when I'm around you." I smile.

"Ben, you can have any girl you want, you're so hot and look at me — I'm short, dumpy and plain looking. What are you doing with me?" she says as a tear rolls down her face.

I'm stunned. Doesn't she see how beautiful she is? I place my hands on her face. "I have the girl that I want and I'm looking at her. Carly, I love you, I never thought I could love someone this much, you have turned my world upside down. You are not dumpy and plain, you are beautiful and have the sexiest curves. I love your body and I'm telling you now I never want to hear you say that about yourself again because that will piss me off."

Carly is about to say something when I place my hand around the back of her neck and pull her in for a kiss. The kiss becomes hot and heavy very quickly. I move my hand down her back pressing her body further into mine as Carly moans into my mouth. I place both hands on her bum and then lift so she can wrap her legs around my waist and I slowly walk us to the bed.   "Sweetheart, if you were dumpy I wouldn't be able to pick you up as easily as I do." I smile against Carly's mouth as I lay her down. Her hair fans out on the pillow and she gives me the most loving smile that travels all the way to her stunning eyes. "Fuck, you're beautiful," I say breathlessly as I gently touch my lips to hers. I get lost in the kiss as I press my body against Carly's. Her body fits me like a glove and I can't get enough of her, I run my hands over her sexy as fuck curves; she's perfect for me. As we slowly make love we look right into each other's eyes, it's like I'm looking into her sole, the connection is so strong and I know I will do anything for this amazing woman. Words can't describe how it feels to be buried deep inside her. Carly's my drug of choice and I'm unashamedly a full blown addict.

CARLY | 12

I wake up late the next morning and I feel like someone has hit me over the head and shat in my mouth. My head is thumping. Just as I focus on my surroundings I leap out of bed and make a dash for the toilet, just making it in time before I throw up. I don't know where all the vomit comes from because I can't stop, and when did I eat carrots? I hate carrots. I feel someone behind me and my hair being pulled off my face.

"Babe, you ok?"

I try to shake my head but that's a bad idea, I start to groan and Ben places his other hand around my waist and holds me until I finish. I sit on the floor with my head on the toilet seat feeling very sorry for myself when Ben gets up and gets me a cold wet face cloth and he pats it down my face and neck.

"Do you have a bucket?" I nod and motion to the laundry. "Go get ready for a shower, I'll put the bucket in our room and then I will join you. We need to get you cooled down. I have some Berocca in my bag you can have that when we have you back in bed."

"Thank you for taking care of me, how did I get so lucky?" I groan.

Ben goes to kiss me but I pull away because I have just thrown up my entire body weight.

"I do this because I love you." With that he kisses my forehead and leads me to the bathroom, turns on the shower and gets me under the warm water. He disappears for a minute then gets in the shower with me. He washes my hair so gently and washes my body like I'm made of glass, I feel so cherished.

We get out of the shower and Ben places a towel around my hair and proceeds to dry me with another towel. When I'm completely dry he places a towel around his waist and takes the one off my head. When he runs a comb through it keeps getting snagged in a few knots, and Ben apologises every time. When he finishes he leads me back to the bedroom, which feels cooler because he has turned on the fan. There is a Berocca waiting for me on my bedside table. I drink it and then lay down. I have to admit I do feel a little bit better. Ben kisses my forehead and then places kisses on each eyelid. "Sleep, Beautiful, and I will be here when you wake." I sleep for the next few hours.

The first thing I see when I wake is Ben's beautiful smiling face. "How's your head and stomach?"

"Better I think, have you been here the whole time?"

"I told you I would, you are so bloody cute when you sleep, you snuggle into your pillow and make these soft little sounds, plus you drool."

I smack his chest "I do not drool."

"Oh yeah you do, don't be embarrassed, it's nothing to be ashamed of. But tonight I might bring a snorkel and goggles to bed with us coz I don't want to drown," he laughs.

"You fucker, that was mean," I screech as I push him on his back and straddle him.

"But you love me."

"Yes, I love you more and more each day. I'm going to miss you, I can't believe you are going tomorrow."

"It's only a few weeks and then it'll just be us, I can't wait for you to move in with me, to hold you and make love to you every day. I want to christen every room and also the backyard. We'll make as much noise as we like and run around the house naked," he says with a wink.

I lean down and kiss Ben on his mouth and slowly move my way to his ear, I nip his ear lobe and I can feel Ben getting hard beneath me, just the reaction I'm after. I giggle in his ear and kiss my way down his neck ever so slowly. I can feel and hear Ben's breathing change as I make my way down his amazing body.Between kisses I tell him I love him so much and that I can't believe he's mine. I stop at his waist, which is covered by the sheet. "I wonder what's under here," I ask in a sexy voice.

"Babe, why don't you move the sheet away, I know you will be very happy with what you find," he says with a sly smirk.

I lower my head but look at Ben through my lashes. I smile and I work my way lower kissing, sucking and nipping at his skin, Ben twitches every now and then. I stop at his rock hard erection, I grasp the base of his penis in my hand and start to lick his balls.

Ben lets out a moan, closes his eyes and grabs a handful of the sheet. "Fuck Carly, you make me feel so good..oh god...suck my balls babe..that's right..just like that."

I smile as I take his balls in my mouth and roll my tongue around them. Ben's hips buck forward. I lick his cock from base to tip making sure I run my tongue up the main vain because I know that drives him wild. I flick my tongue around the head and taste a bit of pre come, I take him in my mouth and I try to go deeper than I did last time. Ben starts to thrust upwards and controls the pace. All of a sudden I sit up. "Honey keep your eyes closed," I say as I lean over to my bedside drawer and pull out a packet. I place the contents in my mouth and then I go down on Ben again.

"What the fuck..Carly...fuuucccckkkk that feels so..different... what is it?"

"Pop rocks, it's popping candy," I say as the last of it dissolves on my tongue.

Ben sits up and pulls my body on top of him as he lies back down. "I love you so much, Carly." He rolls us so I am underneath him. "My turn." He leans over to his side of the bed and takes a mouthful of water and then places his mouth over my nipple, I feel something cold and I arch my back and push my nipple further into his mouth. Ben moves his hand to his mouth and pulls out an ice cube and rolls it over my hard nipples.

"Oh god, Ben," I moan as my body reacts to the cold sensation, he drags the remainder of the ice down my sides and stomach with his tongue licking behind. He gets to my belly button and I feel sick. I grab his hand. "Ben, please don't ever touch my belly button, it makes me feel sick if anything goes near it. Please, I'm serious, don't ever touch it or be in the vicinity of it."

Ben lets out a throaty laugh and just nods his head, he puts another ice cube in his mouth and crawls further down my body so he's between my legs, he parts them wider and runs the ice up and down my inner thighs as a delicious shiver goes through my body. Ben asks me to lift my hips and then he places a pillow underneath me, he gets another ice block, pops it in his mouth, parts me with his thumbs and blows cold air on my clit. My toes start to curl and I grab handful of his hair and pull his face into me, Ben starts to lick me like I'm his favourite flavour of ice-cream. The contrast of his tongue and the ice is mind blowing and

I start to moan his name and move my hips in time with his strokes.

Ben looks up at me and he moves a hand up to play with my nipples. I take his hand and move it towards my mouth, I take two of his fingers in my mouth, I suck, lick and gently bite them. Ben places his other hand under my thigh and holds me firmly because I am all over the place, I can't keep still, he is making my body move in ways I never thought it could, he knows how I like to be touched. Ben removes his hand from my mouth and runs it down my body until I can feel it between my thighs, I feel him insert two fingers inside me and my hips thrust upwards to meet them, he places his other hand on my abdomen and gently but firmly pushes down while his tongue and mouth play with my clit. My eyes shoot open and my body jerks, I can feel my orgasm coming at a frantic pace. "Ben I'm coming," I gasp. He doesn't let up and I experience a very intense orgasm, my whole body is convulsing and I love it.

Ben slows his movements down and my body starts to relax. I am spent but I want him inside me. I lift my head up and Ben is laying there with a wonderful grin, I can tell he is very proud of himself. I smile. "Can we try another position?" I ask between pants.

"Anything for you."

"Can we try with you taking me from behind because I have heard the angle is amazing but be careful where you put that thing, it's fuckin' huge," I say. Ben can't get to his knees fast enough. "I'll take that as a yes," I say laughing. He asks me to turn around and get on my knees, he parts my legs and moves in behind me, placing his hands on my hips and leaning in to kiss my back. I turn my head to look back at him and he kisses me while his hands play with my hard nipples. I moan and arch my back which makes my bum rub against Ben's cock. Ben leans us forward and he kisses my back towards my hips. He gets me to place my hands on the bed and widen my legs. I can feel the tip of his cock enter me and slowly push inside until he is all the way in. "Ooooohhhhhhh-hhhhhhh....babe....fuuuuuucccccccckkkkk that's...wow that...what an angle...please move."

"Am I hurting you, do you want me to pull out?"

"NO!" I yell "You pull out and I will never go down on you again. I mean move, thrust, pound into me, just fuck me."

"With pleasure." Ben grabs my hips and starts to move in and out.

I lean down on my elbows so my arse is in the air.

"Ben fuck me hard..please…this feels amazing." He growls and starts to pound into me. I have never been fucked like this before, it is so wild and just what I need. Ben leans forward and grabs a handful of my hair and pulls it back so my head is off the mattress, I feel a tingle shoot straight to my inner thighs, holy hell this is really turning me on, who'd have thought that I would like it rough. Ben continues to pound into me and I can feel my orgasm building.

"Carly, you feel so good…babe…come for me," he chants as he pounds into me. I tilt my arse up just a little bit more and then my orgasm crashes over me. Ben grabs my hair harder and pulls my head closer to him as he lets out a moan and comes inside me.

I'm spent, we collapse onto the bed, heart's pounding and I can't wipe the smile off my face. Ben lies next to me holding my hand as we try to catch our breaths. "WOW, that was, well, there are no words on how fantastic that was. Each time is better than the last," I say, completely satisfied and exhausted.

We fall asleep holding hands. I wake first and lay there taking him in, he is so sexy and all mine. I can't believe my luck. I know our initial meeting didn't go well but I thank god every day that he saw something special in me and never gave up. I'm smiling like a fool when he opens his eyes, turns his head to me and smiles back.

"Hello Beautiful, how long have you been awake?"

"Not long," I say, stretching. "I'm hungry, you have worn me out, I need to fuel up." I say, raising my eye brows. "Are you hungry?" Ben gives me that sexy smile. "I mean are you hungry for food? There is stir-fry in the fridge."

"Sounds great. I'll cook while you keep me company," he says, pulling on his jeans and t-shirt.

I look at him and think what a shame that he has to cover up that wonderful body. I wonder if he will cook naked for me in our own place, I could really get used to that I thought with a giggle.

"What's so funny?"

"I'm just picturing you cooking for me in our new home, naked, but you have your glasses on."

"I will make that happen for you Beautiful, as often as you want," he says with a kiss, and then leaves the room to cook our dinner.

I get dressed and join Ben. Our bodies are in sync as Ben cooks and I set the table and get us a drink. The conversation flows and this feels so natural I can't wait until we are in our own home.

We eat our meal and go to bed early because this is our last night before Ben has to fly home. It has come too soon, I'm not ready to let him go, I am so used to seeing him every day. We lie in each other's arms, kissing, caressing and talking.

"Babe do you have any oil like baby oil?" Ben asks.

"Why?" I reply.

"I want to give you a massage because I think you will like it and besides I love putting my hands over your naked body." I get the oil and a few towels from the bathroom. Ben takes the oil from me as I place the towels on the bed. "Carly, take your clothes off, put your hair up and out of the way and lay on your stomach."

I do as he asks and place my head on my pillow, I feel so relaxed and I can't wait to have Ben's talented hands all over me. He drips the oil on my shoulders and I shiver because it's cold. He straddles my lower back and starts to rub the oil in. He applies the correct amount of pressure and it feels divine; he works the knots in my back and I can feel my body start to relax, oh my god this feels amazing; I let out a low moan as Ben works his way lower.

"Your curves are so fuckin' sexy I can't get enough of them." Ben shuffles lower and is now straddling my thighs, he drips oil down my butt crack, I squeal and wiggle because it tickles. Ben moves his hands lower and massages my bum spending a lot of time kneading each cheek and he is really turning me on, I can feel myself getting wet between my legs. Ben moves further down my body and massages my thighs, legs and feet hitting all the pressure points.   "Turn over, Beautiful," he commands in a low, sexy voice. I roll over and look at him, he's smiling and has a rock solid hard on.

"Is that for me?" I smile at him.

"It's yours and only yours."

"I want you inside me." I purr.

"All in good time, I haven't finished your massage yet." Ben massages the rest of my feet moving up my legs to my thighs, paying special attention to my inner thighs but not actually touching me where my body aches for his touch. As he works higher I moan louder and my body is so responsive to him, he massages his way up my stomach and spends a lot of time on my breasts, kneading and pinching my nipples. I arch into his hands and wrap my legs around his waist, lock my ankles behind his back and pull him to me. I feel his hard cock rub against my clit and my body starts to spasm, I rub faster and faster and I can feel my orgasm building, I start to pant and my body convulses as I come.

Ben runs the back of his hand down my cheek "You look amazing when you come, so wonderful."

I smile and look up at him, "Make love to me all night."

"It will be my pleasure."

I place my hand around his cock and guide him to my wet pussy, I push my hips forward and I take in all of him. We start to move slowly and he feels amazing, we get our rhythm and move as one. Ben kneels while still inside me, puts his hand around my lower back and pulls me to him. He thrusts faster and my body starts to respond, I lightly push his shoulders so he is lying on his back and I am straddling him, his cock is so deep, I lean back to change the angle and to play with his balls; I know this will drive him crazy. I take over and thrust into him hard and with long strokes. He starts to moan and places his hands on my hips, with every thrust he tightens his hold on me and I'm pretty sure that I will be bruised tomorrow.

"Fuck Carly, I can't hold out much longer."

I lean down so my mouth is level with his ear and I whisper, "Come for me, I love you Ben." I bite his ear lobe and he comes inside me while he wraps his arms tightly around my shoulders.

We lie like that for such a long time, enjoying the closeness and not wanting to let one another go, Ben running his hands up and down my back. I fall asleep with him still inside me.

The morning comes too soon, I wake to find Ben curled in behind me, arm around my waist and his face nuzzled into my neck. A tear falls down my face as I realise that he is flying out today and I won't see or touch him for about a month; it's killing me, my heart is aching for him already. Ben stirs and pulls me closer. During the week he packed up his room on the base and brought all his things to my house. He returned his hire car late Friday afternoon so all he has to do this morning is have breakfast and shower before I take him to the airport.

He rolls towards me and kisses me good morning, and notices that I have been crying, "Sweetheart, we will be together very soon, hopefully our new home will be ready a little earlier than expected so you can come over earlier than planned. I can't wait to start our new life and get our four-legged, furry child," he laughs. "I love you so much Carly. Come and shower with me." Ben gets out of bed, and I put my robe on while Ben puts on shorts and a t-shirt. I take his hand and we made our way to the bathroom. Ben adjusts the taps to the correct temperature, then undoes the tie on my robe and pushes it off my shoulders. I lift his t/shirt off his head while he undoes the button and zip on his shorts and they fall to the floor to join my robe.

Ben washes my hair and then we take it in turns to wash one another's body, we don't say much to each other. I memorise his features and body as Ben does the same with mine. We make soft slow love in the shower until the water goes cold. I try to eat something but my stomach can't hold much. All too soon it's time to go.

Ben says goodbye to Mum and Dad, promising again that he will look after me when I move in with him. He puts his bag in my car and I start the drive to the airport.

Ben places his hand on my leg and doesn't move it; we don't talk much, we just listen to the radio. As I'm parking the car at the airport Ben plugs his iPod in and presses play. Then he turns to me, touches my face so I am looking at him and starts to sing to me.

It's a slow song called *All of Me* by John Legend. Looking into my eyes he sings, *"What's going on in that beautiful mind, I'm on your magical mystery ride.*

"Cause all of me loves all of you, love your curves and all your edges, all your perfect imperfections. Give your all to me, I'll give my all to you, you're my end and my beginning, even when I lose I'm winning."

I can't stop the tears streaming down my face, the words are so beautiful and I know he is making a memory for us to hold onto until I can be with him.

"How many times do I have to tell you, even when you are crying you're beautiful too."

I laugh at that line, how perfect.

"The world is beating you down, I'm around through every mood. Cause all of me, loves all of you."

The song finishes and I throw myself at him, kissing and hugging him, I don't want to let him go.

Ben slowly pulls away. "Carly, I have to go, please stay with me until I have to board the flight." I reluctantly nod my head. He gets his bag out of the boot and takes my hand in his as we walk towards the terminal. Once his bag is checked in and he has his boarding pass we go to a café. Ben gets a coffee and I have a cup of tea. We sit cuddled next to each other in a booth and we hardly touch our drinks, we are so lost in one another. Then Ben's flight is called and we make our way to his gate; I feel like a dead man walking, it's torture. We hold onto each other's hands like it's our life line. Ben waits until the last minute before he boards. We have said *'I love you'* a thousand times and he promises to call me when he lands. My heart is being ripped out of my chest.

I watch his flight leave and then I make my way back to my car. I'm not paying too much attention to where I'm going when I bump into someone. I start to say sorry and as I look up I see Nicole leaning against my car. My knees buckle underneath me and she catches me before I hit the ground. "What are you doing here?" I ask once I have calmed down.

"Hun, I couldn't let you drive home alone after saying goodbye to Ben. Your dad called me last night to see if I would drive you home today because he thought you might need a friend, and he was worried about you driving home on your own. He picked me up just as you left and dropped me off a few rows away from your car." I'm speechless and all I can do is give a small smile. "You're welcome, hun. Come on, let me take you home," Nicole says as she places he arm around my shoulder and pulls me close.

I don't remember much about the drive home. I'm very thankful that Nicole was with me and I love my dad even more for setting this up. We get home and Nicole walks inside with me. When I see Dad I run into his waiting arms and cry until I think I have no more tears to shed. Once I have calmed down I give Nicole a hug and Dad drives her home as I go to my room for a lie down. I can smell Ben on the sheets and I bury my nose in his pillow and cry some more.

I must have fallen asleep because I wake with a start when my mobile rings. it's just after 6 pm and its Ben calling. I try to pull myself together before I answer it.

"Hello beautiful, how are you?"

"Miserable."

"Yeah me too. Usually I'm excited to come home but today I left my heart in Perth and I need you to bring it back to me. My heart will always be yours, so the sooner we are together the sooner I'll be whole again."

We talk for a couple of hours and I don't want to say goodbye but Sydney is two hours ahead of Perth and he has to get some sleep before work tomorrow. Ben promises we will speak daily, he tells me he loves me and he will see me soon. When I hang up I feel empty and I cry myself to sleep.

13 | BEN

I groan when my alarm wakes me at 6 am. I haven't slept well. I'm used to having Carly sleep next to me in her big bed and now I'm sleeping in a single bed on board the Naval Base and it sucks. All I want to do is talk to Carly but I can't because she is two hours behind me and even if I did talk to her I will be late for work and I don't want to get charged. I have a squeaky clean record and I want to keep it that way.

I pull myself together, go for a shower, get dressed and go to the mess for breakfast. As I start to eat I feel a hand on my shoulder.

"When did you get back, Richo?" asks Hayley Carter as she sits down next to me. Hayley and I joined the Navy in the same intake.

"Hi Hayls, I got back last night. How you been?"

"Not too bad. How was your course?"

"It kicked my arse, it was so full on. In the beginning I didn't think I had a hope in hell of passing, but as time wore on I got into the swing of it and it was cool catching up with Davo, Rabbit and Kiwi."

"I heard Davo hooked up with a girl while he was there" Hayley laughs and rolls her eyes. "Bloody typical, he's such a man whore."

"Yeah her name is Nicole and she's a great girl. Actually I met someone too. Her name is Carly and I met her in the first week I was there."

"Oh yeah. So you also had someone to play with while you were in the West," Hayley giggles.

"No it's more than that. Carly's amazing and I'm in love," I smile.

"OH MY GOD. I never thought I'd see the day that ladies' man Richo admits he's in love," scoffs Hayley.

"Since when have I been a ladies' man? I've had my fair share of women but no more than anyone else. Besides, I am officially off the market, Carly's it for me."

"Isn't it going to be hard to do the long distance thing?"

"No, because she's moving over here in a few weeks. We went online and secured a place but it's being painted and the floors are being re-sanded and stained before we can move into it."

"I'm shocked," says Hayley as she sits silently next to me.

"I'm so happy Hayls, I can't wait for you to meet her," I say, but something's off with Hayley. "You ok Hayls?"

"Yeah I'm ok."

I'm surprised by her mood change but she's a woman and in my experience they are moody creatures by nature so I let it drop. "How's Sophie?"

"Yeah, she's good."

"Her parent's know about the two of you yet?"

"Nah and I doubt that they'll ever know. She thinks her mum knows but she is scared to have that conversation with her just in case she's wrong," Hayley says sadly.

"How do you feel about that?"

"I feel like a dirty little secret. My family and friends are so cool about my relationship with Sophie it's really hard not having it acknowledged with her family and friends. I can't be myself around them and it hurts," Hayley says with glassy eyes.

I reach my hand out to touch hers "I hope things change for you."

"Hope is all I have, Richo. Anyway it's time we made a move," Hayley says as she stands up.

"Have a good one," I say as I walk out the mess.

The day drags and my hearts not in it. I think of Carly all day, wondering what's she's doing, whether she's thinking about me. Is she missing me as much as I'm missing her? Fuck me I have definitely grown a vagina. Before you know it I'll have to buy some tampons coz I've got my period. Finally it's home time and I can call Carly.

She picks it up after two rings. "Hey babe how was work?"

"Long, boring and thankfully over. How did you sleep last night?"

"Terrible," she sighs. "My bed is so lonely without you and I hate sleeping alone."

"I know, but we'll be together soon, Beautiful. What did you get up to today?"

"Not a lot, I've been throwing things out that I'm not going to need. You should see how full the wheelie bin is," she laughs.

My heart constricts at the sound of Carly's laughter. It's only been twenty-four hours and I'm already lost, I miss her face, smile, laugh, smell, how her body feels against mine when I make love to her, the sounds she makes when she's about to come, and the way she sighs my name as I enter her. I just really miss her.

"Only throw out the stuff that you really don't want, I would hate for you to throw something out just because you don't think we'd have the space."

"Don't worry everything that is important is coming with me."

"I just want you to feel comfortable and happy in our new home."

"Ben, as long as I'm with you I will be happy. I miss you so much," Carly sighs. "I never thought I could love someone as much as I love you. I have to admit it scares me sometimes."

"What scares you, Beautiful?" I ask, knowing Carly has a lot of insecurities from her childhood and last relationship. I can hear her struggling on the other end of the phone. "Babe, talk to me," I plead.

"It's just....ummm..." I give her time to get her thoughts together. "I'm wor...worried you will ch...change your mind."

I take a deep breath because it upsets me that she doubts herself and us as a couple. "Carly, if I need to say this to you every day to make you believe me I will. I love you, I will always love you, there is no other woman for me, you are perfect for me and I'm counting down the days until we can be together again. Please don't ever doubt my commitment to you. I would never have asked you to uproot your life and move across to the other side of the country if I wasn't serious about you."

"I know I'm just being silly but you have to remember things don't usually work out for me and I'm scared," Carly says quietly.

"I wish you could look into my heart and see how much I truly love you. Promise me something, when you are having doubts call me and we will talk them through; I don't care what time of day or night it is, we will work through this together. Can you promise me that you will call?"

I can hear Carly's breathing start to even out. "I promise."

"That's my girl," I say with a smile in my voice. We talk for another two hours before my stomach starts to rumble and it's time for dinner. Over the next few weeks we talk daily and make plans for when Carly is able to move over.

On Saturday afternoon there is a knock on my door. "Hey Richo how's it goin?" asks Ringo. Ringo's real name is David Starr and everyone in the Navy is called by a nickname, some good, some bad.

"Just watching some TV. What you up to?"

"A few of us are heading up to Kings Cross tonight for a feed and a few drinks. You up for it?"

"Yeah sounds great. What time are we leaving?"

"We're all meeting at the gate about 7 pm."

"Thanks mate, I'll see you then," I say as Ringo shuts the door.

Just after 7 pm I walk up to the gate and meet the guys. There's Ringo, Philly, Sterlo, , Ando and Jax. We walk up to the Cross and have a feed at a Mexican Restaurant we drink Margaritas and beers as we eat the mouth-watering food. We decide to put all the food in the middle of the table and to help ourselves. The restaurant is packed and the banter flies around our table. I notice a few of the waitresses pay our table extra attention, one in particular is very touchy feely with me and it makes me very uncomfortable. A while later I get up to go to the toilet, which is at the end of a narrow passageway. After I finish I am walking back to the table when one of the overly attentive waitresses stands in my way. I go to move around her but she moves with me, putting her hands on my hips and leaning into me.

"My name's Skye and I finish work in an hour. How about we go for a drink?"

I move her hands off my hips and move around her as I say, "No thanks."

I make my way back to the table and finish the last of my drink as the guys get up to leave, we pay the bill and head to O'Malleys Pub. It's a great Irish pub in the heart of the Cross that has live music and the place is packed. We make our way to the bar and as I place my order I feel a hand on my arm, I look to my left and I see a girl I had a one night stand with about a year ago; her name is Gemma or Emma something like that.

"Ben it's great to see you. How've you been?"

"Good, and you?"

"Not bad. I haven't seen you since that night. I'm being honest when I say it was the best fuck I've ever had; no one since you has been able to make me come so hard and I'm more than happy to have a repeat performance," she whispers in my ear as she pushes her tits into my arm.

I pull my body away from hers. "No thanks, I've got a girlfriend."

"I don't care," she says as puts her arm around my waist.

"I DO," I say angrily as I remove her arm and take a step back. "Now get the fuck away from me." I notice her wince at my words as I turn to the bar but I don't care. I get the drinks plus a shot which I down straight away before I hand the guys their drinks.

"Cheers Richo," Jax says as he grabs his beer. "Looks like that girl was into you."

"Not interested, I have a girlfriend."

"So it wouldn't bother you if I had a crack?"

"Be my guest," I laugh as I take a pull of my beer.

The rest of the night is incident free and I get smashed. We stumble out of the pub about 4 am and make our way to the kebab shop for a feed. After we have demolished our food we head back to the base. Once inside my cabin I try to strip off my clothes but I'm flopping around like an untrained seal. As I fall on my bed I spot the photo of myself and Carly that's sitting on my bedside table. I wrestle my phone out of my pocket and search for the number. After a few rings I hear a sleepy voice say "Hello."

"Babe I really miss youuuu," I slur.

"Ben is everything ok? You sound weird."

"I'm just lonely without you that's all. I miss you so much."

"I know, I miss you too honey," Carly says with a yawn.

"Babe you're tired, I'm sorry I woke you."

"No it's ok, I'm here if you want to talk. How was your night?"

"It was ok, we went for Mexican and then to the pub with the boys. I wish you could have come out with me."

"Me too, babe, but I'll be there soon. Sounds like you've had quite a bit to drink," she giggles.

"Yeah, and those bitches put their hands on me and they weren't you. Your hands are the only hands I want on me."

"Ben what are you talking about?"

"The waitress and Gemma/Emma at the bar."

"You're not making sense. What the fuck is going on?" Carly yells.

"Babe why are you yelling?"

"You wanna know why I'm yelling? You have just told me that two 'bitches', to use your word, had their hands on you tonight and you want to know why I'm yelling? If you want to be free just say so and I'll leave you to it."

"Whoa whoa, hang on a minute. What makes you think that I want to be free? I love you and only you. I don't want anyone else. I felt sick when they touched me, babe. Please believe me, nothing happened, I promise." I listen to her breathing and I can tell she's upset and trying to calm herself down. "Babe please talk to me."

"What do you want me to say Ben?"

"Babe, I'm telling you the truth. As soon as they touched me I moved."

"So how do you know one of their names?"

Oh fuck I didn't think she would ask me about that. I take a deep breath. "A year ago I had a one night stand with Gemma/Emma whatever her fuckin' name is. Tonight was the first time I have seen her since that night."

"That's just fuckin' great."

"Now you're being ridiculous, I can't control what other people do or where they go. What do you want me to do be a hermit until you get here?"

"No that's not what I'm saying at all. Arghhhhh. This is getting us nowhere, we both need to get some sleep and talk about it later with clear heads."

"I agree, Carly, but I don't want to leave it like this," I say as I take a few breaths. "Just know that I love you and I would never do anything to upset you or jeopardise our relationship. So have a good sleep and we'll talk tomorrow. I love you Carly."

"I love you too. Nite," Carly says as she hangs up the phone.

I fall back onto the bed, how the fuck did that happen? I just wanted to hear her voice and it turned into an argument. Why did I have to mention the girls, I'm such and fuckwit. Even though I've had a skin full of beer and margaritas I find it hard to fall asleep.

I groan as I'm woken by banging on my door. I look at my watch and see that it's 3.25pm; oh god I feel like shit. I pull my jeans on and stumble to the door. "All right, all right stop your fuckin' banging," I yell as I swing open the door.

"WOW who kicked you in the balls?"

"I'm tired, hungover and not in the mood. What do you want Hayley?"

"Okaaay...I was just wondering if you wanted to go for a few drinks, but considering the mood you're in I don't think that's a good idea."

"Sorry Hayley, I have a banging headache and I haven't had a lot of sleep. I don't think going out drinking again is a good idea." Just then my mobile rings and as I walk to the bed I see that it's Carly, I'm in two minds as I reach for the phone. I want to talk to her but I don't want another argument.   "Hey babe," I say as I press answer.

"Hi," Carly says softly. I know she's nervous to talk to me because I can hear it in her voice, but I can't wipe the smile off my face just hearing that one word. Hayley motions to me that she is going and she shuts the door behind her.

"Are you ok, Beautiful?"

"Yeah, but I'm not happy that we argued."

"No, me neither. I promise you nothing happened, as soon as they touched me I either shrugged them off or removed their hands. You are the only one for me Carly."

"I believe you, I was just being irrational. It's hard when my track record with guys isn't good."

"It's ok, I understand, as long as we're good."

"We're good. I love you Ben."

"I love and miss you so much. I'm counting down the day's until you're here and we are living in our own home. It's going to be great." Carly and I talk for the next two hours and when we finish the call I know we are good and back on track.

CARLY | 14

For the next couple of weeks I pack up my room and throw out a lot of things that I don't want or need. I will be taking very little from my previous life into my new life. I even sell my car, it's old so I don't get much for it. Nicole and I hang out as much as we can and I talk to Ben daily; unfortunately I don't have a laptop so I can't Skype with him. I really miss seeing his face.

It's the middle of June and even though it's the first month of winter the weather is relatively warm, but then again winters in Perth are usually mild. My mum wants to take me out to lunch. I'm dubious because usually when she wants to see me alone she wants to talk about George and he's the last person I want to talk about. Mum drives us to my favourite café on the beach front, and we are seated inside but have a clear view of the beach; the waves are rolling in and there are pelicans and sea gulls on the sand.

We order our drinks and meals and make small talk. I notice Mum keeps glancing at the door like she's expecting someone and I start to get an uneasy feeling. "Mum, who are you waiting for?" I ask.

"No one, Carly, what are you talking about?"

"You keep looking over at the door like you are waiting for someone." I lean in close and say, "If you have invited HIM to meet us here you will never see or hear from me again." I can feel the hairs rise on the back of my neck, my heart starts thumping in my chest, the room starts spinning and I can hardly breathe. I look at my mum and she has tears running down her face and her eyes are fixed on the door. I turn around and George is standing at reception, looking our way with a smirk on his face. I stand and stumble my way to a waitress that is in the opposite direction to the reception. I touch her arm and as she spins around she can see that I'm in trouble; she holds my hand, puts her arm around my waist and leads me into the kitchen. Once we reach the kitchen the waitress calls for her manager.

As the manager reaches me, I say, "Dad" and give her my phone. She scrolls through my contacts and calls my dad, explaining who she is and she describing me. The manager asks me if I'm Carly and I nod that I am. I motion for the phone, put it against my mouth and say just one word, "George." Dad says he is on his way and not to move, then he asks me to hand the phone to the manager. The manager takes my mobile and says 'yes' to what he had said to her. She hangs up and then grabs the restaurant phone, walks to the waitress who had helped me, whispers something in her ear and the waitress comes over and sits with me.

After a bit of time had passed the manager comes back and says, "Carly, your dad told me that you have a violence restraining order against George." I nod. "He asked me to keep you safe and to call the Police, which I have just done. The Police and your dad are on their way. It looks like the lady you came here with and George have gone, but we have looked at the CCTV and they are both on there, and we will give that to the Police. Is there anyone else you would like to call?"

I want to call Ben, but how could I do that to him while he is on the other side of Australia? I just shake my head and start to cry. The waitress holds my hand and just sits there with me, I hold onto her like my life depends on it.

My dad arrives before the Police and he is shown to me. As soon as I see him I get to my feet and stumble to his waiting arms, he holds me tight, rocking me saying over and over, "It's ok, I've got you."

Dad turns to the manager and asks to see the CCTV footage, although he knew I was having lunch with Mum today, he needs to see her reaction for himself to see if this was planned or just a chance meeting; I think he already knows the answer but he needs confirmation. Dad asks the waitress to sit with me again as he follows the manager to her office. I'm not sure how long they are gone. The Police turn up and ask to see me. A waiter brings them to where I am and they ask me if I'm ok, and I say I'm a little better. Just then my dad and the manager re-appear, and my dad looks like he has been crying, he keeps wiping his hand across his face and looking at the floor.

The Police introduce themselves "I'm Constable Isaac and this is my colleague Constable Michaels. Can you tell me your name please?" I tell him who I am and that I have a VRO out on George.

My dad tells the officers there is CCTV footage of George on the premises and that the manager can show it to them. They leave me with the waitress again. I turn to her and ask her name.

"I'm Tess. Are you feeling better?" I nod weakly.

Dad and the Police and the manager come back and the Police have a copy of the CCTV footage. They inform me that they will go to George and take his statement and they will be back in touch. My dad put his hand out to thank Tess and the manager, whose name is Alicia, for helping me. I stand up and hug Tess, then my dad puts his arm around my waist and walks me to his car.

"Carly, I'm pretty sure you were set up and I'm disgusted that your mother either instigated it or was a willing participant. I have spoken to Nicole and you are staying there tonight."

We go to Nicole's, using my key because Nicole is still at work and won't be home for a few hours. We go inside and I make us a cup of tea and then we sit on the lounge.

"Carly, after today I think it would be a good thing for you to go to Sydney early," says Dad. "I don't want you to go but I don't think your'e safe here, and unfortunately I can't be with you 24/7."

"I would h..have nowhere to l..live because the house w..w..won't be vacant for another week or s..so, and I can't stay on the base with B.. Ben."

"Ratbag, I will pay for a room close to Ben's base until your house is ready." I look at him and shake my head. "Carly, please don't fight me on this. My job is to protect you and keep you safe and I have done a crap job at it so far, so please let me do this for you."

"You have been a wun...wonderful Father so pl..please don't say you have done a bad job. Y..you didn't know about George and Shaun be...because I didn't tell you, you can't ch..change or help what you are unaware of, it's n..not your fault, it's theirs."

"Are you ok with me booking a room and flight for tomorrow?"

"C..can I talk to Ben fir...first to make sure that he's ok w..with this?"

"Of course, I'll give you some privacy."

I call Ben "Hello Beautiful, what great timing. I have just finished work."

I try to calm myself down "Hi, how was your day?" I try to speak normally but Ben senses something is not right.

"Babe, what's wrong?"

I explain to him what happened and what my dad has suggested. Ben goes quiet. "It..it's ok, I can g..go down s..s..south for a few d..d.. days to hide out until th..the house is re..ready if it's not con..con..convenient," I stutter.

"Carly, please take deep breaths and calm your breathing." I start to do as he asks. "That's it, babe, nice and slow, in and out, in and out," Ben says over and over. I started to calm down. "Is that better?" Ben asks.

"A little, I'm s..sorry."

"What are you saying sorry for?"

"Aren't you b..bored and over all my dra..drama? I know I am, th..this is not wh..what you signed up for. B..Ben if you decide th..that this is to..too much and want to fin..finish with me I will n..not think any l..less of you, I..I wouldn't blame y..you."

"Have you finished?" Ben asked angrily. I say I have. "None of this is your fault, George is a sick fuck who enjoys nothing more than making your life hell and don't even get me started on your mum, I am more disgusted in her than him. How could she do that to her own daughter? When we have kids I will never turn my back on any of them. Don't you ever blame yourself for what they chose to do, it is not your fault and I don't ever want to hear you say that again. Also, when are you going to understand that I love you more than anything and I will never ever leave you? Remember the song at the airport? 'All of me loves all of you', and that will never change. Is your Dad there?" I say he is. "Can I please speak to him?"

I go to my dad and explain that Ben wants to talk to him. I hand Ben my mobile and I leave them to it. I lay down on the lounge thinking about what Ben said. He said 'when we have kids.' Holy shit he is thinking of forever. For the first time that day I smile.

As my dad is talking to Ben, Nicole arrives home. "Hey Chica, sounds like you have had a fucked up day."

"You could say that," I say as I get to my feet to give her a hug. "I just can't believe my mum either set it up or went along with it, what the fuck?"

"Where's your Dad?"

"He's talking to Ben, Dad wants me to go to Sydney tomorrow he's just checking that Ben will be there and I won't be alone."

Just then my dad enters the room and hands me my mobile. "Hi Nicole," my dad says as he gives her a hug and kiss hello. I look at my phone and I see that Ben has hung up, and my stomach drops.

"Ratbag, Ben and I have a few arrangements that we need to get to. Nicole, do you have a computer I can use? I don't want to do it on the one at home in case Kath is around. Besides, if I do everything here she won't find out."

Nicole shows him to her PC and then she comes back to join me on the lounge. "Hey, what was that look for when your dad gave you your mobile back?"

"I was surprised he had hung up without saying goodbye, I thought that meant…well…that it was all too hard and he didn't want me anymore."

"Hun you really have to have some faith in your man; blind Freddie can see that he loves you more than life itself. You need to cut him some slack and stop waiting for him to let you down."

"I'm scared to allow myself to think that. Why would a guy put me first when my own mother sets me up, and she is supposed to love me unconditionally. Thank god I have you and Dad."

"And Ben, you have Ben. Please Carly, believe that, he would move heaven and earth for you, he's a good guy."

After about an hour Ben is calling my mobile. "Hello," I say softly.

"Hey babe, can I talk to your Dad please."

"Can you tell me what's going on?"

"Once I have spoken to your Dad."

"Why not now?" I ask angrily.

"Carly, please, can I just talk to your Dad."

"I'm not a fuckin' ch..ch..child. I have a right to know what is happening as l..l..l..long as it concerns me, I am s..s..sick of people doing things behind m..mm..my back even if they think it is for my own good…I have a v..voice and I wan..want to be heard."

"OK babe, please control your breathing, slow things down; you are stuttering again."

"Coz you're t..t..treating me l..l..like a fu..fuckin' idiot." Nicole holds my hand and gently pulls me to her. I start to cry, I am a fucking idiot.

Nicole grabs my phone. "Hey Ben, I have you on speaker. Carly's in no state to be kept in the dark, could you please tell her what you and Andrew spoke about and also what you have done since you last spoke to him. Andrew has locked himself away with my PC and looks like he's shutting down so we are not going to get anything out of him."

"Ok. Carly, I'm sorry for shutting you out but I'm not there to protect you and this is my way of helping. I get so focused that I have pushed you out, the person I'm trying to help."

"She's nodding, so what's going on?"

"I have been in touch with Defence Housing and they say that our house will be ready later next week. I have also booked a room in a hotel within walking distance of my base for the next week, with the option to add extra days if needed. Your dad is going to book the flight and hopefully that will be sometime tomorrow."

"She's booked on the 2.20pm flight," my dad says as he enters the room.

"That's wonderful news, thanks Andrew I will be there to pick her up. Carly, are you ok to have a private conversation with me?"

Nicole hands me my phone, I take it off speaker, walk into the bedroom and shut the door. I lay on the bed before I start to speak. "What do you want to say?"

"Babe, please don't be angry with me, I just got carried away and really focused on getting you safe and here with me where they can't hurt you anymore."

"Ben, you have to remember how my life has been, I have always been controlled and manipulated by George, Shaun and my mum. I know you have the best intentions, but you shut me out and made decisions for me without even discussing them with me and that's not cool. You can never do that again."

"I'm sorry Carly, please accept my apology. I love you so much and the thought of your Mum and George hurting you made me wild, and as I said, I just wanted you to be safe and that's with me. My world starts and ends with you."

"Ok."

There is silence for a while and then Ben says "So, in regards to our furry child do you want a boy or a girl and what do you want to call it?"

That question throws me but I understand that Ben is trying to lighten the mood. "Ummmm, a boy I think, because if we decide to breed him we don't have to have a pregnant dog on our hands. And as for a name, I like human names. I like the name Roger...Roger the Rottweiler."

Ben roars with laughter. "Carly, that is an awesome name, I love it. When we get settled we will contact a few breeders and see how we go about getting one with papers. Carly can you please promise me one thing?"

"If I can."

"Please don't go back to your house tonight or even tomorrow. Let your dad pack what you need."

"Ben, I have no intention of stepping foot in that house again. I told my mother at lunch she will never see or hear from me again. My dad will get what I need and if there is anything I have forgotten he will send it to me. I will inform the Police and Courts tomorrow that I am moving interstate and as soon as I have it I will give them my new address and new mobile number."

"New mobile number?"

"Yeah, only a few people will have it, and I will make sure that it's a silent number, so there should be no way that Mum or George can track it down. I have asked Dad to store it in his phone under a false name in case she decides to get nosey."

"What do you think is going to happen to them, Carly?"

"I'm not sure. I just know that I haven't seen my dad this sad before. I know when George attacked me he was very upset; actually I think he was more angry than upset with George. But this time it's my mum too, and I'm not sure if their marriage will survive this. I'm worried about him, Ben." I say sadly.

"I don't know what to say to you to help. This is all new territory for me. We just have to be there for him."

Just then there is a knock at the door and Nicole enters. "Hun, the Police are here and would like to speak to you."

"Don't hang up, take the phone with you and explain to them that you have them on speaker and that I'm on the other end."

I do as Ben asks. Constable Michaels starts to talk. "Carly, after watching the CCTV footage today we spoke to your brother George, and he states that it was a coincidence that you and he were at the same café at the same time. Once it was pointed out that the female you were with is your and George's mother, we started to take more notice of her movements and actions. We noticed that she seemed nervous while watching the door and didn't look overly surprised when George walked in. We have spoken with Mrs Nelson and she states that it was a coincidence that George walked into the café where you and she were about to have lunch. So, with no evidence to point to a set-up we are unable to follow through with any charges. But this will be written down and added to your file. Carly, we are sorry we are unable to be of more assistance."

I thank them for their time and Nicole shows them the way out. I forget Ben is on the line until I hear him talk. "Fuck me, is he made of Teflon? Nothing sticks, I'm sorry Andrew, I know he's your son, but he has to get his dues one day and I hope I'm there to watch his downfall."

"You and me both son." my dad replies.

I go back into my room to talk to Ben. "I'm going to go because I would like to spend some time with my dad to see if he is alright and find out what he intends to do. I love you and I will see you tomorrow night. You'll be there to pick me up right?"

"Nothing would keep me from picking you up, this is the only good thing that has come of today's incident, I get to be with you sooner than expected. I love you too. Try to get some sleep. Night babe."

I hang up and go into the lounge to talk to my dad, Nicole gives us some time alone. I sit next to him and lean my body towards him, he puts his arm out so I can snuggle into his side. "Dad are you ok?"

"I'm fine, Ratbag. I'm just going to really miss you that's all."

"What about you and Mum?"

"That I can't answer. I haven't always agreed with how she has treated you and George, but today has devastated me. The woman I married would not have set that up, so in saying that, who am I married to? Anyway, I am going to go, I will be back in the morning with your things. Now are you sure you have everything on this list?"

"I think so, if not I will let you know and you can send it to me. Dad, promise me you won't give her my new address and number."

"Sweetheart she won't get it from me." He stands, gives me and Nicole a kiss and hug goodbye and leaves.

Nicole and I sit silently on the lounge just absorbing the day's events. She turns her head to me "So you're leaving tomorrow."

"Yep, looks like it."

"Hun, it's earlier than we planned but it's for the best. You'll be safe but I'm sure as hell gunna miss ya," she says as a tear runs down her face. I pull her to me and we cry together, we cry for our amazing friendship, our crazy sense of humour and because we are going to miss each other so much.

I don't sleep very well that night, I suppose it is crazy to think I would. I get up early to say goodbye to Nicole before she goes to work. We hug, cry, and laugh, and I promise her I will call as soon as I land.

My dad comes around just after 9 am with my suitcase and the items I asked him to get. As I pack I ask him how things went with Mum and he just shrugs his shoulders and says he doesn't want to talk about it. Dad takes me to get a new silent mobile number and then to the Court House and the Police Station to inform them that I'm moving interstate. I give them my new number and as I'm about to walk out I hear a familiar female voice. I turn around and there is Constable Smyth talking to one of her colleagues. I get her attention and she walks over to me. "Carly, is that you? What are you doing here? Is everything ok?"

"Yes and no, but I am here to inform you guys that I am moving interstate and that I have a new silent mobile number."

"You look so much better than the time I met you. I have to admit I only recognised you because of your dad. Where are you going?"

"I'm moving to Sydney to live with my boyfriend Ben. It is happening a bit quicker than expected but things change."

"Yes, I saw the report from yesterday. Carly, I wish you all the best."

"I'll be back when it goes to court so I might see you then. Thank you for everything you did for me that night. I know you were doing your job but you were very kind to me and I will never forget that." We smile at each other and say our goodbyes.

"Dad, before we make our way to the airport can we please stop off somewhere?"

"Of course we can."

I get my dad to stop off at the florist and get bunches of flowers for Tess and Alicia. As we arrive at the restaurant I notice the sign on the door said closed. I hadn't considered that, I walk up and I'm about to knock when I see Tess round the corner.

"WOW Carly, you look so much better than yesterday. I was so worried, it's great to see you," she says with a huge smile.

I throw my arms around her and hug her like my life depends on it. "Thank you so much for taking good care of me yesterday, I will be forever grateful." I pull away and hand her a bunch of flowers. "It's not much but I just wanted you to know much your kindness meant to me." Tess smiles and I can see her bottom lip wobble a bit. "No more tears, this is a happy day. Can you give these to Alicia for me?"

"You can give them to her yourself because she's working today and should be in her office. Come with me and we'll go and find her. I'm pretty sure she would like to see that you're ok."

Tess knocks on Alicia's door and we walk in. "Alicia there is someone here who would like to see you."

Alicia stands up, smiling, as I walk to her. "Carly, it's great to see you, how are you?"

"I'm better, thanks to you and Tess. Thank you for taking care of me yesterday. I will not forget your kindness. These are for you as a thank you."

Alicia takes the flowers from me and holds my hand for a few seconds just smiling and looking into my eyes. "You are going to be just fine, I can feel good things are coming your way."

Ratbag

As we get closer to the airport I notice Dad goes quiet. We park and he gets my case out for me. He starts to walk towards the terminal and I put my hand on his shoulder to stop him. "Dad, can we please say goodbye here? If you come into the terminal it's going to be torture just hanging around waiting to be called, this way we can say goodbye our way and without a time limit hanging over our heads."

Dad reluctantly agrees, and we hug, kiss and laugh. I love my dad so much and I am a very lucky girl to have him. "I will call you when I get there, I have put my new number in your phone under the name Roger." He raised his eyebrows. "When Ben and I get a dog we are calling him Roger; he will be your furry grandson." We both laugh and then it's time to say goodbye.

"I love you Dad, I could not have wished for a better father, I'm so damn lucky."

"I'm the lucky one, I just wish things would have turned out differently for you," he says with a sombre look.

I kiss and hug him one more time and then make my way to the terminal, I'm just about to walk inside when I feel the need to turn around, and as I turn I see my dad standing there about five feet away. "I'm just making sure you get inside safely," he says. I rush up to him, crying and hugging him. I can feel his body shake and as I pull away his face is wet with tears. I wipe them away, smile at him and mouth *'I'm going to be ok.'* He nods and says "I know."

We let go and I walk into the terminal. I don't look back again. I check in my suitcase, get my boarding pass and make my way to my gate. I sit down and send texts to Nicole and Ben to let them know I'm about to board, and to ask Nicole to keep an eye out for my dad. Just as I press 'send' my flight is called and my stomach does a flip. I know once I board this flight my life is going to be very different.

The five hour flight is fairly uneventful. I try to watch a movie but it's hard to concentrate, so I give up and put in my head phones and listen to my favourite play list. I have two seats to myself so I stretch out.

As I feel the plane start to make its decent I start to get butterflies in my stomach, I'm excited and I can't wait to see Ben. It seems to take forever to taxi down the runway to the terminal. The Captain announces that the local time is 9.35 pm. I unlock my seat belt, grab my hand luggage and line up to disembark. We move so slowly that I start bouncing on the pads of my feet to try to calm myself. I walk through the gate scanning the crowd for him; there are so many people and I can't see him, I just hope we can find each other. As I scan the crowd for what feels like the hundredth time I see my Ben, he is standing there in front of me, with the showing off his dimples with the biggest smile, and he is wearing his glasses. I clutch at my chest, he takes my breath away. I rush towards him, throw my arms around his neck and kiss him, and he pulls me closer as he wraps his arms around my waist. All of a sudden I realise *I'M HOME* and I let out a breath that I didn't know I was holding.

Ben places his hands on either side of my face just smiling and taking me in. "Come on, let's go home." He takes my hand. As we wait for my luggage I send Nicole and Dad a text.

We arrive at the hotel at about 10.40 pm. The room is nothing spectacular but it has what I need: a queen size bed, bathroom and, most importantly, Ben. Ben sits my suitcase down and holds his hand out for me to take. I place my hand in his and he pulls me to him, engulfing me in his wonderful arms. We stay like that for a while just taking it all in. I look up into his eyes. "I'm finally home," I say.

Ben's lips come crashing down on mine as he walks me to the bed where he lays me down, undresses me and tenderly makes love to me. Wrapped in his arms, I sleep so well that night.

15 | BEN

I wake in the morning and wrap my arms tighter around Carly, I can't believe she's actually here. I know the circumstances weren't the greatest but I'm so happy she's here because I really missed her. I take a look at my watch and if I don't get a move on I'll be late for work. I snuggle into Carly's neck and breathe her in before I get up and make my way to the shower. Before I leave for work I kiss her goodbye. She stirs and tries to get up. "Babe, go back to sleep. It's really early and I've got to go."

"You should have woken me and I would have got up with you," Carly yawns.

"You were out for the count, making those cute little noises and I didn't have the heart to wake you. Your key for the room is by the TV, I'll be back about 4.30 pm. I'm sorry I can't spend the day with you."

"It's ok, I'll be fine," she says with a smile. "Now go to work."

At lunch time I call Carly. "Hello Beautiful, how is your day going?"

"Good. I spoke to my dad this morning, but he didn't want to speak about himself. Hopefully he will open up one day. Then I realised that my clothes aren't warm enough for Sydney weather so I came into the city and I bought myself a jacket to wear because it's bloody freezing and now I am sitting in a lovely café with a couple of magazines enjoying a toasted sandwich while talking to my guy," Carly replies.

"Sounds like a good morning. Babe, would you like to have a look at our house after work today? The previous tenants have moved out and they are about to paint the walls and re-sand the floors. We can get a sneak peak before that happens."

"That would be fantastic, I'm excited," Carly squeals.

"I thought you'd be happy. Well babe, I have to get back to work and I will see you later. I love you, have a great afternoon."

"I love you too, see you soon.

Just after 4.30 pm I walk in the door. Carly's so happy to see me that she throws herself into my arms. I pull her in tightly and press her up against the wall, I put a hand under her bum and lift her up, she wraps her legs around my waist and I let out a growl. My erection is pressing between Carly's thighs and it feels amazing. She reaches down and starts to undo the button and zip on my jeans, she places her hand inside my boxers and grasps my cock. I get harder with her touch and I suck in a breath. I gently lower her legs so she's standing and she switches places with me pushing me against the wall while she is kissing my neck. She pushes my t-shirt up and kisses her way down my chest paying particular attention to my nipples, she licks and sucks each nipple as I let out a moan and grab a handful of her hair. She kneels and pulls down my jeans and boxers as I take my t-shirt off. Once I'm naked Carly looks up at me, smiles and lick her lips before taking me in her mouth. My hips jerk forward and I tighten my hold of her hair. "Carly...fuuuucck... that's right..just like that..lick my balls babe...ooooohhhhhhhhhh." Oh my god, I'm in heaven. "Babe you have to stop, I'm close and I don't want to come in your mouth," I moan as I help Carly to her feet, still holding a handful of her hair. I gently pull her head back, spin her around so her back is against the wall again and as I kiss her exposed neck I command her to remove her clothes. Once she's naked I kiss my way down her chest licking and biting her nipples and skin. She arches her body towards my mouth and lets out a moan, I'm in heaven. I kneel at her feet and kiss my way towards her inner thighs. I place her right leg over my shoulder so her pussy is exposed. She shivers as I blow cool air on her clit and softly lick her pussy. She grabs my head and guides me closer. I look up into her eyes. "So beautiful," I say as I place two fingers inside her and start to finger fuck her while my tongue flicks and sucks, her orgasm is building rapidly and her body convulses as she comes around my fingers and in my mouth.

I kiss my way up Carly's beautiful body and wrap her legs around my waist. She reaches down and grabs my erection, places it against her pussy and sinks onto my cock. Oh god she feels wonderful. I pump into Carly hard and fast and I feel like I'm going to push her through the wall. My body stills as my orgasm takes over and I come inside her. It takes a while to catch my breath and come down from my high. I'm spent as Carly takes my hand and leads me to the bed, we lay down facing each other, basking in the moment.

After a while we get dressed and drive over to see our new home. We don't have a key but we are able to look through the windows at the front. I can see Carly really likes it and I know she can't wait to put her stamp on it.

We decide to get some dinner at a Chinese restaurant close by. Halfway through our meal I put my fork down, take a deep breath and say, "Carly, I would like to take you to meet my parents this weekend, if you're ok with that?"

"Ummmm…I'm not sure."

"What aren't you sure about?"

"Who knows and how much do they know?" Carly asks quietly.

"Mum and Dad know some things but not everything. No one else in my family knows."

"What specifically do they know?" she ask as she puts her head down.

"They know about the 2nd attack, the VRO, what happened at the café this week and also that you can suffer panic attacks."

I can see that Carly's body has grown stiff and she holds onto her fork tighter trying to slow down her breathing. I lift Carly's hand to my mouth and kiss the back of her left hand. "Carly what's worrying you?"

"I don't want their pity or to be treated like I'm made of glass, I don't want anyone to watch what they say around me and I want to be treated like everyone else. I just want to be normal," Carly says with a sigh.

"Explain to me what's normal. This, our life here, is our new normal. It's entirely up to us what happens next, we are in control. My parents want to spend some time with the girl that I love, the girl that has made me so happy and is the future mother of our four-legged fur baby," I say with a laugh. "Just think about it and if you have any questions please ask."

"I want to meet your family but I have to say it's really overwhelming. Everyone is so nice, they get on really well and I'm just not used to it. When I agree to meet them can we *please* do it one at a time, I don't think I can handle the whole clan in one go."

"Of course we can, this weekend would be just my parents, they would like us to have a meal and a few drinks and stay the night on Friday. They want to get to know you in a relaxed setting. What do you say?"

"Ok, but just them no one else."

"Done, they are going to be thrilled," I say with a smile. I fill Carly in on my parents, siblings and my beautiful, funny niece Chelsea. I try not to overwhelm her with too much information because I know she is anxious about meeting them. It's not surprising considering the family she grew up in. I can't imagine being scared of my brother and having him torture me all my life. And if that wasn't bad enough, to have your Mum take his side all the time. When Carly and I have kids they will know that their parents love them equally and I will always protect them.

I notice Carly tosses and turns through the night. I pull her close to me and assure her that everything will go well tomorrow.

16 | CARLY

Ben finishes work at lunchtime on Friday and we make our way down to Wollongong. My nerves kick in when we start making our way down Mount Ousley because I know that we are not far from his parents' home. Ben puts his hand on my knee and gives a gentle squeeze. About ten minutes later he pulls into the driveway of a beautiful two story brick and tile home across the road from the beach. I just sit there as he turns off the car, my mouth wide open. Ben starts laughing. "Babe, close your mouth."

"Why didn't you t..tell me where your pa..parents live? Did y..you grow up here?"

"Yeah all of us grew up in the house. Kelsey and Damon still live here but they are gone for the night so we can have some time alone with Mum and Dad."

I look down at my jeans, jumper and runners. "I'm un..under dressed, I should have worn som..something better, th..they are going to th..think that I'm a bag lady."

"Carly you are hilarious, you're not here to meet the Queen, relax will you." He gets out and walks round to my side and opens my door. "Come on, time to go in."

"Ben, I can't, th..this is too much, you should h..have explained where y..you grew up, I'm n..not good enough for you, I..I can't compete with th..this," I ramble on and on. I start to hyperventilate and my mouth goes dry, my heart is pounding in my chest and I feel trapped, I have to get out of here. I push Ben out of the way and start making my way to the beach, I wish my dad was here, the beach is where I go to talk to him.

Ben catches up with me and grabs me by the elbow to stop me going any further. "Ben I'm not r..r..ready for this, t..t..they are going to know I'm not g..g..good enough for you, that I'm n..nothing."

"Carly stop, please don't, you are everything to me, I love you more than life itself." he says as he pulls my body into his and holds me tightly, rocking me back and forth until my panic attack finishes.

After a while a woman walks up slowly, I don't take much notice until Ben stands up and gives her a hug. Oh shit, it's Ben's Mum. She looks at me with a warm smile and then asks me if it's ok if we talk in private. My eyes flick between her and Ben, he squeezes my hand and mouths *'it's ok.'* I nod, Ben leans in, kisses me on the mouth, tells me he loves me and then leaves me alone with his mum.

She takes my hand and walks me to a bench seat facing the water. "Are you feeling better?" she asks.

"Yes, I'm s..sorry that you have s..seen me like this, I'm b..better now," I say, wringing my hands in my lap and avoiding looking at her.

We sit there for the longest time in silence just watching the waves crash on the beach and the birds flying overhead. Even though it's cold it's not raining and the sea air feels great against my skin. My body starts to relax and my breathing is back to normal.

Ben's mum reaches for my hand and I let her. "Carly, I am pleased that you and Ben are here, you have made my son extremely happy and he is so in love with you, I have never seen him like this over a girl before."

"How can I..I make him happy? Y..you saw what happens wh.. when things get too much. He has always g..got to watch out for me, be ca..careful what he does and s..says around me; that will get old pr.. pretty quick."

"It won't always be like this, everything is still so fresh and raw. You have to give yourself time to heal and the first step was moving to Sydney where you are away from any danger."

"H..How much do yo..you know?" I ask quietly.

"Enough to know that you haven't had the best life. I know you are close with your Dad and your friend Nicole, but other than them you have pretty much been on your own. We would love the chance to get to know you and welcome you into our crazy family, that's if you'll have us," she smiles.

"Mrs R..Richardson, why are yo..you being so nice to m..me?"

"Firstly, my name is Lucy — Mrs Richardson makes me sound so old — and secondly Ben loves you, and that's enough for us. Please come back to the house, James is dying to meet you." Lucy stands and holds out her hand for me. "Come on, I promise you it'll be ok." I place my hand in hers and stand, and as we walk back Lucy drops my hand and then places a reassuring arm around my shoulder and when we reach the front door she gives me a light squeeze. "Ready?" she asks. I smile and nod as we walk inside.

The Richardson's house is amazing. We walk into a huge foyer; to the right is a room that looks like an office and to the left is a massive floor to ceiling mirror wide enough that three people could stand side by side in front of it and see all of themselves. At the end of the foyer on the right is a beautiful staircase that hugs the wall and has a slight curve, and on the wall beside the staircase there are family photos, and I make a mental note to have a good look at them later. At the end of the foyer is a door, which we walk through to enter an open plan area containing the lounge room, dining room and kitchen. We find Ben and his Dad having a beer at the kitchen bench, deep in conversation. Both men look up at us and I can see Ben eyes searching mine to see if I am ok. I give a small smile and Ben looks like he relaxes.

Ben puts his beer down and walks over to me, takes my face in his hands and asks if I'm ok. I say I am and he gives me a quick kiss on the lips. He holds my hand and walks me to his Dad. "Carly, I would like you to meet my dad, James. Dad this is Carly."

I put my hand out to shake his but he just smiles and pulls me in for a hug. James is a big man and his body engulfs me; he kisses the top of my head and says, "Welcome to the family, I am so happy to meet you, Carly." As he releases me he takes a step back and puts his hands on my shoulders, and looking at me he says, "You are beautiful, my son has great taste." I blush and put my head down. Why are they being so nice to me?

"Time for a drink. Carly, what can I get for you?" Lucy asks. "We have wine, most spirits, cider, beer, soft drink or juice."

"Cider is good th..thanks." James gets me a drink while Ben motions for me to sit down on the lounge. He sits next to me and puts his hand on my thigh and lightly squeezes, I turn to him and he gives me a smile and a wink, which makes me giggle.

I listen to the three of them talk about people they know, such as Ben's brothers and sisters and what Chelsea is up to; she sounds like a handful but a lot of fun. They let us know that Chelsea's birthday party is the following weekend at Piper's house and they have an invite for us that Chelsea made. Lucy hands it to Ben and it is so cute, she has drawn a picture of herself on a swing with Ben pushing her. Ben tells Lucy he will call Chelsea later to thank her for the invite.

Lucy announces that dinner is ready. I offer to help and she asks me to set the table. There is a vase of pink and white lilies on the table that look and smell beautiful. Ben and I sit across from Lucy and James. The meal is amazing; we have roast beef, roast potatoes, corn, peas, cauliflower, broccoli, Yorkshire pudding and gravy, and for desert there is homemade apple pie and ice cream. I am in heaven, Lucy is a wonderful cook and I have relaxed and started to join in the conversation that flows throughout the meal. After dinner James and Ben load the dishwasher and clean up the kitchen while Lucy and I sit down.

Lucy takes my hand "How are you feeling now?"

"I'm much better, thank you, the meal was wonderful. You and James have made me feel very welcome and I thank you for that."

"Carly, you are great company, Ben loves you and it is very clear that you love him, and as his mother it's a beautiful thing to see. I know you moved here a little earlier than you expected, but how are you feeling about everything?"

"It's for the best, but under the worst circumstances. I know I was moving here anyway and I'm thrilled to be with Ben because I really missed him. Though I wish things were different."

"How so?"

"I wish my mum didn't feel the need to set me up. She always takes George's side even though she has witnessed firsthand what he has done to me. Lucy, I just don't get it. How can a parent do that to her child?"

"My sweet girl, I can't even begin to explain what she's thinking or why she does the things she does because I don't understand it myself. I try not to take sides where the kids are concerned. It's not always easy but I do try to stay out of their issues. Has it always been like that?"

"For as long as I can remember, but in her defence I didn't tell my parents what George had done to me over the years because I was scared of him and I thought he would kill me, which he nearly succeeded in doing twice," I say, lowering my head.

Lucy squeezes my hand tighter. "Darling you have nothing to be ashamed of, so please don't lower your head. You were the victim, I know you don't like to think like that but you did nothing to provoke these attacks. You have every right to expect your mother to protect you, that's what normally happens. I would give my life so my kids could live;

my kids call me Mother Bear because I'm that protective," she says with a laugh. "James and I are here for you, I just needed to let you know that."

I was just about to thank her when Ben and James return to the lounge. Ben looks at us. "Everything ok with you two?"

"Couldn't be better. Carly and I are just getting to know each other," Lucy says as she gives my hand a reassuring squeeze.

Ben asks if I would like a tour of the house. He takes me out the back first and there is a spa and swimming pool and beautifully landscaped garden beds and green lawn. As we walk up the staircase I slow down so I can look at all the photos; there are years of memories for the Richardson family. James and Lucy's wedding photo takes centre place and photos of all the kids, from birth to present day, are around it. This is how a family should be. We get to the top of the stairs and turn left. Ben points to the end of the hall. "This is Mum and Dad's room, the spare room, then the toilet and bathroom, and here is my room when I stay, next to Damon's, and at the other end of the hall is Kelsey's room."

I look into Ben's room and see our overnight bags in there. Ben must have put them in there while I was at the beach with Lucy. Ben pulls me into his room and shuts the door behind us. He walks me to the bed giving me that sexy smile that shows his dimples and he has a sparkle in his eyes. He lays back on the bed and pulls me so I'm lying on top of him. I can feel he is hard so I rub myself against him, pleasure jolts through me and I let out a low moan. Ben pulls my mouth down to his and he kisses me slowly and deeply. I get lost in him until all of a sudden I can hear loud voices downstairs. I pull my head up and look at Ben. I roll off him and we go to see what's going on. Once we get to the bottom of the stairs and we can hear the voices better, Ben stops, looks at me and says, "That's Damon, he was supposed to be gone for the night. If you don't want to deal with him go up to my room and I will sort this out."

"No it's ok…ummmm…I'll meet him. Your folks are lovely so let's get the next one out of the way," I say with half a smile. Ben holds my hand as we walk towards the lounge. I walk as slowly as I can and I'm chewing the inside of my cheeks.

I hear James' voice and I can tell he's not happy "You knew that this was hard for Carly, we need to take things slowly with her and introduce the family two at a time. What are you doing home?"

"It's not my fault that Gibbo got food poisoning, I don't want to sit there all night listening to him spew and shit himself," says Damon.

"You're such a good friend," Lucy says sarcastically.

Ben opens the door and we walk in. I walk up to Damon. "Hi Damon, I'm Carly, it's nice to meet you."

Lucy is about to say something but Ben holds up his hand to stop her.

Damon looks at me and then at Ben. "Dude you did good," he says with a smirk. I just shake my head. "Nice to meet you too, Carly."

We talk and have a few drinks. Ben and Damon are so funny how they take the piss out of each other. Lucy brings out Ben's baby photos, Ben isn't very happy but he was so cute when he was little. If we ever have kids together I hope they take after him. It is about 1 am when we decide to go to bed. I had a great night.

I tell Ben I am going to go for a shower. I grab my pj's and head for the bathroom, but when I go to close the door Ben pushes it open, closes it behind us and locks it. Before I know what's happening his mouth is kissing my neck and his hands are cupping my breasts. "Ben we can't have sex in your parents' bathroom, especially when they are just down the hall," I whisper.

"Babe I have been dying to get you alone since I showed you my room earlier; we can be quiet; well I can, but I know I'll have you screaming my name," he whispers with a huge grin on his face. Ben continues kissing my neck and is slowly moving around so he's standing behind me, he knows I am putty in his hands when he is behind me kissing the back of my neck. He is not playing fair. Ben starts to undress me and I let out a low groan at his touch on my skin; once I'm completely naked I push my bum back into his groin and grind into his erection. Ben spins me around and crashes his mouth to mine. I undress him as quickly as I can and we make our way to the shower, where he lifts me up and makes love to me quietly.

As we leave the bathroom we run into Damon. He laughs and says, "Saving water hey bro?" and keeps walking.

We make it to Ben's room before we burst into laughter. We lay in bed talking about the day, his family and how well everything went. I start to yawn. Ben kisses me goodnight, tells me he loves me then gets me to turn to my other side so he can cuddle me from behind and I fall into a blissful sleep.

In the morning I wake with a start to find a little girl jumping up and down on our bed, and I realise pretty quickly it's Chelsea. All of a sudden Ben wakes, and nearly shoots out of bed — thank god he is wearing his boxers — but before he can get out of bed Chelsea misjudges her bounce and she lands on his crotch. He doubles over in pain. I don't know why, but when a guy gets hit in the balls girls generally laugh and I am no different; the more he complains the harder I laugh and because I am laughing so hard Chelsea laughs too.

Ben scowls at me and says, "Not helping Carly."

That makes me burst into hysterics and I fall off the bed. I have not laughed like that in such a long time. I am rolling around on the floor when I hear a knock on the door, Chelsea jumps off the bed and runs over to open the door and I see Lucy, James, Kelsey and Piper staring at me — I recognise Kelsey and Piper from Skype and also the photos I have seen. They look at me as if I have lost all my marbles, and I point at Ben because I can't speak. Ben is doubled over with tears in his eyes but manages to tell them when has happened. James sucks some air through his teeth and crosses his legs, whereas Lucy, Kelsey and Piper start laughing. Piper manages to stop laughing long enough to say, "What's the story morning glory?" Even James thinks that's funny and starts to laugh. Piper gets Chelsea out of the room and says they will see us downstairs.

I get up on the bed and crawl to Ben, I put my arms around his waist and ask if he is ok, Ben just glares at me and says, "What do you think?" I apologise for laughing but it takes a while for Ben to calm down and talk to me again.

There is a bit of sniggering when we walk into the lounge, mainly from Piper and her husband Justin. Chelsea runs up to Ben and throws herself into his arms, I notice when he bends forward to pick her up he pushes his bum out further so there was no way she can kick his balls again. Ben looks at Chelsea and says, "Between you and Carly I doubt I'm going to be able to Father children."

His family look at me and I proceed to tell them about the night we met. James and Justin just shake their heads while Lucy, Piper and Kelsey start to have a go at him. "We brought you up better than that Benjamin," Lucy scolds him.

Ben walks with Chelsea in his arms to the lounge and sits down, putting her on his knee and holding his hands up in surrender. "I know, I know, I was a complete D.I.C.K and I am thankful Carly took the time to get to know the real me."

"Uncle Ben, what's a dick?"

Ben's eyes are as large as saucers. "When did she learn to spell?" Ben asks without trying to laugh. We all look anywhere but at Chelsea, I can see bodies shaking trying really hard not to laugh out loud. Ben seems to compose himself. "Chelsea, Uncle Ben said a naughty word and I'm sorry."

Chelsea throws her arms around Ben's neck and kisses him "I love you Uncle Ben but you have to put money in the naughty jar because you said a bad word."

"I will do that next weekend at your party if that's ok with you?" Chelsea just smiles at him and snuggles into his chest. It is lovely to see the special bond they have.

As we all sit down to breakfast Damon walks in the door. Chelsea sits between myself and Ben and I help her cut her food. Piper talks about her morning sickness that doesn't just happen in the morning, it seems to go all day. Kelsey talks about her upcoming Higher School Certificate (HSC) exams. Damon talks about university (uni) and his job as a bouncer at one of the local pubs. Chelsea just chatters away. Lucy and James join in the many conversations, while Justin chimes in every now and then; like me he is quiet most of the time. I sit there watching the dynamics of this amazing family and I am very lucky to be welcomed into it.

As I am getting lost in my thoughts Chelsea puts her hand on my face. "Aunty Carly are you coming to my party? I'm going to be a fairy."

I smile at Chelsea. "I think you will make a beautiful fairy and I would love to come to your party. I saw the invitation you made and the pretty picture you drew for Uncle Ben, you did a very good job."

Chelsea smiles then gets off her chair and climbs onto my lap, she sits facing me. "Aunty Carly can I please play with your hair?

"Of course you can, but we will have to wait until everyone has finished breakfast and everything is cleared and cleaned away."

After breakfast Ben pulls me aside. "Mum has asked to talk to you to see if you're ok with meeting Darcy today, if you are she will call him and invite him for lunch."

I kiss his lips and smile. "That sounds good to me. Your family are so nice and it's a shame that Darcy is not here."

As promised, I let Chelsea play with my hair. She sits on the lounge and I sit at her feet. She has a water bottle, brush, comb, clips and hair ties. Chelsea sprays so much water on my head it's soaking wet, so

Ben goes and gets a towel for my shoulders. She brushes it and puts it up in all kind of weird and wonderful ways. "Aunty Carly, can I please cut your hair?" Before I get a chance to answer everyone in the room yells no. "I was only asking," says Chelsea, "no need to yell."

I stifle a laugh and turn around to face her "Do you want to be a hairdresser when you get older Chelsea?"

"Yes I do and I will cut your hair."

"That sounds great to me Chelsea, I look forward to it. Have we finished? Because I need to have a shower and wash my hair and get ready for lunch." Chelsea nods and I excuse myself and make my way to Ben's room to get my toiletries bag. As I am coming out of his room I bump into Damon. "I'm just going for a shower but I can wait if you need the bathroom."

"No it's ok, you go ahead Carly. Hey, before you go, I would like a word with you first." I nod and take a deep breath. "Please don't hurt him, he's a good guy and I can tell he loves you. I have never seen him this way with any of his other girlfriends and I have to admit it worries me."

"Damon I am so damned lucky that he found me and persevered every time that I pushed him away. Ben makes me so happy that sometimes it scares me how much I love him and he loves me. I promise you that I will never deliberately hurt him. He is very lucky to have you look to out for him. I wish I had that from my brother." I say with a sigh. "Are we ok?"

"Yeah, we're cool," he says with a smile. "You better go and wash your hair because you look like a drowned rat."

I laugh. "You are such a charmer."

I shower quickly, dry my hair and change into clean clothes. As I make my way downstairs I can hear voices and I hear my name. I stop to listen even though I know I shouldn't.

"Carly seems nice enough but there is something about her that I'm not sure about, I just can't put my finger on it. Something doesn't add up," I hear Piper say.

"What do you mean by that?" Ben asks angrily.

"It seems there is something bubbling just under the surface and that it will explode without much provocation, I think she is a loose cannon and I'm worried for you."

"You have only spent a few hours with her, she has been nothing but nice to everyone, especially Chelsea, and you come out with this bullshit. You are so far off the mark. Carly has not had an easy life by any stretch of the imagination but she is the best thing that has ever happened to me. I have never been so happy and if you can't see that you are blind."

"Piper you need to get to know Carly. Give her a chance," Lucy says.

"I'm just looking out for my little brother, is that a crime?"

"No, it's not, but this time I think it's unwarranted. She's a lovely girl," James says.

"Only time will tell but I have a really bad feeling about her," Piper sighs.

I can't move, I'm frozen to the spot and then I hear the front door open. I turn my head around to see a guy and girl walk in holding hands. They just look at me for a few seconds, then the guy speaks. "Hi Carly, I'm Darcy and this is my girlfriend Lily. It's nice to meet you."

"It's n..nice to meet you too Dar..Darcy, and you Lil..Lily," I say as I walk past them with tears starting to fall. "P..Please excuse m..me I will be back in a..a..a minute."

"Carly, are you ok?" asks Darcy.

"Yeah, yeah I'm f..f..fine I just need a b..b..bit of fresh air that's all, I..I won't be lo…long,"I say as cheerfully as I can. I make my way outside and run to the beach, just as my feet hit the sand it starts to rain, fuckin' typical, could this day get any worse? I walk along the sand away from the house trying to calm myself down. I focus on the waves rolling in and try to calm my breathing, I don't want to have another panic attack. I sit down facing the water and just breathe in and out, trying to relax my body. After a while I hear Ben calling my name, I wrap my arms around my legs and I try to be as small as I can. A few minutes later I hear Ben's voice and he sits down next to me.

"How much did you hear?" Ben asks.

"E..Enough," I whisper.

"Carly, please look at me, I don't want to talk to the side of your head." I lift up my head but I can't look at him. "I'm sorry you heard that, Piper had no right talking about you like that, I am so fucking angry with her. Are you ok?"

"But she's right th..though." Ben tries to interrupt but I stop him "There is always som..something just under the surface and it d… doesn't take much to s..set me off, I have panic attacks, I st…stutter and have b..bad dreams. I had a panic attack yesterday wh..when we arrived here, that's not nor..normal."

"Carly, please slow your breathing down. And what's normal? Everyone has something, I don't care who you are. You have had a hard life and things are bound to affect you. Hopefully with time things will become easier and you will have some control, that's my wish for you." Ben puts his arm around me and we just sit there in the rain watching the waves roll in. After a while I start to shiver, Ben stands, offers his hand to me and helps me to my feet "Are you ready to go back? I will make her apologise to you for what she said about you."

I lift my head to look at Ben "Please don't do that, she has nothing to apologise for, Piper is entitled to her opinion and as I said, I agree with her."

We walk back to his parent's home in silence, Lucy meets us at the door with towels and a hug. "I'm sorry for what Piper said."

"Lu..Lucy it's ok. As I said to B..Ben, Piper is entitled to h…her opinion and I think sh..she is right. She is only lo…looking out for Ben a..and that's a wu..wun..wonderful and caring thing t..to do. I wish I had a si…sibling that loved me th..that much." Just then Piper enters the foyer and everyone goes silent.

Piper walks up to me and before she can talk I hold up my hand. "Piper I am u..use to people not l…liking me, or thinking I'm we..weird, and that's ok, but in future if y…you have any concerns about me pl… please talk to me about it a..and don't talk about m…me behind my back. For the record, you are r…right, I have issues th..that affect my day to day life and th…they do bubble just under the s..surface. I am ho… hoping that one day things will settle d..down and I can start t..to live a normal life. I have one more hur…hurdle to go and once th..that is over I hope I c..can start the healing pro…process, so I ask you, in the meantime ju..just get to know me and th..then form an o…opinion. Now if you w..will all excuse me I would li..like to take another sh..shower because I'm free…freezing."

As I make my way up the stairs I can hear Ben behind me. I reach the handle to the bathroom as his hand covers mine and gently squeezes. I turn to face him and he has his arms open wide for me, I step forward and bury my face into his chest. He wraps his arms around me, kisses my forehead and rocks us back and forth.

After a while he pulls away. "Come on, Beautiful, let's get you warmed up." He shuts the bathroom door behind us, turns on the taps and starts to undress me. Once I'm naked he tests the water and when he is satisfied with the temperature he guides me under the stream of water. He steps back to remove his clothes and then joins me in the shower. Ben takes his time washing my body and hair, showing me how much he loves me. He is so gentle and loving I feel so safe with him, and I start to relax. When we are finished Ben dries me and puts a towel around my body and one around my hair. He wraps a towel around his waist and goes to open the door.

"Wh..what are you do…doing? I can't wa..walk around practically na…naked in your parents' home. Can y..you please get me some cl..clothes and bring them in h..here for me?"

"You're kidding me right? Carly, we are the only ones up here and my bedroom is right next door. I will go out first to make sure we are alone." Ben opens the door and walks into the hall. "Carly, everyone is downstairs. Come on you'll get cold again."

I race out of the bathroom and into Ben's room and shut the door behind me. Ben stands there laughing, shaking his head.

We get dressed and I dry my hair. I sit on the end of the bed, not wanting to go downstairs because I know it's going to be awkward. Ben sits next to me and takes my hand in his. "Babe, we can't stay up here all day, please come downstairs and let's see if we can salvage this day. Plus I'm starving," he says with a cheeky grin that shows his dimples.

"You are not playing fair, you know I can't resist those dimples," I say laughing.

"If they didn't work on their own I was going to bring out the big guns." He leans into his bag and grabs his glasses case, takes his glasses out and puts them on. He wags his eyebrows up and down and I burst out laughing.

"I will just about agree to anything you want when you wear them, you are so sexy," I say as I lean in to kiss him.

"Come on babe, I'll be right by your side, I promise." I take his hand and we walk downstairs. Just before we enter the lounge room I take a deep breath. The conversations stop as we enter the room and I feel like a deer in head lights.

"Aunty Carly, that was a very long shower, Nanny won't have any hot water left. That's very naughty because everyone else has to have cold showers now," Chelsea chastised me.

I kneel down so I am face to face with Chelsea. "I'm sorry for taking a very long shower, Chelsea. I promise I won't do that again."

"Ok Aunty Carly, you are forgiven. Come and draw with me,"

Chelsea says as she pulls me to the large breakfast bar where her colouring books and pencils are. As I sit down the conversations start up again and after a while Piper makes her way to us and sits down next to me.

Piper touches my hand to get my attention, I turn to face her and I notice she had been crying. I start to say something but she stops me. "Carly, I was so far out of line before and I am really sorry for what I said and for hurting your feelings, that was not my intention. I am so protective over my siblings I tend to talk without thinking," she says in a hushed voice so Chelsea can't hear. "Please forgive me?"

"There is nothing to forgive. I am thrilled that Ben has all of you looking out for him. Do you know how special that is?"

"Can we please start again? I would like to blame it on pregnancy hormones but my mouth has always gotten me into trouble. Mum has said to me for as long as I can remember to engage the brain before opening my gob. I'm twenty six and I still haven't mastered that," she says and we both burst out laughing.

I relax a bit more. "I would really like to start again," I say with a smile.

We have an amazing lunch. Lucy made lasagne from scratch and served it with salad and garlic bread. As we eat I watch the whole family interact and I notice how much they resemble one another. Lucy and Piper are the only two who don't have dimples, but Kelsey only has one dimple in her left cheek. All the guys are about six foot and the girls are between five foot five and five foot nine. Ben and James wear glasses and have brown eyes, while the rest have deep blue eyes. Lucy, Piper and Kelsey have blonde hair and James, Ben, Darcy and Damon have brown hair. They are all genetically blessed. Chelsea is a combination of Piper and Justin, who is about six foot with black hair and brown eyes. Chelsea is tall for her age, with black hair, stunning blue eyes and those beautiful dimples. She is going to break some hearts.

After lunch I help clean away and load the dishwasher with Lily, Darcy's girlfriend. It's nice to talk to an outsider. I find out that Darcy and Lily have been together since high school, and that they live together in Wollongong so she is close to uni and Darcy to work. Lily is doing a Batchelor of Arts in photography and eventually she wants to work for National Geographic; she also works part-time to help with their finances. Darcy is an electrician and does the odd cash jobs for extra money.

I want to ask her questions about the family but Ben and Darcy come over. I didn't realise how tiny Lily was until she stood next to

Darcy; her head only comes up to his chest. She has hazel eyes and light brown hair that reaches the middle of her back and her smile lights up her whole face. She has an infectious laugh, I really like her.

Ben pulls me aside. "Babe, Darcy has asked if we would like to go to the pub with them tonight. Damon is a bouncer there and he will be working. It'll be great to let our hair down."

"I have nothing good enough to wear, I only have my jeans and a t-shirt, I'll look like a bogan."

"That's crazy, your t-shirt is from the Kings of Leon concert and you've hardly worn it, your jeans are new and you have your black converse runners, there is nothing bogan about that. We can stay here again tonight. Come on, what do you say?"

"Ok, sounds good, but can we catch a taxi? That way we can both drink. You deserve to let loose after everything you have had to put up with lately."

"Great, I'll let them all know. You ok to get ready early and head over to Darcy's place with them? We can leave from there. And we can grab a bite to eat before we go to the pub."

Ben informs his folks of our plans and I start to get ready, thankfully I don't go anywhere without my hair straightener and makeup bag. As Ben gets a key off his Mum I start to apply my makeup.

Chelsea enters Ben's room. "Aunty Carly, you look pretty. Can you make me look pretty?"

"Chelsea, you are already pretty, you don't need any of this makeup."

"Please Aunty Carly."

"Let's go and check with Mummy first and if she says yes then I will put some makeup on you, ok?" Chelsea grabs my hand and races down the stairs yelling 'Mummy' as loud as she can. We get to the bottom of the stairs and Piper rushes over to see what's wrong.

"Mummy, can Aunty Carly put some pretties on me?"

Piper looks at me confused. "Chelsea was watching me put on my makeup," I say. "She asked if I could put some on her and I said that she would have to ask you first."

Piper lets out a breath. "I thought you were hurt the way you were yelling and running down those stairs. If Carly has time and she wants to I guess it's ok to have a little bit of makeup on, but not too much."

"I have put makeup on little ones before for photo shoots so I promise I won't put on too much, she will still look like a five year old," I reassure.

Chelsea and I made our way back upstairs where I put on a little bit of powder, eye shadow and lip gloss. I take a photo of her with my phone, she looks so cute.

"Aunty Carly, can you take a photo of us?"

I say I will but I have to finish my makeup first. When I finish I sit Chelsea on my lap and take a few photos of the two of us, we are laughing and taking photos with silly faces when all of a sudden Ben appears in the doorway.

"You two are crazy but you both look very pretty," he says with a wink.

"Uncle Ben, can you take a photo of us?" Ben smiles and goes to take a photo of Chelsea and me. "No silly," says Chelsea, "I want you in the photo too."

Ben sits down next to me and places my phone in front of the three of us and takes a few photos. "Two of my favourite girls," he says as he kisses us both on the cheeks.

Chelsea pulls away "Don't mess up my pretties Uncle Ben."

"I am very sorry," Ben says, trying not to laugh. "Aunty Carly and I have to go now. We are going out with Uncle Darcy and Aunty Lily but we will see you next weekend for your birthday party, ok?"

Chelsea starts to cry "I don't want you to go, I want you to stay and play with me. Please Uncle Ben."

"Sweetheart we have to go but I promise we will see you next week and we will play then."

Chelsea nods, gives us both a kiss and cuddle and makes her way downstairs to say goodbye to Darcy and Lily. Ben grabs his jacket and we make our way out of his bedroom. Just as I am about to go down the stairs Ben puts his arm around my waist and pulls me back so I am pressed up against him. "Have I told you how beautiful you look and how much I love you?" he says as he leans down to kiss my neck.

I smile. "You just have, and I have to say you're looking damned fine yourself, plus I love you too. Now let's go and have a good time."

CARLY | 17

We travel to Darcy and Lily's place in their car. They live in a cute little town house with two bedrooms and a bathroom and toilet upstairs, and a lounge, kitchen, laundry and toilet downstairs. Ben and I sit on the lounge waiting for them to get ready; it's nice just to spend some alone time with Ben.

We enjoy a meal at the pub, it has such a chilled atmosphere. The conversation is flowing, Darcy and Lily share stories about Ben, most are funny but a few have me raising an eyebrow. Then we go in to the bar and find a table close to the dance floor. It has been too long since I had a good dance and I need to blow away the cobwebs.

As Ben and Darcy go to the bar to get the drinks a guy walks past our table and says hello, I smile and say hello back, but Lily doesn't look to happy and just scowls at him and then looks away. I'm about to ask her what's going on when the guys come back with our drinks.

"Ahhh cider, a girl after my own heart," I say as I clink Lily's glass with mine. Over the next hour the pub starts to fill up and I am definitely buzzed. It doesn't take much to get me drunk, I'm what's commonly known as a two pot screamer. What can I say, I'm a cheap date.

Before Damon starts work he comes over to say hello and sits down with us for a while. He is about to get up and start work when we hear a girl screech Ben's name, and we all swing our heads around to see where this god awful noise came from. I notice Ben tense up, and I place my hand on his thigh to see if he's alright. Then a girl launches herself at him and sits on his lap with her arms around his neck. My hand is trapped under her and I have to really yank at it to get it out.

"Ben, when did you get back? I've missed you," she says. Ben looks really uncomfortable as she tries to pull him in for a kiss.

He grabs her hands from around his neck and stands her up and gently pushes her away from him. "I've been back a while. Whitney, this is my girlfriend Carly," Ben says, gesturing to me.

I hear Damon mutter, "This ought to be interesting."

Whitney takes a step back, folds her arms and slowly looks me up and down.

I let out a laugh and start to turn around. "Here you go, now you can see all of me. Is one spin enough or would you like me to do another?" I ask sarcastically. Our table erupts in laughter.

"Who is this bitch?" Whitney asks Ben.

"Watch your mouth," Ben says angrily. "As I said before, Carly is my girlfriend and if you can't be civil to her you can leave now."

"What do you mean your girlfriend? You said you didn't want to get tied down and that's why we weren't together."

"He meant he didn't want a relationship with you because you're a bunny boiler," Damon says. "Whit, when are you going to understand that Ben doesn't want you, never has never will."

"Damon there is no need for that," I say as I hold my hand in front of him. "You don't need to humiliate her like that."

"I don't understand why you are sticking up for her, she called you a bitch."

"I've been called much worse in my time but that doesn't mean that you have to belittle her." I turn to Whitney and hold out my hand. "Whitney, I'm Carly, it's nice to meet you."

Whitney just stands there, with mouth open and tears in her eyes that threaten to fall. She straightens up, looks at my hand, turns to Ben and says, "Your loss."

Ben takes my hand and pulls me into him. "I'm sorry about that, she has always had a thing for me but I have never looked at her that way, Carly. I promise I have never touched her."

"Ben there is no need to explain, it's all good. Besides I can't blame her for having a crush on you, you're so damned hot," I say with a wink as I kiss him.

Damon was about to walk off to start work. "Damon, are we cool?" I ask.

"Yeah we're cool," he says with a smile, "Well played." I curtsy and he walks away shaking his head.

We are about to sit back down at the table when the DJ starts to play John Newman's *Love Me Again* "I love this song, Lily you wanna dance?" I ask excitedly. We practically run to the dance floor and we dance to the next six songs. Then a song comes on that we don't like so we head back to the table. I need to cool down so I motion to Ben that I am going to the bar to get a glass of water. The bar is three deep with people so I have to wait a while to get served. I make my way to the bar and as I am waiting my turn a guy next to me starts talking to me. I turn to look at him and realise he's the guy that said hello to Lily and I earlier, so just as I smile at him as the barman taps me on the arm for my drink order. The music is loud so I lean across the bar to place my order. I feel a hand cup my right breast. I turn my head to look at the guy again; I smile and he smiles back at me. I move my body so I'm facing him, take a small step towards him and then raise my knee to hit him in the balls, and as he goes down I knee him in the face, splitting his nose open. He falls to the floor with blood pissing out of his nose. He looks up at me in complete shock, and I notice some people are laughing at him and then I see the crowd part. Oh fuck this can't be good, I say to myself. I look up and see two huge bouncers coming my way. I brace myself ready to be thrown out but they lean down, pick the guy up off the floor and walk away with him, leaving me standing there. I don't know what to do, I just stand there like a stunned mullet.

Next thing I know Damon is next to me asking me to go with him. I follow him to an office. Ben, Darcy and Lily are already in there. Damon shuts the door behind us and they burst into laughter. I look at them as if they have lost their marbles.

"Babe, you never cease to amaze me. Damon told me what that dirt bag did to you at the bar and how you handled the situation. I am so proud of you," Ben says as he pulls me into him.

"How do you know what happened?" I ask Damon. "The bar was really crowded."

"I had collected some glasses and just walked behind the bar when I saw what Alex did to you. Before I could react you had sorted him out so I radioed the other guys to collect him and told them that I would speak to you. Would you like to see the footage?"

"Why not?"

Damon presses play and a grainy black and white scene shows up on the TV, the camera must have been over the guy's head because it shows a clear view of what he did to me and then what I did to him. Ben, Darcy and Damon groan and cross their legs when they see me knee him in the balls.

"What is going to happen to me?" I ask. "Am I going to get

charged?"

"I seriously doubt it. Alex has done this before but no one has either put in a complaint or done anything about it, until you. He has been put in a taxi and more than likely he is on the way to the hospital. I'm pretty sure you broke his nose," Damon says with a smirk. "I will make sure a copy is made and we keep it in the safe just in case he tries anything."

I look at Lily. "You know him don't you?"

"Yes, unfortunately. I used to go to School with him and he tried many times to split me and Darcy up. He generally made my life hell throughout high school. I'm lucky I don't see much of him since we graduated."

"So what now? Do I have to leave?" I ask Damon.

"No, we removed the problem so you are welcome to stay and enjoy the night. But please don't get into any more fights, I am busy enough without watching you all night, ok Rocky?" Damon laughs.

We all laugh at Damon's comment and make our way back out to the bar, we're about to get a drink when I hear the DJ play *Blurred Lines* by Robin Thicke/Pharrell and TI, and I grab Ben's hand. "Come dance with me." We make our way to the dance floor and we dance like no one was watching, we are grinding on each other, laughing and just having a great time. The next song they play is *Daft Punks Get Lucky*, and I whisper in Ben's ear that he is going to get very lucky tonight. I pull back so I can see his face and he has the biggest smile; he mouths *'I love you.'* We dance to a few more songs and are about to get a drink when Darcy and Lily join us.

I really like Lily, I think we are going to become good friends. She is so sure about what she wants and is focused, so I know she will get what she wants out of life. Darcy is such a solid guy and he is besotted with Lily. It's a beautiful thing to be in their company, they are so in love. I realise that this, right here and now is normal. Couples are out having a good time and it really drives home how not normal my life had been. Thank god Ben came into my life, I am one very lucky girl and I intend to show him how lucky I am later.

At the end of the night we see if Damon wants to share a taxi with us but he says he is going to his mate's and won't be home tonight. Ben and Darcy announce they are hungry so we head to the kebab shop just up the road. Watching two grown men inhale a kebab is a sight to see. Lily and I sit there laughing at them, it's like we are watching lions devour their latest kill. Once they finish we walk back to the pub and wait for a taxi.

Whitney walks up to us with two other girls behind her. "Ben, your girlfriend is a bitch, I saw what she did to Alex. You really are slumming it with her."

I can feel Ben's body tense up and his arms get a bit tighter around me, he starts to say something but I stop him. "Whitney, after a rocky start I tried to make nice with you but you weren't having any of it," I say. "You have every right to be jealous of me. Ben is a great boyfriend, he's hot as hell and the most amazing attentive lover. He won't stop until I've had mind blowing orgasms. The things he does to my body... well, let's just say it's a work of art. So you run along with your little friends because no one here is interested in your bullshit."

"Ugh…ummmm," Whitney stutters.

"Yeah that's what I thought," I say as I snuggle into Ben's chest. Just then a taxi pulls up and the four of us get in.

As we pull away the three of them start to laugh. "Holy shit, Carly, you don't mess around. I have never seen her lost for words," laughs Darcy. "Though I really didn't need to know how my brother operates in the sack."

"Well what can I say?" Ben says smugly.

We drop Darcy and Lily at their place and are halfway back to Ben's parents' when he pulls me closer. "You've been quiet since we got in the taxi, are you ok?"

"I'm not proud of what I said to Whitney," I reply. "I intentionally said things to hurt her and that was wrong."

"Babe, she was being a total bitch to you, she is jealous of you and that's not your fault. If she had of minded her own business or been nice to you none of this would have happened. Please don't beat yourself up about it."

Ben's parents' home is in total darkness and we try to be as quiet as we can as we make our way inside. Thankfully everyone is asleep; walking up a flight of stairs is hard when you're pissed. Note to self, never live in a place that has stairs. We make it to Ben's room and collapse on the bed. The curtains are open and because it is a clear night the moon shines through and gives the room a romantic glow. We start to kiss and undress each other, as Ben makes his way down my body to remove my jeans and I let out a yelp.

"Did I hurt you?"

"Yeah my knee is sore, I think it's the one that I kneed that guy with."

Ben turns on the bedside lamp and we see that my knee is swollen and a massive bruise has broken out. "Babe, how did you not notice this before?"

"Ummm I don't know, maybe I didn't notice coz of all the cider I've drunk," I say laughing.

"I will just have to be careful and concentrate on the rest of your body," Ben says with a sexy smile, and then he proceeds to treat my body to two amazing orgasms before he makes love to me.

BEN | 18

I wake mid-morning with Carly wrapped around me. I pull her closer and hear her groan, "Ben my knee's killing me and I can't straighten my leg." I roll away from her and sit up so I can look at her leg. Carly lets out a scream as I touch her knee, which is swollen to the size of a melon and is a lovely shade of purple. "Oh fuck it hurts," moans Carly.

"Babe, you need to get dressed and I'll take you to the hospital."

Mum asks Carly if she can have a look. She pokes and prods Carly's knee, causing Carly to cry out in pain a few times.

"Carly, I can call Piper to come and have a look at this. She's a Nurse at Wollongong Hospital and hopefully she can help so that you don't have to wait for hours in the Emergency Department," says Mum.

Piper arrives about thirty minutes later with her massive first aid kit. Carly's sat on the lounge with her leg elevated. "So, what happened here then?" Piper asks. Carly explains what happened and everyone is silent until Piper says, "Shit Carly, I think I got off easy yesterday."

"My dad is a Prison Officer and he taught me how to defend myself. He said the trick was to smile at the guy and that makes them think that you're up for it, then they let their guard down and that's the time to make your move."

Piper looks at Carly's leg and she is pretty sure that she has ligament damage. The best treatment is to put on a compression bandage, apply ice for about twenty minutes every two hours, elevate and use crutches. Piper also advises me to get some over the counter pain relief for Carly. I give Carly a kiss as I go to the Chemist to get what she needs.

I put Carly's seat back as far as it can go for the drive home but I can see that she's very uncomfortable. Thank god the hotel has a lift and we don't have to take the stairs. Once we get to the room I phone down to get some more pillows so Carly can prop up her leg. We order room service that night and watch a few movies. Carly fidgets all evening.

At bed time I help Carly remove her bandages and get undress so we can have a shower, I then wash and dry below her knees and help her get settled in bed. She takes two more pain killers and settles in to go to sleep.

Sometime in the early hours of the morning I wake and realise Carly's missing from our bed. I discover her asleep on the lounge, so I walk over to her. I can see the pain etched all over her face as she groans in her sleep. I place my hand under her shoulders and the back of her good leg and start to lift her from the lounge. She wakes with a start. "Ben what are you doing? I'm too heavy put me down."

"Don't be crazy, you're as light as a feather. What are you doing all the way over here?" I ask while I carry her to bed.

"I was tossing and turning so much I was worried that I would wake you and you have to work tomorrow, you need your sleep. So I got up and went to sleep over there."

"Promise me you will never sleep on the lounge again, your place is with me in our bed. I don't care if you keep me awake, I would prefer that to waking up in an empty bed."

I wake up exhausted because both of us didn't sleep well. Before I leave I place a glass of water and pain killers on Carly's bed side table. I lean down to kiss her goodbye "Make sure you take those pills babe."

"I will, love you," she says sleepily.

"Love you too."

My morning goes really quickly. As I'm going to lunch I bump into Hayley.

"Hey Richo, how's it goin?" she asks.

"Great Hayles, and you?"

"Same old, same old."

"That don't sound good."

"I'm just having a hard time with a few things at the moment but I don't wanna talk about it."

"Fair enough. Hey Carly's here in Sydney, she arrived last week," I say with a smile.

"I didn't think she was moving here until the end of the month."

"Things changed. It's so great having her here, I really missed her. Anyway I'm going to give her a call so I'll see you later."

"Catch ya."

I pull out my mobile and press Carly's number and when she answers my heart skips a beat, just the sound of her voice makes me smile. "Good afternoon, Beautiful. How's the knee?"

"Sore but I can't lie around anymore. I know while I'm in the room I have to elevate it, but I was hungry so I thought I would come and get some lunch and a few magazines then head back to our room."

"Sounds like a plan. By the way I heard from Defence Housing this morning and our home will be available for us to move in this Friday, so I have organised for our things to be delivered Friday morning. We can pick up the key Thursday after work."

Carly squeals. "Ben that's wonderful, I am so excited to have our own home I just hope that I will be mobile enough to help with the move."

"If not it'll be ok. You just meet the delivery guys there in the morning and I'll arrive just after lunch to move things to where we want them. You can tell them what room you want things in before I get there and I will put our bed frame together when I get there. I'm so excited, Carly, I can't wait."

"I might do some research to see if there are any Rottweiler pups being born soon and I will also see if there are any jobs in and around the Ultimo area because I need to get a job soon."

"Carly, don't feel any pressure to get a job, if you want to work that's fine but only look if you want to, I am more than happy to support us."

"You are a wonderful guy Ben Richardson, but I need to work, I'm not one to be idle. I'd get bored and then I would become a pain in the arse and that's no good for anyone," Carly says laughing.

"Ok babe I have to get back to work, I'll see you later, I love you."

"I love you too," I hear Carly say as I hang up the phone.

The afternoon goes fairly quickly and I can't wait to get home to Carly. I find her fast asleep on the bed. I strip out of my clothes and lay down next to her, gently kissing and nibbling her neck.

"What a wonderful way to wake up," Carly says with a sigh.

I say as I unbutton her shirt and kiss my way down her fantastic body, only pausing to tell her how much I missed her. I suck a nipple into my mouth and gently bite. Carly moans and arches her back towards my mouth. For the next couple of hours we explore each other's bodies thoroughly.

By Thursday the swelling in Carly's knee is going down and the bruise has turned an ugly shade of yellow. When I finish work we drive to get the key for our new home. The place is freshly painted and the floors are polished. We walk around deciding where we will put everything. When we walk into what will be our bedroom we discover that it has French doors that open out onto the back patio, there is a huge walk-in robe along one side of the room and we have an en-suite.

"I'm so in love with this room, it is perfect," says Carly as she leans against the frame of the French doors.

I wrap my arms around her waist and pull her back against my chest. "I can't wait to move in and start this new chapter with you. I love you so much, Carly, I know we are going to be happy here." I move her hair and start kissing her neck, my hands roam up and down her sides as she pushes herself further into me, giving me the green light. I turn her around, her lips press against mine, she opens her mouth and our kiss becomes deeper.

Then she pulls away, looking me in the eyes. "You have made me so happy, I never thought I deserved or was worthy of happiness but you have changed all that. I love you with all my heart. Thank you for finding me."

I hold her tighter, there's no need for words. We stand there for a while before we take one more look around, lock up and then leave. We drive to the local pub and have a meal then go back to the hotel to pack our things. I will bring them over tomorrow after work. Once we are packed we jump on the internet and look for Rottweiler breeders. I make a few calls and we find two breeders that have young or newborn male pups, and we arrange to go and see them on Sunday. One is in Albion Park and the other is in Nowra.

CARLY | 19

Friday morning Ben makes love to me before going to work. What a way to wake up! I catch a taxi to our new home. The guys who deliver the furniture are great; they can see that I'm on crutches and they move things for me that they wouldn't normally, and they set up the washing machine and dryer so I can wash the sheets and towels. They leave mid-morning and that gives me time to wash the dinner set, glasses, and cutlery etc. before Ben arrives.

It is a dry and windy day so I hang the sheets and towels on the line. I have just finished and am heading back inside when I hear a woman's voice say hello. I stop and look around and see a woman wave to me from the house next door.

"Hi, my name is Amber. I'm assuming you have just moved in."

"Yeah we have. I'm Carly."

"Well nice to meet you, I will leave you to it because I know how hectic moving day is. I just wanted to say hello, and if you need anything please don't hesitate to ask. Have a good one," she says as she disappears inside.

As I'm putting the washing basket and trolley away in the laundry I hear something at the front door. "Hi honey, I'm home," Ben yells out. He has a huge smile on his face as he walks into the kitchen. "I brought lunch because I thought you might be hungry."

"You're a star, I am so hungry."

"I have our clothes in the car could you come and give me a hand?"

I follow him thinking it's a bit strange he asks me to carry something because I am still on crutches. I step outside then Ben stops me.

"I should have done this last night but today is officially our first day in our new home." He leans down and sweeps me into his arms. He

- 143 -

seems to have no trouble picking me up, he must work out a lot because I'm no light weight.

"Ben, what are you doing? Put me down," I laugh.

"I'm carrying you across the threshold." Ben smiles and looks puzzled.

"Honey you only carry me across the threshold if we marry."

"Consider this a trial run," he says with a cheeky smile and wink.

He walks inside and puts me down at the kitchen table, I take a seat and point to where I have put everything, Ben pulls out two plates and hands me my lunch and a can of coke, then he sits next to me and we chat over our lunch.

Ben puts our bed together as I take the sheets and towels down from the line, I place the towels in the bathrooms and then make my way into our bedroom with the bedding. We make our bed and it looks so comfy, I can't wait to get in it tonight.

When everything is set up we go to the shopping centre to buy food. Because we are starting from scratch the bill is huge, but what can you do? As we're leaving I notice a little shop that has wind chimes, we walk over and I find one that I really like, it is made of bamboo and the sound is lovely and soothing, and Ben reluctantly agrees to let me buy it. I hang it under the patio when we get home.

We put the shopping away and decide to order pizza for dinner, I phone in the order while Ben sets up the TV and DVD player. I sit on the lounge watching Ben frown because the TV won't work; he looks so confused, he re-reads the instruction manual and it still won't work. I watch him get frustrated and throw the manual on the floor. I have never seen him like this before, I find it funny and I start to laugh.

"Are you laughing at me?"

"No honey, I wouldn't do that," I reply sarcastically.

"You are going to pay for that," Ben says while he pounces on me. He lays on top of me on the lounge and starts to tickle me.

"No Ben, please don't!" I scream while trying not to laugh.

There's a knock on the door and I thank god for the pizza delivery guy.   "You will get yours later," Ben laughs as he walks to the front door.

As we are eating I look at the TV. "Ben what does that wire do?"

Ben looks up and sees the wire that I am talking about. "Fuck, I can't believe that I didn't see that before." He puts his plate down, connects the wire and the TV comes to life. "Way to go, babe," he says with a smile.

We cuddle on the lounge, attempting to watch a DVD but we get too wrapped up in each other. Ben gets up to lock the front and back door then comes back to me, he holds out his hand and says with a sexy grin "Come on beautiful, let's go and christen our bed." He leads me to our bedroom where he has lit some candles for a romantic glow. He lays me in the middle of the bed, turns on his iPod and sexy music starts to play. I can tell the song isn't recent and I sort of know the tune, so I must have heard it when I was younger.

Ben just stands there at the bottom of the bed, I lean up on my elbows and I'm about to say something when he puts a finger to his lips, "Shhh-hhh." Then he starts to move in time with the music and sing to me. The first couple of lines are a bit corny and I have to stop myself from laughing, but then I listen to what Ben is singing. *"All day, I've been thinking about you babe, you're my one desire."* All of a sudden I realise he is stripping for me. OH MY GOD, this is so fuckin' sexy. *"Oh babe I wanna taste your lips, I wanna be your fantasy, yeah. I don't know what I'd do without you babe, don't know where I'd be, you're not just another lover, no, you're everything to me. Every time I'm with you, babe I can't believe it's true, when you're layin' in my arms and do the things you do."* Ben is stripping so slowly and his eyes never leave mine, the way his body is moving is really turning me on and I can't wait to feel him inside me. *"You can see it in my eyes, I can feel it in your touch, you don't have to say a thing, just let me show how much, I love you, I need you, yeah."* He's down to his boxers. *"I wanna kiss you all over, and over again, I wanna kiss you all over."* His eyes are burning into mine, he is looking at me with a combination of love and lust, moving very slowly towards me. *"So show me, show me everything you do, cause baby no one does it quite like you."* He climbs onto the bed and slowly starts crawling to me. *"I love you, I need you, oh, babe I wanna kiss you all over and over again, I wanna kiss you all over."*

I'm breathing heavily. "That was the hottest thing I have ever seen," I say as I place my hand around his neck and pull him to me. As our lips meet Ben places his body against mine and leans forward so I am flat on my back and his body is pressed against mine. I feel him rub his erection between my legs, it feels so good I moan with pleasure.

Ben kisses his way down my neck and then kneels between my legs "You have too many clothes on, Beautiful."

"I think we need to rectify that," I say breathlessly. Ben holds his hands out for me, I place my hands in his and he pulls me into a sitting position. He lifts my t-shirt off over my head and then leans in to kiss me while he unclasps my bra. He slowly slides the straps off my shoulders and down my arms all the while kissing, sucking and gently biting down my neck towards my chest. He lays me back down and I place his hand over my heart "Can you feel it beating?" I ask Ben.

He nods, never taking his eyes off mine. "It beats for you and only you, you have my heart and my love, always." He leans down and kisses me like his life depends on it and then he makes his way down my body, stopping to suck, lick, kiss and nip at my breasts along the way. It feels so good, I arch towards him and my body shudders with pleasure. He works his way down my stomach and stops at the waistband of my jeans, undoes the button and with his teeth he pulls down the zip, blowing warm air onto my skin. He starts to pull down my jeans and underwear, I lift my bum to help him and I hear them land on the floor. He parts my legs and places his head between my thighs. "Babe you are so fuckin' wet, I'm gunna make you come til you nearly pass out," he says as he places two fingers inside me and slightly curls them in a come here motion, then he flicks my clit with the tip of his tongue.

I grab handfuls of the doona underneath me, moan and arch my body into him. "Ben…I….ohhh…fuck…oh yes just like that…it feels… feels…ama..zing..please don't stop." I place my hands on Ben's head and grab his hair.

Ben pulls his fingers out and parts my pussy so my clit is exposed then he licks and sucks my clit harder and doesn't stop.

"Ben!" I scream as I experience an amazingly powerful orgasm, my whole body convulses and shudders, I can hardly breathe and I think my heart is going to jump out of my chest. Ben doesn't stop, he licks and sucks until I can take no more. He slowly kisses his way up my body, giving me time to recover. "WOW, you definitely made good on your promise, words aren't enough to describe how wonderful that was," I say as I try to catch my breath.

Ben reaches my mouth and kisses me with passion. I can taste myself on his lips. I roll him onto his back and as I try to kneel pain shoots through my knee and I let out a cry.

Ben wraps his arms around me. "Babe, are you ok?"

"I was so caught up in everything I completely forgot that my knee hurt, see what you do to me?" I say with a laugh. "I would like to try something that I saw in a movie once." Ben says ok. "Honey, can you please stand at the bottom of the bed and remove your boxers?" Ben gives me a confused look but he does as I ask. I move down the bed, lie on my back and place my head over the edge. I position Ben so he is level with my head, I raise my arms and drop them behind my head so they rest on the outside of his thighs, I ask Ben to lean forward and to place his hands on my hips, then I take his cock in my hand and move it towards my mouth.

"Carly, what movie did you see this in?"

"A Disney movie, why?" I say with a straight face.

"No way!" Ben yells.

"Ben, it was in a porno," I say laughing. "I have never tried it before, but I heard I could deep throat you in this position and I thought we might try it if you're ok with it?"

"You never cease to amaze me, I can't believe how willing you are to experiment."

"That's because you love me and I know you will never do anything to hurt or degrade me," I say with a smile. "Now lean forward because I want your cock in my mouth. You will have to control the pace but don't go too fast coz I don't want to gag, and gagging isn't very attractive," I laugh.

Ben slowly runs his hand down my cheek as he leans forward so I can take him in my mouth. I feel his body tense as I place my lips around his cock and start to suck. Ben moves in and out of my mouth slowly, I start to feel a bit weird because the blood is rushing to my head but I try to focus on Ben and making him feel wonderful. I relax my throat so he can go deeper, and I reach up and play with his balls. He sucks air through his teeth and throws his head back. "Ahhh, god Carly." He increases the pace, his breathing gets faster and he starts to groan, I can feel his body start to tense and then he pulls out. "That feels so damn good, babe, but if I kept going I would have come in your mouth and I don't want to do that tonight."

He stands, helps me up and guides me back to the middle of the bed so my head is resting on my pillow. He kneels between my open thighs, and as he leans forward to kiss me I say, "Ben I want you inside me." I can feel his hard cock press slowly inside my pussy, I moan with pleasure as he stretches me. He starts to quicken the pace as I run my nails up and down his back; I dig my nails in his bum and bite his shoulder as I feel another orgasm build. I pull my head back and look Ben in the eyes as I come.

"That is the most amazing sight," he says, leaning down to kiss me. I smile and urge him to go faster. I look deep into his eyes as he comes hard and long. Exhausted, he collapses on me and I wrap my arms around him, kissing his face and forehead. We lay like that for a while until we come back down to earth.

Ben leans up, kisses me and then rolls to his side of the bed. He looks at me, smiles and then drags me across the bed into his arms. "That's better," he says as he cuddles me tightly.

"Ben, I love it when you sing to me. Where is that music from? It sounds familiar."

Ben starts to laugh. "It's a seventies song by a group called Exile and it's called *Kiss You All Over.*"

"Where did you hear it?"

"You are going to find this funny, but when I was on duty a few weeks ago we watched the movie Happy Gilmore with Adam Sandler in it, and he sings that song. I thought it would be great to play it for you on our first night in our new home — the strip was a spur of the moment thing," he says with a nervous laugh.

"You my darlin' make me a very happy girl, that strip was so fuckin' hot, you have no idea. Have you done that before?" I asked not really sure if I wanted to know the answer.

"No, as I said it was a spur of the moment kind of thing. This was just for you and no one has ever seen it before you."

I have to admit I'm relieved that was for my eyes only and that I bring it out in him. I feather kisses over his chest as our bodies relax. "Ben, what's duty?"

"Sorry babe I forget you're new to this lifestyle. It's when we have to spend the whole day and night on the base."

"Fair enough, I suppose I will find out more about the Navy as we go along."

"If you have any questions please ask me and I will try to answer them as best I can, but there will be times when I can't say anything. Some things are classified and if I say anything I will get into deep shit."

"I understand," I say with a smile.

"Hey I have a question, when are you twenty one?"

"On my birthday," I say with a smirk.

"Ok smartarse, what date and month were you born?"

"I will be twenty-one on November 30th."

"It's going to be a big year for the Richardson's because Kelsey is eighteen on November 29th."

"Holy shit, that's crazy. I knew I liked her, us Sagittarians are amazing people," I say with a laugh.

"Well I think you're pretty amazing, so I would have to agree with you. It's been a big day and the weekend is going to be hectic, so how about we get some sleep?" Ben asks with a yawn.

"Yeah, that's a good idea because we have to go shopping for Chelsea's present before we head down there tomorrow. Have you any idea what she would like?" I ask.

"I asked Piper and Justin and they came up with a few ideas. They said she would like a Barbie and a Barbie campervan, things she can put in hair and some things called Monster High dolls, there are over fifty characters. I'm thinking the Barbie and campervan because there are too many of those dolls, it could get very expensive for Piper and Justin."

"Every girl should have at least one Barbie in her lifetime," I say with a smile.

"Yeah I agree, we will go shopping in Wollongong. The party doesn't start until 2 pm so we get to have a bit of a lay in."

"That sounds like heaven. Good night honey, I love you."

"Nite Beautiful. Not as much as I love you," Ben says with a contented sigh.

I turn around and Ben pulls my back to his chest. I sleep soundly in our new home, wrapped up in Ben's arms.

20 | BEN

We wake about 9 am and christen the shower in our en-suite. After a late breakfast we make our way to Wollongong. We were about halfway there when Nicole calls Carly's mobile.

"Nicole is everything ok? And why are you up so early on a Saturday?"

"Hey Chica, I have to work today, the office is getting changed around and Management want us there to help. It better not take all day. Now the main reason I am calling, other than to hear your voice... Have you spoken to your Dad lately?"

"No why? Is he ok?"

I ask Carly to put her phone on speaker.

"Nicole I have put you on speaker, Ben and I are driving to his niece's fifth birthday party."

"Hey Benny boy, you better be treating my girl well and giving her lots of explosive orgasms."

"NICOLE!" yells Carly.

"Nic, you don't have to worry about that, I am keeping Carly very satisfied," I say with a laugh. I love that girl.

"Good to hear it otherwise I will make my way over there and kick your arse," she says, laughing.

"Sweetie, what's going on with my dad?"

"Oh yeah, sorry I got off track. Well, he left your mum last weekend and has moved into a unit on the other side of town."

The colour drains from Carly's face. I tighten my grip on her hand and find somewhere to pull over.

"Carly, you there?"

"Yeah she's listening, Nic, just hang on a sec." I say as I hold my hand over the phone. "Babe, say something please," I plead with Carly.

"I always th..thought this would happen but n..now it's a reality I don't know what to s..say, I need to talk to him."

I remove my hand from the phone. "Hey Nic, can Carly call you later, she wants to call her Dad."

"Yeah no problem. Carly, I promise you I will keep an eye on him. Luv ya girl."

"Love you too," Carly says as I hang up the phone. "I have to c… call my dad." It goes to voicemail so she leaves him a message to call her as soon as possible. We sit there in silence as I rub my thumb over her hand and give Carly time with her thoughts.

"We need to get going, there's nothing I can do and sitting here is a waste of time. I just have to wait for him to contact me." She gives me a slight smile and I kiss the back of her hand just before we pull back onto the road.

We reach Wollongong around lunch time, then we buy Chelsea's Barbie and Barbie's campervan, wrapping paper, sticky tape and a card. We go to a café for lunch and as we are waiting for our order Carly wraps the presents and I write in the card. "I can't believe she is five," I say. "I remember when she was born; I was lucky enough to meet her on her first day in this world. It was my final year in high school and I was so excited about becoming an uncle. I went up to the hospital later that night and luckily for me everyone had gone home so it was just Piper, Chelsea and me. It was such a special moment. I got to hold her and talk to her without anyone else butting in. She had her tiny hand wrapped around my finger. She opened her eyes and looked right into my soul and I have been putty in her hands ever since," I laugh.

"You are so good with her, it's beautiful to watch. How do you think she is going to go with the new baby?"

"I think if she is included in a lot of things with the baby and also has alone time with everyone she will be ok. It just has to be handled properly, that's all. She's an intelligent girl."

"Yeah, but you can be a genius and still do and say crazy things because of jealousy. I just hope everyone understands she is only five and gives her room to express how she is feeling."

Just then our lunch arrives. I take my first bite, look up and notice a strange look on Carly's face. I turn to see what she's looking at. Seriously WTF. "Whitney, nice to see you," Carly says.

"What can we do for you Whit?" I ask angrily.

"I just wanted to talk to you in private."

"Not gunna happen, anything you want to say to me you can say in front of Carly."

"Ok, well I would prefer some privacy but you want it this way," Whitney says as she sits next to me, "I'm pregnant."

"Umm…congratulations," I say with a shrug.

"Well it's congratulations to you too, considering you're the father."

Thank god I'm sitting down because I think she could have knocked me over with a feather. I'm in total shock. This girl is mentally unstable.

"How could you?" Whitney continued. "You said you loved me and you sleep with someone else.

"Carly, I thought it was best to tell you so you can pack up and go back to where you came from. I'm carrying his child and you will never know how that feels," Whitney says, looking very pleased with herself.

I feel like I'm in the twilight zone. "Carly, it's not true, you have to believe me."

"I have to know, when did this happen? How many times?" Carly asks Whitney.

"You shouldn't torture yourself," says Whitney in a condescending voice.

"It's the only way I am going to come to terms with this. Please tell me, Whitney, I need to know."

"Ok if it'll help."

"It will, thank you Whitney."

I can feel my future slipping away from me, this can't be happening. I have never touched Whitney before or since Carly.

"Ben and I hooked up a few times in the last week of May, I won't give you the details but obviously we didn't use protection and I am six weeks pregnant."

"Are you sure it was May?" asks Carly.

"One hundred percent because it was on the night of my parents' 30th wedding anniversary. Ben came out to dinner with my family and then we got a room in a hotel for the night. It was amazing, and yes, you are right, he is a very attentive lover," Whitney says with a smirk.

Carly bursts out laughing. She places her hand in mine. "Babe, I need to be careful around you because it looks like you have super sperm. You got a girl pregnant from another State."

"Wh…what are you talking about," Whitney stammers as the colour drains from her face.

"What she means, you evil bitch is that I was in WA the last week of May!" I yell at her. "Carly and I were picking out furniture for our new home here in Sydney."

"It must have been the first week in June, it's the baby brain, I'm so forgetful at the moment," she says with a nervous smile.

"Still in WA. You need to find the real father of this baby, that's if there is one. Now get the fuck out of here before I forget that I have been brought up properly and I don't lay my hands on females out of anger."

Whitney struggles to her feet, grabs her bag off the table and storms away from us in a flood of tears. I let out the breath I was holding, shake my head and sink back into my chair. I open and shut my mouth a few times but words evade me. "Honey are you ok? I tilt my head, shrug my shoulders and look at Carly. "Yeah, I know, stupid question. What a mind fuck. I'm being deadly serious when I say that there is something seriously wrong with that girl. Who does that?"

"I don't know. Are you ready to go? I have lost my appetite."

I drove to Piper's on auto pilot, hardly registering that I had pulled into the driveway. That bitch could have cost me my relationship. I feel Carly's hand on my arm. "Carly, I am so fucking angry I'm scared that if I start to talk I will hit someone. She could have split us up over a lie. Thank god you knew she wasn't telling the truth."

"Honey I know and love you and I know you would never cheat on me. If you can't talk to me please let me get either your dad or one of your brothers. I'm not angry but you really need to get this out."

"Can you get Darcy and Damon for me, please?"

She leans over to turn the car off and kiss me on the lips. "I'll go get them."

I watch Carly walk to the front door and wait for someone to let her in.   She's inside for a few minutes when Darcy and Damon walk outside. I get out of the car and lean against the bonnet as they walk towards me.

"What you doing out here mate?" asks Damon.

"Carly said that Whit said something to upset you," says Darcy.

I take a moment to calm down before I say anything. I look up. "That fuckin' cunt told Carly that I got her pregnant," I growl through my teeth.

"Fuck me, what a bunny boiler," Damon says as he shakes his head.

"Understandably, you're pissed at Whit, but how's Carly?" asks Darcy.

"Darc I'm really worried about her. She seems to be ok, but it had to have affected her in some way. Though at the moment she is more concerned about me so she's putting on a brave face."

"At the moment you're my main concern. You wanna tell me how you're feeling?" asks Damon.

"Damon I want to strangle the bitch, how dare she do that to me, to us? Why would she do that? She's knows I've never touched her and never will. I don't understand. It makes no sense."

"Mate you never will understand. She obviously has a screw loose and she chose you as her target. Luckily for you and Carly there was no possible way that it could have been true, so there was no way Carly could have doubted you. My suggestion is to put it behind you and come inside to enjoy Chelsea's birthday party. She's been asking after you," says Darcy.

"Would you mind asking Carly to come out?"

"No worries. We'll see you inside," says Damon as he pats my shoulder.

I watch the boys go inside and I make fists while I wait for Carly. The door opens and I see her walk towards me. I can see hesitation in her eyes as she slowly approaches me. I hold out my hand for her and as she takes it as I guide her to stand between my legs.

Carly places her arms around my neck as I place mine around her waist. "How are you?" Carly asks quietly.

"Better now I have you in my arms," I smile. "You do know that the allegations are not true."

"Of course I do. For me there was never any doubt. My main concern is you. Honestly, how do you feel?"

"I'm sorry I shut you out, I was so fucking angry with that bitch, all I kept thinking was you were going to believe her and leave me, even when I knew you didn't believe her and you were trying to get her to trip herself up; a part of me still thought I had lost you and that scared the life out of me. Carly, I love you so much sometimes it's overwhelming. I can't imagine my life without you," I say as I pull her tighter into my body.

"As soon as she said the baby was yours I knew she was lying.

The time of the year she said she got pregnant was irrelevant. As I said before, I know you would never cheat on me, I trust you more than I have ever trusted anyone, I wouldn't have moved in with you if I didn't. Please let's not let this ruin today, everyone's here to celebrate your gorgeous niece's fifth birthday. Besides, we have a fairy castle cake to enjoy. I love and trust you Ben," Carly says as she leans in to kiss me.

"I love you too, Beautiful."

We walk in holding hands and as we reach the games room Mum comes over. "Is everything ok?" she asks with a concerned look.

"Yeah Mum everything with us is good, that bitch could have ruined my relationship with her lies and I will never forgive her for that, she needs help."

"There is definitely something not right with her. I just hope she has realised she has gone too far this time and seeks help," Mum says with a sigh.

Just then Piper calls us over because Chelsea is going to blow out the candles. Chelsea has five little friends from school and the rest are family. I look at everyone and I realise I am so lucky to be a part of this family, there is so much love in this room and Carly is a very welcome addition.

We have a good time at the party. Justin's parents Craig and Donna and his two sisters Melissa and Laura are there. Both sisters are older than Justin, and neither is married or has children. Piper's and Justin's families get on well together and the party is a huge success. After Chelsea has cut her cake, opened her presents and her friends have left, she climbs onto Carly's knee and snuggles in, and before too long is fast asleep. I look at them and smile. "She loves you," I whisper.

Carly smiles back "The feeling is very mutual. How could you not love her?"

After a while Chelsea stirs and calls out for Justin, he comes over and lifts her off Carly's lap. She looks at him and says, "I love you Daddy" and snuggles into his chest. I see and hear Carly sigh, I know she misses her Dad.

When we arrive back at Mum and Dad's I turn off the ignition and take Carly's hand and rest it on my thigh. "Babe, I need to tell you about Whitney. As you know, we went to school together. We weren't great friends but we got along ok, though all that all changed when she started to develop a crush on me. I never encouraged it but that didn't stop her.

She would turn up at parties that I went to, and when I went to movies with my mates she would be there. Love letters would come to my home and she would call my mobile and not say anything. It was crazy, I had to speak to her and try to get her to stop. I tried to do it as gently as I could but it made no difference. It got worse when I had a girlfriend, she really stepped things up and tried everything in her power to split us up. Sometimes she would succeed and other times she wouldn't. When I joined the Navy she would tell anyone that would listen that she was my girlfriend and that she was waiting for me to finish Recruit School and would move in with me when I got posted. Totally delusional. Every time I come to Wollongong I try not to go places where she may turn up. I'm sorry I kept this from you, I should have told you the full story."

"Ben we all have a past and there are things that aren't easy or that are uncomfortable to explain, its ok. My concern is you. Are you ok?"

"Yeah, I'm better now that I have explained everything. I'm sorry I didn't tell you earlier and that I spoke to Darcy and Damon first."

"I'm just happy you spoke to someone and were able to work through it," Carly says as she leans over to kiss me. Just as we are getting out of the car Andrew calls. Carly puts it on speaker so I can hear.

"Dad, where have you been?"

"Hey Ratbag, I have been busy. Listen, there is something I need to tell you. I have left your Mother. I moved out last weekend. I just couldn't take things anymore. I don't want to bore you with the details but I couldn't stay there anymore."

"Are you ok? Do you want me to come home?"

"I'm getting there, and no, I don't want you to come home. Your life is with Ben and you are safe there. I have moved into a two bedroom unit and when you and Ben come back for the trial I would like you to stay with me. That reminds me, have you heard when it's going to trial?"

"No, but I'm expecting to hear soon. When I find out I will call you. I love you and miss you Dad."

"Right back at ya, Ratbag. Take care and I'll talk to you soon."

Carly hangs up and takes a deep breath. I give her moment to collect her thoughts then we go inside. What a day.

CARLY | 21

The next day we leave mid-morning and head about thirty minutes south from Wollongong to Albion Park to look at the Rotty pup. The puppy is cute, as most puppies are but I wasn't feeling anything special for him. We thanked them for their time and headed to Nowra forty minutes south.

This time we are able to see the parents of the puppy. The female is tall with longer hair and a thinish head while the male is shorter with short hair, a stocky build and a big head; he is beautiful. The breeder brings out the male pup and I fall in love; he has the build of his father, with a big head and huge feet that he will grow into. She places the pup on the floor and I sit behind him and click my fingers to check his hearing, the puppy spins around straight away and runs over to me, I'm in love. I look at Ben, nod and smile. Ben laughs and pays a deposit for our new puppy Roger. He is only four weeks old so we can't take him yet. We have to wait until he is eight weeks old. We take a few photos and head for home. I am so excited, I can't wait to bring Roger home.

The rest of the week is pretty quiet. I am finally off my crutches but I am still not walking properly, that will take some time. I have re-arranged the lounge room and placed a few pot plants around the patio; it's starting to look like home.

On the weekend we decide to go sightseeing around Sydney. It's a clear but cold day so we decide to go to Taronga Zoo which has been open for nearly one hundred years and is on the top of a hill overlooking Sydney Harbour. We realise that we don't have many photos together so we decide to rectify that this weekend.

Our next stop is Darling Harbour, and we catch a water taxi to Luna Park. We ride the ferris wheel and take a few selfies with the Sydney Harbour Bridge in the background, then we go on the dodgem cars, down Devil's Drop — that's where you sit on a mat and you go down this huge slide — through the mirror maze, along the Wonky Walk — where you walk like you're drunk — and on the Wild Mouse roller coaster. We have such a good time, I feel like I have no worries in the world.

On Sunday morning we go to The Rocks, have breakfast and look around the markets. We buy some photos of Sydney in the early nineteen hundreds and some of Perth in the nineteen fifties, plus some homemade chilli and jam. You can see the Harbour Bridge real close from The Rocks so we get some good photos taken. When we finish we take our things back to the car and then take a walk to Circular Quay where the ferries depart. We hop on one that is going to Manly. I'm excited because I have never been on a ferry before. The water is choppy and the ferry rolls around a lot, and I have to really concentrate on the shore because I feel sea sick; of course Ben has no such trouble.

When we get off the ferry in Manly we go to the Manly sea life sanctuary. It's so cool, I love animals. I notice that you can dive with the sharks, and I take note because that would be a great Christmas present for Ben.

We have a late lunch and sit in the mall watching the world go by. I reach across for Ben's hand. "Thank you for this weekend, I have had the best time," I say with a huge smile.

"You are very welcome, Beautiful. I agree this weekend is just what we needed, it's a shame it has to end," Ben says with a sigh.

"Our weekends are going to be busy once the puppy comes to live with us. We won't spend all our time with him but in the beginning we'll have to toilet train him and get him to sit on command and all that stuff. I can't wait.

"I miss not having a dog, we had one when I was little and she was gorgeous but when she died my mum said there and then we would never get another dog because it was too hard losing her, so that was that," I say sadly.

"I guess the only question is what rugby team will Roger support? The Dragons or The Storm," Ben says laughing.

"Ben, that is a very silly question, of course it'll be the Storm."

"You keep thinking that, babe." Ben winks at me.

After lunch we catch the ferry back to Circular Quay. It wasn't a good idea to have lunch beforehand, it's a miracle I don't throw it up. I can't wait to get onto dry land, I don't think I will be joining the Navy any time soon.

When we get home we put the photos we bought on the wall. It's looking more and more like a home, and this makes me happy. We go to bed very early that night, partly because we are exhausted and partly because I want Ben's body and I want to take my time exploring it.

Monday morning Ben kisses me before leaving for work. I get the laptop out and start looking for work. The house is all organised and I have to admit I am bored, there is only so much housework I can do. I open up a few job websites and apply for five beautician jobs. Next I decide to look up things to cook for dinner. I find something that looks easy and only has a few ingredients, so hopefully it'll be edible.

I walk to the shopping centre which is only ten minutes by foot to get the ingredients. As I'm coming out of the supermarket I bump into Amber, my new neighbour. She asks if I have time for a drink to get to know each other. I have come a hell of a long way but there is no way am I opening up to someone I just met. I reluctantly accept the offer and we make our way to a café. Amber orders some kind of fancy coffee and I order a pot of tea. I don't drink coffee, I have never tasted it, I just can't stand the smell. I have tried to drink it but every time I get my lips near the smell just takes over and it makes my stomach roll.

The conversation is a bit awkward, I am not happy to offer too much information and I don't want to ask many questions because that will give Amber the impression she can ask me questions and I'm pretty sure I won't want to answer most of them. I find myself feeling very uncomfortable.

We talk about generic stuff, and about our partners. Amber's husband is called Matt and he is in the Navy; she is 25 and Matt is 28, she's from Darwin and he's from Melbourne, , they met three years ago when his ship pulled into Darwin, and they have been married for one year. They have lived in the house next door for about six months. Amber works in administration but is on leave at the moment. That's about all the information I can handle, so I finish my tea and go to stand up. Just then my mobile rings; it's a Perth number. I excuse myself and walk out of the café to answer the call.

"Hello is that Carly Nelson?"

"Yes, who is this please?"

"Miss Nelson, my name is Michael Dawson, I am a representative from the Perth Courthouse and this is a courtesy call to inform you of the court date for your case against Mr George Nelson. The date is Monday the fourth of November. You will be sent confirmation in the mail. If you are unable to attend on this date you are to contact the Perth Courthouse and another date will be set."

"Thank you for the call Mr Dawson," I say as I hang up the phone. I just sit there for a while staring at my phone. I have been expecting a date to be set, but now that it's here I'm not so sure I want to go through with it. My heart starts racing and I'm feeling dizzy. I try to calm my breathing and I picture Ben talking me through this. I sit on the bench with my elbows resting on my knees and my head in my hands trying to calm down.

I hear my name being called. "Carly, are you ok?" Amber asks as she sits next to me.

"I will be, please just give me a minute," I mutter. Amber sits next to me in total silence, keeping a respectable distance but close enough to catch me if I fall. I'm not sure how long we sit there for but once I feel better I lift my head and look around. "Thank you" is all I can say.

"Don't mention it. Hey I'm heading home now, would you like a lift?"

"That would be good, thanks." I smile at her.

When I get home I put the food in the fridge and call Ben to let him know what had happened. My call goes to voicemail and then I remember he has fire training all day. It can wait til he gets home. I decide to lay down on the lounge for a while because the panic attacks take a lot out of me. It doesn't take long for me to fall asleep.

I wake with a start when I feel lips on my lips. I open my eyes and Ben is kneeling down at my side. "What time is it?"

"It's 4.45pm, are you ok? I got a missed call from you but I was at training all day. I tried to call you when I finished but my call went to voicemail. How long have you been asleep for?"

"About five hours." I say. I explain to Ben about meeting up with Amber, the phone call and the panic attack. Ben gets me to sit up and then he sits where my head was and gets me to lay down again. He runs his fingers through my hair as we talk about the day's events. I explain that I am really scared about going to court and I am thinking of withdrawing the charges.

Ben tenses up underneath me. "Carly, please don't make a decision now, you have time to think it through and hopefully get used to the idea. You know I want him put away for what he did to you, but I will back your decision no matter what, and I have already told you I will fly to Perth with you so you're not alone. When is the date?"

"It's November the fourth, it's a Monday. Do you think you will be able to get leave?" I ask worriedly.

"That won't be a problem, I promise."

"Ok, well I have a lot to think about. Do you mind if we don't talk about this anymore?"

"Of course not, babe, whatever you want," Ben says as he leans down to kiss me. "I can see you have been shopping, what did you get?"

"I bought the ingredients to make shepherd's pie, it looks fairly easy so I thought I would try to cook that tonight, what's the worst that can happen?" I ask with a half-hearted smile.

The shepherd's pie turns out ok, I didn't burn it and I didn't kill Ben: good result. As we are showering I tell him that I have applied for a few jobs and how good Amber was with me when I had the panic attack, and Ben tells me about his fire training.

Ben snuggles into my back and I fall asleep as soon as my head hits the pillow. I wake with a start when I feel hands around my throat and a knee on my chest, I grab at the hands but he is too strong, I'm finding it hard to breath. I slap at his face but because it's dark I can't see him, I try to scream but I only manage a squeak. "I'm going to fuckin' kill you, you fat, ugly, pig," whispers George. With the last little bit of strength I have I dig my nails into his arms. If he kills me at least I'll have his DNA under my nails.

"Carly, Carly, babe, please wake up." I hear Ben's voice.

I jolt up to a sitting position and I see the room is lit up, Ben is next to me with blood on his arms. I look around the room expecting to see George, my heart is thumping so hard, I'm shaking and wet through. "Wha..What happened?"

"Babe you had a nightmare, I tried to wake you but you wouldn't wake up. Are you ok?"

"W..What happened to your ar..arms?"

"It's not important, when you have settled down I'll get you in the shower."

"I..I did that to you didn't I? B..Ben I am so sorry," I cry. "I th.. thought you were George, h..he was st..strangling me, I tried t..to get him off me b..b..but he was too strong, I sc..scratched him so I had his DNA un..under my nails for when the p..police found my b..body." I start to sob.

"Ssshhhhhhhh," Ben says as he climbs in behind me and rocks me until I calm down. He walks me to the shower, sets the temperature, washes me and takes good care of me. While I am drying myself he changes the sheets because they are wet with my sweat from the nightmare. He returns to the bathroom and I look at his arms, he has multiple scratches on both arms, so I get out the antiseptic and bathe his wounds. I can't believe I did this to him, my heart sinks.

I sit on the edge of the bath with my head in my hands, rocking back and forth. I've hurt the guy I love, I'm no better than George, I say over and over in my head.

Ben crouches down, removes my hands from my face and kisses away my tears. "Please don't cry, Beautiful, it wasn't your fault, you had a nightmare."

"But I..I hurt you, l..look at your arms, they're a m..mess," I cry.

Ben picks me up and carries me to our bed, lays me down, wraps his arms around me and just holds me until I calm down. I sit up, take his hands in mine and I kiss the scratches softly and slowly, making sure I kiss every inch of every scratch, as I do that as I mutter I am sorry in between each kiss.

Ben places his hand on my face and pulls my lips to his. "Let me make love to you, Beautiful." He lays me down and we make love softly and slowly, looking deep into each other's souls.

Neither of us sleep well for the rest of the night, I'm surprised Ben is able to get up for work. He kisses me before he leaves and I sleep in until mid-morning. I'm exhausted mentally and physically. Ben calls me at lunch time to see how I am, we chat for a while and then he has to go back to work.

The rest of the week is blissfully uneventful and we settle into our life together. It's a learning curve living with your partner, there are some things that annoy you and you try to let it go but really, how many times do I have to tell him to put the toilet seat down? I have nearly fallen in twice when I wasn't paying attention...

On the weekend we go food shopping and also buy things for our new puppy. We go a little overboard but he's our baby, what can you do! We get him a bowl, collar and lead, chew toys, doggie treats, two dog beds — one for the lounge and one for the bedroom, because he has to have options — a water bowl for inside and a water dispenser that looks like a water cooler for the outside. I can't wait to bring him home.

The following week I get three calls for interviews, all of the salons are between ten and thirty minutes away from home, I'm very hopeful. After the interviews two salons call me in for a trial. I have to say I'm nervous, not in my ability, because I know I am a good beautician, but what if they don't like me? I'm not easy to like.

Luckily the trials are on different days because sometimes they can last one hour or several hours. The first salon has been open for about two years so it has regular clientele and is very busy. The manager has arranged for a few regular clients to come in for me to wax them, give a facial and do a few piercings. I was there about two hours and the Manager only corrected my technique twice. I think it went well the staff seemed nice even though we didn't talk much because it was that busy.

The next day I have my trial at the other salon, it's smaller and not as busy. I do treatments on the Manager and she doesn't give me much feedback, but the staff are ok. It doesn't have the same feel as yesterday's salon but beggars can't be choosers. Hopefully one of the the jobs comes through.

On Friday night we decide to go out to the local pub for a meal and a few drinks. The restaurant is on one side the bar and the stage and dance floor are on the other. Exposed beams, lead lighting panels, and dark wood give the place a nice atmosphere.

After our meal we make our way into the bar and discover there is a band playing tonight, and I get excited because I love live music. We are stood at the bar when I feel a tap on my shoulder. I turn around to see Amber standing there. I am a little embarrassed because I haven't seen her since the panic attack and I really don't want her to bring it up. Amber introduces us to her husband Matt and the four of us chat while we are waiting for the band to start.

Ben and Matt seem to get on well and talk Navy which goes over my head, so Amber and I chat away getting to know one another, I find she has a very sarcastic sense of humour and I feed off that. We banter back and forth and laugh our arses off at stupid things. A few times the guys stopped talking to look at us with curious expressions on their faces.

It turns out the band is a cover band and they play anything from Kings of Leon to Foo Fighters, they are awesome. Luckily for me Amber loves to dance so it doesn't take long for us to hit the floor. She dances like Nicole and I, like no one is watching, and it's so much fun. After a while the guys tear themselves away from their beers and come and dance with us. I love it when Ben dances with me, I feel alive because he sees is me and no one else. We drink and dance the night away. We're enjoying ourselves and we all decide to go to the night club, but not before Ben and Matt inform us that they are hungry. Really, what is it with guys when they have been drinking they always want a feed? I never have any room.

We walk to a burger place, it's pretty busy. Amber and I sit down at a table while the guys line up to place their order. Just as the guys get to the counter a fight breaks out on the table next to us between a group of kids in their mid-teens. Amber and I get up and walk our way to the counter while we wait for them to get thrown out.

Once the guys have devoured their burgers we make our way to the night club. We have to walk up a steep flight of stairs to get into the club, which isn't easy when you have been drinking and wearing heels. It has two levels. The bottom level has a bar that runs against the full length of the wall, and in front of the bar is a bit of carpet then a large dance floor, and on the back wall facing the dance floor is the DJ booth. The top level has chairs and tables and a balcony so you can see down to the bottom level, it also has a bar on the back wall. It's such a cool place.

The place is packed and Ben sees a few guys he knows from the base. He introduces me to them but I'm so pissed I can hardly remember my own name let alone theirs. As Ben is talking to his friends I go to dance. I have no one to dance with because we have been separated from Amber and Matt, so I dance alone, which doesn't bother me. I used to dance alone back home when Nicole had picked up a guy.

The DJ plays great songs so I dance for quite some time on my own. I get tired so I head back upstairs to get a drink and to see Ben. I get a cider for myself and a beer for Ben and then make my way through the crowd to where Ben and his mates are. I get bumped and a little bit of his beer spills over my clothes, fuck I hate the smell of beer. As I get through the crowd I see Ben and a girl standing very close to each other, whispering in each other's ears and leaning against the railing on the balcony. I stand there for a while just
watching them. The girl laughs at something, she flicks her hair and runs her hand up and down Ben's arm, she is flirting with him and he does nothing to stop her. She keeps her hand on him and he doesn't remove it.

"Are you fucking kidding me?" I mutter. I walk over to where they are, slam his beer on the table and storm off. I just have to get out of here. I hear Ben calling after me but I ignore him and duck into the ladies' toilet, I stay in there for a while. I go into one of the stalls, put the lid down, sit there and try to calm myself down. I can't believe that he allowed her to touch him like that, it wasn't just a simple touch it was more intimate. I can't believe this is happening, he tells and show's me he loves me but he allows another girl to touch him that way.

To some people it might not be such a big deal but to me it's huge, it took a lot for me to let Ben in. I would never touch or let another guy touch me that way. I have to get out of here, I decide I'm going to stay in a hotel for the night and then get a flight out tomorrow. I can't stay here anymore. I should never have trusted him, how stupid am I? Guys are all the same, they pull you in, convince you that they love you and then screw you over. I'm such a fuckin' idiot.

I stand up, dry my eyes and walk to the sink to wash my face. I take a few deep breaths and walk out into the night club. I start to make my way to the exit when I feel a hand on my shoulder, I swing around with my fist clenched and I see its Ben. "Fuck off!" I yell at him and continue to walk out of the club.

"Carly stop, what's wrong?"

"Go back to the slapper who had her hands on you. We're through."

"Carly, slow down, talk to me."

"Go fuck yourself Ben!" I yell over my shoulder as I walk down the stairs.

Ben races down the stairs, grabs my right elbow and spins me around to face him. "Talk to me Carly, what the fuck is going on?"

"She had her hands on you and you allowed it, I would never touch or let a guy touch me that way, I would never let a guy get that close to me. We are over, through, done. I will not allow you to use me!" I scream at him as I wrench my arm out of his grasp and storm off.

I take my shoes off and run towards the taxi rank, thank god there is a taxi waiting, I get in and tell the driver to go before Ben can catch up. We drive off before he can reach us. Ben calls me on my mobile but I ignore it and put the phone on silent. The driver asks where I want to go and I say I need a hotel room for the night. We drive around for a while and he drops me off at a decent hotel, I pay him the fare and thank him. I walk inside, book a room and then go upstairs. As I open the door I look at my phone and there are ten missed calls and voicemails, all from Ben.

I call Nicole.

"Hey Chica, how you goin?"

"Nicole." That's all I can say before I burst into tears.

"Awww Carly what's happened?"

I tell her about what that girl did and that Ben didn't stop her, and that I left him at the club and I'm now at a hotel.

"Carly, I know you're upset but did you see Ben kiss her, hug her, put his arm around her or touch her in an intimate way?"

"No, but that's not to say it hadn't already happened while I was dancing," I sobbed.

"What did he say about it?"

"I didn't give him a chance to lie to me, I ran off and booked a room for the night."

"Does he know where you are?"

"No, I won't answer his calls, I don't want to speak to him or see him again and I'm going to try to get a flight home tomorrow."

"Carly, you are home. You live with Ben now and that's your home. You need to talk to him and sort this out. I can tell you have been drinking and might not be thinking straight, please talk to him."

I started to cry again. "Don't you want to see me?"

"Carly don't, please. You know I miss you but I want to see you happy and that's with Ben, please give him the chance to explain, you owe him and yourself that."

We talk for another half an hour and I reluctantly agree to talk to Ben. We say good bye and I promise I will call her in the morning.

As I hang up I look at my phone and see that I have twenty seven voicemails from Ben and one from my dad. Fuck, why did he have to call my dad?

I call my dad. "Carly, thank god. Are you ok?"

"No Dad, I'm not," I cry. I explain what happened tonight and my dad listened to everything I had to say without interrupting.

"Ratbag, Ben called me, he's beside himself. Have you spoken to him? Does he know where you are?"

"No and no, Dad, I have nothing to say to him, he allowed her to touch him in a way that is disrespectful to me and he looked like he was enjoying it. I won't stay around for that. I'm in a hotel for the night and then I'm going to try to get a flight back home tomorrow. When I have the information can you please pick me up at the airport?"

"Please don't make any rash decisions. Talk to Ben first and then if you still want to come back I will be there to pick you up."

"Dad, I don't think I can," I whisper. All the fight has left me, I'm exhausted and I just want to go to sleep. I tell my dad that I love him and that I will call him tomorrow.

I lay back on my bed as tears roll out of my eyes. I don't know how long I been lying there for when I hear a knock on my door. I close my eyes because I know Ben has found me. I'm not sure how he did it but I ignore him.

"Carly, I know you are in there, please open the door," Ben pleads. He starts to bang on the door a bit louder. It's in the early hours of the morning and if he doesn't shut up he will wake the other guests.

Reluctantly I open the door. "What do you want Ben?"

"Thank god, babe. What's going on? Why did you run like that?" he asks as he walks past me into my room.

"You must really think I'm stupid. That bitch had her hands on you, you were snuggled in against the balcony whispering to each other, smiling away and you want to know what's going on? How would you react if you saw a guy do that to me?"

"Babe, nothing is going on with me and Hayley, we were at Recruit School together and we work together, that's all."

"You're full of shit. You can go now. We're over and I'm going home tomorrow. I never want to see you again," I say as I walk to the door for Ben to follow me. I turn around and he is standing by the bed. "Ben, you need to leave, now," I cry.

"Carly, I don't know what you think you saw but nothing is going on with me and Hayley."

"BULLSHIT!" I yell, cutting him off. "She had her hands on you. How would you feel if a guy had his hands on me and we were laughing snuggled up against the balcony whispering in each other's ears? You would go ballistic."

"If you would let me finish, I was about to tell you that there is nothing going on between Hayley and myself." I go to interrupt again but Ben holds his hand up. "Would you let me finish? Carly I want and love you, no one else. Hayley and I met at Recruit School, we instantly hit it off as mates and there is nothing other than friendship. Besides, she's a lesbian." Ben said.

"You're going to play that card? You only want to make yourself look innocent and you think that lying to me by saying she is a lesbian will make this better," I say angrily. "B..Ben we are o..ov..over, just go please," I stutter and collapse to the ground sobbing. Ben rushes over and puts his arms around me. I pull away from him and he sits next to me on the floor, playing with his phone.

"Texting her t..to let her k..kn..know you're on your wa..way?"

"NO," he says angrily. "I want to show you something."

"Ben please, I can't h..ha..handle seeing photos of y..you..you two together," I say, completely defeated.

Ben holds his phone up in front of me. "Carly, please look at the screen."

I shake my head and whisper "Don't." My heart can't handle anymore.

Ben places his phone in my hand. "Please Carly, just look at the screen." I open my eyes and I see it's Hayley's Facebook page. I go to hand him back his phone.

"Look at the relationship status."

It says that she is in a relationship, I look at Ben with a 'so what' expression. People cheat.

"Carly, look at the name of the person she is in a relationship with." I look back at the phone and it says Hayley Webb is in a relation-ship with Sophie White. I read it twice and then look up at Ben. He's nodding. "Yes, that's right, she IS a lesbian," he says smugly.

"That doesn't mean anything, she might be bi-sexual and she and her partner are after a threesome with you. Isn't that every guy's wet dream?" I say angrily.

"Not mine."

"You really must think I'm a complete idiot!" I yell at him.

"Carly you are all I want, all I need. I love you like I have never loved anyone. Have I ever given you reason to think that I am cheating on you? Carly I can't keep my fuckin' hands off you. You are so damn sexy, I can't wait to get home to you every day, I miss you when I am at work, you're all I think about, I want to grow old with you, you make me so happy, why would I look elsewhere?" Ben pleads.

I sit on the floor rocking back and forth, mumbling to myself. I don't know what to think, I don't know what to believe, I'm so fucking confused. "How di..did you find me?"

"What?"

"It's not a hard question," I say raising my voice. "How did you find me?"

"When you got in the taxi I thought you were going home. so I grabbed a taxi and followed you there. But I found the place empty, I called you. When you wouldn't answer, I called your Dad and he hadn't heard from you, so I phoned the 24hr emergency line for the credit card. Because our cards are connected you are authorised to get information about my card and vice versa. They told me you had booked a room and I came to talk to you."

I get up off the floor and make my way over to the bed, I'm exhausted and I can't handle this anymore. I look at the clock and it's 3.51am. I need some sleep, I lay down on the edge of the bed and close my eyes hoping for sleep to end this nightmare. After a few minutes I feel the bed dip on the other side as Ben lays down, he faces towards the middle of the bed and gently runs his hand up and down my back. "Don't fuckin' touch me," I spit out. Ben doesn't say anything, he sighs and rolls away from me. I silently cry myself to sleep.

I wake about 8 am with Ben wrapped around me, I slide out from underneath him and make my way to the bathroom. I make sure I take my phone with me. I send Nicole and Dad a text to let them know that I'm alive and that I will contact them later with my flight details. I open the bathroom door as quietly as I can, grab my shoes and bag and make my way to the door.

"Where are you going?"

"I told you, we're over, I'm going home."

Ben bounces off the bed and rushes to shut the door before I can get out. "Babe, you can't leave, we need to talk this out."

"We talked last night, I said all I had to say, there's nothing more to talk about," I say coldly.

"Like fuck there isn't. Carly, I love you. Please believe me when I say Hayley and I are just mates, I have never looked at her that way and I will never look at her that way." Ben holds my face in his hands and tilts my head up so he is looking in my eyes. "I love you and only you Carly Nelson, you are my life, I was just existing before you came along but now that I have you in my life I am living. I love the life we have, I look forward to waking up with you in my arms, making love to you, laughing with you and experiencing new things with you. Carly, please don't leave me, I'm begging you," Ben says as his body slides down the door. He sits on the floor with his head in his hands, crying.

I stand there completely confused for a minute or two. I don't know what to do. I look down at Ben and my heart breaks. Fuck, fuck, fuck, fuck, fuck I say in my head, what am I supposed to do? I sit down on the floor between his legs and tilt his chin up with my index finger and look into his eyes. "I'm not going anywhere," I say.

It takes a while for Ben to register what I said. He places his hands in mine and gently rubs his thumbs over my skin. He slowly moves towards me and places a soft kiss on my lips, he holds my head in his hands and deepens the kiss, I respond by grabbing a handful of his shirt and pulling him towards me. As the kiss deepens his body covers mine and he lays me back so I am lying on the floor. Ben kisses me with such passion and our breathing gets faster. He starts to pull at my clothes and removes them one by one.

He carries me to the bed, places me on the edge of it and kneels between my thighs. He kisses me and then kisses down my body and stops just as he reaches my waist and pulls down my underwear. He looks up, lifts both legs so I fall backwards and places my ankles over his shoulders. He lifts his head and looks at me and growls, "I am going to show you over and over how much I love you and I will keep showing you until you believe me." He parts my thighs and begins to lick and suck my pussy, there is nothing gentle about it, his purpose is to make me come as quickly and as hard as he can.

After my second orgasm I have to pull him away from me. "Ben, please, I can't take anymore, it's too much. I want you inside me," I pant.

"Not yet, I want to give you one more, babe."

I sit up, grab his hands and move him so he is sitting next to me. "Ben this is not necessary, just be normal with me."

"Carly, I nearly lost you, I don't know what to do," Ben whispers.

"Make love to me, that's all you need to do," I say as I straddle him, kissing and removing his shirt. I lean back on his legs so I can undo his jeans, I stand up and get him to do the same, then I remove his jeans and boxers, sit him back down and straddle him again. I take his cock in my hand, holding it as I place myself over him and slowly lower myself.

"Babe, I love you so much," Ben says as he thrusts up into me while kissing my face. Ben comes, moaning my name. He wraps his arms around me and won't let me go.

I need to use the bathroom, and it takes me a while to convince Ben that I will be back and that I'm going anywhere. I come back into the bedroom and Ben is sitting on the bed with his back up against the wall. He holds out his hand for me to join him. I climb onto the bed and cuddle into his side.

After a while Ben asks if we can talk, I nod and he starts things off.

"First I want to apologise for allowing Hayley to touch me like that. She is a very touchy feely person, but, you're right, I wouldn't like it if another guy put his hands on you like that, irrespective of who he was. It was disrespectful and I am so sorry I hurt you and I promise it will never happen again. Secondly, I should have paid you more attention at the night club, I got so wrapped up talking to everyone that I ignored you and that's not cool."

"I was ok dancing by myself, I love to dance and I wasn't expecting you to dance with me the whole night. Just because we are a couple doesn't mean that we are joined at the hip, we are allowed to do different things. You were happy talking and I was happy dancing, no problem there. The problem was how close you and Hayley were, that she touched you intimately and you let her. I felt like such a fool when I saw the two of you."

"Carly, I promise you that you are the only girl for me, I don't think of anyone else that way. I feel so free with you, I have never sung to anyone or stripped for anyone before," he says with a laugh. "You are everything to me, Carly, and I'd be lost without you."

"It's ok," I say as I place my hand on his heart.

"Carly, my heart is yours and only yours," Ben says as he places his hand over mine.

It is quiet for a while, we are lying there holding each other when my mobile rings. It's my dad. "Carly, are you ok?"

"Yes, Dad, Ben and I have talked and we are working through it, so I won't be flying back today."

"I'm pleased to hear it, he's a good guy and he's good for you. I was hoping you would sort things out. Well Ratbag, I will leave you to it, I'll talk to you soon. I love you."

"I love you too Dad."

After a while Ben asks another question. "I noticed tonight that when you were angry your speech was fine but when you got upset you started to stutter. Does it always happen that way?"

"For some reason when I am pissed off I don't stutter, maybe it's because I have a bit of control but when I'm upset I lose control and that's when I tend to stutter. I have seen people who stutter all day every day but when they sing it is beautiful and perfect," I say with a sigh.

We are exhausted mentally and physically so we decide to head home. As soon and I get in the door I start to take my clothes off and head for the shower, Ben is right behind me. It's like he is afraid to let me out of his sight, I go with it because it's what he needs at the moment. We wash and dry each other and then crawl into bed, Ben wraps himself around me and we fall asleep.

I wake with a start to a clap of thunder, it's dark outside even though it's only 2 pm. We are in the middle of a wild storm, there is thunder, lightning, hail and it's pissing down with rain. Thank god we're inside. I go to turn on the bedside lamp and it won't work, and I realise the power is out. I look over at Ben and I see that he is flat out, poor bugger. I slip out of bed, get dressed and go into the kitchen to get a drink and then walk to the front door to see how bad it is. I open the door and I can hardly see the house across the road because the rain is so heavy. I step outside and stand under the eaves, sipping my drink, and watching the weather. Then I hear Ben yell my name. I turn to see him running out of the bedroom in a panic.

"Carly, where are you going?" he asks breathlessly.

"Nowhere, I'm watching the storm. The thunder woke me so I got up to see what was going on."

Ben bends over, put his hands on his knees and takes in a few deep breaths. "For a split second I thought you'd left me," he says, trying to calm himself down.

I walk over to him, take one of his hands in mine, lead him through the front door and lean against him watching the storm. "Ben, I am not going anywhere, you're stuck with me," I giggle, trying to lighten the mood.

Ben holds me tightly and I can feel his heart thumping in his chest. I look up at him and I see that his head is leaning against the side of the house and his eyes are closed tight but a tear escapes and rolls down his cheek. I place my hand on his cheek and wipe away his tear. "Ben, look at me please." He slowly opens his eyes and they are filled with unshed tears. "We are ok, I'm not leaving you, I promise." He smiles but it doesn't reach his eyes, I can see that it will take a while for Ben to believe what I am saying.

We go back inside and wait out the storm. I try to make conversation with Ben but he is closed off and gives me one word answers. I quieten down and leave him to sort his feeling out as I read my book. I glance up at him every now and then and I notice he has a pained look on his face.

The storm passes about 5 pm and the power comes back on about thirty minutes later. Ben gets up from the lounge, walks into the kitchen and starts to make dinner. Usually I would sit at the kitchen bench and talk to Ben as he cooked but tonight I will leave him to his thoughts.

Ben comes and tells me that dinner is ready and as I walk into the kitchen I notice he has lit a few candles and has opened a bottle of wine. I smile at Ben and kiss him on the cheek as he pulls out my chair for me. We eat our meal in relative silence. When I finish I thank him for the meal, take my plate to the sink and start to wash the dishes. I have just about finished when I feel Ben's body press up against my back and his arms wrap around me. I stop what I am doing, I lean my head so it's resting on his shoulder and I place my hands over Ben's arms.

We stand like that for a while then Ben leans down and kisses the side of my neck. "I love you so much, Carly."

I turn in his arms and look up at him. "I love you too." I stand on my toes, wrap my arms around his neck and pull him in for a kiss. Ben presses me against the sink as he deepens the kiss, his hands run up and down my sides. He pulls away and leads me to the bedroom where we make love twice before falling asleep.

Ben doesn't sleep well even though he's exhausted, he tosses and turns, which keeps waking me up. He mumbles in his sleep and calls out for me, and I place my hand on his chest to try to give him some comfort. He starts to settle down so I remove my hand and I cuddle into him. I fall asleep listening to his heart beating strongly in his chest.

22 | BEN

I wake with a start and bolt up in bed.

"Ben, are you ok?" Carly asks as she places a hand on my arm.

"How long have you been awake?"

"A few hours."

"Why didn't you wake me?"

"You were tossing and turning all night so I wanted you to sleep," she says as she rolls towards me to cuddle into my side.

I put my arm around her and pull her closer, kissing the top of her head. I take a deep breath, life is perfect when she's in my arms.

After a while we get up and have a late breakfast and decide to go to the movies. We choose a comedy because we need a good laugh. The movie is great and it really brings me out of my funk. We go to the pub just down the road from the cinema and watch a replay of the State of Origin game three between Queensland and New South Wales. It's a great match and QLD win the series 2-1. Carly's loving it because she goes for QLD but I'm not happy because I go for NSW.

We're chatting and watching the game when Hayley appears, I sink back into my seat. Just when things are back on track, this is all we need.

"Hi there, what happened to you the other night Richo?"

"Nothing much, how are you? Where's Sophie?" I ask while holding Carly's hand that little bit tighter.

"I'm good, I had a massive hangover yesterday though, so today has been a quiet one."

"And Sophie?"

"She's gone to visit her folks, they don't know about me so I never go with her," she says with a shrug.

After an awkward silence I announce I'm going to the bar and ask Hayley what she would like to drink. I lean down to kiss Carly on the lips and mouth *'sorry'* as I stand up. I can tell by the look on Carly's face that she is going to have words with Hayley, so I stand just off to the side so they can't see me but I can hear them.

Hayley leans in towards Carly. "I think I should introduce myself, I'm Hayley," she says as she thrusts her hand towards her.

Carly takes her hand. "Carly."

"Marley?"

"You know damn well it's Carly so don't try that shit with me." I smile and think, that's my girl.

Hayley actually looks shocked and then she recovers. "Well Carly, I have heard nothing but bad things about you and I don't think you are good for Richo," she says with a smirk.

"Up until Friday I had never heard your name so I couldn't give a toss if you think that I'm not good enough for Ben. The only opinion I care about is Ben's."

I can tell she is surprised by Carly's reaction because she is very quiet and looks nervous. Carly leans closer to her. "I know you have a thing for Ben." Hayley goes to interrupt Carly but she stops her. "As I said, I know; it's as obvious as dog's balls. Ben's under the impression that you're a lesbian but you and I both know you're bi-sexual and you're after Ben. Now, I believe that you went to Recruit School together and he has never made a move on you, and that tells me he doesn't fancy you. So from where I'm sitting you have two choices: you tell him you fancy him and see how that plays out or you get over it and continue the friendship you have. It's your choice."

I can see what Carly said has rattled Hayley and she is thinking about it, so I go to the bar and get the drinks. When I return to the table there is a noticeable atmosphere and because they don't know I witnessed the confrontation I have to play dumb. "OK, what's going on?" I ask as I put the drinks on the table.

"What?" Carly asks trying to sound calm.

"Carly, don't play dumb."

"Hayley and I were just getting acquainted while you were getting the drinks. Isn't that right Hayley?"

She just nods, skulls down her drink, stands and lets us know that she has to go. She won't look at Carly as she says goodbye. After she leaves I look at Carly. "What the fuck happened while I was at the bar?"

"Just as I said before, we had a chat and got to know one another," Carly smiles as she gives me a kiss and then asks what I want to eat for dinner.

The rest of the night is uneventful. We enjoy our meal, watch the rest of the rugby and then go home and make love. All in all a great end to this day.

On Monday I get an excited call from Carly saying one of the salons she had a trial in has offered her a job and she starts next Monday.

"Babe that's awesome. Let's go out for dinner tonight to celebrate."

"That would be lovely, I'll book somewhere. I love you," Carly says as she hangs up the phone.

During the week I call the breeder and we arrange to go and pick up our puppy on Friday afternoon. We call Piper to see if we can pick Chelsea up on the way because she is so excited to meet him.

On Friday I finish work at midday and pick Carly up before we make our way to Wollongong to pick up Chelsea. She is waiting on the front porch for us, and when she sees our car she starts jumping up and down, how cute. We go inside for a little while and let Piper know what we are doing and roughly what time we will be back. I get Chelsea's booster seat from Piper's car and put it in ours. We say goodbye and then make our way to Nowra.

We just pull onto Princes Highway when Chelsea starts asking questions about the puppy. "Uncle Ben and Auntie Carly what is the puppy's name?"

"We are calling him Roger," I say with a laugh.

"Where is he going to sleep?"

"He will sleep inside because he is a baby and he needs to be with us," says Carly, even though I'm not happy about it. She keeps telling me that he's not just a dog he's our baby.

"Can I come and visit him?" asks Chelsea.

"Of course you can," I say.

Chelsea talks nonstop the whole way there, she is so cute and funny. We pull up at the house, Carly undoes Chelsea's seatbelt and helps her out of the car and she races to the front door. Chelsea squeals with excitement when she sees the puppy, and Roger bounds up to her; she sits down and he climbs all over her. He starts nipping at her and jumps on her lap, pushing her flat on her back. I race over to help and when I get there Chelsea is crying so I pick her up and she cuddles into my chest.

"Uncle Ben, I don't like Roger, he bites me and pushes me over," she cries.

"Sweetheart, Roger is a baby and he needs to be taught not to do those things, he doesn't mean to hurt or upset you, he's just excited to meet you. How about we play with him for a while and then take him home?" I say trying to calm Chelsea.

She reluctantly agrees as long as I hold her hand. The breeder was good and left us alone for about ten minutes so we could all get use to each other. After a while Chelsea got used to pushing him away when he nipped at her and jumped up. Her confidence grows and by the time the breeder comes back out she is laughing and playing with him. We walk to the car and Chelsea insists that Roger ride in the back with her. We have a blanket ready for him to lie on and we place that next to Chelsea's booster seat. Once they are settled in the back we made our way back to Wollongong. Everything is quiet so Carly turns around in her seat and notices that Chelsea and Roger are asleep. He has his head on her lap, one of her arms is resting around his stomach and she is holding one of his paws with her other hand. It is so damned cute that Carly gets her phone out and snaps a few photos and sends them to my family.

When we pull up at Piper's, Chelsea and Roger are still asleep. I open my door which wakes Roger, and he yawns and stretches which wakes Chelsea. She looks around confused but happy when she sees Roger by her side.

I help Chelsea out the car and she runs up to her front door with Roger behind her, opens the front door and the two of them run inside. I put Chelsea's booster seat back in Piper's car and then we walk inside to find Piper cuddling Roger and Chelsea pouting.

"You can't have him all to yourself Chelsea, I want a cuddle too," Piper says.

"But he's my friend Mummy and I want to play with him."

"First I think he needs a wee, Chelsea can you please take him out the back so he can have a wee on the grass," Carly asks.

"Aunty Carly he can use the toilet like everyone else, I will help him."

We try not to laugh.

"Chelsea, animals go to the toilet outside. Only people use the toilets inside," Piper explains.

"Yuk." Chelsea says as she screws her face up. "So he will do poo's out there too?"

"Yes he will, and Uncle Ben and I will clean it up," laughs Carly.

Reluctantly Chelsea takes Roger outside and as they reach the grass he has a wee, then they run around while we sit and have a cuppa and a chat.

"How is the pregnancy going? Do you have a date yet?' I ask.

"Not too bad now the morning sickness has gone, though I do have a bit of difficulty sleeping because he's kicking me under my ribs at night and I am forever going to the toilet," laughs Piper. "I'm five months and due second of December."

"Wouldn't it be cool if your baby was born on Kelsey's eighteenth birthday, she would be over the moon," I say.

"I'll see what I can do," Piper says with a smile.

We finish our drinks and call Chelsea to bring over Roger so we can take him home. We promise her that we will bring him back and she can visit. As we walk outside Justin pulls up, and Chelsea runs to him with Roger right at her heals so she can show him. We have a quick chat with him and he plays with Roger for a little while then we have to get moving.

Roger lays on Carly's lap all the way home, Chelsea must have worn him out because he hardly moves. We get home, put him on the grass for a wee and then go inside. After Roger has had a look around it's time for a feed. We are feeding him raw chicken wings and raw meat, he needs protein to grow into a strong Rotty. He eats his dinner as I order spring rolls, a king prawn chow mein, a king prawn satay, fried rice and prawn crackers.

Once we have finished our Chinese, Carly and I sit on the floor to play with Roger and his toys. Carly takes lots of photos. Carly intends to take a photo of Roger every month so we can see how much he has grown, and we promised we would keep in touch with the breeder and send her some photos from time to time.

When it is time for bed we set Roger up in the laundry. He has a bed, water bowl and toys, and newspaper on the floor that he will hopefully go to the toilet on, fingers crossed.

As we shower Carly says, "If I'm lucky enough to have children I would love them just to be like Chelsea." I stop what I'm doing and just smile at her.   "What?" she asks, looking a little confused.

"You have never spoken about having children before."

"I never thought it was on the cards for me so I pushed it to the back of my mind, but the more time I spend with Chelsea I find myself getting hopeful that kids are in my future. She's smart, funny and so damned cute. I know I haven't known your family very long but I am very fond of everyone, especially Chelsea."

"Ok, so now you have broached the subject, how many kids do you want?"

"I think I would like three because, god forbid, if one of them is like George the other two would have each other," she says with a pained look.

I hold her face in my hands. "That will never happen, none of our children will be like George. I want them to have your looks and eyes, you're inner strength and brain and the boys to have my height."

"They have to have your dimples," laughs Carly.

I roll my eyes. "You really have a thing for my dimples," I smile as I pull Carly's mouth towards mine and kiss her deeply. I push her up against the shower wall, put my hand under her bum and lift her up. Carly reaches down and grabs my hard cock and rubs it against her pussy. She bites my bottom lip and I let out a low growl. "I need to be inside you now." I push into her slowly never breaking eye contact. "I love you Carly and you're my world, I love you so much," I say as I pump into her.

Carly screams my name and calls out that she loves me and her body shudders when she comes. My body tenses and I bite her shoulder and come inside her soon after her release. I pull out of Carly and set her on her feet and pull her close as we come down from our high. Once our breathing is back to normal Carly starts to move out of the shower.

I grab her hand and turn her to face me. "Can we please revise the number of kids? Carly, I would like to have at least four kids, I want a house full of kids, love and laughter, what do you think?"

"WOW…ummmm….you really want kids with me? What if George's behaviour is genetic and I pass that on? I would never forgive myself if I did that to you," she says sadly.

"Carly, George's behaviour is just that, behaviour. I seriously doubt it's genetic because he's not like that all the time and it seems it's directed only at you, so please don't let him dictate your decision to be a mother. And of course I want kids with you, why wouldn't I?"

"Again I just never thought it would be in my future. I would love nothing more than to be the mother of your children but I want to wait until I'm at least twenty five, I'm too young."

"I'm not saying I want them now, we need time to be a couple first and we have only been together for about five months. Plus I want to get married before we try for kids."

"You have really thought about this haven't you?" Carly asks.

"After our first date I started thinking about it, Carly. I knew then that you where special and I wanted you in my life and I could see a future for us."

"I don't know what to say to that, I'm speechless," she whispers.

"Have I said too much?" I ask as I put my head down.

She reaches up to touch my cheek. "No, you haven't said too much, if this is how you feel I want to know. I just never thought I was loveable and I thought that no one would love me. That all changed when I met you."

We get out of the shower, dry off and crawl onto the bed and she pushes me so I'm on my back and she's straddling me. Carly's kissing my chest, paying a lot of attention to my nipples before she starts to make her way south, moving down until she has my rock hard cock in her hand and mouth. Carly slowly moves her hand up and down twisting at the tip as she blows cool air on the head of my cock and it jerks in her hand. I let out a groan and slowly thrust my hips up. She leans forward and flicks the tip with her tongue, fuck that feels amazing. Carly licks my cock slowly from root to tip and she's knows she's driving me crazy. She lowers her mouth and takes as much of me as she can. "OH MY GOD," I moan as Carly goes to town. I thrust up as she is going down on me, sometimes I go a little too far and she gags but generally we have a good rhythm going. I wrap my hand around hair. "Babe....oooooohhhhhh that....fuuuccck...wow...soooo good." Carly moves her mouth so she's sucking and licking my balls because she knows this drives me crazy. "Carly...babe...please....please don't....feels....oh god," I cry out. I pull her head up. "I will...come...if you keep...that up," I pant. She gives me the most beautiful smile as she crawls up my body, kissing me as she goes. I wrap my arms around her and position her so she's underneath me.

"Man you're quick," giggles Carly as I kiss my way to her breasts and suck a nipple into my mouth and play with the other.

"Fuck I love your tits," I say around Carly's nipple as she lets out a laugh.

I make my way south kissing, licking and biting her soft skin. I love how she feels against my skin. I reach her pussy and flick out my tongue and taste her as her hips buck off the bed into my face and she grabs the doona cover with her hands. Soon she's screaming, "Ben I'm coming, please don't stop."

I lick and suck until she can't take any more. She grabs my head and pulls me up and he kisses me with so much passion. "I want you to take me from behind, I fuckin' love that angle," Carly breathlessly tells me. A huge smile erupts over my face. "I'm guessing you like that position too," she laughs.

"Any position with you is amazing, but I have to say this is my favourite. Now get your arse back here so I can fuck you til you scream my name again."

"I love it when you are like this," Carly laughs.

I position myself behind her, place my hand in the middle of her shoulder blades and slowly push Carly down so her face is resting on the bed and her arse is in the air. "Fuck me Carly, you look so hot in this position."

"All you can see is my arse," she laughs.

"Babe it's not all I can see; I can see the curve of your back, your beautiful pale skin and I can see the side of your face. I can see all the emotions that you are experiencing while I plough into you, it's such a turn on," I say as I place my hands on her hips and pull her towards me and enter her.

"Fuuuuccccckkkkkkk babe… sooooooo goood… fuck me hard," Carly moans.
"Ben I'm gunna come…don't stop," she cries as she comes so hard around my cock.

"Oh god, Carly..you are so tight…oh..god…I'm coming," I groan as I come inside her. We're exhausted so we fall to the side just lying there trying to catch our breath. "That was wonderful," I pant as we hold each other's hands. We fall asleep sated and exhausted.

Roger cries off and on through the night so we don't get much sleep. In the morning I get up before Carly and let him him out the back to go to the toilet and so I can clean the laundry. We stay home that weekend so Roger can get used to us and we can start to train him. Carly is really good and patient with Roger.

Sunday night Carly doesn't sleep very well because she's nervous about starting her new job. We both get up when my alarm goes off in the morning and we feed and play with Roger before I have to leave for work. I give Carly a kiss goodbye and wish her luck for her first day at work.

23 | CARLY

The nerves really set in as I get myself showered and dressed for work. My uniform is all black, including my closed-in shoes, and I must wear makeup and put my hair up. I get to work about twenty minutes early and I wait at the front of the salon while one of the girls gets the Manager. The Manager, whose name is Donna, introduces me to the rest of the girls. The beauticians are Kirsten, Jo and Georgie and there is a junior called Melissa but she only works Saturdays because she goes to school.

We all have our own rooms, which are our responsibility. There are two piercing rooms and two massage/facial rooms, it's a good sized salon. I put my bag in a locked cupboard out the back and then have a look at my room. I wipe my tweezers with alcohol wipes, move a few things around and then have a look at my client list.

I'm pretty busy considering it's my first day and the clients don't know me yet. The day goes pretty quickly and even though I don't get much of a chance to chat to the other girls because everyone is busy, they seem to be nice and happy to answer any of my questions.

I go home happy but knackered. Luckily for me the bus stop is at the end of my street so I don't have far to walk. I open the front door and the smell is amazing; Ben has cooked Lucy's lasagne for dinner and I can't wait, I am starving. I walk into the kitchen and find Ben cooking for me, naked, wearing only his glasses. I start to laugh.

"How was your day Beautiful?" asks Ben, as if this is normal.

"Ben what are you doing?"

"I'm cooking dinner."

"But you're naked," I laugh.

"You told me once that you pictured me cooking for you naked and I thought tonight was as good a night as any," Ben says with a sexy smile.

I walk up to him, wrap my arms around his neck and kiss him. "You're crazy," I laugh.

"I just wanted this day to be memorable."

"You managed that," I smile.

"How was your day?" Ben asks as he holds me around the waist.

"It was good, I had forgotten how much I love what I do. The girls seem great and I have a permanent roster and nearly all the clients from today booked back in with me. The only thing is that I work all day Saturday's but I have every fourth one off."

"It's the nature of your profession, you were just lucky that you didn't work weekends in your previous salon. We'll be fine, we just have to make the most of Sunday's. Now are you hungry?"

The rest of the week goes quick, work is good, and because I work late on Thursdays Ben picks me up. He has offered to pick me up from work every day, but I'm happy catching the bus and that way he can relax after work.

On Sunday we take Roger to the vets to get him microchipped and to have his second needle. Once he has had his third we can take him out for walks. Ben is trying to get Roger use to his lead, but at the moment he hates it, whenever it is around his neck he rolls on the floor like when a crocodile has been captured, or he just lies down and Ben drags him across the floor boards, it's hilarious. I think Roger thinks it's a game and is playing when he gets dragged.

When I get home from work on Monday Ben has dinner waiting for me and as I sit down at the table there is an envelope on my plate with my name on it. I open it and squeal with delight. There are two tickets for Pink's concert on Saturday the 10th August at Sydney Entertainment Centre. I race over to Ben and throw myself into his waiting arms.

"Darcy and Lily will be coming with us. You ok if they stay the night?"

"Of course they can stay, I'm so excited, thank you so much Ben, you are too good to me."

"You deserve it and I remember from our first date that you said that she was touring this year and that you and Nic were going to go. So as soon as they were on sale I made sure we had tickets."

"You remember that?" she whispers.

"Babe, I remember everything you tell me about you," Ben says as he kisses me.

The next couple of weeks fly by and before we know it it's the night of Pink's concert. We have a meal before the concert which is great because it gives us a chance to catch up with Darcy and Lily, who we haven't seen since Chelsea's party. Lily and I buy a concert t-shirt. I make sure I get at least one t/shirt at every concert.

We take our seats and settle in for the show. Pink is an amazing entertainer and the show is fantastic. Luckily the block where we are gets up and dances. I hate sitting down at concerts. We sing and dance through Pink's show. I would have to rate this among the top five of all the concerts I have been too.

After the concert we go to a pub for a few drinks. We chat about how great the show was and how inadequate she makes Lily and I feel because she is so damned talented. The guys just shake their heads and laugh at us. There are a few pool tables and Ben and Darcy go and see if a table is free. Darcy comes back to get us because the game is just about to finish and the guys are up next.

Ben and Darcy play the first game and Darcy wins, then they want to partner up with Lily and myself. I explain that I have never played before so Ben gives me a quick lesson and then the game starts. I suck big time, I hardly get the stick to hit the ball. I am reminded often that the stick is called the cue. Ok then. When I did actually hit the ball it was too hard and I need to be a bit gentler. Give me a softball bat any day, if I'm going to hit something I want to hit the shit out of it. I don't think pool is my game. Anyway we lose. Badly.

Ben's not happy that we lose and Darcy really rubs it in. I can see that the rivalry is huge between them because Lily rolled her eyes and says it has always been like this. Ben wins the next one and then asks if I want to play again, I think he is relieved when I say no. Lily and I talk while the guys play again. All of a sudden Ben yells and does a victory lap around the table. Apparently they played another two games because they had both won two games each and Ben won the decider, Lily and I are too busy talking to take notice.

"Really?" I say to Ben when he has stopped jumping around.

"What? I won the game."

"Babe, I think the whole of Sydney knows you won. It's just a game of pool not the Olympics."

"Carly, you clearly don't understand. It's more than a game, I can't have Darcy or Damon beat me."

"Why not?"

"Because I'm the oldest and as the oldest it's my job to beat them in everything."

"Are you fuckin' kidding me? You can't win everything it's impossible."

"Carly I always win and get what I want. I got you didn't I?" he says raising one eyebrow.

I laugh. "Well honey you will lose one day and when that day comes I hope you're able to handle it. If not, don't come bitching to me because I'm not interested."

I look at Lily. "You say it's always been like this?"

"Yep afraid so, it gets old pretty quickly." she says, rolling her eyes.

Once back home we let Roger out of the laundry and he is excited about the extra attention. Lily and Darcy play with him on the floor while Ben and I get them a drink. The night is great, we put some music on low, it's great to see Ben and Darcy together because they get on so well and Lily and I have really hit it off. Maybe because she is an outsider like me.

Lily asks how I'm finding it in Sydney and if I miss Perth.

I take a deep breath before I answer. "I'm happy here with Ben, I miss my dad and my best friend Nicole though."

"Do you have any plans to go back for a holiday?" Lily asks. Ben and I look at each other, unsure how to answer. "Did I say something wrong?" Lily asks.

I grab a hold of Ben's hand and he gives me a reassuring squeeze, I take a deep breath "We will be going back in early November for a court case."

"Oh we had no idea." Darcy says.

"No, I know you didn't." I look at Ben "I suppose they are going to find out soon enough, so maybe now's a good time?"

"It's up to you babe, whatever you think."

"What's going on, you're freaking me out," says Darcy.

"What do you know about me?" I ask.

"Just that you have had a bit of a tough life and you came over to Sydney earlier than expected, nothing specific," replies Darcy.

"Ok, well I have a brother called George that I have a violence order against because he nearly killed me. The court case in November involves the last attack."

"Carly, you said the last attack, how many have there been?" asks Lily.

"They started when I was nine and throughout the years the beatings varied. He put me in the hospital when I was eighteen and then again a few days after Ben's birthday this year. I didn't press charges the first time because I thought it was my fault and I was ashamed, plus my father is a Prison Officer and I didn't want it to interfere with his career. But this time I know it wasn't my fault so I have pressed charges. I came here earlier than expected because my mum set me up: she took me out to lunch and George just happened to turn up at the restaurant we were at. Even though we can't prove it I know she set it up. My dad and Ben flew me out the next day, so that's why we stayed in a hotel while waiting for this place to be ready."

There's total silence. You could hear a pin drop. Ben leans in and kisses my cheek. Lily has her hand over her mouth and tears rolling down her face, Darcy is shaking his head, clenching his jaw and looking at Ben.

"Guys it's ok," I say.

Lily jumps up, sits next to me and puts her arms around me. Ben is about to say something when I stop him, I'm ok with Lily hugging me.

"Carly, it's not ok, it's anything but ok. Who knows?" asks Darcy

"Your folks know, they were told before I met them. I intend to tell the others when the time is right so I would appreciate it if you wouldn't say anything to your sisters and Damon until I have a chance to tell them."

"Of course, that goes without saying. Fuck we had no clue," Darcy replies.

"Why would you, your family get along so well and you look out for each other. My upbringing is so different from yours, I'm very envious but thrilled to be a part of your family now," I say with a slight smile.

"Are your parents together?" Lily asks.

"No, my dad couldn't get over my mum setting me up. Mum has always taken George's side and Dad finally had enough so he left her a few weeks ago. Ben and I will stay with Dad when we go back in November. Mum doesn't know where I am, I also changed my mobile number and made sure it was silent."

"Do you think he'll get jail time?" Darcy asks.

"I fucking hope so." Ben spits out "I hope he gets a lengthy sentence and he gets the shit kicked out of him daily and becomes someone's bitch because that's what he deserves the fucking coward."

I lean in, place a kiss on his cheek and I smile at him and when our eyes meet, his body relaxes as he presses his forehead against mine. We take a moment before looking back at Darcy and Lily. "Wow, that brought a downer to the night," I say with a laugh. "I think it's time for more drinks and we need to crank up the music. Come on Lily, let's pick something we can dance to."

The guys go to the kitchen to get us some drinks. I glance up and they are deep in conversation, Darcy has his hand on Bens shoulder and I can tell they need some brother time. I turn back to Lily and we go through my iPod and select the playlist called dance. The first song starts and it's *Wake Me Up* by Avicii. Lily and I let loose, we dance all around the lounge room doing stupid moves and laughing our arses off to a few more songs. The guys are still in the kitchen talking and I think it's long enough. "Hey you two, the entertainment is in here so please bring us our drinks and come and join us."

They bring us our drinks and sit on the lounge, and a few minutes later Jason Derulo's Talk Dirty To Me starts. Lily and I look at each other and we both have a wicked look in our eyes, we turn to our men and start dancing for them. The dancing gets very hot when we give our men a lap dance, I can tell that Ben is really enjoys it when I grind my bum into his groin, he is rock hard, exactly what I was hoping for.

After the lap dance Ben and Darcy are speechless. Lily and I get up to dance to a few more songs, the guys join us when Do I Wanna Know? by Arctic Monkeys come on, it's slow with a great beat. Ben and I dance in each other's arms, grinding our bodies together and getting very turned on, we start to kiss and all I want to do it tear his clothes off. I look over to Darcy and Lily and they aren't there. "Babe they left just after the song started," Ben laughs.

I race to the bedroom while Ben puts Roger in the laundry, I can hear giggling from the spare room, Ben stops in his tracks. "I can't hear my brother having sex it'll scar me for life."

I turn on the music in the bedroom to drown them out. "Better?"

Ben launches himself at me. "Much better, now come here coz

I'm gunna fuck you til you can't walk anymore, you are going to end up bow legged before I finish with you."

I burst out laughing, "You are crazy but you are my crazy and I love you so much, thank you for tonight," I say as I kiss him. Ben thoroughly explores my body for the next three hours, god he has some stamina. I'm one lucky cow.

Two weeks later we all gather at a pub in Wollongong for James' surprise 50th birthday party. Lucy has hired out one of the rooms and there is about eighty family and friends there. It's a great night and James has no clue about the party, he just thought we were all going out for dinner. I meet so many people that night, and they say they have heard wonderful things about me from James and Lucy. Everyone is so nice to me.

Ben, Damon and Darcy end up getting shitfaced with their cousins. Ben is such a funny drunk. He is tactile when he is sober but when he is drunk he can't stop touching me and kissing me and telling anyone who will listen how much he loves me. I love it.

A stretch limo picks us up at the end of the night. James, Lucy, Piper, Justin, Chelsea, Ben, myself, Darcy, Lily, Damon and Kelsey go for a ride around Wollongong before we get dropped off at different points. Chelsea has a great time in the limo, she opens the sunroof and wants to look out the top. Lily and I get on either side of Chelsea and lift her up so the three of us are looking out, Chelsea is having a wonderful time but we can't stay up too long because it's bloody freezing. Piper, Justin and Chelsea are dropped off first, then Darcy and Lily, and finally the rest of us at James and Lucy's house.

Everyone is exhausted so we all go to bed straight away. I have to help Ben up the stairs and James helps Damon, they are so funny. Ben keeps telling his family how much he loves me and that we are going to get married and have at least four children. Lucy smiles broadly, Damon tells him not to play his hand too soon and to keep something as a surprise, and Kelsey swears she will never drink alcohol because she doesn't want to act like an idiot.

When I finally get Ben in his room I have difficulty getting him undressed because he wants to fool around. Generally I'm right there with him but tonight he is so drunk that he has no coordination and has brewers' droop, he couldn't get hard if his life depended on it. I strip him to his boxers then I pull back the covers and get him to lie down, I turn the light off and I am making my way back to the bed when I hear Ben groan and mumble he's going to be sick.

"Fuck!" I yell. I run to turn the light back on just in time to see Ben lean over the side of the bed and throw up in his backpack. I am no good when someone is throwing up; it's not the vomit, it's the noise that you make when you are heaving; I am what's called a sympathy vomiter. I open the door and call for Lucy, thankfully she's awake and goes in to sort Ben out, I feel really bad but I know if I tried to help Ben I would have been throwing up myself and then there would be two of us to clean up after.

I go downstairs and get two glasses of water and Berocca from the pantry. As I get to the top of the stairs Damon runs past me with his hand over his mouth, he just made it to the toilet in time before he throws up. I go into his room and put one of the glasses of water down on his bed side table and put a Berocca next to the glass.

I enter Ben's room and find him dry reaching whilst still hanging over the side of the bed. Lucy is sat next to him rubbing his back. I can just imagine her doing that for him when he was little, she is such a caring Mother. She notices me in the doorway and asks me to bring the water to Ben and to get a wet flannel. I do as I'm asked and she wipes Ben's forehead with the flannel. Ben looks like death, poor baby. Lucy gets him to lie on his side on the bed and to take a few sips of the water before he goes to sleep. She gets up and takes the down to the laundry and washes it out. She comes back upstairs and makes sure Damon is ok before coming to talk to me.

"Are you ok?" she asks me.

"Lucy, I am so sorry that I couldn't help Ben but I'm no good with vomit, if I tried to help you would have been cleaning both of us up."

"Carly, not everyone can do that, though having five kids helps. I have to say I'm not that great with blood, and with having three boys you can only imagine how many times I have had to clean their cuts and scrapes. Don't worry about it. There is a small bucket under the sink in the bathroom, go and get it just in case he throws up again," she says as she hugs me good night.

Ben is moaning and coughing in his sleep. I don't sleep very well that night scared he might throw up again and choke on his vomit.

"Oh god, I'm dying." groans Ben as he wakes up in the morning. I roll over and he is lying on his back with his head in his hands. "Babe, who the fuck hit me over the head? It's pounding."

"What do you remember?"

"Ummm..I remember drinking with the guys but I don't remember leaving the party or coming home. Did you undress me?"

I touch his face "Yeah I did honey. I got you a Berocca last night but you were not in a fit state to have it. It might be an idea if you had it now."

Ben lifts his head off the pillow and groans, "Babe I can't move, can you please get it for me?"

I stifle a laugh and walk to his side of the bed, put the Berocca in the glass, dissolve it and hand it to him.

Ben slowly sits up in bed and drinks it down. "Ohhhhh god I feel like hell, why did I drink so much? Did I make a fool of myself?"

"First, you drank so much because you were with family, you were happy, you were relaxed and having a great time; second, you did not make a fool out of yourself, you were lovely, sweet and wonderful just like you always are," I say as I lean in to kiss him. "Are you hungry? What do you have as your hangover food?"

"Babe, I need ice cold coke and a burger with the lot."

"I'll go get it for you. Go back to sleep and I'll wake you when I get back." I get dressed and ask the others if they want anything. Damon has wants a large bottle of Fanta and KFC hot and spicy, he looks as rough as Ben. Kelsey comes with me into town and thankfully she knows were Ben's favourite burger bar is. While we're waiting for our order Whitney walks in. "Fuck me, every time we come to Wollongong that bunny boiler turns up, she has to be a stalker," I whisper to Kelsey.

Kelsey has her back to the door so she has to turn around to see what I am talking about. "Just ignore her Carly, she's not worth it."

"I'm happy to do just that but she makes it her mission to get in my face." My number is called and as I walk to the counter I hear pig noises coming from Whitney and her cronies. I start to laugh, it's so juvenile. I get Ben's burger and as I start for the door Whitney stands in my way. What the fuck. "Whitney what can I do for you?"

"There's nothing I want from you."

I step to the side and try to walk around her but she puts her hand out to stop me. I see red. "You really need to get your hand off me." I say through my teeth.

"Or what, you're going to hit me like you did Alex?" She smirks.

I calm myself. "No, because that's what you want me to do."

"Why would I want that?"

"Because you're bat shit crazy, now get the fuck out of my way." We push past her and make our way to the car. We stop at KFC to get Damon his food and then make our way back to the house.

When we get home Ben is still in bed and Damon is moaning on the lounge. Kelsey takes Damon his food and I head upstairs to get Ben. I walk into the bedroom and Ben is sat on the side of the bed with his head in his hands. "Babe, please shoot me and put me out of my misery."

Poor thing, he looks really bad. I sit next to him. "I have your coke and burger downstairs, have a shower and then go eat, hopefully you will feel better. Is there anything else I can do for you?"

"You could help me shower," he said with a wink.

I laugh. "No matter how sick you are you are always up for it." I grab his hand "Come on you, let's go." We walk into the bathroom and lock the door. I undress and Ben takes off his boxers. I can't believe he has a hard on. I look at him. "Really?"

"What can I say, babe? I am a sex machine and you are so fuckin' hot, now come here and give your man some lovin."' I squeal as he wraps his arms around me and pulls me under the shower. After our water sports we go downstairs, where I watch Ben devour his burger and drink the coke while I have tea and toast.

The next couple of months are pretty uneventful. We go to work, come home and have dinner, play with, walk and train Roger, make love and go out on Saturday nights. Life is great, my client base is growing at work and the girls are great.

Ben and I open a joint account, he has a direct debit set up and he said I should only put in what I want, I make sure that I put in at least twenty five percent of my fortnightly wage. Ben won't let me pay towards the rent, bills or when we go out. We have a bit of an argument when I insist on paying the grocery bill but I won't back down. I explain that I want to contribute and because I am working there is no reason why I can't, and he finally relents. I make sure that our pantry and fridge is fully stocked with food and drink that Ben loves, especially his favourite biscuits, Tim Tams.

24 | CARLY

As we near the end of October my nightmares and panic attacks start to come back. I become very argumentative, especially with Ben. If he says black I'll say white, poor buggar, I give him a really hard time.

We book our flights back to Perth and make sure that we can stay with my dad. When I interviewed for my job I told them that I had a holiday booked in early November for two weeks, they were ok giving me the time off. I decided not to tell anyone about the court case because it's no one else's business.

The Friday night before the court case we go out for dinner to the local Thai restaurant. We sit across from each other in total silence; Ben's afraid to talk to me in case I bite his head off and I'm lost in my thoughts. It's a total disaster. We eat in silence, we drive home in silence, we watch TV in silence at opposite ends of the lounge, then we shower on our own. This is the first time I have showered alone since we've become a couple, and I hate it.

I wake up in the morning with a migraine. I race to the bathroom and throw up, then I wet a cloth and wipe the back of my neck and forehead. I stumble to the kitchen to get my migraine medication. My eye sight's not the greatest and I walk into the dining room table. There are times when I lose my eye sight completely, but hopefully today's not one of those days. I open the draw to get the medication and as I grab for a glass it slips out of my hand and smashes on the floor. "Fuck," I say as I bend down to start picking up the shards of glass.

"Don't move." Ben says sharply as he gets up off the lounge.

"What are you doing on the lounge?" I say as I jump with surprise.

"I slept there last night, and you didn't even notice," he says angrily.

"Fuck you!" I scream as I run out of the kitchen, I can feel the glass cutting my feet as I run but I'm numb to the pain.

Ben yells after me, "Carly, stop, you've cut yourself!"

"I don't care," I say as I run into the bedroom to get dressed, I have to get out of here. I start to pull on my jeans and jumper, Ben is grabbing at me to stop, I push him away and get my socks out of the draw. I sit on the floor and pull the glass out of my feet.

"Carly that one looks deep. Please let me have a look at it?"

I ignore him, put my socks on and then lean over to grab my runners, I slip them on my feet and walk back to the kitchen. I take my meds and walk out the front door. Ben's yelling for me to come back, I just keep walking. After a while the pain starts to hit me, I sit down in the gutter in between two parked cars and put my head in my hands, the pain in my head is excruciating and my eye sight has nearly disappeared. I have no idea where I am, no ID and no phone. Everything goes dark and I lay down. I've given up. George wins I mumble over and over.

"Is she ok?" I vaguely hear a woman ask.

"I've called the Police and an ambulance. She doesn't look good and her shoes are red with what looks like blood," says a male voice.

"Ma'am, Ma'am, can you hear me?" I just lay there. "Ma'am can you tell me your name? Are you hurt?" I don't reply. I hear sirens and doors opening and closing. I feel someone touching me but I don't say anything, I open my eyes but all I see is darkness. I feel my body being lifted and I groan in pain.

I hear car tyres screech on the road and a door slam shut.

"Carly!" I hear Ben yell. "What happened to her?"

"Who are you?"

"I'm Ben Richardson, Carly's boyfriend. Is she ok?"

"Sir we don't know what has happened to her, we got a call that there was a woman on the side of the road. Where is the blood from?"

"She broke a glass and then walked through it, I tried to get her to stay and let me have a look but she ran out of the house. I've been looking for her ever since."

"She hasn't said anything. Has she consumed any drugs or alcohol?"

"Carly has a migraine and took some medication before she left the house. She has been under a lot of stress lately and we're flying back to Perth tomorrow for a court case against her brother. She has a violence order out against him."

"We have to get her to Hospital, I need to take some details from you and then if you want to you can follow the ambulance."

I just lay there listening to everyone talk. I don't say a word, not even when Ben kisses my forehead and tells me he loves me.

I'm put in the back of the ambulance and a man starts talking to me. "Carly, how do you feel?" I don't respond. "Carly, you need to tell me where the pain is so I can help you." I say nothing because there is nothing to say, my whole body is in pain, he can't help me with that. "We are nearly at the hospital where they will take good care of you," the man says.

I'm wheeled out of the ambulance and into the hospital. I hate the smell and the noise. I'm moved into a bed and I hear the curtain being pulled, I roll onto my side and tuck my knees up.

"Carly, I'm Belinda, your nurse," says a woman's voice. Can you please give me your arm so I can take your blood pressure." I roll onto my back. "Thank you. I need to check your temperature and also have a look at your feet." I remain silent and let her do what she wants. Belinda takes my shoes off. "It looks like two of your wounds need sutures. I need to get the kit, I won't be long."

I hear the curtain move again. I hear Ben's voice before he places my hand in his. "I was so worried, why did you run out?"

"Hi, I'm Belinda, Carly's nurse. I am going to clean these cuts on her feet and I'm pretty sure two of them need sutures." I can feel pressure on my feet as Belinda goes to work, I don't move or make a noise when she puts the local anaesthetic in or when she stitches me up.

When she leaves the cubicle Ben speaks. "Carly, please talk to me, I'm sorry I snapped at you this morning, I shouldn't have, we are both under a lot of stress, you needed me to be there for you and I've let you down."

"Y…you said th..that my p..p..place is wi…wi…with you in our b..bed and yu…you slept on th..the lounge," I stutter.

"I know babe, and that was such a dick move. I'm sorry, no matter what happened I should have come to bed with you. You needed me and I was being a selfish prick. I know this court case is going to be hard on you and it has been affecting you for the last couple of weeks. You have been tossing and turning and having nightmares most nights."

I can't talk to him anymore, I have nothing to say. Ben sits there holding my hand rubbing his thumb across the back of my hand silently, I hate the silence. I hear the curtain move again.

"Carly, my name is Doctor Rossum, can you tell me what happened to you?"

I say nothing. Ben explains to the Doctor what happened, and the Doctor asks questions about the court case, about how long the abuse went on for and whether I seen anyone to talk about it.

Doctor Rossum sits on the side of my bed. "Carly I'm a Psychologist and I was paged to come and see you because you have been exhibiting unusual behaviour. After talking to Ben I have an idea why. Are you ok if you and I have a private talk?" I nod my head and Ben is asked to go wait in the waiting room. "Carly, are you able to tell me how you are feeling?"

I take a while to answer because I don't want to stutter. "I'm scared."

"What scares you?" he asks.

"George will get off and he will come after me again and kill me this time. Ben will realise that I'm too much trouble, that I'm nothing and not worth the effort," I whisper.

"Your concerns about George are valid, no one knows how the trial is going to go. However, the fact that you live on opposite sides of the country is a help. Why do you think you are too much trouble, that you are nothing and not worth the effort?"

I take a deep breath, I have never spoken to anyone about how I really feel before, and the fact that I can't see is unnerving me. There could be a room full of people in here with us. I feel naked and exposed.

"Carly, you need to open up to someone and I hope I'm that someone. You can't keep bottling it up inside because it effects every aspect of your life."

Slowly I start to talk. "I have never spoken about my deep down feelings and fears before, I just talk about the events — you know, just the facts, it's easier."

"Ok, how about we confront one thing at a time. Why do you think that you are nothing?"

"Because that has been drummed into me from a very early age. George told me daily that I was a worthless, fat, ugly pig and when you hear that from someone who you're related to and should love you, you believe it. And when you add that my mother takes his side, and set me up, even though he nearly killed me, what am I supposed to think?"

"It is hard when you are told daily that you don't measure up. Eventually you believe it. Tell me two good things about yourself."

"Ummmm that's not easy....ummmmm....I'm good at my job

and I'm a loyal friend."

"They are good qualities but I would like you to tell me two things about you, personal things that you like about yourself."

I'm silent for a long time. "I can't think of anything."

"If I brought Ben in here do you think he could name any?"

I don't answer I just pull my knees to my chest and shut down again. After a while the Doctor excuses himself and he comes back in the cubicle with Ben. When I hear Ben's voice I open my eyes and I realise my vision is coming back because I can now see shapes.

Doctor Rossum speaks: "Ben I have brought you in here because when I asked Carly what she liked about herself she said that she is good at her job and is a loyal friend. I then asked her to tell me two personal things that she likes about herself and she couldn't come up with anything. Ben, can you tell Carly two things that you like about her?"

Ben starts to talk. "She's beautiful on the outside and on the inside, she has a wicked sense of humour and her laugh is so contagious, she makes me want to be a better person because she gives so much of herself to me and my family, when she smiles at me my heart skips a beat, she has the most stunning eyes and they are so expressive, I think she is the sexiest woman on this planet and I am so fuckin' lucky she loves me."

"WOW. Carly, how do you feel after hearing what Ben has just said?"

Tears roll down my cheeks. "I don't k..know how you c..can feel that way because I br..bring so much drama to your life. Y..your life was so dif..different and drama free be..before you met me, this is m..my normal, this is how I gr..grew up and I don't want t..to burden or tain… taint you with my bullshit."

Ben sits next to me on the bed, places his hands on my cheeks and wipes away the tears. He leans his forehead against mine and I can just about make out his features. "Carly, that was your normal but it isn't anymore. Your life with me and Roger is your new normal. I promise to show you how much I love you every day, I am here for you to confide in, to lean on and you can always count on me to have your back. My life is nothing without you in it, I love you so much. Carly, please don't ever doubt that."

"Carly, I think we have made a great start today but you need time to process, I would like to see you again, hopefully when you come back from Perth. Is that something you're willing to do?" I just nod and Doctor Rossum leaves the cubicle.

Ben leans in and kisses my forehead. "How's your migraine?"

"Bearable, my sight is slowly coming back. Ben I want to get out of here, can you please see if I can go home?" Ben goes to find a doctor and I slowly sit up. My head is pounding but I need to go home to my own bed. Ben comes back with Belinda the nurse.

"Carly, I just need to do some obs before we can discharge you." Belinda takes my blood pressure, temperature and shines a light in my eyes to see how my pupils react. Inside I'm screaming because it feels like she's stabbing my eye with a knife, but because I want to get out of here I don't react or say anything. When she is finished she finds a doctor and I'm discharged. Belinda gives Ben Doctor Rossum's details and then shows us to the exit. Ben holds onto me because my sight is fuzzy, my feet hurt and I am fairly weak. He settles me in the car and drives us home extra carefully.

At home Ben lies with me, holding my hand until I fall asleep. I wake in the early hours of the morning, and I'm hungry because it's been over twenty four hours since I last ate. I make my way to the kitchen and decide to have a toasted cheese and onion sandwich and a cup of tea. As I get the bread out of the pantry Ben walks into the kitchen yawning and rubbing his stomach.

"Sit down and I'll make that for you," he says.

"I'm capable of doing it myself," I growl.

"Babe, I know you are, but standing must hurt your feet. Besides, I want to do this for you." I move to sit down at the kitchen table and stare into space. Ben makes us both a toasty, and gets himself a glass of milk and a cup of tea for me. The sound of us crunching our sandwiches is deafening.

"Carly, please talk to me."

"What do you want to talk about?"

"Anything, everything, I just want us to get back to normal, to talk and act how we usually do. I miss you, I miss us, I want you to let me in," Ben says as he holds my hand. I look up and he gives me a reassuring smile.

"I want that too but I don't know how. I'm scared and I feel lost."

"Beautiful, we will do this together. What scares you?"

"That he will get off, find out where we live, then come after me and finish what he started before coming after you and your family. I am so scared, I have nightmares that he is chasing me with a knife or trying to drown me or strangle me. All I see is his face, he's smirking at me while he's killing me. I don't know how I'm going to face him in Court, I don't think I'm strong enough," I cry.

Ben pulls me onto his lap. "Carly, I promise I will not let him near you, I will protect you until my last breath and we can do this together. Irrespective of the Judge's decision, we as a couple will not let him win." He pulls me in for a cuddle. "Are you ready to get some sleep? We have to be packed and at the airport in eight hours."

BEN | 25

The alarm wakes us, we pack, and I call Damon to make sure he is still staying at our place while we are away because we don't want to put Roger in a kennel. Then we drive to the airport. Once we check in our bags we go for a drink and something small to eat.

The flight seems to take forever and Carly fidgets the whole way. I try to make sure she has everything she needs and also to keep her mind off the Court case. Andrew and Nicole are at the airport to meet us and as soon as Carly sees them she starts running as fast as she can. She throws herself into Nicole's arms and hugs her with tears streaming down her face. I know she has really missed them. Nicole and Carly cling to each other and chat away while Andrew and I get our bags. I smile to myself as Carly and Nicole sit in the back of the car and catch up with all the gossip, it feels good to listen to her laugh and talk so freely.

We arrive at Andrew's and Nicole stays for dinner. At about 10pm Nicole goes home and Carly gives her a really long hug goodbye. Carly and I stay up for a while chatting to Andrew but because of the time difference we are really tired so we go for a shower about 11 pm and then try to get some sleep.

I toss and turn all night, I put my ear buds in and play my iPod. I'm not aware that Carly's awake until she takes one of the buds out of my ear and places it in her own ear. We lie in bed facing each other, holding hands and listening to the music. After a while I place my hand around Carly's waist and pull her body into mine and kiss her deeply, we haven't had sex for about two weeks, which is so unlike us because we are usually at it like rabbits. Come to think of it, we have hardly kissed either. We have been consumed with this Court case and we have let it infect our relationship.

Carly lets out a small moan as I start to kiss her neck. She runs her nails down my back and digs them into my bum pulling me closer "Ben, I need you," she whispers.

"I'm right here, I'm not going anywhere and I'm going to take my time with your beautiful body. I love you so much, Carly."

The next day we arrive at court and Carly is ushered into a room where she's meeting her lawyer. Andrew organised Jack Cooper to represent Carly the first week she was in Sydney. We've spoken to him a few times over the phone.

I knock on the door of the room. "They are ready for you, babe." Carly freezes and she doesn't move. I go over to her. "I will walk in with you, it's going to be ok," I whisper as I kiss her forehead.

Carly takes my hand and we walk into the courtroom. I have to let her hand go as she walks to the desk and sits with Jack. She turns her back to George's Lawyer while she's talking to Andrew, Jack and myself. All of a sudden I see Carly tense up, and I know without looking that George has entered the room. She starts to shake and I reach my hand over and take her hand in mine and squeeze gently, she closes her eyes and tries to control her breathing. After a while I feel her body relax and she opens those beautiful hazel eyes and gives me a soft smile. I love her so much but I'm worried how she is going to handle this week. I know this is going to tough and I'll be there for her the whole way.

Judge Harvey enters the room at 9 am and we all have to stand up until he sits. There is no jury so the Judge will be deciding the verdict. The first day is taken up with the lawyers having their say about what had happened to Carly and what should happen to George. It is so long winded and I don't understand much of what is said. Nicole isn't allowed in court because she is to give evidence, she had been a witness to how he treated Carly and also the first attack. Even though Carly didn't press charges after the first attack there was still the police and hospital report, which should count for something.

When we break for lunch we go to a café and sit in a booth in the back. We have just about finished our meal when Carly's mum walks up to the table. "You need to turn around and walk out of here," Carly says, not giving her a chance to speak.

"Carly, I just want to see how you are and tell you that I miss you."

"You don't care about me, I have always come second to George, and even though he put me in hospital twice you still take his side. I have nothing to say to you so go away before I get really angry. You disgust me and I don't want to look at your face anymore." Kathy has the nerve to look upset.

"Kath, I think you need to go. No one here wants anything to do with you and you're embarrassing yourself," Andrew says. We all keep eating our lunch and ignoring her like she isn't there, and eventually she leaves. I'm assuming she went back to George. I look at Andrew and he looks sad.

That night we all go to bed early. Carly's mentally and physically exhausted so after our shower I lay a towel on the bed and get Carly to lay on her stomach while I give her a massage with scented oils.

On the second day of the trial Constables Smyth and Hadden, Ambos Martin and Steve plus the attending doctor at the hospital go in the witness box. It's surreal hearing in their words what had happened to Carly. After lunch it's Carly's turn in the witness box and I can see that she's petrified. After every question she has to take a moment to calm herself so she doesn't stutter.

Jack stands up first and asks her questions about her life growing up with George and the attack, it was really hard watching her struggle to talk to a room full of strangers about something so personal. I could see she was embarrassed at times. She looks at Jack when he asks her questions but when she answers she focuses on me. Before I know it the Judge calls an end to the day and announces that George's Lawyer will cross-examine Carly tomorrow.

That night Carly and I decide to get fish and chips and eat it sitting on the beach. We need to unwind, and the sea air plus the sound of the waves always calms her. After we finish our meal we just sit there watching the world go by and eventually the sun goes down. Carly sits between my legs and leans against my chest. For the first time in such a long time she relaxes. We sleep really well that night, I think it is a combination of the sea air, exhaustion and feeling relaxed at the beach.

Carly wakes early, has a shower and tries to eat breakfast but she can't stomach it. On the drive to the court house Andrew has to pull over because she needs to throw up. He pulls over just in time, I lean across and hold her hair and rub her back until she has finished. My heart goes out to her and I feel so fucking frustrated because I can't take away her pain. We pull into the car park just as Kathy and George are getting out of her car. When George sees us he gives Carly an evil smile and waves at us. Carly tightens her grip on my hand and I can feel her body start to shake. I pull her tightly into my body and just hold her and reassure her that she's safe and that George will NEVER touch her again.

Carly starts the day in the witness stand with George's Lawyer cross-examining her. When she doesn't answer quick enough for him he snaps his fingers or rolls his eyes to make her uncomfortable and stutter. I can hear George laughing at her. Fuck I want to kill him. I have never felt so much rage and anger towards another human being before. Jack asks to approach the Judge and he explains that Carly has a stuttering problem and she's taking her time so she can answer as clearly as she can. The Judge instructs George's Lawyer to allow Carly time to answer. She's cross-examined all morning and George's Lawyer tries to trip her up on many occasions, but my girl stands firm and answer every question truthfully. I'm so proud of her.

We stop for lunch and we're so relieved Carly's time in the witness stand is over. Jack informs us that he has no need to call Nicole, he was only going to use her if things weren't going well. Plus she wasn't there at the second attack and the first one doesn't count because Carly didn't press charges. The up side is that Jack is very happy with her time in the witness box.

After lunch Jack and George's Lawyer give their closing arguments, which go on forever. The Judge states that Court will be back in session tomorrow morning at 10 am so he can deliver his verdict. Nicole comes around to Andrew's that night and we have a BBQ and a few drinks and try to unwind.   We go inside and sit on the lounge watching a movie. Carly falls asleep with her head resting on my chest and her arm across my stomach. I don't have the heart to wake her so I carry her to bed. She starts to stir as I close the bedroom door with my foot. I get her to stand while I help her undress, and once she's naked I ask her to lay on her back and then kiss my way up her beautiful body and give her two orgasms using my tongue. Carly grabs my hair as she pulls me up and then rolls me on my back and straddles me as she guides my cock into her. She rides me like her life depends on it and as I'm getting close to coming she slows her body way down to prolong my orgasm and clenches her pussy around my cock and milks me. Needless to say we both sleep well.

We arrive at the courthouse at 9.45 am and take our places inside the courtroom. At 10 am Judge Harvey enters the room and we all stand until he takes a seat. The Judge reads the verdict on the charge of aggravated assault occasioning bodily harm – 'GUILTY'. The Judge speaks to George and tells him what he did to Carly was despicable and unprovoked and that George will serve time in jail. The sentencing hearing is set for a months' time.

I'm ecstatic, George will finally pay for what he did to Carly. Jack explains to us that Carly doesn't have to be there for the hearing and that he will call her once it is over. He also asks if she wants to say anything to the Judge before he hands down George's sentence. She can write it in a victim impact statement but she doesn't have to decide now. I am so relieved this is finally over, however he's free to go where he wants until the fourth of December.

Carly hugs Jack and then races to us. Nicole and Carly are in each other's arms crying and laughing. That night we go out for dinner to celebrate. Before we go we call my mum and dad and then Darcy and Lily. Carly promises them that we will tell the others when we get back.

26 | CARLY

On Saturday at lunch time Nicole comes around and announces that were going out to see a live band tonight. Nicole's two sisters are coming with us. Sally is twenty-three and Monica is nineteen. She tells me the name of the band and I have never heard it before, but I'm game to discover a new band. We get to Perth about 7 pm and made our way to Metros. It's a great place to watch live
music. We have to line up to go inside, which is strange for a band I have never heard of.

"What's the name of this band again?"

Nicole and Ben burst out laughing. "Babe, we lied to you about the name of the band, we are here to see OneRepublic."

I squeal and jump up and down "You guys are too good to me," I say as I kiss and hug them both.

"As much as I love you, Chica, it was all Ben. He said that you told him once they were coming, and after what has gone down this week you really deserve to have some fun and let your hair down."

"You are way too good to me, Ben Richardson," I say as I hug and kiss him.

As we're waiting to go inside the girls are people watching. "Oh my god, have you seen how many hot guys there are?" asks Nicole.

"Do you remember what a guy feels or looks like now you bat for the other team, Mon?" Sally says with a smirk.

"Sal, be careful, you might opening Pandora's Box," says Nicole.

"Don't talk like you have been around the block when you haven't even opened the front door yet, Sal," Monica says.

Ben gives me a confused look and I laugh. "Sally is a virgin and Monica is now in her first female relationship," I whisper.

"Ohhhh, I see, or at least I think I do," Ben laughs. "This is going to be an interesting night."

"Honey, you have no idea," I say with a smile.

The banter between the sisters is fun to watch. Monica is so quick witted and sarcastic, and when you are a friend of hers she gives you her all; Nicole says what pops in her brain, she has no filter; and Sally is the quietest of the three. Don't get me wrong, she's not backward in coming forward, it's just that the other two are so far out there. They are all so close and because I am best friends with Nicole I am like their fourth sister. Monica is in the final year of her hair dressing apprentice-ship and Sally is a PA.

You can tell they are sisters, they all have green eyes. Nicole and Sally have brown hair — Nicole's is short and Sally's is long and wavy — and they're about five foot nine and of slim to medium build. Monica is shorter and this week her hair is red with long layers; she is very curvy and has big boobs. These three attract attention no matter where they go.

Two young Policemen walk past us. "How I would love to be sandwiched between those two," Nicole sighs.

"Get your muff out Nic," yells Monica. "Show 'em what they are missing."

Ben just looks at me. "It's gunna get worse, babe. Wait til they start drinking," I laugh.

After a while the doors open and we're allowed inside. I buy myself a OneRepublic t-shirt and then we make our way to the bar. The warm up act comes on stage; her name is Emma and she was one of the contestants from The Voice. The drinks are flowing and all of us are having a great time, just what I need. Emma finishes her set, which was good, but I'm excited to see OneRepublic. To get the crowd going they pump up the music and Havana Browns Warrior comes on. Ben stands back watching the four of us dance. Somehow I find myself in the middle of the girls and they are dry humping and grinding into me. I am used to it so I just go with it, I love these girls. I look up and Ben is smiling at me. He mouths '*I love you*' and it melts my heart.

When the song finishes I go back to Ben. He leans into me and whispers in my ear, "Fuck that was so hot, babe."

"You liked that, did you?" I smile.

"Every straight guy does, trust me. It wasn't just me watching, there were a lot of guys enjoying the show," he says laughing.

"Have you had a threesome, foursome, gangbang, orgy?"

Ben laughs. "I thought I was going to have a threesome once but it fell through. What about you?"

"Nah, I'm not into girls, I don't want to play with something I already have. Plus I don't want to be with two guys at the same time. So, is a threesome something you are still interested in?" I ask nervously.

"Babe, I'm not sharing you with anyone, you are all mine and I am all yours." He kisses me and pulls me in close.

The girls come over as the lights dim and I hold my breath with excitement waiting for them to come on stage.

OneRepublic are amazing. Ryan Tedder, the lead singer, interacted with the crowd really well. They sing old and new songs and because Beyoncé is playing at the Perth Arena just a few minutes' walk away and Ryan had written her song Halo, he attempted to sing the song but he couldn't remember the words and asked for a copy. The crowd helped him out and by the time we had finished the song he was handed the words. We dance and sing, the crowd is really chilled and enjoying the show. The song *What Does The Fox Say* by Ylvis plays as One Republic leave the stage, and everyone is singing and dancing to that stupid but very catchy song.

We get more drinks and dance to the great music the DJ plays. Ben dances with the four of us and I think he enjoys being the centre of attention. A guy starts getting closer to the back of Nicole and is checking her out. He is very tall, well over six foot, built like a brick shithouse with light coloured short hair. Nicole notices me looking at her and I mouth '*behind you*'. She turns around and the guy gives her a panty dropping smile. Nicole places her hands behind her back and gives me the thumbs up as she dances with her new friend.

Sally rolls her eyes, I think she would panic if a guy did that to her. Sal doesn't have any confidence when it comes to boys and hopefully she will loosen up a bit after a few more drinks. Both boys and girls are eyeing up Monica, she just oozes sex appeal and people flock towards her. She dances in her own little world, totally oblivious to the attention she's getting.

After a while Nicole comes back and asks me to go to the toilet with her. "WOW Carly, he is so fuckin' hot it's crazy," Nicole beams. "His name is Max, he's twenty-six and in the Army. Carls I bet he looks amazing in his uniform, and hopefully out of it too." She winks.

"He must lift weights coz you don't get a body like that without a lot of work."

"His arms are solid and he has really big hands and feet, so I'm hoping that goes for the size of his cock too."

I laugh and hug her. "I have really missed you Nicole."

"Right back atcha Chica, but one day I will surprise you and move to Sydney. I can't live forever without you."

"That would be amazing. Hey, is he on his own or does he have some mates with him? Sally really needs some male attention."

"He said he is on a Bucks do with some of the guys from the base. I'll speak to him."

We go back to Ben and see him and Max in deep conversation. I stop and look at Nicole, who gives me a confused look. "I don't know what's going on coz I didn't introduce them," she says.

Ben sees us approach, smiles and holds his arm out for me. I walk right up to him and wrap my arms around his neck and give him a kiss.

I whisper in his ear "Everything ok?"

"Yeah, babe, it's all good. When you two went to the toilet Max came over and introduced himself and we have just been talking. He seems like a stand up guy."

The four of us stand there talking for a while before Sally and Monica join us. Ben and Max go and get us more drinks while we talk about Max.

"Holy fuck, Nic, if you don't fuck his brains out tonight I will disown you. He's making me consider going back to taking cock again," laughs Monica.

"Jesus Christ Mon, keep your voice down, people can hear you," Sally scolds.

"You are such a prude, you know what you need? You need a stiff cock up ya. When are you going to give up your V card? Surely it expired a long time ago."

"Fuck off Mon, you are so obsessed with my sex life."

"What sex life? I doubt you know what a cock looks or feels like."

Thank God just then the guys come back with more drinks because I can see that conversation getting completely out of control. I notice Nicole whisper something in Max's ear. He smiles, nods and walks off. I look at Nicole, she winks and has a sly smile on her face.

About five minutes later Max comes back with three other guys. He introduces us to Pedro, Whitey and Richard. I don't know what is in the water in the Army but these guys are hot and buff.

They seem nice enough, though Pedro seems a bit up himself. He is giving it the *'big I am'*, telling us how many times he has jumped out of a plane, about the expensive car he drives and the big house he owns in Melbourne. I believe when a guy feels it necessary to big note himself he is over compensating and is lacking in another area. Whitey and Richard seemed nice and quite taken with Sally. Poor thing, it's like sharks circling their prey; she is so out of her depth.

All of us go to dance, Sally is in the middle of Richard and Whitey, Monica is dancing with Pedro, Nicole with Max, and me with my Ben. We dance for quite a long time, Max can't keep his eyes off Nicole and she is loving it. Pedro leaves after a while, probably realising he is getting nowhere with Monica.

After a while Nicole whispers, "He's coming home with me tonight."

"Glad to hear it because he has been mentally undressing you all night and I would hate for him to go home with blue balls. That's just cruel, bitch," I laugh.

We all decide it's time to go. Both Richard and Whitey ask for Sally's number so she stores her number in their phones. Richard calls her straight away so he knows she had put the correct one in. He also takes her phone, takes a photo of himself and Sally, attaches the photo and puts his name to his number. I think he's really into her, and I have to say they look damn fine together.

Richard walks us to the train station, making sure he walks next to Sal. I can see his hand twitching really close to hers and I think if she just moves her hand a few centimetres he will hold her hand, but I think he's being respectful and I like that.

We say goodbye to Richard as we board the train. Nicole is sitting on Max's lap with her tongue down his throat while the rest of us chat. About ten minutes into the train ride Sally receives a text message from Richard. She wouldn't say what it said but she has a huge smile on her face the whole way home.

When we get off the train we put Sal and Mon in one taxi because they both still live at home, and then Ben, myself, Nicole and Max get in another — we are staying at Nicole's tonight. Max and Nicole don't come up for air the whole taxi ride, and at some point during the ride home Nicole hands me her keys. Max goes to pay the fare but Ben beats him to it. We get out of the car, Max picks Nicole up and she wraps her legs around his waist. Those two are going to get very freaky tonight. I open the door, and Max growls, "Where's your bedroom," to Nicole. She points down the hall and waves to me as they disappear. Ben laughs. "I think we might have to put some music on to drown them out."

"Or we can give them a run for their money." I wink.

Ben pulls me close "I love how you think, Beautiful." He walks me backwards to our room as he is kissing me, he closes the door and guides me to the bed and stops me at the foot of the bed. "Did I tell you how amazing you looked tonight?"

"You didn't say it with your mouth but your eyes did." I smile.

"Well Beautiful, my mouth is going to devour your body all night. I hope you took your vitamins."

As predicted, Max and Nicole are loud so we put on the radio. We undress each other slowly, kissing, licking and biting. When we are completely naked Ben kisses his way down my body. He kneels on the floor and hooks my left leg over his shoulder, he places his hands on my inner thighs and opens my legs wider as he slowly licks my pussy. "Fuck babe you are so wet," Ben says and grabs my bum and pulls my pussy into his face. He licks, sucks and nibbles, it feels amazing. I have to hold onto his head because I'm worried my legs are going to give way. As my orgasm gets closer I grab Ben's hair and the closer I get the more I pull his hair, this spurs Ben on, he places two fingers inside me and I come on his fingers and mouth.

As I come down from my high I pull Ben to his feet. "Now it's your turn gorgeous." I lick and kiss my way down to his hard cock. "Fuck I love your cock especially when it's inside me,." I say as I lick the tip. Ben sucks in a breath and lets out a moan. He places his hands on my head and wraps my hair around his fingers. I look up at him. "Tell me exactly what you want me to do to you."

"Babe, I want you to lick and suck my cock until I come in your mouth and I'm going to control the pace."

"Fuck yeah, I love it when you take control, it's so hot." I lean forward and kiss the tip of his cock, I look up and make sure Ben is watching, I smile and then take him in my mouth while maintaining eye contact.

"Babe…fuck…your mouth is so talented…keep sucking."

I smile around his cock and I take more in of him my mouth and flick my tongue around. His cock pops loudly out of my mouth and I lick my way down to his balls, I know this drives him crazy. I blow on his balls and he lets out a moan. I take one in my mouth and roll it around with my tongue while my hand strokes his cock. Ben grips my hair tighter and holds me in place.   "Carly...don't   stop...fucking amazing."

I go a bit lower and run my tongue against the skin between his balls and anus, and Ben tightens his grip in my hair as he thrusts himself further into my face. I can feel his body start to shake. He moves my head up so I can take his cock in my mouth and Ben moves my head up and down, I hollow my cheeks and suck.

"Oh my god Carly..sooooo good..fuck I love you." I start to play with his balls and then I dig my nails into his bum. "Babe I'm gunna come..don't stop," he growls. His grip tightens and he holds my head still as he comes in my mouth. "Fuck me, that was out of this world."

"You haven't seen anything yet. I'll let you rest a bit and then I want more of your body," I say. We climb onto the bed exhausted. After a while I say I need a drink, so I put my pj's on and make my way to the kitchen. I'm just getting a glass out when Nicole walks in looking freshly fucked. "Looks like you are having a good time," I laugh.

"Carly I think I'm going to be walking bowlegged for the rest of my life, he is huge, definitely a two hander and forget the six pack, he has an eight pack and has the sexy as fuck V down there. He has so much stamina, and he's strong — he picks me up like I weigh nothing. We've fucked against the wall and on my bed. I've had four orgasms, he goes down on me like his life depends on it and when he's inside me won't let me close my eyes. He looks deep into them, like he's looking into my soul. What the fuck, I think he has ruined me for other guys."

"Ahem." We spin around and see Ben and Max standing there in their boxers, smiling.

I take a good look at Max, bite my bottom lip and say to Nicole under my breath, "Holy fuck." Nicole smiles at me like the cat that got the cream, smug bitch.

"Carly, you wanna close your mouth and stop drooling," laughs Ben.

"Sweetheart, we have two hot as fuck nearly naked guys in front of us and you expect me not to react? Really?" I say as I hand him and Max a drink.   We sit down at the kitchen table, Nic and I in our pj's and the guys in their boxers. It feels a bit weird, like it's an interval. Ben and Max get on really well. Max seems easy going and he can't keep his hands off Nicole, it's good to see.

After a little time I give Ben the look, grab his hand and say "Round two," as we hurry to our room. I turn back to Max and Nicole. "By the way can you two please keep it down? I love Nicole but I don't want to hear her scream 'deeper' or 'fuck me big boy'," I laugh as we shut the door.

Ben pounces on me as soon as the door is shut, he strips me of my pj's very quickly and throws me on the bed. "After I make you scream my name as you come, I want to take you from behind"

"I'm all yours sweetheart, anything you want," I reply with a sexy smile. True to his word I scream his name as I come, fuck he's good. I get up, turn around and back into him. He smacks my arse as I press into his cock, I love a sexy spanking and it's such a turn on.

Ben guides his cock into me, taking it slowly, grabbing my hips to make sure we go at his pace. He slides in and out of me easily because I'm so damned wet. He slaps my arse again which makes me clench down on his cock. "Fuuuuucccccckkkk you feel so good babe," Ben starts to pick the pace a bit and he gently pushes my head down towards the mattress so we have a better angle. As he's pumping into me I reach underneath and start to rub my clit, Ben must have looked down because I hear him gasp and then growl, "You are going to kill me, you know that don't you? That's so fuckin' hot babe, don't stop." I am so free with Ben, I'm not shy or uncomfortable about anything.

As Ben is pumping into me he reaches down, pulls his cock out and slams in two fingers, he leans back and watches as they go in and out of me. He pulls them out and slowly runs them up to my anus and rubs a finger around my hole, I let out a small moan, I have never had back door play before but this feels good and I am interested to see where this is going. Ben slams his cock back into me and starts to pump fast and hard, I can feel my orgasm building as I rub my clit, Ben's slamming into me with his cock and his thumb is playing around back there. "I'm so close Ben, make me come," I moan. Ben increases his pace and inserts his thumb in my arse. "Bennnnnnnnn!" I scream as I experience the most intense orgasm that just keeps going and going, my body is shuddering and if it wasn't for Ben holding me around my waist I think I would have collapsed on the bed. As I am coming down from my high Ben cries out and comes inside me, and we fall on the bed exhausted. I roll over so I am facing him. "You are an amazing lover Ben Richardson and I am one lucky girl. I love you so much."

"So that was ok with you? I have never tried that before and I wasn't sure what you would think."

"As I have said in the past I know you wouldn't do anything to hurt or degrade me and I trust you with my body. If I wasn't up for it I would have stopped you, you don't have to worry about that. I enjoyed it," I say with a smile.

"It looked and felt like you enjoyed it, would you be ok if we took it further?"

"Are you talking about anal sex?" Ben just nods and looks embarrassed.   "If you asked me about trying anal before tonight I probably would have said no, but after what you just did honey, I'm up for it. But we will have to take it slow, your cock is a lot bigger than your thumb," I laugh.

"We can do that babe, I will have to get lube."

"Ummmm no need, I have some lube," I say, and now it's my turn to look embarrassed.

"Okay, why do you have lube?"

"Well…ummmm..you see..I have two vibrators and sometimes I need lube."

"I had no clue, were are they?"

"In a purple box under the bed at home," I reply.

"When was the last time you used them? We have sex pretty much every day." He has a concerned look on his face.

I hold his face in my hands "Honey I haven't used them since you and I started sleeping together, the batteries have probably died by now. I have no need for them because I have you. While we are on the subject, I have to let you know that I have a few porno's too."

Ben looks surprised "How many?"

"I think about ten maybe fifteen."

"Carly, you are full of surprises." Ben says shaking his head.

"Is that a good or a bad thing?"

"Babe, it's a very good thing, I had no idea. Would you be comfortable watching them with me? And maybe we could use your toys from time to time?"

"That's something I never thought I would do with anyone else, but yeah, why not? I'm having a lot of firsts with you," I say as I kiss him. We're both turned on by the conversation and we make love for the third time that night. We fall asleep just as the sun is coming up.

It is just after 1pm when I wake. Ben is snoring away and doesn't stir when I get dressed. I make my way to the kitchen because I'm hungry and thirsty. I look in Nicole's fridge and there isn't much there except some eggs, milk and butter, so I look in the freezer and find some bacon. Cool, bacon and eggs it is. I find a loaf of bread in the pantry and I'm all set. I defrost the bacon in the microwave and turn the oven on so the bacon will keep hot while I cook the eggs.

I put on the radio and I'm singing and dancing as I get the eggs out of the fridge, then I turn around towards the stove and find Max sitting at the kitchen table. I scream and nearly drop the eggs. "What the fuck Max, you can't do that, you scared the shit out of me." I place the eggs on the counter and sit down waiting for my heart to slow down.

"I'm sorry, Carly, I didn't want to disturb you," laughs Max.

"No worries, are you hungry?"

"I am starving, I was coming in here to see what there is to eat when I discovered you'd beaten me to it."

"Can you check the pantry and see if there are any tins of baked beans and spaghetti in there because I know Ben will be hungry."

Max walks over to the pantry. "There are baked beans and a tin of tomatoes, do you want them as well?"

"Yeah, may as well." Max passes them to me "Would you like a tea or coffee?" I ask.

"I would kill for a strong coffee, white with two sugars please. How long have you known Nicole?"

"We met first day of high school and have been best friends ever since. She stood up for me against a bully that day, and we hit it off right away. We have quirky senses of humour and we can read each other so well, at times we don't even need words."

"Nicole said that you and Ben live in Sydney now, and are only back for two weeks."

I don't know why, but I found myself telling Max about George and the court case. He was stunned when I finished.

"Fuck…I don't know what to say, Carly."

I hand him his coffee. "It's ok, he's been found guilty and will serve some jail time, and he can't get to me anymore."

"When do you find out what his sentence is?"

"The fourth of December, so it's only a few weeks away. I have to say seeing him in Court was hard, I tried to block him out but it was difficult when the whole time he was sat a few metres away from me. Thank god I had Ben, Nicole and my dad otherwise I doubt I would have gone through with it."

"I hope he gets the book thrown at him. Any guy who physically hurts a female is the lowest of the low. My wish for him is that he becomes someone's bitch while he's locked up, Karma will get him."

"Anyway..enough of that. Tell me about you," I say, trying to lighten the conversation.

"I was born in Penrith NSW, and my family still live there. I have 5 sisters all younger than me, and they all still live at home so when I go back on leave it's like living in a crazy farm," he laughs. "I love my sisters and I'm very protective of them, I'm twenty-six and have been in the Army for eight years. I have been stationed at Campbell Barracks in Swanbourne for just over a year."

"Have you any kids, been married or engaged? How long was your longest relationship?"

He gulps "Okay…ummmm..no kids, never been married or engaged, longest relationship was two years and that finished three years ago."

"Why did it end?"

"WOW, you are really going for broke."

"Nicole means the world to me and even though we don't share the same DNA she is still my sister so I would hate for her to hook up with a douche bag. For the record, I don't think you are but I still need to ask these questions."

"Yeah I get that, I can see how close the two of you are. It ended because she couldn't handle me being away for so long when I went to Iraq. She packed up and left while I was on deployment and I got a Dear John letter four months in. I haven't seen or spoken to her since."

"Do you miss her?"

"I used to, but they say time heals and I believe that is true. She is the only woman I have lived with besides my mum and sisters. I miss coming home to someone."

"That's sad, I understand lonely. Even though I lived with my family I still felt alone. Thank god for Nicole, I don't think I would of survived my teenage years if it hadn't have been for her and her crazy family. I spent a lot of time in her house," I laugh.

"Babe, why are you interrogating Max?" yawns Ben as he walks towards me with that sleepy look on his face.

I pull him in for a kiss. "We're just getting to know each other, that's all. I'm about to make bacon, eggs, baked beans and cooked tomatoes. I'm assuming you're hungry?"

"Of course I am. You wore me out last night, babe," he says with a sexy smirk.

"You sit down and I will make you a coffee."

Ben and Max chat as I cook our food.

"Max, can you please wake sleeping beauty and let her know food awaits her in the kitchen?"

Max salutes me as he walks out. "I like him Ben, he's such a nice guy. I hope something comes of this for Nicole," I say as I place his plate full of food in front of him. After a while Nicole and Max come out of her bedroom. I notice he is holding her hand, how sweet.

That evening we all take Max back to the base. Nicole is very quiet on the way home. When we get home I give Ben the look and he goes to bed, leaving us to talk. I sit down next to Nicole on the lounge and take her hand. "Ok hun, spill."

Nicole starts babbling "Carly, I'm so screwed, he's amazing. I like him, I really like him. I don't do this, I'm a fuck 'em and leave 'em kinda gal. There was a flirty thing with Ryan but it wasn't serious. Max makes my heart skip a beat when he looks at me, touches me, kisses me. I can't think when I'm around him. He is soooo fuckin' hot, and he's the most amazing lover who makes sure I am completely satisfied before he even thinks about himself. And that body, I'm wet just thinking about it…what the fuck am I gunna do?"

"Awwww hun, you have it bad. Did you make plans to see each other again?"

"Yeah, he said he would like to take me out for dinner sometime this week. He said he will call me."

"He's keen Nicole, the two of you had a wonderful weekend and he's a great guy who's into you. This is new territory for you, hun."

"Carly, he has the most talented tongue and his body is rock hard. I swear his cock is so big that when he rams it into me it nearly comes out of my mouth."

"NICOLE…you kill me," I laugh.

"Chica, he is huge. When I gave him a blow job I was concerned I wouldn't be able to get my mouth around it, it's not just long, it's thick too. And it stays up for a long, long time; he has stamina, he wore me out," she says with a love sick smile. "I have a photo of it, you wanna see?"

"Hell yeah, just don't tell Ben." Nicole scrolls through her phone. "How many photos did you take?"

"I took a few of us at the pub on Saturday night, then some later in my room, and a few while he slept."

"Does he know about the ones when he was passed out?"

"Ummmm I don't think I mentioned it," she says with a cheeky smile.

"You are so naughty, Nicole." She shows me a photo where Max is lying on his back with one arm under his head and the other resting on his impressive eight pack; the sheet is just covering his legs and his cock is lying against his right leg...fuck me...it's flaccid and it's massive. I look up at Nicole and notice she is smiling. "Take that smirk off your face you smug bitch. How did that fit inside you?"

"I don't know, but there is no way I could go back to what I'm used to, no other guy will measure up, he's ruined me Chica. I just hope he wants to see me again."

"I have a good feeling about Max, he's a good guy, Nic. He said he will call and I believe he will." I get up and hug her goodnight, then go to bed and snuggle into a sleeping Ben.

On Wednesday Nicole gets a call from Max to see if he can take her out for dinner. She is so excited, I have never seen her like this over a guy before. When she gets home from work I help her pick out something to wear for her date, she is so nervous. She has a few things to choose from and decides on a cornflour blue halter neck dress that is fitted and sits just above her knees. She wears it with silver four inch strappy heels, and I do her hair and makeup. She looks beautiful.

"Shit girl, you look hot, I'd do you," I laugh.

"We're going to head off before Max gets here. We are staying at Dad's tonight so you have the whole house to get freaky in," I say as I kiss her goodbye.

Just as Ben and I get to the car Max pulls into the driveway. "Nice ride mate," whistles Ben. Max is driving a red soft top jeep.

"Just a tip," I say to Max, "but if I was you I would put the top on because she looks amazing and wouldn't appreciate her hair being blown everywhere."

"Carly, you're a life saver. Ben wanna give me a hand?" Ben helps Max and they chat like they have known each other for years, it's great to see. Max leans into the passenger seat and pulls out a massive bouquet of red roses.

"Oh my god your good, she's going to cream herself when she sees those. Make sure you show my girl a good time."

Max stands tall, smiles and salutes me. "Yes Ma'am." Then he walks to Nicole's front door as Ben and I get in Dad's car and drive off.

We decide to have pizza for dinner and watch a DVD. I walk behind Ben as we enter the shop to choose a movie, he stops all of a sudden and because I'm not paying attention I walk straight into him "What the hell Ben, why did you stop?"

"I think we should skip the movie, I just feel like pizza and then an early night," he says with a strange look on his face.

"What? I thought you were up for a movie?"

"Well, well, well if it isn't my lying slut of a sister."

Before I know what's happening Ben has George by the throat up against the wall. "You don't talk to her you evil cunt, I hope they throw the book at you and you serve a long sentence. My wish for you is that you get beaten and fucked in the arse daily because that's what you deserve." Ben turns to me, grabs my hand and we start walking to the car.

We are halfway to the car when George coughs, bends over and puts his hands on his knees "You'll pay for that."

Ben turns to go after George again "NO..please B..Ben, this is what h..he wants. He's n..not worth it. All that ma..matters is you and me..p...please." Ben just stands there staring at George, his hands clenching at his sides and breathing rapidly. I touch his arm and it takes a while for him to look at me. The look on his face tears at my heart, he looks so angry but his eyes are sad.

"Babe we n..need to go, come o..on," I plead.

"You're welcome to the retard. She can't even talk properly, stupid bitch!" George yells as we walk away.

Ben roars as he runs past me knocking George over and they both roll around on the ground throwing punches. The next thing I know Max is pulling Ben off George and he won't let him go. "I'm gunna kill the cunt, get off me Max."

"Can't do that mate, you need to calm down."

"The fuck I do, I can't hold it in anymore, I want to hurt him so fuckin' bad."

"Ben you need to cool it, you're upsetting Carly," Max says.

Ben stops, looks at me and sees I'm in Nicole's arms crying. Max relaxes his hold and walks Ben to us, he reaches his hands out and grab my face. "Carly I am so sorry I wasn't there to protect you, I failed you and I will never forgive myself for that," he says as he collapses to the ground with his head in his hands.

I sit down on the ground and pull his hands away from his face. "B..Ben look at m..me please."

Ben looks up. "I am so ashamed of myself, you told me what he did to you, I should have gotten ready at your place and then it wouldn't have happened, he's a monster, he nearly killed you."

"But h..he didn't. I w..will get jus...justice Ben, he's g..going to Jail wh..where he be..belongs. Ca..ca..can we please g..go home?" Ben takes my hand, kisses the back of it, helps me to stand and leads me to the car. Nicole and Max follow us, I take a breath. "I am so sorry I have ruined your date," I say to Nicole and Max.

"Carly, you haven't ruined anything, I'm just glad that we were driving past when this all happened. Are you two going to be ok?" asks Max.

Ben is silent, his pain is palpable. "I just need to get him away from here, can you help me get him to the car?" I ask.

Max talks quietly to Ben and he finally gets him in the passenger seat. I hug Nicole and Max. "Thank god you were here. We'll be ok, thank you again."

"Call me, Chica, anytime. Love you," Nicole says as I start the car.

Ben is silent as I drive away.

"Do you want to go back to Dad's or do you want to go somewhere else?" Ben doesn't say anything, I'm not sure he even heard me. "Ben..did you hear me?" Still nothing. I pull over on the side of the road, get out and start walking. "Fuck this I don't deserve to be ignored," I say to myself as I walk away.

After a while I hear Ben calling my name. I don't stop. Eventually Ben catches up to me, grabs my hand and spins me around so I am facing him.

I am spitting mad. "You have no right to ignore me and shut me out. He kicked ME, he punched ME, he tried to kill ME, and don't you think I have had enough without you shutting me out? I get that you are angry and that's why you went after him, I totally understand that, but you have allowed that monster to get between us. He robbed me of my childhood, of a safe and loving home and now us... you are letting him win," I say as I wrench my hand out of Ben's grip and walk away. I can't take anymore so I start to run as fast as I can. I just need to get out of here.

After about five minutes I stop running because it hits me all of a sudden that I have nowhere to go. I can't go to Nicole's because she is on a date and I don't want to be there and cramp their style if and when they go there after dinner, and if I go to Dad's he will ask all kinds of questions that I don't want to answer. I stand on the side of the road trying to catch my breath as tears roll down my cheeks. I notice a car stop next to me, and I look up and see Ben get out of the driver's side. He stops just in front of me. "I have nowhere to go," I cry.

Ben pulls me into his arms. "I am so sorry, Carly. I let the whole situation take me over without thinking how it was going to affect you. You are so fucking brave, you stood up in Court and didn't waver when things got tough. His lawyer tried to trip you up but you were so strong and kept to the truth. I was in awe watching you. I'm sorry I let him get to me, but I want him dead, that way I know there will never be a chance of him attacking you again. I have never hated someone so much in my life and it scares me."

"I understand hatred, I really do, but you can't let it consume you because the hate will infect the good and then he wins. The perfect revenge for me is to have a happy and successful life and that's what I intend to do and I want you to be a part of that."

Ben holds my face and looks deep into my eyes. "HE.WILL. NOT.WIN...I promise you we will have a wonderful life together, Carly." He pulls me into his chest and holds me so tight I can feel his heart thumping. "Do you want to go for a walk along the beach?"

"I'd really like that," I say.

Ben takes my hand and we walk along the beach enjoying the view. I'm loving the feeling of the sand between my toes. We stop and watch the last of the sun disappear, then, without any warning, Ben picks me up and runs towards the sea. I scream for him to put me down but he just keeps going. He runs into the water and we fall forward, I go under the surface and come up spluttering.

"You're crazy," I laugh.

"I would have done anything to see that smile and hear you laugh. I love you, Carly," Ben says as he pulls me in for a kiss.

"And I love you, always."

We stay in the water for a while, kissing, until we get cold. We make our way to the car and thank god Dad has some towels in his boot because I'm freezing. Ben drives us home and we go straight for the shower. We explain to Dad what happened with George, and Dad is livid.

"Dad there is nothing we can do, George will continue to say vile and disgusting things about me, he gets off on it. The trick is to try not to react. I know it's hard but that's what he wants. He'll be locked up soon like the animal he is, and fingers crossed it's a horrible time for him."

"I have written to the Judge to inform him which Prison I work at so George won't be sent there," says my dad.

"Dad, I want to ask you something and I want an honest answer no matter what it is."

"Of course, Ratbag."

"I know you have said all along that you hope George serves some jail time, but he is still your son. I want to know how you are coping with all of this."

"I have to admit it's not easy. He has to pay for what he did to you but I'm afraid for him when he enters the system. Plus I had your Mother on the phone begging me to try to convince you to drop the charges before the trial started. The right thing was to go through with the trial and he needs to serve time, I just hope this sorts him out."

"Why didn't you tell me about Mum?"

"Carly, you had enough to deal with and I didn't want to put more on your plate. Besides, in the end I just stopped taking her calls."

"Okaaay…so now that Mum has been brought up..how are things between the two of you?"

"The marriage is over, I should have left years ago and I should have stepped in when she treated you second to George. I don't understand why she does it and I am so sorry I never stopped it."

I walk over and hug my dad. "I don't blame you for what she did, it's not your fault. I love you Dad."

My dad pulls me in tight. "I love you too, Ratbag. Anyway..I'm starving. What's for dinner?"

We order pizza and have a few drinks while we wait for it to be delivered. We go to bed early but Ben is distracted. I put my hands on either side of his face. "I need you Ben."

"I'm right here babe."

"I mean all of you, I have your body but I want your mind too.

Please come back to me."

"I'm sorry, babe. I'm here, you have all of me," Ben says as he lays me on my back and covers my body with his. "Carly, you are so beautiful and I love you with all my heart." I blush and look away from him. "One day you will be comfortable enough to take a compliment from me, and I look forward to that day."

Ben and I make love for the next couple of hours, we need the closeness and we don't want to rush our time together. I feel so loved.

27 | CARLY

A few days before we fly back to Sydney I meet Nicole for lunch alone because we need girly time. And I need her to fill me in on her date with Max.

I get to the café before her and order us a BLT each and pot of tea for 2. Nicole arrives just as the waitress places the tea on the table. I give her a hug and kiss hello.

"First things first," she says, "how are you and Ben after last night?"

"We're ok, after we left you Ben wouldn't talk to me so I pulled over and walked off. I get that he feels guilty because he wants to protect me, but he can't let it consume him because that way George wins. Anyway, long story short, we talked and we're good."

"Do you blame Ben?"

"No, not at all. The only person to blame for attacking me is George and I refuse to let him ruin my relationship with Ben. Anyway enough of that, how was your date? I want all the details, do not miss a thing."

"Well, after we saw you and Ben leave, George decided to start on me."

I slap my hand over my mouth. "Oh my god Nic I am so sorry."

"It's not your fault, Chica, that he's a six pack short of a carton. When you drove away Max and I walked to his car and unbeknownst to us, George followed. Seriously, is he blind? Can't he see the size of Max? Anyway, as Max opens the door for me, George spits at me as he walks past. Who does that? Luckily it only hit my arm. Max saw red and grabbed him by the back of his neck and slammed him down on the bonnet of the car, yelling at him and asking him what was his problem. I thought Max was going to kill him. He told George to apologise to me but at first he refused. He changed his mind and did apologise when Max tightened his grip on his neck and also brought his arm up behind his back. But I know he didn't mean it, so I took matters into my own hands and kicked him in the balls. He would have fallen to the ground if Max hadn't had a hold of him. Hopefully I have prevented him from ever having children," Nicole laughs.

"Way to go, Hun. I have never been able to stand up to him that way. I'm so proud of you. Ok, so what happened then?"

"We sat in the car dumbfounded then Max said, 'Let's not let that scum spoil our night.' So we went to dinner. We went to an Italian Restaurant, I had Osso Buco and Max had Cannelloni and we got a bottle of pink wine, which was really nice, light and fruity. He held my hand while we were waiting for our food. It was like we were the only people in the restaurant, he never took his eyes off me and even during the meal he made sure his foot or leg was touching me. The conversation flowed, there was never a quiet moment. We talked about our families, jobs, travelling, music, movies and what we want in the future. It was so relaxed and normal, it scared me a bit. I'm not like this, I don't talk about my future with guys," Nicole says nervously.

"Hun, you're really into him and it looks like he's really into you. I will say the same thing you told me when Ben came along. You told me to let him in, it was scary but I did and look how great that turned out. Please do the same, let your guard down and I don't think you'll be disappointed. Ok, so back to the story, you have a great meal and then what? Don't leave out anything," I smile.

"After we finish our meal and wine I invite Max back to my house. We get back to mine and we're both a little nervous, which is crazy after the weekend. But he comes in, we sit on the lounge for a while talking and just holding hands when he leans in, touches my face and tells me how beautiful I look, then he kisses me, softly at first, but then things heat up pretty quickly. I straddle him on the lounge and he undoes my dress so the top falls down and because I can't wear a bra with that dress he gets the full view. He growls, sucks on my neck, makes his way to my tits then stands up with me still straddling him and makes his way to my room.

"The flowers he bought me smelled so lovely that I put them in my bedroom and when he opens the door the fragrance hit us, it was beautiful. He stands me at the bottom of the bed, turns on my bedside lamp, places one of my scarves over it, which gives the room a soft glow, then kneels at my feet and slowly removes my shoes while caressing my calves and feet. Once my shoes are off he stands slowly, running his hands up my legs until his hands reach the zip for my dress, he unzips me and the dress falls to the floor. I'm stood there in just my G-string while he is fully clothed.

"He goes to take it off, but I stop him, informing him that he has too many clothes on. I kneel and take his shoes off then stand up and undo every button on his shirt nice and slow, not breaking eye contact once. When the buttons are all undone I slide the shirt off his shoulders and throw it on the chair. I then walk my fingers down his chest to undo the button and zip on his jeans. I can see how hard he is and my heart skips a beat remembering how big he is. I remove his jeans and he is standing before me in his boxers. I start to kiss down his chest, making my way to his cock, but he stops me, saying that I always come first. And then he picks me up and places me on the bed.

"Then his very talented tongue went to work, he licked my pussy through my G-string. Carly, I was so fuckin' wet, it didn't take me long to come once he removed my G-string. He crawled up my body and spent quite a bit of time licking, biting and sucking my tits. When he entered me he looked deeply into my eyes, I was mesmerized by him and he never broke eye contact. He is the best lover I have ever had. He can go for a long time. I had to keep changing positions because my hips would get sore.

"We had sex three times last night and finally got to sleep about 3.30 am. Poor buggar had to get up at 6 am to get to work on time. Before he left this morning he woke me with a wonderful orgasm. I could get used to that. He asked if he could come round and see me tonight because he has something he would like to talk to me about. I said I would cook for us, that way we wouldn't get interrupted. So Chica, that's everything."

"WOW what a night, I'm wet just listening to that. What do you think he wants to talk about?"

"I'm hoping it's about making us a regular thing, I enjoy his company and the sex is out of this world, fingers crossed." Just then Nicole's mobile signalled she had received a text. She looks at her phone and a huge smile breaks out over her face.

"By the look of that stupid grin the message is from Max."

"Yeah, he said he has been thinking of me all morning and is looking forward to seeing me tonight."

"As I have said a few times, he's keen on ya, Hun, and I can see the feeling is very mutual. I'm really happy for you, he's a great guy," I say as I hug Nicole. We finish our lunch and then I walk Nicole back to her office. "Call me tomorrow, I want to know how your night went," I say as I hug and kiss her goodbye.

When I get home I attack Ben, I am so worked up about what Nicole told me happened on the date between her and Max. I make Ben a very happy guy. We have a quiet night in with Dad because we have plans with Nicole for Friday and Saturday. It's nice just hanging with my dad. Ben calls Damon to make sure Roger is ok and to remind him that we were flying home on Sunday.

On Friday afternoon Ben and I make our way to Nicole's house because we are going out for dinner and then to see a local band. Nicole had sent me a text that Max would be joining us tonight and that makes me very happy. We have only been at Nicole's for about thirty minutes when Max arrives. I notice he has a bag with him; I smile to myself because it looks like their talk went very well.

We have a few drinks before Nicole gets home from work, as soon as she drives up the driveway Max gets to his feet and meets her at the door. She squeals and jumps into his arms nearly knocking him over, they start kissing and I think they forget we are there because it gets quite heated. Eventually I clear my throat, "Either take her in the room and fuck her brains out or sit down and let me get Nicole a drink."

They stop kissing and just look into each other's eyes like they are looking into one another's souls. I have never seen Nicole like this before, it's a beautiful thing to witness, she looks so happy. Max kisses Nicole on the nose as she slides down his body so her feet are on the floor. "You are like a massive tree and I love climbing you," she says to Max with a sexy grin as we walk into the kitchen to get her a drink.

I look at Nicole. "Spill, I assume that your talk went well."

"Chica it went better than well. Max told me that he wants us to be exclusive and would like to see where this is going. I told him I am happy with the exclusive but I just don't want to be his booty call. If we are going to do this I want to have a real grown up relationship, and after talking about what we both wanted, Max asked me to be his girlfriend," Nicole says with a squeal.

"Hun, I am so fuckin' happy for you, I have never seen you like this with a guy before. I love him, I think he's great for you, he gets on really well with Ben and from what I see he treats you so well. Other than your sisters, has he met your folks?"

"No way, too early for that. If things go well then I would love for him to meet my folks, but we will see."

"Ok hun, time to get our drink on and join our men." We grab Nicole a white wine and another beer for the guys. We go into the lounge and the guys are talking rugby. Nicole just rolls her eyes because she was brought up in the west and doesn't understand rugby, so we hand them their beers and leave them and go to Nicole's room to pick out something for her to wear tonight.   We pick out a pair of jeans that make Nicole's arse look amazing. To go with them we choose a jade green low cut silk tank top and a pair of jade green flat sandals.

When I enter the lounge on my own Max asks were Nicole is, and he can't get out of his seat quick enough when I tell him she is taking a shower. Ben and I laugh as Max makes his way to the bathroom. Ben holds out his hand to me and pulls me onto his lap. Knowing Nicole and Max are going to be a while, we start to get hot and heavy. I straddle his lap and I can feel his hard on, he winks at me and then carries me to our room and makes love to me.

A couple of hours later there is a loud bang on our door. "Get his cock out of your mouth and let's get moving. I'm starving, my hunk of a man has worn me out." We hear a slap and Nicole yelps and squeals as we hear Max and Nicole run into her bedroom laughing.

We get ready and Ben looks so hot I want to jump him. He's wearing jeans, a black shirt and black converse runners, and he smells amazing, I'm wet just being near him. I wear my typical pub gear: jeans, The Who concert t-shirt and black ballet flats.

As we walk out of the bedroom Nicole whistles. "Fuck me drunk Chica you look hot as hell, I'd do ya."

"Right back atcha Hun," I say as I pull her in for a hug. "I luv ya."

Max and Ben look at each other and shrug their shoulders. "You'll get used to it," Ben says as he claps Max on the shoulder.

We get a taxi to the restaurant and have a wonderful meal with a few bottles of wine. I'm quite buzzed as we walk to the pub. to watch the band. The place is packed and the vibe is electric, I see a few familiar faces but no one I want to talk to. I need to go to the toilet, so I kiss Ben and give him my drink to look after. As I come out of the cubicle I look up and see a familiar face. "Tess is that you?"

"Oh my god, Carly. How are you?"

"I'm really good thanks, and you?"

"Yeah, no complaints. Are you living here now?"

"No. We came back for the trial, we fly home this weekend."

"I have to admit I was pleased when I wasn't called as a witness. I hate being the centre of attention, but I would have done it if they'd asked me. That day in the restaurant still gives me nightmares, so I can only imagine how you are feeling," Tess says with such sadness.

"It's ok. He has been convicted and is to be sentenced early next month. Just to know he is going to serve jail time is a good feeling. Hey, I would love for you to meet Ben and my best friend Nicole."

"I'd love to, lead the way."

As we walk up the three of them are in deep conversation. I put my arm around Ben's waist and he jumps because he didn't notice me walking up. "Ben, Nicole and Max I would like you all to meet Tess. Tess was very kind to me when my mum set me up and tried to ambush me with George. Tess was my lifeline and she wouldn't leave me alone."

Ben leans forward and hugs Tess and thanks her for taking such good care of me. Nicole pulls her into a bear hug and gets quite emotional, while Max just shakes her hand and says hello. We all stand there for a while chatting then Tess says she has to go because she is out celebrating a friends twenty first and everyone is waiting for her. As I give her a hug goodbye I become quite emotional; Tess has a very special place in my heart.

When the band starts up the place is alive and the dance floor crowded. ACDC's *Thunderstruck* starts and Max goes crazy, it turns out he is a massive ACDC fan and just loses himself in the music, I can relate. Because of his size he takes up a lot of room but when he's in the zone he needs a lot more room. It's funny to watch him, he's a great dancer and it's like the songs go right to his soul. When the song finishes he looks like he has run a marathon, he's so hyped up. We stay on the dance floor for the rest of the night.

We have a few more drinks before we move onto the nightclub. It's a strange place because when you go through the front door you walk down two flights of steps that are on a ninety degree angle, not great when you are pissed and wearing high heel shoes, but luckily I'm wearing flats tonight. At the bottom of the steps you walk into a huge room the has three bars against three walls and a sunken dance floor. The carpet is disgusting because of all the spilt drinks, so your shoes stick to it. Thank god you can't smoke in pubs and nightclubs anymore. The DJ is playing some great music and Nicole and I hit the dance floor straight away. As we are dancing we look to the guys and they are talking, oblivious as to what is going on behind them. There is a group of five girls eyeing up Ben and Max. I look at Nicole and she looks like she is going to rip someone's head off.

"It's ok, he's really into you and doesn't look at other girls the way he looks at you," I say trying to calm Nicole down. "The boys will be polite but just watch, they will not encourage anything."

We watch for a while, waiting for the girls to get the courage to approach the guys. Two girls break away from the group and they make their way to Ben and Max, egged on by the other three girls. I can see Nicole tense as one of them puts her hand on Max's arm, he spins around with a huge smile, probably thinking it's Nicole, but when he realises it's not her his smile fades and he takes a step back. The girl that approaches Ben is a bit more forward, she grabs his bum, Ben is not happy and tells her to fuck off. Just then Max puts his hands up to get the first girl to back up; he shakes his head and points to Nicole on the dance floor. He gives Nicole his panty dropping smile and walks towards her, leaving the girl standing there like a stunned mullet. I look at Ben and he's really not happy.

Once Max reaches Nicole I walk to Ben, put my arm around him and whisper in his ear, "It's not nice being felt up by a total stranger is it?"

Ben snaps his head around to look at me and then puts his head down, he knows I am talking about the first time we met. He finally looks up, places his hands on my cheeks, and looks me in the eyes. "I am so sorry for that night, I always knew I was in the wrong but now I get it."

I lean forward, kiss him and then drag him to the dance floor. I'm not angry with him, I just needed to make a point and thankfully he gets it.

We dance and drink some more until I'm really pissed and find it difficult to stand up. Ben grabs me around the waist and announces to Nicole and Max that it's time he took me home, the other two agree and we make our way to the stairs. Ben and Max have to help me because there was no way I can navigate the stairs in my condition. As soon as we get outside the fresh air hits me and I nearly pass out, thankfully Ben is still holding me and he guides me to the taxi rank. I have trouble walking, and when I announce I'm going to be sick, Ben pulls me to the side and leans me over a small wall, grabbing the back of my t-shirt so I won't fall while Nicole holds my hair. As I empty the contents of my stomach someone rubs my back. Ben leans his body into mine and speaks softly to me.

"Oh god I feel like shit," I moan as I wipe my mouth. My throat is burning and my eyes are watering, I must look like death.

"Here Chica," Nicole says as she hands me a mint "Your breath stinks," she says with a chuckle.

"So would yours if you threw up and when did I eat carrots, I fuckin' hate carrots." Really, how does that happen? Ben holds me up as we walk to the taxi, Max gets in the front while I lay across Ben and Nicole in the back. "I'm never drinking again, I'm going to die," I moan.

"Babe, you are going to be fine, I will look after you. Nicole do you have some Berocca at home?"
"Yeah, with the amount I have consumed in my lifetime I think I deserve shares in that company. I'll sort you out Chica," Nicole laughs.

I think I passed out because I don't remember the ride home. One moment I'm stretched out in the back of the taxi and the next I'm wrapped around Ben as he carries me inside Nicole's home. He places me on the lounge and follows Nicole into the kitchen to get me a drink. I look across from me and Max is sat on the lounge laughing. "What's so funny?" I slur.

"You are, can you even see me?"

I take a while to answer because it's taking a bit of time to get my thoughts from my brain to my lips. "I have to admit you are a bit fuzzy, but yeah I can see you and you look damned fine too. Just wanted you to know that," I say as I wave my index finger at him.

"Hey bitch, stop hitting on my man," Nicole laughs as she and Ben walk back into the lounge. Ben hands me a Berocca and encourages me to drink it down while it is still fizzing. I finish it and let out a burp and wipe my mouth because I don't have good control of my body and I think I spilt a little bit.

"Nicole, how about you put a porno on. I know you have some coz we bought them and our toys at the same time," I snort.

Max and Ben nearly choke on their beers. "Carly, what the fuck?" yells Ben.

"What? You said you wanted to watch them with me, so what's your problem? Unfortunately I don't have my toys with me, so that will have to wait until we get home."

"Seriously Carly, you have no filter when you're wasted. That was a private conversation."

"Okaaaay," I say slowly. "Sorry if I offended you."

"You didn't, but there are some conversations that should stay private and this is one of them. I would hate for Max and Nicole to feel uncomfortable around us because of what you said."

"No issue here, Benny boy. Carls and I don't have secrets; nothing we say to each other makes us uncomfortable, that's just how we roll baby."

I start laughing, I have no idea why, but I can't stop, I laugh so hard that I fall off the lounge and start to roll around on the floor.

"Alright, I think it's time for bed," announces Ben as he crouches so I can jump on his back.

"Oh babe, I'm gunna to ride you like we're in the Kentucky Derby, giddy up," I say as I smack his arse.

"Now I get why you two are such good friends, are you sure you're not related?" laughs Max.

"Hot stuff, Carly is my sister we just don't share DNA." Nicole waves at me as Ben carries me into our room. Ben shuts the door, sits me down on the bed and starts to undress me while trying to stop me from straddling him.

"Carly can you please sit still while I get these clothes off you."

"Ben hurry up coz I wanna suck your cock dry and then fuck you all night long and I want you to put your huge cock in my arse," I pout.

"Carly, firstly keep your voice down because you're yelling; secondly, you can suck my cock any time you want; thirdly, I would love nothing more than to fuck you all night long; and fourthly, we will try anal sex but we need to work up to that and we need lube, so for now that has to wait."

"Ok we can wait but you have to smack my arse as a consolation prize and you have to smack it good. I want to feel it tomorrow when I wake up. Make sure you leave your hand print and…and you have to pull my hair coz that shit turns me on big time," I purr.

Ben laughs. "I can promise you that, you are fuckin' crazy but I love you. You make me so happy, Carly." Ben lays me back on the bed and kisses me all over. As promised, I ride him hard, and as he promised, he pulls my hair and smacks my arse so hard it leaves a hand print.

CARLY | 28

I wake mid-afternoon with the worst hangover I have ever had. I'm alone in the bed and I can hear talking coming from the lounge room. I roll over and see a note wrapped around a glass of water with a Berocca and two pain killers on the bedside table. I grab the note and I see Ben has drawn a heart with Ben and Carly written in the middle of the heart. I smile, drink down the pills with the Berocca, clutch the note to my chest and lay back on the bed. I send Ben a text to meet me in the bathroom so I can thank him for the lovely note. I hear his phone receive the text and then I make my way across the hall and wait for him. I only wait a short time until he joins me.

"How are you feeling beautiful?"

"My head is pounding and my mouth feels disgusting. I'm pretty sure I threw up. How bad was I last night?"

"Yeah, you did throw up just as we left the nightclub and you were ok. You talked about watching porn and using toys, your filter was non-existent last night," he laughs.

"Oh god, please don't tell me I offended or upset Max."

"Nah babe, he's cool. We had a chat and he found you funny and could understand why you and Nicole are friends. Come on let's get you in the shower because it's 2.30pm and you must be hungry."

We get in the shower and even though I have a thumping hangover we have sex, a girl has needs. I work up quite an appetite and Ben makes me a toasted cheese, tomato and onion sandwich and a cup of tea.

Nicole looks up as we enter the lounge. "Nice of you to join us, Chica, how you feeling?"

"Hun, this has to be the worst hangover I have ever had. Max, I'm sorry if I said anything to make you uncomfortable last night."

"Carly, it's all good, you were enjoying yourself and you're funny when you're wasted. As I said to you last night, I understand why you and Nicole are friends," laughs Max.

"I don't remember you saying that. Actually I don't remember much after we walked up the stairs from the nightclub. Fuck I'm such a lightweight," I groan.

We decide to have a BBQ for dinner. The guys go and get the food while Nicole and I relax.

"Hun, I have never seen you this happy. I really like Max and he is so good for you. I just wish things were different and we didn't live on the other side of the country, I'm really gunna miss you."

"I'm gunna miss you too, I feel like half of me is missing. Hopefully one day things will be better and we can live near each other again. I have to believe that is going to happen, it's the one thing that keeps me going," Nicole says sadly.

When the guys come back we are crying and hugging. Max looks at Ben and Ben motions for Max to follow him. He understands and hopefully will be explaining things to Max while they prepare the BBQ. After a while we stop crying and walk out the back. The guys hold their arms out for us and we walk up and snuggle in. Ben kisses the top of my head, leans down and whispers in my ear, "You ok?" I nod and hug him tighter because I will be ok. But it's going to be hard to say goodbye tomorrow.

The guys cook us a lovely dinner and we sit out the back eating, talking and laughing the night away. We stay up pretty late. I don't want to drink so I just drink tea or water, there is no way I'm going to board that flight with a hangover. Ben and Max exchange numbers because Max will be going home to Penrith for Christmas and he wants to catch up with us, and I'm really happy about that.

Dad comes to Nicole's to pick us up and take us to the airport for our 11 am flight. Nicole and Max come to see us off but take Max's car, and Ben rides with them to give me and my dad a bit of alone time. We just chat like we usually do, something very normal after a very abnormal couple of weeks.

As we pull into the car park the tears start to fall. Like last time I ask them to say goodbye here because I can't handle long drawn out goodbyes. I hold onto Dad as we wait for the others to arrive. I spot Max's jeep park a row away from Dad's car. Nicole is crying as she comes over with Ben and Max behind her. She reaches Dad and I, and Dad puts his arm around her and hugs us both as we cry. The guys get the bags out the back of Dad's car and they wait for us to say our goodbyes. My heart is breaking again, I'm not sure when I am going to see them again and it's killing me.

Dad pulls away and leaves me and Nicole to it, he walks over to Ben and shakes his hand and says something to him but I can't hear what it is. Ben and Max come over. "Babe, we have to go and check in," Ben says. Nicole and I part but we still hold hands looking into each other's eyes, we don't say a word, we don't have to.

I look at Max, walk to him and give him a hug while Nicole hugs Ben. "Please take care of our girl, coz I'm sharing her with you and I expect you to take good care of her. She's my family and I love her to bits," I whisper in Max's ear.

"I promise, Carly, I will take good care of her. Look after yourselves, have a safe flight and hopefully we can catch up when I go home on leave. I will keep in contact, Ben has my number," Max smiles as he pulls away.

I give Dad and Nicole one last hug as we turn to catch our flight. My tears fall until halfway through the flight. I try to get some sleep but I just sit there with my eyes closed while I lean my head on Ben's shoulder.

Damon meets us at the door with Roger sitting at his feet. I call for Roger and he comes running, he has grown in the two weeks we have been gone. I am happy to see him.

We settle back into our normal life but the sentencing is always in the back of my mind. I try not to let it affect my moods but it isn't easy. This time I make sure I speak to Ben about how I'm feeling because I won't let it come between us again.

Thankfully Ben's family include me in the planning for Kelsey's eighteenth birthday party. Kelsey decides to have her party at one of the nightclubs in Wollongong. She is the last one of her friends to turn eighteen so everyone will be allowed to enter the nightclub. Including family and friends, Kelsey invites about one hundred people and decides the decorations will be purple and silver. I've spoken to the girls at the salon and swapped my shifts around so I have Friday and Saturday off so I can celebrate Kelsey's eighteenth and my twenty-first.

Late Tuesday night Ben gets a call from Lucy that Piper had gone into labour. Word spreads through the family and we were all excited to meet the new addition.

Ben is eating his breakfast when Lucy calls his mobile so Chelsea can speak to him. "Hey Mum, how's Piper? Has she had the baby?"

"Morning Ben, Piper is good, she had a boy at 4.50 am and his name is Noah Alex; he weighs nine pounds and certain little lady would like to speak to you," says Lucy.

"Of course, put her on."

"Uncle Ben I have a brother," squeals Chelsea.

"Chelsea that's fantastic, you're a big sister now. Is Nanny taking you to meet your little brother?"

"After we have brekky. Uncle Ben are you coming too?"

"I have to go to work, but Aunty Carly and I will come and meet him after work. Can you let Mummy know we will see her later?"

"I will Uncle Ben, I love you."

"I love you too, Chelsea, see you soon."

"Bye."

Ben comes into the bedroom picks me up and swings me around. "I have just spoken to Mum and Chelsea and we have a nephew. Noah Alex was born a few hours ago. He's a chunky buggar too, weighing nine pounds. I worked it out and that's four kilos," laughs Ben.

His excitement is contagious. "That's wonderful, are we going to see them after work?" I ask.

"Yeah if that's ok with you?"

"Of course. Do you want me to get some flowers and a card for Piper and a present for Noah and Chelsea?" Ben looks at me strangely when I mention a present for Chelsea. "It's a huge adjustment for everyone and the older siblings always seem to miss out. A present is a small way to say that they are just as important as the new baby and haven't been forgotten."

"That's a wonderful idea, I'll go shopping after work and then I'll pick you up when you finish and we'll head down."

"Sounds like a plan," I say as I kiss him. Ben has a huge smile on his face as he leaves for work. The day goes really quickly and I'm excited to meet Noah. Ben picks me up when I finish work and we make our way to Wollongong. "The flowers look beautiful, Piper will love them," I tell him.

"Yeah they are so her, pink lilies are her favourite flower. I got Noah blue towels with his name monogrammed on them and a silver photo frame engraved with his name, date of birth, time of birth and what he weighs. For Chelsea I got a Barbie dream house, I think she's going to love it."

"You did great honey, they are going to be thrilled. Are we going straight to the hospital?"

"Yeah she should have finished dinner and we will get the last hour in before visiting hours close. I can't wait to see him," beams Ben.

"I'm excited, but I have never held a baby before so I think I will just watch you and maybe in time I will be able to hold him."

"How come you haven't held a baby before?"

"Hello, have you met me? I don't have any friends other than Nicole and my cousins live interstate. A few of them have kids but we are not close so I haven't met them." I say sadly.

"Well when you are comfortable I'll show you how to hold him. It's such an amazing feeling, especially when they look at you and hold your finger. They smell wonderful and the noises they make are so damn cute."

"You really love kids don't you?"

"What's not to love? I can't wait to be a father and would love a big family, you up for that?" Ben says with a cheeky smile.

"In a few years, I'm too young for kids at the moment."

"I'm not saying today, but hopefully in our future." I blush and put my head down. "Babe why are you blushing? You know I see you as my future, I'm not backwards in coming forwards about it."

"I know you do it's just that you know I haven't had a relationship like this before and it's not easy for me to allow myself to look that far ahead. Please don't be mad at me, I know you love me and I hope you know how much I love you, but this is foreign territory for me; I'm not used to being treated so well and I have to admit it scares me at times," I say nervously.

Ben reaches for my hand and lifts it to his mouth and kisses the back of it. "One day you will be comfortable enough to accept and believe that you are the one for me and my future is with you. I am a patient man, Carly, and I will wait for as long as it takes."

"Thank you," I say with a smile. We chat for the rest of the trip. We arrive at the hospital just as Justin is walking out with Chelsea.

When Chelsea sees Ben's car she comes running up. "Uncle

Ben!" Ben gets out of the car and Chelsea jumps into his waiting arms. She squeals as Ben picks her up and cuddles her tightly. "Uncle Ben, my little brother is so small."

"That's because he was in Mummy's tummy but he will grow and he needs his big sister to help him. Do you think you can do that?"

"Of course I can Uncle Ben, I love him."

Awwww my heart skips a beat, Chelsea is an amazing little girl. I can't believe how much I love her already. I walk over to Justin, give him a hug and kiss on the cheek. "Congratulations Justin, I can't wait to meet Noah. How is Piper?"

"She's good but exhausted. She will be thrilled you and Ben have come tonight. Everyone has been up today so you have them all to yourselves."

"How are you doing?"

"Carly, words can't describe how I'm feeling at the moment, I'm walking on air. Piper is amazing, she has given me two beautiful children and I am one very lucky man. Noah's perfect, ten fingers and ten toes and the Kinney black hair," Justin laughs.

Ben puts Chelsea into her car seat and we both give her a kiss goodbye and let her know that we will be seeing her soon. Ben shakes Justin's hand and pulls him in for a hug. "Congratulations mate, I'm happy for the three of you."

As we enter the room Piper is asleep and Noah is in the basinet next to her bed. Ben sits down next to Piper's bed. I want to give Ben time alone with his nephew and sister so I go to get a drink for the three of us and a vase for the flowers. I'm gone about fifteen minutes.

"There you are," Ben says as I return. Piper is awake now and Ben is holding Noah. Ben has the biggest smile on his face and I can see that Noah is holding his little finger.

I put the flowers on the bedside table, and lean in to give Piper a hug and kiss. "Congratulations Piper, he is beautiful, and look at that hair," I laugh.

"I know, the Kinney genes are very strong," Piper smiles. "But he has the Richardson dimples, both sides," she says proudly.

"Where were you babe?"

"I wanted the three of you to have a bit of time alone, just like you did with Chelsea. It's a special time and I wanted Noah and Chelsea to have the same experience on their first day in this world with you."

I pull the drinks out of my bag and hand one to Piper and put the other two on the table. "Come over here and meet Noah," says Ben.

I walk over to Ben and crouch down so I can have a better look at Noah "He's so tiny Piper."

"You don't think that when you are giving birth, his head is big for a start. I tore; with Chelsea I was cut, so that means a shit load of sutures; neither was fun, but thankfully labour was only seven hours this time, and only four hours of that was serious labour. It was much better than being induced, like when I had Chelsea. That shit works quick and I was in serious labour for about seven hours. Going naturally was much better," Piper laughs. "Do you want to hold him Carly?"

I look at Ben, he smiles at me. "Ummm I h…have never held a ba..baby before, Pi..Piper. I d..don't want to dr..drop him," I stutter.

"Carly ,there is nothing to be nervous about. Sit down and Ben will show you how to hold him."

"Are y..you sure?"

"Of course you're his Aunty and I would love to have a photo of the three of you on Noah's first day in this world."

"I co..could sit next to B..Ben and you can t..take a photo of the th..three of us."

"Stop being such a sook, I trust you with my son, Carly."

Ben stands up and motions for me to take a seat. I take a deep breath and sit down. I fidget for a while trying to sit in a comfortable position. I look at Ben and give a small smile to let him know I am ready. Ben gives Noah a kiss and he wriggles and makes a noise. My heart skips a beat, the colour drains from my face and I give Ben a panicked look.

"Babe its fine, he is moving because I just disturbed him. Take a deep breath and I will place him in your arms. I will place his head in the crook of your arm and his body will rest against your arm, just hold him against your body, he will snuggle into you."

I take a deep breath and nod that I'm ready, Ben leans towards me with Noah. He places his hand under Noah's head and moves him to my arms. Ben places Noah's head in the crook of my right arm and I automatically lift my right hand to meet the rest of his body. Noah lets out a sigh and snuggles in, I'm mesmerised by him, I can't take my eyes off him. His little hand is out of the blanket that he is wrapped in and I gently rub my finger against his skin, it's so soft. I am taken by surprise when Noah wraps his tiny hand around my finger, tears begin to pool in my eyes, this is such a magical moment and I feel quite emotional. For a moment I forget that we were not alone, I look up and see Piper and

Ben sitting on the bed smiling at me. A tear escapes my eye. "Piper he is so beautiful."

"Yes he is, I produce beautiful children," smiles Piper. "Ben go over there so I can take a photo of the three of you." Ben gets off the bed and crouches next to me, he puts his arm around the back of the chair, kisses me on the cheek, kisses Noah's head, places his hand on Noah's tummy and then turns to Piper ready for the photo.

Ben holds my hand as we walk to the car, I'm lost in my thoughts when we reach his car, as he opens the door for me he leans in to give me a kiss. "How did it feel holding Noah?"

"Ben I have no words to explain how that felt, it's a feeling I have never experienced before and the strength of it took me by surprise. He smelt amazing and when he took my finger in his hand I just fell in love."

"Yeah I understand, that's how I felt the first time I held Chelsea and when I held Noah tonight. I'm so happy you were here to experience this with me. I love you, Carly."

"I love you too, Ben," I say as my stomach growls. "I hate to break this moment, but I am starving. Let's find somewhere to eat."

We go to a gourmet pizza place and enjoy a delicious meal. Ben shows me the photos that were taken tonight, I hadn't realised that so many where taken of Noah and myself, I look up at Ben with a confused look on my face. "Babe you were so into Noah that you didn't notice me taking the photos, I wanted to capture it all and I think I did that. You looked so beautiful holding him, the love was oozing out of you and I fell more in love with you tonight."

"I never understood why people get all gooey about other people's babies. You are supposed to love your own but I never believed it when someone said that they loved someone else's baby until tonight. It's hard to explain how much I love that baby, when he held my finger and made a little sound my heart just melted. I know I love Chelsea but I have spent time with her and interacted with her, Noah's not even a day old. I'm just blown away." I look up and Ben is just sat there smiling at me. "What?"

"I was just thinking how lucky I am that I found you and that you actually love me, I'm a very lucky man."

"What's there not to love? You're a great guy, hot as all fuck, and you have an amazing family that have accepted me, and did I mention that you're hot?" I giggle.

Ben just laughs and shakes his head "You are so good for my ego, Beautiful."

"Right back atcha."

29 | CARLY

I have the day off on Friday so I get everything ready for the weekend. We have Kelsey's party tonight and then we have my twenty first on Saturday, it's going to be a huge weekend. Ben won't tell me what he has planned for my birthday, but knowing him it will be wonderful. All I know is that I need comfortable clothes in the day and a dress for the night.

I'm in the bedroom putting our clothes and toiletries into a suitcase when I hear Ben walk in the front door just after midday. As I go to turn my head to say hello I feel his hands around my waist pushing me onto the bed. He covers my body with his, moves my hair aside and kisses the back of my neck. "I have really missed you this morning Carly, I need to be inside you," Ben says as he starts to pull my pants and underwear down. I can feel myself getting wetter and let out a moan as he kisses his way down the back of my legs while removing my clothes. I hear Ben unbuckle his belt, undo his button and pull down his zip, then his clothes thud as they hit the floor. He kisses and nips his way back up my legs, my body is on fire and I want him so bad. I can feel his erection press into the crease of my bum and I part my legs. Ben runs his hands up my side, slowly removing my top and unclasping my bra. He straddles my lower back, grabs both arms and pulls them behind my back and with my bra he binds them. I gasp and Ben stops "Are you ok with this?"

"Fuck yeah, this is hot, I'm all yours handsome, do what you want."

Ben lets out a low growl as he kisses his way down my spine and pulls me to my knees. "Get on the floor and kneel." I do as I'm told and Ben stands in front of me. He runs his hand over my cheek as I look into his eyes, I see so much love and lust I can hardly stand it. Ben rubs his erection on my lips as he holds my hair. "Open your mouth beautiful." I do as I'm told and Ben just puts the tip in my mouth, I try to take in all of him but because he is holding my hair he has control. "Suck and lick it." I poke my tongue out and flick it over the head before sucking the tip. "Fuck babe." Ben slowly pushes forward so I can take more of him, he controls the pace as he moves my head, I suck and lick him like there is no tomorrow and he is falling apart. "Babe...fuuucccckkk..don't stop... so good." After a while Ben pulls his cock out of my mouth and assists me to stand.

"Now it's your turn," he says with a sexy smile. "Kneel on the bed up near the pillows coz I want you to ride my face."

Oh my god, I nearly come on the spot. Ben helps me onto the bed and positions me so that my head is resting against the bed head. He gets me to spread my legs as he lies on his back and shuffles through my legs so that his mouth is in line with my pussy. Ben wraps his arms around my legs, places his hands on my thighs and lowers me down onto his very talented tongue. My eyes roll into the back of my head as he goes to work, I start to move my hips in time with his tongue. "Oh god Ben...so good..so close...don't stop," I pant as he sucks and licks my clit until I come. He slides out from underneath me as I try to catch my breath and come back down to earth.

I can feel the bed dip as Ben positions himself behind me. He slaps my arse which takes me by surprise and I let out a yelp, this is fuckin' awesome. Ben grabs my binding, pulls me so I'm kneeling up and my back is resting against his chest "Where's the lube?" he whispers in my ear. A shiver runs through my body. I motion to the bottom draw and Ben gets off the bed to get it. I hear the cap pop as he kneels behind me again. He guides me back towards the middle of the bed, spreads my legs and gently pushes my head to the bed so that my cheek is resting on the mattress. Ben slaps my arse again as he thrusts his cock in my pussy and starts pumping hard into me. I feel something cold against my hole and I realise it's the lube, as Ben is pumping into me his finger is moving in and out of my arse. I moan with pleasure, my senses are in overdrive. I don't know what's gotten into Ben but I know I'm lovin' it.

"Are you ready for me to fuck your arse Carly?" Ben growls.

"Yes, yes, please Ben," I pant.

Ben pulls out and places his cock against my arse and slowly pushes forward, he is holding my binding with one hand while the other hand is spreading my cheeks. He pushes in a little and lets me get used to it and then pulls out, pushes back in a little further and repeats until he is all the way in. He stills. "Are you ok?"

"Honey I'm more than ok but please take it slow unless I ask you to speed up. Please don't come inside me, I don't want to be leaking out of my bum all day," I laugh.

"Ok. Fuck you feel good Carly, so fuckin' tight I don't think I will last very long."

As Ben starts to move he holds the binding with one hand, grabs my hair with the other and pulls my head off the mattress so we are looking into each other's eyes. As promised he goes slow until I give him the signal to speed up a bit. I can see that Ben is close and in total heaven, all of a sudden his breathing becomes heavier, he pulls out and comes on my back as he kisses me and tells me how much he loves me. As he let's go of my hair and undoes the binding I fall onto the bed totally exhausted.

Ben goes to the bathroom to get a wash cloth to wipe my back. He rubs my shoulders and arms because they were tied up for a while. He lays on the bed facing me.

I place my hand on his cheek. "That was mind blowing, you took me by surprise and the fact that you tied my hands and told me what to do was so fuckin' hot I nearly came before you touched me. Thank you," I say as I lean in to kiss him.

"I wasn't sure how far you would let me go, I wanted it to be a surprise so we couldn't over think it. You're right that was so fuckin' hot, I don't know how I held out so long." Ben laughs.

We lay there for a while basking in what we have experienced, looking into each other's eyes and running our fingers gently over the each other's skin. Eventually we get up and go for a shower, it would be poor form to turn up at Ben's parent's home with his come on me.

We grab our things, pack up Roger's food, blanket and toys and head down to Wollongong for the weekend. Roger is staying at Pipers while we are at the party. When she offered Ben wasn't so sure because she had just had Noah, but she insisted because Chelsea really wants to play with him.

As a surprise we got Piper to alert the School that we would be picking up Chelsea. We get to the School about fifteen minutes early so we let Roger out of the car and let him stretch his legs. Because Roger isn't allowed on the school grounds Ben goes to Chelsea's classroom to get her while I stay outside the perimeter fence. The bell sounds and I can see the kids come out of their classrooms. I can't see Chelsea but I heard her squeal when she sees Ben, she runs into his arms talking a mile a minute. Ben points our way and as soon as Chelsea sees Roger she squirms out of Ben's arms and runs to us. I thought Chelsea was going to say hello and maybe give me a hug and kiss before she went to Roger, but no, she totally ignores me and throws her arms around Roger and starts kissing him. I'm laughing when Ben gets to us, he looks at me funny and when I explain what had happened he started laughing to.

We decided to buy a booster seat for when we have Chelsea and also for when Noah gets older, so we are all set to take Chelsea home. Roger sits in the back with Chelsea and she shows him her reading book and a drawing she did at school. It's so cute I take a video of it on my phone.

We pull up at Pipers and let Chelsea and Roger out, they go running to the front door and Chelsea knocks, waiting for Piper to let us in. Piper came home from the hospital yesterday afternoon because both her and Noah had no complications and she wanted to get home to Justin and Chelsea. Piper opens the door as Ben and I reach it with Rogers stuff. Chelsea and Roger run in and go straight to Chelsea's room.

Noah is asleep in Piper and Justin's room, so we head into the lounge while Justin makes sure that Chelsea and Roger are behaving and Ben puts the kettle on. "How's it all going Piper?"

"Pretty good. Because Noah is our second we have an idea what to expect even though every baby is different. He slept pretty well last night, waking every four hours for a feed. And because he is bottle fed we took it in turns getting up to him. Justin is going to watch them so I can come for a while tonight. I can't miss Kelsey's eighteenth."

"That's fantastic, I was hoping you'd be able to go, Kelsey will be thrilled."

Noah wakes up and Ben is up and out of his chair before anyone else can move. Justin heats up the bottle and Ben feeds Noah, he is so good with him. Once he has fed and burped him he changes his nappy, I am amazed how comfortable he is with all of that and I know he's going to make a wonderful father.

After a while we say goodbye and head to James and Lucy's to get ready. Kelsey has a few of her girlfriends there getting ready and I promised to do all their makeup and hair. Ben brings me a sandwich to eat because even though there is food at the venue it's only finger food and I need something in my stomach before I start drinking.

Ben and I get Kelsey a DKNY ladies stone set watch, it is beautiful and sleek and Kelsey loves it. The whole family buys her jewellery. James and Lucy get her a ruby ring; Piper, Justin, Chelsea and Noah a necklace with an eighteen key; Darcy and Lily a Pandora bracelet with a few charms, and Damon gives her an anklet. She is all blinged out.

Kelsey looks beautiful. She is wearing a red strapless to-the-knee dress and her is hair down; I put in some curls and her makeup is perfect, even if I do say so myself. Lucy takes heaps of photos of the girls before the limo turns up and the girls go off for a ride in it. They'll take photo's along the way and also stop off at Piper's so Kelsey can see Chelsea.

While we were back in Perth we came across a beautiful cornflower blue dress that has a sweetheart neckline and sits just above my knees. I have decided to wear it tonight with strappy black heels. Ben is wearing black pants and shoes with a lavender long sleeve shirt. I nearly cream myself when he walks into the bathroom to see how long I will be, he looks so hot. "Oh my god Ben you look amazing, very handsome, I'm a lucky girl," I beam as I kiss him.

I take another ten minutes before I am happy with my hair and makeup, then I go into the bedroom to get dressed and spray on my favourite perfume, Flora by Gucci; it's fruity and floral and an added bonus is that Ben loves it. As I am about to descend the stairs Lucy comes out of her room. "Holy hell, Lucy, you look amazing," I say. "You are one hot Mumma." She is wearing an aqua coloured dress that looks fantastic with her blonde hair and blue eyes.

"Carly, you are good for my ego. Come on let's go get our men and make our way to the party before Kelsey makes her grand entrance." We walk down the stairs with our arms linked and make our way into the lounge to let the men know we are ready. As we walk into the lounge James and Ben have their backs to us and are deep in conversation. "We're ready," Lucy announces.

The men stand, turn to look at us and stop in their tracks. "Ben, we are very lucky to have two beautiful women on our arms tonight," says James.

Ben takes my hand in his. "You take my breath away, Carly, you look so beautiful," he says as he kisses my cheek.

The nightclub looks amazing with the purple and silver decorations and the DJ is the best in NSW. There is a photo booth set up and it has props with it like feather boas, big glasses, hats and tiaras.

One of Kelsey's friends send Lucy a text that they are five minutes away. We stand with Piper, Damon, Darcy and Lily waiting for her to arrive. I look around the room and I see family and friends and they have all gathered here for Kelsey. There is an excited atmosphere in the room and we all erupt when she walks in. Kelsey loves the room and is a little overwhelmed by the welcome.

The music is pumping and the drinks are flowing. The bar staff make a special cocktail for Kelsey's eighteenth that is purple and she loves it. About an hour after Kelsey's arrival Lucy and James bring out the cake, which is beautifully decorated in purple and silver and is in the shape of the numbers one and eight. It has eighteen sparklers on it that Kelsey tries, unsuccessfully, to blow out. Lots of photos are taken with family and friends. We all have an individual photo taken with Kelsey, it's wonderful being a part of the Richardson family. After the cake is shared and photos are taken Piper says she is going home. Ben and Darcy walk her to her car while Lily and I dance.

The guys come back and join us on the dance floor. As I'm dancing I notice a guy watching Kelsey. I watch him for a while and he doesn't take his eyes off her. I turn to Lily and ask, "Who's that guy?"

"Oh that's Ethan, why?"

"He hasn't taken his eyes off Kelsey for the last ten minutes. What's he to her?"

"Ummm I'm not too sure. They go to school together and have been friends for years but that's all I know."

"I think he has a thing for Kelsey," I say with a knowing smile.

I continue to watch Ethan as we dance and I notice Kelsey looking at Ethan every now and then, she smiles and then looks away. "I think there is more going on than friendship because I have watched them look over at each other," I say to Lily.

"We'll just have to wait and see what happens. Who knows, when they've had a few drinks they might get the courage to approach one another."

"I hope so, because there is a definite attraction." Ben pulls me close and asks me what we are talking about. I explain and he doesn't look to happy. "What's the face for?"

"She's my little sister and I don't think I'm too happy with a guy checking her out."

I look at him "Are you kidding me? She's eighteen, she's beautiful, funny and smart, who wouldn't be attracted to that?"

"It's just hard, she's the baby of the family and my little sister, the one I always protected when we were growing up," he says sadly.

"Honey, she's an adult now, you have to let her live. I think it's beautiful how you all care for one another but you can't wrap her in cotton wool, she needs to live and experience life and that includes boys"

"I know what you're saying is right but it's not easy."

I put my arms around him and kiss him on the lips. "You are a good brother, Ben. I love you so much."

"I love you too, babe. I have to say you look phenomenal and I can't wait to get you out of that dress. This afternoon's activity keeps running through my mind."

"Ben, it was so hot, to begin with I wasn't sure if I liked it because it was painful and you're a big boy you know," I say with a cheeky smile. "But when I relaxed I started to enjoy it. I don't think it's an every time thing but I am more than willing to have a repeat performance. Did you have that planned or was it a spur of the moment thing?"

"All spur of the moment, when I walked in and saw you in the bedroom bent over with your back to me I knew I wanted you and I know you are ok with me taking control so that's what I did. Using your bra to tie your hands up was something I saw in a movie but have never tried, it worked very well I think."

"Oh hell yeah, that was amazing I nearly came when you did that, it turned me on so much. I have never been tied up before so that was another new experience for me and I loved it," I smile. "You are an exceptional lover, Ben, and I am always very, very satisfied."

"I'm pleased to hear that,Beautiful." We dance for a while longer and then I excuse myself to go to the bathroom. On the way I notice Ethan standing there on his own. I walk up to him and introduce myself. Ethan is about five foot ten, has a stocky build as if he plays rugby, shaggy light brown hair and an electric smile.

"Are you having a good night?" I ask.

"Yeah, this is a great party."

"How do you know Kelsey?"

"We go to school together and we will both be attending Wollongong Uni next year."

"What are you going to study?"

"I'll be studying Civil Engineering, it's a four year course."

"That's wonderful, I hope all goes well for you. Now Ethan, I don't want to embarrass you but you have not taken your eyes off Kelsey, does she know how you feel about her?"

Ethan is speechless and tries to regain his composure before he speaks "What are you talking about?"

"Ethan, I am a people watcher and I can see that you're into Kelsey, does she know?"

He puts his head down. "I don't think so, I have had a thing for Kelsey since our second year in high school but I have never had the courage to say anything."

"Well honey, I have noticed her looking your way quite a lot tonight, so the feeling might be mutual. Do you dance?" Ethan looks at me as if I asked for his first born child. "Ethan I will give you a tip, if a guy can dance then the girl has a pretty good idea what kind of lover he will be because if you can move on the dance floor you have the moves in the bedroom." Ethan stands there with his mouth wide open. "I am a straight shooter, I tell it as I see it. Please believe me, I am not trying to embarrass you, but life is too short, go after what you want, if you don't ask you don't get." Ethan looks at me, smiles, kisses my cheek and announces that he is going to ask Kelsey to dance. "Thata boy, you go get her Ethan," I yell as he walks towards Kelsey. My work here is done, I say to myself as I walk to the bathroom.

When I come out of the bathroom I notice Ethan and Kelsey dancing to The Fray's Love Don't Die, and boy can he move, I smile to myself. The party is a huge success, I have a few drinks but not too many because I know I have a big day tomorrow. Everyone is in a great mood. Ethan and Kelsey look very cosy and dance the night away. He gets her drinks and they go into the photo booth quite a few times. The photo booth is a fantastic idea and everyone has their photo taken.

We arrive back at James and Lucy's place after 4 am. As I reach the front door Ben turns to me. "I want to be the first to wish you a happy twenty-first birthday, beautiful," he says before he kisses me.

"Thank you honey. I am so happy to be spending my birthday with you and because I'm the birthday girl I want you to take me up to your bedroom and I want you to fuck me until I can't see straight," I say laughing.

"That will be my absolute pleasure," Ben says as he opens the front door and chases me upstairs. We take our time undressing each other and exploring one another's bodies. I am a happy woman as I fall asleep entwined in Ben's arms.

CARLY | 30

It feels like I have just closed my eyes when Ben is shaking me awake. "Wake up, birthday girl everyone is down stairs waiting for you. Mum and Piper have prepared a fantastic late breakfast."

"What time is it?" I groan.

"It's 10.30 am and you need to get up."

I reluctantly get up and have a quick shower, put my hair up in a ponytail and put on a pair of jeans and a t-shirt.

I walk down the stairs and take a deep breath before I open the door, I'm not use to being the centre of attention. My nerves are on edge as I can hear the laughter on the other side of the door. I count to three, open the door and walk in. *"HAPPY BIRTHDAY!"* the family yells, and Chelsea comes running up and jumps into my open arms. "Happy birthday, Aunty Carly," Chelsea says as she kisses my cheek and hugs my neck tightly. "Sit next to me, Aunty Carly," she says as she grabs my hand and drags me to the table.

Lucy, James, Piper, Justin, Damon, Darcy, Lily and Kelsey all give me a hug and kiss before I sit down. I sit between Ben and Chelsea and Ben hands me a glass of champagne and make sure everyone else has one, Chelsea and Piper have orange juice. He stands up. "I would like to make a toast to my beautiful girl Carly on her twenty-first birthday, but I really don't think it's my place to do that." I look at him with a confused look.

I start to get nervous. "Wh…what's going o..on?" I stutter. Ben leans forward, kisses me and takes my hand in his.

"Well Ratbag, it's the Fathers job to make the speech for his daughter's twenty-first."

My head spins around towards the kitchen and I see my dad walking towards me with a huge bouquet of beautiful flowers. I struggle to my feet with the help of Ben, I'm shaking and crying as I stumble into my dad's arms. I can't speak, I just stand there hugging him, letting it sink in that he is really here. I pull back and look at his face. "You're here, how?"

"While you were in WA Ben and I got our heads together and organised everything. Darcy and Lily picked us up at the airport this morning."

I cut him off "Wh..what do you me..mean us?"

"Bitch, you didn't think I would miss your birthday did you?"

I look towards the sliding door and I see Nicole and Max entering from the back yard. I scream as I run over to them hugging Nicole like my life depends on it. I can hardly see because I am crying so much. I hear laughter behind me and the whole family are looking at us but I see tears in Lucy, Piper, Lily and Kelsey's eyes. I turn towards Ben and I fall more in love. I slowly walk to Ben, take his head in my hands and look deep into his eyes "Thank you," I whisper before I kiss him passionately.

"Put him down!" yells Damon. Everyone laughs as we separate.

"Have you met everyone?" I ask as I give Max a hug and a kiss on the cheek.

"Yeah, Chica, we are all good. Now it's time to eat coz I'm starving," laughs Nicole.

We all sit down for a wonderful meal, I look around the table and I feel so loved, I have never felt this before. The conversation and laughter flows, and Chelsea is in her element because she has a large captive audience.

"Aunty Carly ,me and Roger made a card for you," Chelsea says as she passes me the card. Chelsea has drawn me, her, Ben, Noah and Roger, and she has put hers and Noah's hand prints and Rogers paw print in the card.

"Chelsea, this is wonderful, thank you so much," I say as I pull her close and hug her.

We talk about how good the party was last night and Lily brings up Ethan. Kelsey starts to go red, something definitely happened last night. "Ok spill, what happened with you two last night?" I ask.

Kelsey squirms in her seat "Nothing much, we danced, we talked and he asked if I wanted to go to see a movie later this week."

"He's a nice boy, I hope you said yes." I say as Ben glares at me. "What? He is nice. I had a lovely chat with him last night."

"Yes I did," Kelsey smiles.

"Way to go," I say as I raise my glass to her.

My dad stands. "I would like to say a few words if I may?" Dad looks at me. "Carly, you have always made me very proud. No matter what you do, you do it with the utmost kindness and integrity, I'm in awe of the woman that you have become. I know your journey has not been easy and at times I wasn't sure you would make it but you're a fighter and thankfully you pulled through. Now you have the love of a fantastic young man, and I know with Ben by your side you will continue to grow and blossom. So I would like you all to raise your glasses to Carly, my beautiful daughter."

"*TO CARLY*," everyone toasts.

I stand and give Dad a kiss and hug, I take a deep breath and calm myself. "WOW I am one very lucky girl, thank you Dad. I have to admit this is quite overwhelming, I have never felt so much love from so many people in my life before. Everyone I love is in this room. James, Lucy, Piper, Justin, Chelsea, Noah, Darcy, Lily, Damon and Kelsey thank you so much for accepting me into your family. I love you all so much. Nicole, even though we're not blood you're my sister and I miss you more than you know, thank you for flying across the country to spend this time with me. Max, you know I think you're awesome and hot as all hell."

"Hey bitch, eyes off my man," Nicole laughs.

"I'm only stating the obvious, am I right ladies?" Lucy, Piper, Lily and Kelsey all agree quite eagerly.

"BABE!" yells Ben.

"Honey you know I think the same about you, but I can also appreciate other guys."

"It's ok Benny boy I think you're hot too," Nicole giggles.

"Dad, you have always shown me unconditional love and I am truly thankful you are my father. Ben, you and my father are the most important men in my life. Our introduction was…ummmm different, but even though I was being a total cow to you, you persevered. Thank you for not giving up on me, you make me so happy that it scares me sometimes. You saved me, I know you don't think so but you did. I love you more than words can ever express." As I finish I look around the room and there's not a dry eye.

Ben stands and pulls me in for a kiss as he hugs me tightly. "It's time for your present."

I'm shocked "I was..wasn't expecting anything, th..the fact that your all h..here is enough for me," I stutter.

"Carly, slow your breathing," Ben says gently, "Of course I have something for you," he says as he places a square box the size of my palm in my hand.

Tears roll down my face as I slowly unwrap my gift. Ben has bought me a heart shaped locket and on the back is engraved TO MY BEAUTIFUL GIRL HAPPY 21st BIRTHDAY LOVE ALWAYS BEN XX. I throw my arms around him. "Thank you so much it's perfect, I love it, can you please put it on me?" I pass the necklace to Ben and turn around so he can put it on me. It's beautiful, I can't believe how lucky I am.

I feel Chelsea tap my leg, and I crouch down. "Aunty Carly, I made this for you at School." She hands me a fan made out of pop sticks with cotton wool on the ends.

"Chelsea, this is beautiful. Would you be ok if I take it to work with me because it gets pretty hot in the salon and I could use a good fan."

"Yes you can, Aunty Carly."

I thank Chelsea with a kiss and a cuddle.

James and Lucy come forward, stand on either side of me and cradle my shoulders, I melt into them. "Carly the rest of us pooled together to get you a present you can use when you want to."
I look at them confused, as James hands me a card, kisses my cheek and motions for me to open it. My hands are shaking as I rip open the envelope. I open the card and something falls out, I pick it up but before I look at it I read the card. It has the most beautiful words in it and for the umpteenth time today I'm crying. I finish reading the card, and I turn to hug James and then Lucy. I take a look at the piece of paper that fell out and it's an eight hundred dollar travel voucher with an airline. "OH MY GOD, I can't believe you got this for me," I run around the room hugging everyone.

"You can use it when it's safe to go back," Lucy says before she realises what she actually has said. Heads swing my way. "Carly, I'm so sorry."

"Lucy it's ok, it's about time everyone knew."

"Know what?" asks Piper.

"Can we get Chelsea out of the room first? I would prefer her not to hear this."

Lily stands up. "Come on Chelsea, how about we take Noah

outside to see the garden? And we can play with Roger." She picks Noah up out of his bassinet and holds Chelsea's hand as they make their way outside. Lily looks back and gives me a reassuring smile, and I mouth *'thank you'* as she shuts the door behind them.

"Dad are you ok with this?"

"It's your story to tell," he says as he squeezes my hand.

I take a deep breath as Ben takes my hand in his. I take my time as I tell my story. I try to tune out the gasps and the crying because I need to get it all out and that way everyone knows. As I finish I explain that he will be sentenced on Wednesday and as soon as I know how much time he will serve I will let everyone know. Piper and Kelsey come over to me slowly and hug me while they are crying.

Damon and Justin walk to Ben and do the man thing, where they say nothing but show him and me their support.

"I'm s..sorry I didn't tell yu..you before, but I wanted it all d..done and dusted before you were t..t..told. James and Lucy were told be.. before I moved over here, Dar..Darcy and Lily were told the ni..night of the Pink concert, I didn't intend to t..tell them. Please don't be angry with m..m..me."

"We're not angry with you, we're so sorry this happened to you," Piper says as she hugs me tighter.

After a while I say, "I'm pleased you all know. If it's ok with everyone I would like to push it aside and enjoy the rest of today."

Darcy walks to the sliding door to let Lily know it's ok to come back inside with the kids. Ben leans into me and says "How about a BBQ lunch?"

"That's sounds perfect," I say as I kiss him. I motion to Kelsey to follow me "We are having a BBQ lunch, you are very welcome to invite Ethan if you like, he's nice and I like him." Kelsey thinks about it for a while, thanks me and then grabs her phone and goes somewhere private to make the call. I walk back to everyone and ask if some music could be put on to lighten the mood.

It's a beautiful day and we sit outside chatting and drinking, Lucy puts out some snacks and it feels amazing having all the people I love with me on my birthday. James and Lucy make my dad feel so welcome, everyone loves Nicole and Max, Justin is holding Noah while he has Chelsea on his lap singing nursery rhymes with her. I'm sitting there smiling when Ben whispers in my ear, "Are you ok?"

"More than ok, this is the best birthday I have ever had, thank you so much," I say as I lean in and kiss him.

Just then the doorbell chimes, Kelsey jumps up and races to the front door. Everyone looks at each other trying to figure out who might be at the door. I sit there just smiling to myself as I watch the shocked expressions on everyone's face when Kelsey walks in holding Ethan's hand. I stand up to greet them. "It's great to see you again, Ethan, did you have a good time last night?"

"Hi Carly, yes I did. Thanks for inviting me to the BBQ and happy birthday," he says as he kisses my cheek.

"Thank you, I'm thrilled you could make it today, would you like a drink?"

"Yes please, can I have a coke?"

"There's alcohol if you want?"

"No thanks, I had a lot to drink last night, Kelsey convinced me to have a few of those purple drinks and holy hell they packed a punch so I need to dry out today. I think my liver will love me for it," Ethan laughs.

Kelsey motions for him to sit down while she gets him a drink. I notice Ben, Darcy, Damon and Justin scowling at Ethan. I give them all the *'what the fuck'* look as I can see that Ethan is feeling very uncomfortable. I touch Ben on the leg and when he finally looks at me I mouth *'stop.'*

Ben has a confused look on his face. "What?"

I lean into him and whisper in his ear, "Ben really? You and the boys have been scowling at Ethan since he walked in the door, he's a nice guy who has been into Kelsey for quite a few years and it looks like she feels the same about him."

"She's my little sister and it's my job to look out for her, besides I don't like him."

"For fucks sake Ben, you don't even know him, how can you say you don't like him? Give Ethan a chance. How would you like it if your family treated me like that? It's not right, you're all making him feel very uncomfortable and I expect more from you," I say, very disappointed.

Ben is shocked with what I have just said. "I didn't look at it that way, it's just that Kelsey is the baby of the family and we have always been there to watch out for her."

"I get that, but Ben, you can't treat people that way. Please have a chat to the guys and get them to back off." Ben nods, gets up and asks Darcy, Damon and Justin to follow him. They are gone for about ten minutes and when they come back I notice their attitudes have all changed. I give Ethan a wink as I see him relax a little.

After we eat lunch I get some alone time with Nicole. "How's it all going with Max?"

"Chica, it's amazing, I just can't believe how good this man is. I see him most nights and he spends the weekends with me. The sex is out of this world and gets better every time. He has met my folks and my dad loves him and as you know, he has never liked any guy I have brought home. I am a bit worried because I am meeting his family for the first time this weekend and he has five younger sisters. I am going to have to think about what I say before it comes out of my mouth." We both laugh.

"Yeah, I hear ya on that one."

Nicole slaps my arm. "Bitch."

"I only speak the truth. I can see that you are crazy about him, have you told him?"

"We have hinted to each other that we are in love but neither of us have said the words. I don't want to be the first one to say it in case he doesn't feel the same, I know I couldn't handle the awkwardness that would cause."

"I think if you utter the words he will say them back, he is head over heels in love with you. Since we have been sitting here talking he has hardly taken his eyes off you. He looks over here pretty much every thirty seconds."

"I'm not ready to put it out there yet, I think it's too soon and I don't want to scare him off."

"You will know when it's the right time to tell him and I know he feels the same way as you do."

Just then Ben comes over. "Babe, I have to interrupt because you and I have plans, so I would like you to go upstairs to have a shower and do your hair and makeup. I have put something on the bed that I would like you to wear tonight."

"I can't leave. Dad, Nicole and Max have flown all this way it would be rude of me to leave."

"Chica, it's all good, we are going to see Max's family. We will catch up tomorrow. Now be a good girl and do as Ben says," Nicole smiles.

I look around and everyone is smiling at me. My dad walks over. "Ratbag, go get yourself glammed up and let Ben take you out for your birthday. I will be spending the evening with James and Lucy and I am sleeping here the night, so I will see you later."

Ben and I make our way upstairs and when he opens the bedroom door I notice a beautiful one-shouldered fuchsia coloured knee length dress lying on the bed beside a box containing a new pair of Badgley Mischka five inch platinum strappy shoes. I'm gob smacked and turn to look at Ben. "When?" is all I can say.

"When we were in WA and you picked the dress you wore last night I saw this one and bought it while you were in the change room, I got the owner of the store to ship it here. I knew your shoe size and my sisters helped me with the style."

"I..I..I don't know wh..what to s..s..say." I stutter as tears stream down my face, how did I get so lucky I think to myself.

Ben pulls me in for a kiss "Babe, I would give you the world if I could. Now get your beautiful backside in the shower and let's get this show on the road," he says, and he turns me around and slaps my arse as I walk towards the bathroom. I make sure I walk slowly and swing my hips a little more than usual because I know Ben is watching. I lean on the door frame, turn to look at Ben and blow him a kiss. I hear him growl as I shut the door.

I usually straighten my hair but this time I put in curls and waves that are different sizes, and when I am happy with my look I make my way to the bedroom. I notice there is a matching fuchsia strapless bra and G-string lying next to my dress. Ben has thought of everything I think as I smile to myself. I spray myself with Ben's favourite perfume, put moisturiser on my body and then get dressed. I look in the mirror and I am happy with what I see. I have huge butterflies in my stomach and as I reach the door to the lounge. I rub my fingers over the necklace Ben has bought me.

Everyone stops talking as I walk in the room. "Aunty Carly, you look so pretty."

"Yes she does, Chelsea, Uncle Ben is a very lucky man," says Ben as he walks towards me with his killer smile. Ben is wearing a three piece charcoal suit, polished black shoes, white shirt and a fuchsia coloured tie.

"WOW you look so handsome," I say as he pulls me into his arms. I can hear ooohs and ahhhs all around us. I look up and I notice that Nicole, Kelsey and Piper are all taking photos of us. Lucy and Lily are smiling but have tears in their eyes and all the men are just smiling.

We pose for some photos with everyone and some just on our own.

Damon nods at Ben, and Bens says, "Time to go, Beautiful."

"Where are we going?"

Ben takes my hand in his. "You'll see."

A black stretch limo waiting for us out the front. Ben hands me a bouquet of twenty-one yellow roses before we get in.

"Ben, they are stunning."   "Just like you," he says as kisses me and then helps me into the limo.

"Where are we going?" I say as I hand the roses to Lucy.

"We are going to the base of the Sydney Harbour Bridge, to the Opera House, Luna Park and the Rocks. A professional photographer will be meeting us at the bridge and will be with us until the end because I want to capture this night with photos. Carly you look so beautiful you take my breath away, I love you so much and I am a very lucky man that you love me too."

Ben puts his arm around my shoulders and I snuggle into him just enjoying the moment. Every now and then he kisses my forehead and I run my hand up and down his thigh. When we reach the base of the bridge the photographer is waiting for us; he takes some photos in the limo and some outside, we have fun with it and use some props that he has brought with him. The photographer follows us to each destination. He takes some photos at Luna Park, when we are at the top of the Ferris Wheel as the sun is setting and the sunset is a beautiful orange and yellow. I can't wait to see the photos.

We say goodbye to the photographer as we get back into the limo.

"Thank you so much for today, I will never forget it," I say to Ben as I lean in to kiss him.

"It's not over yet, we have dinner reservations," smiles Ben. The limo stops in a street in Sydney and the driver opens the door. Ben gets out first and then offers his hand to me, I grab my flowers and then place my hand in his as he helps me from the vehicle. We thank the driver and walk into a building holding hands. I still have no idea where we are until we stop at the lift and get in. Ben presses the button that says 'Sydney Tower'. A huge smile breaks out over my face. "Do you know where we are?" Ben asks.

"Yes, it's the revolving restaurant, I have seen this on TV. You are really spoiling me tonight."

"Only the best for my girl."

We walk up to the Maître de and Ben tells him his surname.

I look out across the restaurant and I can see the lights of Sydney, it looks so beautiful. The Maître de calls a waitress over and she walks us to our table. Ben is walking in front of me holding my hand and I have to admit I'm really not watching where I'm going, I'm too interested in looking out the windows. All of a sudden Ben stops and I bump into his back. I'm about to apologise when I notice he is smiling a really cheeky smile. I give him a confused look and I'm about to ask what's going on when he steps to his right and I look ahead.   Everyone from today is sitting there at a table waiting for us. I can't speak or move, I just stand there while everyone calls out *'SURPRISE!'* Thank god Ben is holding my hand because there is a good chance that I might faint.

Ben leans into me. "You didn't think I could whisk you away while your Dad, Nicole and Max were here did you?"

We say goodbye to everyone and Ben grabs a taxi for us. He hands a piece of paper to the driver so I won't know where we are going. I look at Ben and he has that *'I'm a clever fucker'* look on his face. I smile and go with it because I know it is pointless asking him where we are going. When the taxi stops the door is opened for me by a suited man wearing a hat. He is wearing a Hotel Quay Grand Suites Sydney badge with the name 'Andrew' on it. "Thank you Andrew," I say with a smile. Andrew tips his hat and opens the hotel door for Ben and I.

We walk past the front desk to the elevator and Ben pulls out the card for the room. "Our folks signed us in and dropped an overnight bag in our room before they went to the Restaurant, and our car is here also."

"Have you robbed a bank or something?"

Ben laughs. "Only the best for you."

"You have really thought of everything haven't you?"

"I hope so, I really wanted today to be the best birthday."

"It is. Ben, I can't believe all you have done for me today. The fact that you arranged for my dad, Nicole and Max to come over would have been enough but everything else is beyond words. thank you so much," I say with a tear in my eyes.

Ben places his hands on either side of my face and wipes away the tears that have fallen. "No more tears," he says as he leans in for a kiss. The elevator stops at our floor and we head to our room. Ben gives me the card, leans down and gathers me in his arms. "Open the door beautiful," he says. I do as he asks and he carries me into our room.

I turn on the lights and I am amazed on what I see. Ben walks to the sliding door and motions for me to unlock and open it. He walks onto the balcony, sets me on my feet and pulls me into his arms. We are both entranced by the view of the Sydney Harbour Bridge, it is lit up and so beautiful. After a while Ben pulls me inside the bedroom and I notice there are rose petals scattered over our king size bed. There is a bottle of Champagne, some strawberries and a box of chocolates. Ben opens the Champagne, placing a strawberry in each glass before pouring. "Happy birthday my beautiful girl," he says as we clink glasses.

Ben and I take the bottle and glasses and head outside to look at the beautiful view. We sit on the balcony wrapped up in each other's arms, sipping our Champagne, watching the world go by. I'm in Heaven.

"Carly, are you ok with me taking a few photos of you?"

"Ok, where do you want me?"

"Can we start with you on the balcony and then we will go from there."

"How many do you intend on taking?" I laugh.

"Ummmm would you be ok if I took some different kind of photos?"

I start to get nervous "Wh..what k..k..kind?"

"Babe, it's nothing to get nervous about, it's just that you look so fuckin' hot in that dress and I know what you are wearing underneath, I would just like some photos that would remain private, for my eyes only."

"B..Ben I'm n..not sure." I say nervously as I wrap my arms around myself.

"If you like I will take a few photos of you as you are. And I would love some with you just in that sexy underwear."

"Ben I do..don't think I..I c..can do th..that." I stutter, feeling more nervous.

"How about I take them from the neck down, I won't show your face. Would that be ok?" I look at him like a deer stuck in headlights. "Please Carly, I promise I will be the only one to see them." After a while I put my head down and nod. "Carly, that's wonderful. I promise I will not show your face and you can see every photo I take and if you're not happy I will delete them, I promise."

I have another glass of Champagne to hopefully loosen me up and calm my nerves. Ben takes a few photos of me with the bridge in the background and then we head back inside. I take a look at them and they are pretty good. Ben leans in, grabs my hair and pulls me in for a kiss. He kisses me so passionately that I am starting to get turned on. He lets go of my hair, grabs the camera and starts taking photos of me. "Fuck Carly you look so damn hot, your eyes are smouldering." Ben shows me the photos and I hardly recognise myself. They are close ups of my face. "You look so sexy in these. This is what I see when I look at you."

I feel a bit more confident so I slowly start to unzip my dress. I keep my eyes focused on his as I pull my dress down my arm and then let it fall to the floor. Ben is taking photos the whole time and I can feel myself relax and start to play for the camera. Ben starts to direct me and asks me to pose a certain way. Thankfully he never asks me to remove my underwear because I don't think I could do that.

I have a look at the photos and delete the ones I'm not happy with. There are a few that show my face but they are very tasteful so I am happy to leave them on the camera. "Even though you look amazing it's about time you got out of your suit," I tell Ben, and I take the camera and start taking photos of him. He plays up to the camera and is finally down to his boxers. Ben then takes the camera from me, puts his arm around me and takes a photo of the two of us.

"Honey, I would love to test out the spa," I say.

Ben can't put the camera down fast enough. He takes my hand and leads me to the bathroom. There are tea candles lined up around the spa. I light them as Ben turns on the water. Then I lean down to take my shoes off. "Babe, please leave them on," Ben says. "I would like to take them off you."

I go and get us another glass of Champagne. When I get back the spa is ready for us. I pass the glass to Ben and we both take a sip. "Come here, Beautiful," he says. He takes my glass and puts it on the side of the spa. He pulls me into his arms, kisses me as he starts to undo my bra. Ben pulls back and sucks a breath in "My God Carly, your beauty is breath-taking." I blush and put my head down. "One day, babe, one day," Ben says as he pulls me back into his body, I can feel his erection rub against me and I start to get wet.

I kiss his neck and run my finger nails up and down his chest, I hear him take in a breath as I kiss and lick my way down his chest. As I kneel I look up into his eyes as I slowly pull down his boxers, his erection springs free. I lick my lips and then take him in my mouth while maintaining eye contact.

"Oh my God babe," Ben moans as he runs his hands through my hair. I don't look away and Ben keeps his eyes focused on mine as I pleasure him. After a while he places his hands on my face and starts to pull me to my feet. "It's your turn, Beautiful," he says as he runs his hands down my sides towards my G-string. He leans forward, taking one of my nipples in his mouth while his hands remove my G-string. I stand there naked, wearing only my amazing Badgley Mischka shoes. Ben moves to my other nipple as his hands run slowly up and down my inner thighs. He kneels and parts my legs, and I place my hands on his head to steady myself. "Watch me, Beautiful, I want to see your face," Ben says as he leans forward while looking deep into my eyes, his tongue gently flicks my clit and I nearly fall apart. I force myself to maintain eye contact but it's not easy.

"OH MY GOD I love your mouth and tongue," I pant.

Ben winks at me and goes to town on my pussy. I grab his hair tightly as I come in his mouth. "You taste amazing, I could do this all day. Watching you fall apart is a sight to behold," Ben says as he stands and pushes me up against the bathroom vanity. "Turn around because I am going to fuck you from behind as you wear those sexy as hell shoes." I do as I'm told, and Ben grabs hold of my hair and pushes me forward and positions my head so I can see him in the mirror. "I want you to look at me while I'm inside you, keep your eyes on me and don't look away." Holy hell this is hot. I nod because I am unable to speak.

Ben slaps my arse before he slowly enters me. "Fuck Carly, you are so damned wet, you feel so good, it's heaven," say's Ben as he slowly moves in and out of me, I maintain eye contact and I see so much love in his eyes. Ben starts to speed up, he puts both hands on my waist and starts to pump harder "Babe, your tits look amazing bouncing around as I fuck you," Ben growls. "I'm so close, I want you to come with me." I place my right foot up onto the vanity, reach down and rub my clit. The mirror is low enough that Ben can see what I'm doing. "Fuuuccckkkk that is so hot, keep playing with yourself while I fuck you," pants Ben.

"I'm close Ben," I say as I start to close my eyes.

"Don't close your eyes, keep them on me, I want to watch you when you come around my cock."

"Soooo close…Ben…so close…don't stop…please..."

Ben slaps my arse again and that sends me over the edge. He grabs me around my waist, pumps harder and growls into my neck as he comes inside me. Ben pulls me close as we come down from our orgasms, he kisses the side of my neck as he pulls himself out of me.

I place my foot on the floor and turn around to face him. "That was amazing, honey, but I think the water has gone cold," I giggle.

Ben turns the hot tap on to warm the water. I bend to take my shoes off and Ben stops me. "Let me," he says as he runs his fingers down my legs, undoes my shoes and slips them off my feet. He takes my hand in his and helps me into the spa. He sits across from me and lifts my left foot into his lap and rubs it. "Babe, those shoes looked so sexy on you but I'm pretty sure your feet are a bit sore."

"It's a price a girl has to pay to look good," I giggle.

"Babe, you really have no idea how beautiful you are. You would look sexy in a bin bag," Ben says as he kisses the instep of my foot.

"You're biased."

"I only speak the truth," says Ben as he lets go of my foot and starts rubbing the other one.

"Oh god that feel's amazing, I didn't realise that my feet were hurting, you kept me very distracted," I smile. I take a sip of my Champagne, lean back and bask in the afterglow of amazing sex and a wonderful foot rub. As the water starts to go cold we decide to move to our massive, comfortable bed.

"Thank you for the most fantastic day. You are the love of my life Ben Richardson. I never believed in soul mates before but you have changed my mind because I believe you are my soul mate," I say as I lean in to kiss him.

"Beautiful, I have known you're my soul mate since the first night we went out for dinner."

"What, the night where I practically ran from the restaurant?"

"Yeah, why do you think I didn't want to take you home straight away? I knew you were it for me. You captured my heart that night, Carly."

"If it's possible, I have just fallen more in love with you," I say as my mouth crashes down on Ben's. I position myself so I am straddling him and I can feel him getting hard underneath me, I take his cock in my hand and rub it against my clit.

"Fuck Carly that feels amazing," growls Ben. I lift myself up and then I slowly lower myself onto his hard cock. Ben places his hands on my hips and moves me up and down.

"Ride me, Beautiful, ride me hard."

Ben sits up and I place my hands on his shoulders and dig my nails in as I get closer. "You feel so good," he grunts as I come again, tightening around his cock. A few moments later Ben comes inside me. "I love you so much, Carly." I lean into his body as his cock twitches inside me. We sit there in each other's arms coming down from our intense encounter. After a while I reluctantly lift myself off Ben's lap and lay on my back on the bed, completely satisfied.

I punch my fists in the air and scream "BEST.BIRTHDAY. EVER."

Ben laughs as he rolls into me, places his right arm across my stomach and nuzzles into my neck. I run my hand up and down his arm as we fall asleep wrapped up in each other.

Thank God we have a late checkout because we don't wake up until 1 pm. I roll off the bed to go to the toilet and I groan because my body is so stiff and sore but it's a good feeling because I know I have had an amazing time. Ben is still fast asleep on his back, and I lean against the wall watching him sleep. The sheet is halfway down his body and for a moment I think about getting my phone out and taking a photo of what is covered by that sheet, but I decide not to because I wouldn't like it if Ben took a naked photo of me.

"Stop staring at me like I'm a sex object. I'm not just a piece of meat, I have feelings you know," laughs Ben.

"You're my piece of meat, pull down the sheet so I can see all of you."

"It turns me on when you take control, babe," Ben growls as he slowly pulls the sheet away from his body. "Is this what you want?" he asks as he lay there completely naked.

"You know it, now I want you standing to attention and ready to service me, Navy boy."

Ben motions to his cock that is getting harder every second. He salutes me "Yes Ma'am." I run and jump on the bed. Ben pulls me on top of him and he fucks me until I scream his name as I come.

31 | BEN

As we drive back to Mum and Dad's I sneak a look at Carly and I see that she has the broadest smile plastered on her face. My heart soars because I know I had a major part in putting that smile on her face. Carly's dad Andrew flies back to WA tonight, and no one wants to cook so we decide to get fish and chips. We call Darcy, Lily, Justin and Piper to see if they would like to have dinner with us.

Chelsea bursts through the door and runs straight up to Andrew. "We're havin fishy chips for dinner."

"Well Chelsea, that's funny because we are too, do you think we could have fishy chips together?"

"Of course we are, silly, that's why we're here," Chelsea laughs as she cuddles into Andrew. Carly says he has always been great with kids, he has the right amount of silly in him that kids are attracted to.

We enjoy our meal with the whole family. Carly gets to feed Noah even though it wasn't very successful, I think most of the milk went on his clothes. He wriggles so much and he sucks so hard that he takes more than he can swallow, greedy little buggar. She's not up for changing his nappies yet, so Mum does that. Hopefully one day she'll be comfortable enough.

After dinner Andrew packs his things and we say goodbye to the family.   On the way to the airport Carly says to Andrew, "Thank you for flying here for my birthday, it wouldn't have been the same without you. It's the best birthday ever."

I raise her hand to my lips and kiss the back of it. As we get close to the Airport I can feel Carly tense and hear her breathing change. I know she doesn't want to say goodbye to her Dad.

I get out of the car, shake Andrew's hand and he pulls me in for a hug. "I know you are a good man and will take very good care of my girl.

I look forward to the day I am surrounded by my grandchildren from you and Carly. Thank you for loving and taking care of her," Andrew says quietly in my ear. There is no need for words so I just nod and smile at him.

Carly's crying before Andrew gets to her, she wraps her arms around him and hangs on for dear life. "I don't want you to go, I've loved having you here getting to know Ben's family."

"They're great people, Ratbag and I know they love you and will look out for you. I couldn't have chosen a better partner for you, I know you're in good hands."

She cries harder. "I'm going to miss you Dad."

"Me too, Ratbag, I'll call you when I land." He hugs her just a little bit harder, pulls back a bit, kisses her forehead then makes his way to the terminal.

I wrap my arms around Carly "You ok?"

"I will be," she says as she leans against my body. "Take me home."

"My pleasure, Beautiful."

Monday and Tuesday goes by quickly but the sentencing is hanging over our heads and Carly's on edge. Tuesday night Max and Nicole come over for dinner and to stay the night. Nicole and Max pick Carly up from work, which she's happy about because she can introduce them to her work mates. I make sure all the salads are done so when they get home we can all go out the back and the girls can chat while Max and I cook the BBQ.

"Soooo..how did it go with Max's family?" asks Carly.

"I was shitting myself on the drive there, you know how it is when you meet the family for the first time. They are so close like Ben's family and they all live at home so it was like I was the new toy. He has five sisters: Helen 24, Sara 21, Molly 20, Alice 18 and Claire 17. They all look alike but their personalities are all so different. Helen is a primary school teacher, is a straight talker and loud; Sara is the drama queen, she's an accountant; Molly is a florist, she wants to please everyone and is a born romantic; Alice is fuckin' hilarious and so sarcastic, she's at uni training to become a vet; and then there is Claire, who is still in high school, she is a bookworm and you don't hear much from her.

"We stayed in a hotel the night of your birthday because we get freaky and loud in the bedroom and I can't do that at his folk's house."

Max and I laugh because that's very true.

"Yeah, I know how loud you and Max are." Carly giggles.

Nicole slaps my arm. "Shut up bitch!". "Anywaaaay..there was a luncheon planned for us with the whole family. I was so intimidated when I walked into Max's folk's home, they were all there waiting for us. And because I'm not the average girl I decided to tone things down, I wanted to make a good impression and for them to like me. The sisters all rushed to Max when we walked in the door and I sorta got pushed out the way until his Mum and Dad came over to introduce themselves. His mum Louise gave me a hug and apologised for her daughters, but she said they miss Max so much that they have tunnel vision when they see him and everyone is pushed aside, so I shouldn't take it personally. Max's dad Bobby is taller than Max and a little intimidating; he just nodded and shook my hand."

"He's a pussy cat when you get to know him Nic," says Max.

I look at Max and then move my eyes to Nicole and she doesn't look too sure about that. "Did things settle down?"

"Yeah after a while, Max tried to include me but the girls are intense and all over him so I just sat back and talked to Louise. Bobby doesn't say much but Louise is very talkative and when I say talkative, I mean she never shuts up," Nicole laughs. "But she has a heart of gold, she loves her family and is very proud of everyone. We sat out on the back patio for lunch and all the boyfriends were there so there were fourteen people in total and I was the odd one out. The sisters are a tough crowd, they get along well and I'm pretty sure the boyfriends have been around for a while because they are very comfortable in the Flynn house. Max tried his hardest to include me in the conversations but because I don't have history with the family it was hard so I just watched and listened."

"Hun, did things get better?" Asks Carly.

"It took a while. After lunch I excused myself and went to the toilet for a break. I put the lid down and just sat there enjoying the peace and quiet. After a while there was a knock on the door and it was Max. I opened the door and walked into the hall with my head down."

"Oh hun, you poor thing," Carly sighs as she hugs Nicole.

"Yeah they are so intense and want all my attention when I'm home, which I understand but it's a bit overwhelming at times," says Max.

"Max apologised for his sisters and promised it would be better when I came back to the table. I told him I just needed a minute and he pulled me in for a hug. We stood there for a while and as I was about to let go Louise came up and asked if I was ok. I put a smile on my face and said I was and started to pull away from Max, and he leaned down and kissed me on the lips, then we walked back outside. When we got back to the patio everyone was quiet. Helen apologised for their rudeness; she said that because everyone knows each other so well they forgot that I have no history with them. The afternoon got better, we had a few drinks and it looked like everyone relaxed a bit, and I started to enjoy myself and get to know Max's family."

"Hun, that's great, I'm sorry that happened to you though," Carly says as Max and I bring the food over to the table.

"Did you have a good time on Saturday, Nicole?" Asks Ben.

"I had a fantastic time, how could I not? I was with my best friend, my amazing boyfriend and you, my unofficial brother. Your family is so cool and I'm in love with Chelsea, that kid is hilarious and so fuckin' cute. God help her future boyfriends," laughs Nicole.

"There will be no boyfriends for Chelsea. She will not be having sex, just ask Justin," Ben says with a serious face.

"Ben, you're crazy, you and Justin can't stop her from growing up and dating. Do you feel the same about Noah?" asks Carly.

"That's different, Carly."

"Oh my god you are a chauvinist, and what a double standard. I can't believe you feel that way. Who are you?"

"Dude, I would quit while you're behind, you are not going to win this," pleads Max.

"Anyway…when do you get the photos the photographer took?" Nicole asks as she looks my way.

"He'll be sending us the proofs via email on Friday and we can forward them on to you. I'm hoping he got some good ones," replies Ben.

"I'm looking forward to seeing them. Everyone looked amazing on Saturday night and I would really like photos as a memento of the best birthday ever," Carly says as I reach out and kiss her hand.

"So Chica, I am going to address the elephant in the room. What time is he being sentenced tomorrow?" asks Nicole.

"Ummm, I think it's about 11 am WA time, so we should hear from 2 pm onwards. I just want to keep busy until I get the call from my lawyer Jack Cooper, he said he would call as soon as the sentence has been handed down."

"I'm up for keeping you busy. Finish dinner and drink up, bitch, you don't have to go to work in the morning so we can let loose tonight."

Max and I clean up as Carly and Nicole sit on the lounge drinking. I put on some music on in the background and it's great to see Carly relax with her best friend. After a while Max and I join the girls with more drinks, this is going to be a big night, just what we need.

We drink and laugh the night away telling stories about ourselves and one another. Because Nicole and Carly have known each other for so long they have heaps of stories to tell, most funny but some sad. Like the time Carly and Nicole went to the movies to see 'Clash of the Titans', they were running late so they got their tickets, drinks and food, showed the guy the tickets and raced into the cinema. The previews had started so they sat down and waited for Sam Worthington to come on screen but instead they got Natalie Portman and Mila Kunis. They'd walked into the wrong cinema and ended up watching that weird arse movie Black Swan. I didn't understand it then and I don't understand it now. Max and I can't stop laughing at them.

"Why didn't you go to the correct cinema once you realised what you had done?" Max asks.

"Well that would have been the logical thing to do, but Carly and I couldn't stop laughing at what we had done and we had sat there too long. So it would have been a waste of time changing cinemas."

"What about the time you found a stray kitten, Carly?" Nicole giggles.

"I pulled into our drive way one day and noticed this stray kitten in the gutter, I thought it was dead until I walked up to it and heard it meow. I took it to the vets and they scanned it for a microchip but there was none. It was so cute so I decided to keep it. They gave the kitten an ultrasound and said it was a girl and she may be pregnant, but if she was then it was right at the beginning so they could safely perform a sterilization. I decided to call her Chloe. She had her shots there and then and I booked her in to get sterilized and microchipped the following week. I got her a pink collar, pink name tag, pink bowl, pink kitty litter tray and some toys.

"Mum and Dad weren't happy because they're not cat people but eventually agreed to let me keep Chloe. I dropped her off at the vets to get sterilized and about two hours later I got a call from them. The first thing I said was 'Please tell me you didn't kill my cat,' and the vet laughed and said, 'No, but when we shaved Chloe we discovered she has a penis.' And I said, 'So she's not pregnant then?'"

Max and I nearly fall on the floor because we are laughing so hard. "Babe, you're telling me they gave the cat an ultrasound and they told you it was a girl when it was really a boy, isn't that Vet 101?"

"Yeah I know. Needless to say we didn't go back to that vet again. Anyway I had to think of another name and I decided to call him Isaak after the singer Chris Isaak."

"That's the cat you had when I met you."

"Yeah, that's him. Unfortunately after everything that happened I didn't get the chance to bring him with me to Sydney, but Mum loves him so I know he is ok with her. She treats him better than she does me," Carly says sadly. "So that's Isaak's story."

"Babe that's hilarious, thank god Roger's vet is switched on."

After a while we put on Sing Star and it gets really messy because of the amount of alcohol we have consumed. Carly and Nicole sing Beyoncé *Crazy in Love*. Well when I say sing, I mean they try to sing and fail miserably.

Max and I sing Good Charlotte's *I Just Wanna Live*, and even if I do say so myself we did a pretty good job. The four of us sing Robbie Williams and Kylie Minogue's Kids and finally stumble into bed about 3 am.

32 | CARLY

I wake about 11.30 am after what I think is the most amazing sex dream until I realise Ben has his fingers inside me, rubbing my clit and sucking my nipple. I moan and arch my back as an orgasm erupts through my body.

"Carly, that was wonderful to watch."

"What a way to start the day," I say with a smile. "Now lay back coz I'm gunna rock your world," I say as I straddle his cock and ride him until he comes inside me.

When Max and Nicole wake up we go into the city and go out for lunch. We find a beautiful restaurant in Sydney CBD and take a seat near the window. Ben, Nicole and I continually look at our watches, we are very mindful that it is getting close to the sentencing. We have a few wines with our delicious lunch and I start to relax a little until my phone rings. We all jump because it's only 2.45pm.

Ben holds my hand while I answer the phone. "H..H..Hello Carly spe..speaking," I stutter. Fuck, I hate stuttering.

"Carly, it's Jack Cooper, Judge Harvey has handed down his sentence."

"Babe put it on speaker," whispers Ben and I nod. "Jack, it's Ben Richardson, Carly has you on speaker, is that ok with you?"

"Of course, I know Carly's nervous about the sentencing. He got two years and eight months. With good behaviour he can apply for parole after eighteen months. They took him away and he is on his way to prison as we speak."

"Pl..please tell me h..he hasn't gone to the pris...prison my dad w..works at."

"No, the Judge got the letter your dad wrote and he took that into consideration."

"I'm pl..pleased, th..thank you J..Jack for ev..everything."

"It's my pleasure, enjoy your day and you will receive all of this in writing. Take care, Carly."

"You t..too Jack, th..thank you," I say as I hang up the phone. I look at my phone as I place it on the table. I don't know what to think, what to feel. All these years he has gotten away with hurting me and now justice has been served. I never thought this day would come, I nick-named him Teflon because everything slid off him and nothing stuck. Tears start to pool on the table as they fall from my eyes. Nicole hands me a napkin as Ben squeezes my hand. I look up. "I sh..should be happy b..but I feel so empty. Wh..why did it have to come to th..this?"

"Try not to think about it, Carly. Hopefully this will make him realise what he did was wrong and he will be remorseful, you never know. Plus you are safe now," says Max.

"Umm is it ok i..if we get out of h..here. I wo..would like to go for a walk down by th..the water."

"Of course, how about we go to Circular Quay and watch the ferries come and go," suggests Max, and I smile and nod.

It's a beautiful summer's day and the sea air is soothing. We sit on a bench and I start to relax as we watch the world go by. Ben sits next to me with his arm around my shoulder and he kisses my forehead every now and then.

There are a few street performers along Circular Quay and Nicole decides to have a bit of fun with one of them. There is a guy walking on stilts juggling all kinds of things and Nicole walks towards him with that look and a cheeky smile that means only one thing — the performer had better watch out.

I start to laugh. "Our girl is crazy, he doesn't know what is going to hit him," I say to Max.

"Yeah, that girl is crazy but you can't help but love her."

"Do you?" I ask Max.

"Do I what?"

"Max, don't be coy, you know what I'm asking. Do you love Ni-cole?"

"Carly, you can't ask him that."

I turn to Ben, and say, "Yes I can, Ben, and I just did." I turn back to Max. "So do you love her Max?"

Max takes a deep breath, looks towards Nicole. "Yes I do. I have never met anyone like her before, she's fuckin' crazy but that's one of the things that I love about her. She says what she thinks and feels, she will do anything for you, she's beautiful, she's sexy and she makes me so happy."

"Have you told her?"

"No, I'm not sure she feels the same way."

"Man you're blind if you can't see how much she loves you," says Ben.

"I'm not sure, it's pretty early in the relationship, I don't want to chase her away."

"I was petrified the night I told Carly, but I just had to tell her how I felt even if it meant losing her. Trust me when I say Nicole's in love with you, it's obvious."

Max looks at Nicole again, gets up and walks towards her. Ben and I look at each other. "I hope we didn't upset him," I say to Ben.

We are both nervous as we watch Max walk up to Nicole. He takes her hand and walks her to the edge of the water and leans against the railing. He pushes a piece of hair behind Nicole's ear and holds her face in his hands. We can't see or hear what he's saying to her. Max has his back to us but we can see Nicole's face. First we see confusion on her face, then shock, and all of a sudden and huge grin covers her face and she throws her arms around Max and kisses him passionately. He swings her around and carries her over to us laughing.

They reach us and they can't stop laughing and kissing. "Wanna tell us what's going on?" I ask.

Max and Nicole look at each other. "We told each other that we're in love," says Nicole.

"Who with?" I ask.

"Cheeky cow, who do you think? I love Max and he loves me."

"About time, it's obvious that you two are crazy about each other."

We spend the rest of the afternoon talking, eating ice-cream and people watching. We go to a pub in The Rocks for dinner. Once we have finished our meal we make our way to the adjoining room to listen to the DJ. I notice there are a lot of men there, more than you usually find in a pub. I realise that something is different.

I turn to Nicole and squeal, "It's gay night." I'm jumping up and down. I love gay pubs, Nicole and I used to go to The Court Hotel in Perth quite a lot. That's a gay and lesbian pub and the atmosphere is amazing.

Ben and Max get us drinks as we find a table. There are four guys on the table next to us and the one to my right smells lovely. I make eye contact and lean over. "I just wanted to let you know that you smell fantastic."

"Thanks Hun, that's kind of you to say. I'm Matt," he says as he holds his hand out to me.

"Nice to meet you Matt, I'm Carly and this is Nicole."

"Hi Nicole. This is Mitch, Joe and Nick. Who are you here with sweetie?"

"We're here with our guys Ben and Max, they're at the bar." Just then the guys come over to the table and I make the introductions. I'm really impressed because Ben and Max are very comfortable interacting with them. I have witnessed quite a bit of homophobia in my time but there is none of that tonight. Nicole and I dance with Ben and Max for a while and then they decide to sit down and drink. We stay on the dance floor and dance with our new friends. We have a great night and I soon forget about what happened today.

Luckily I don't start work until midday but poor Ben has to start early in the morning. We go to bed as soon as we get home because even though I love Nicole like a sister I need a bit of time alone with my man. We get into bed and snuggle facing each other.

"How do you feel about how things went today?"

"I'm surprised about how upset I got, I thought I would be re-lieved and maybe a little happy but all these emotions just bubbled to the surface and I couldn't control the tears. The tears weren't for him, they were for me, for my lost childhood, my innocence, and the fear and pain he inflicted on me. I believe it's finally over, I really believe I'm safe now and I can breathe for the first time since I was a little girl."

Ben pulls me a little closer and kisses me. "You are safe, Beauti-ful. I'm a bit surprised you didn't hear from your dad."

"I'm not sure what I would have said to him. Irrespective of what George did to me, he is still Dad's son and Dad has to be hurting because he was forced to choose between his children. No parent should have to go through that."

"You never cease to amaze me, you are always mindful of other people's feelings no matter what has happened to you."

"I can't be happy when someone else is miserable, especially when I love them. I will call Dad tomorrow."

"What about your mum?"

"That ship has sailed; she will have no involvement in my life anymore, and I have no interest in talking to her. She has got to be hurting but if I do talk to her she will try to convince me that it's all my fault and I don't want to deal with that."

"Fair call, babe." Ben rolls onto his back and pulls me against his side. I snuggle in, putting my head on his chest and my left arm across his waist and he wraps his arms around me. He holds me as we fall asleep.

I feel something lightly touch my shoulder, and I move thinking it's a bug. Then I feel a tap on my shoulder. I slowly turn my head and all I see is a light in my eyes. I squint as I put my hand up to try to block out the light and as I do that I see what looks like the barrel of a gun. I suck in my breath. I can't move, I try to speak but nothing comes out.

I feel hot breath on my neck before I hear the voice of the devil, "Move your fat, ugly arse out of this bed, do it slowly and quietly or I will shoot him."

I do as George tells me. I grab my robe which is lying next to my bed, put it on and quietly slip out of bed. The house is so quiet and I'm surprised that Roger isn't barking. We make our way to the lounge room and George tells me to sit down. I do as I'm told and I watch him nervously pace the floor.

"You have ruined my life, I'm going to jail and it's all your fault, so now I'm here to ruin your life."

George walks to the kitchen and gets a knife out of the butchers block and then makes his way back to me. He sits next to me on the lounge, grabs a hold of my hair and pulls my head back. I feel something cold against my neck and I know it's the knife, I flinch as he runs it across my neck and feel a stinging sensation as I realise he has cut me. I try not to make a sound because he thrives on fear, the more noise I make the more he gets off on it.

"I'm going to slowly cut you from head to toe and then I'm going to chop you up into little pieces and feed you to the sharks," George whispers in my ear.

All of a sudden the hall light turns on and I watch Nicole walk towards us, rubbing her eyes and yawning. She doesn't see us. I start to panic and I try to warn her, but George places his hand over my mouth. I can't let him hurt her. I struggle and make enough sound for Nicole to hear. She stops and tries to focus on were the noise is coming from.

I bite George's hand and yell to Nicole to run. She turns back towards the hall and I think she is getting away but she flicks on the lounge light and then turns back towards us. Her eyes adjust to the light and then she realises what is happening. "Get away from her you fuckin' arsehole!" Nicole yells.

George just laughs his evil laugh. "Once I've finished with this ugly, fat, cow it'll be your turn. I'm really going to enjoy this because I've always hated you and you have stuck your nose in too many times."

I can't sit back and let this happen, I have to do something. George still has a hold of my hair but he has loosened his grip a little because his focus is now on Nicole. I realise I am sitting on something and slowly move my hand underneath me to grab it. It's Roger's choker which is made out of metal chain. I take a good hold of the choker and swing it up as hard as I can into George's face. He screams as it hits his eyes and he lets go of my hair. The gun falls to the floor but he still has the knife in his hand. I dive for the gun as Nicole runs towards George. It all happens so quickly, I pick up the gun and turn around to see Nicole and George fighting over the knife when George gets the upper hand and plunges the knife into Nicole's chest. All I see is blood, so much blood as Nicole falls to the floor.

I let out an almighty scream and I feel hands on my shoulders shaking me. "Carly, wake up please." I can hear Ben's voice, "Babe, wake up, you're dreaming."

All of a sudden my eyes spring open and I see Ben kneeling next to me on the bed with his hands on my arm. "NICOLE!" I scream and go running into the spare room where Nicole and Max are sleeping. I throw open the door, turn on the light, run and jump onto their bed. Max and Nicole wake with a start. I pull back the covers and check Nicole for a stab wound, I see nothing. I throw my arms around Nicole. "You're ok, he didn't stab you?"

"What the fuck?" says Max as he pulls the sheet up his body and rubs his eyes.

"Did you have a nightmare, Chica?" whispers Nicole as I continue to hug her.

"George broke in, held a gun and knife against my throat and then stabbed you," I sob.

"Chica, he can't hurt you anymore, you're safe," says Nicole as she hugs me harder.

After a while I calm down and I start to let Nicole go. Ben is leaning against the door frame in his boxers. "Babe, I have to say seeing you and Nicole hugging each other while you're naked is sorta turning me on."

"I'm right there with ya mate," laughs Max.

"Fuck off you two, that's gross. Ben, I see you as a brother… ewwwww you perv," laughs Nicole.

"Really? You're getting turned on by my nightmare?"

"Babe, that's not what I said. You have to see it from our points of view, you're both naked and hugging each other. How can that not look hot?"

I turn to Max and point at his groin "Since we're being honest, WAY.TO.GO."

Nicole lies back on the bed laughing, "I'm one lucky bitch."

"CARLY!" yells Ben.

"What? I'm just being honest," I laugh.

"Come on, it's time to go back to OUR bed," says Ben as he holds his hand out for me. Max has already seen me naked so there is no use in covering up. I hug and kiss Nicole, get up and make my way to our room. Ben turns off the light and shuts Nicole and Max's door. We get into bed and Ben cuddles me from behind, he moves my hair and kisses my neck. "Good night Beautiful, no more nightmares, I got you."

I push as far back as I can go into Ben's body, take a few deep breaths and relax. "No more nightmares," I repeat and I quickly fall asleep.

Ben's alarm wakes us up at 6 am and I get up with him. "Babe, go back to sleep you had a rough night."

"So did you," I say as I lean in to kiss him. "I want to get up with you, do you want a coffee?"

"That would be great. I'm going for a shower first, care to join me?" Ben winks.

"If I get in that shower with you, you will be late for work. You shower and I'll have your coffee waiting," I smile as Ben pulls a face. "I will make it up to you tonight, I promise."

I make my way to the back door to let Roger out then go into the kitchen to put on the kettle, I pop some bread in the toaster, turn around and see Max walking my way rubbing his stomach. "What are you doing up?" I say.

"I always wake up at this time whether I'm at work or on leave. I usually stay in bed but I heard you and Ben so I thought I'd get up and grab a coffee."

"Do you want something to eat or just the coffee?"

"I'm always hungry, Carly," laughs Max.

"No worries, sit down and I will make you something to eat and get you a coffee." I get a tin of baked beans out of the pantry and take tomatoes, mushrooms, bacon and eggs out of the fridge. Once I have finished chopping the tomatoes and mushrooms I turn to Max. "I just wa..wanted to apologise f..for last night, f..for barging in your ro..room like that."

"Carly, no apology necessary, you had a terrible nightmare and I hope for your sake that's the last one you have. Please don't be angry, but Nic told me that you saw a counsellor when you were in hospital just before the trial. Have you been to see him since?"

I put my head down. "No."

"Can I share something with you?" Max asks. I look up and smile as I start to cook the breakfast. "When I deployed to Iraq I saw things that people should never see. I won't go into detail because I think you have enough going on up there without my crap too, but I have to admit it really screwed me up. When we came back not only had I been to war but my girlfriend had left me so I was in a bad way. My Warrant Officer set up counselling sessions for me but I refused to go, I thought I could sort through things on my own and that I was weak if I asked for help. Eventually I was ordered to go after I saw the Medic and was diagnosed with Post Traumatic Stress Disorder (PTSD). For the first two sessions I sat there refusing to talk, but then on the third session I just let it all out. I had many sessions after that and it was easier every time. I also went on a low dose of anti-depressants for a while, just enough to even out my moods and to make things clearer for me."

"How long did you see the counsellor?"

"I went fortnightly for five months and then monthly for four months, and I was on the anti-depressants for approx. six months. It was hard to begin with but I really believe that they both helped me. I would hate to think how I would be now if I hadn't accepted the help."

"I know it's the right thing to do but I'm afraid what the counsellor may unearth. A lot of what happened to me I have buried deep inside me. I believe I have done that for a reason and I'm not sure I want to go there."

"Just think about it."

"I will."

Just then Ben walks into the kitchen, wraps his arms around me and kisses my neck before he says hello to Max.

"You want some breakfast before you go?"

"Hell yeah, babe, it smells amazing." I get the guys to take their coffees and sit down at the table while I pile their plates high with food. I know they both have big appetites. I get my plate and join them. We decide to let Nicole sleep because she is a grumpy cow first thing in the morning, ain't nobody got time for that.

"I'm going to go for a run," Max says. "Are you ok if I take Roger with me?"

"Of course you can, he'll love it," I reply. "But please don't let him off the lead because he might not come back."

"No problem." says Max as he goes to his room to get changed. As he leaves with Roger Nicole walks out of the bedroom.

"Did you shit the bed?" I laugh.

"Fuck off bitch, Max woke me when he was getting changed to go for a run. How are you feeling after last night?"

"Nicole, it was so real to me, I could feel his breath on my neck and the knife against my throat, I was so fuckin' scared and then when he stabbed you it just tore my heart in two. When Ben woke me and told me I was dreaming I had to see that you were ok, that's why I ran into your room to check on you."

"Yeah, buck naked," Nicole laughs.

"That was crazy, I just flew off the bed and didn't think about covering up. You and I have seen each other naked heaps of times but I think it shocked the guys a bit."

"Chica, once everything had died down and we knew you were ok we lay there laughing our arses off that you ran in naked, that you saw Max's junk and that we were hugging each other. By the way he loved it when you said way to go, that really pumped his ego."

"I hope you used that pumped ego to its full capacity."

"Does a bear shit in the woods? I was all over that," Nicole winks, and I high five her.

When Max and Roger get back Roger is panting so much he can hardly walk. He heads straight for his water bowl and drinks so much I think he is going to drown. He stumbles to his bed and flops down. I think that's it for him today.

"Max, I think you broke my dog," I laugh. "He's not had that much exercise before."

"Yeah, he was getting a bit slow near the end so I slowed down a little, I think he was happy about that. Do you mind if I grab a shower?"

"Knock yourself out hun, but if you intend on taking Nicole with you just remember I need a shower before work so please leave me some hot water."

Nicole jumps to her feet and grabs Max's hand as they walk past me to the bathroom.

I slap her arse. "Go ride him cowgirl." I turn on the TV and turn the sound up because I know they get loud.

33 | CARLY

As Nicole and Max drive me to the salon on their way to Max's parents' home we make plans for the weekend.

"Ben will be home about 1 pm so come over when you want, there is a great pub down the road or we can stay in. Hey Max, when you drop me off at work why don't you come inside and I will tidy you up down there."

Max nearly runs off the road. "WHAT.THE.FUCK."

"We both got an eye full last night and I noticed you trim but I think you can benefit from getting waxed."

"I'm actually speechless and that says a lot considering I'm with Nicole and the things that come out of her mouth."

"So, what do you think?"

"Carly, I'm not letting you near my junk, that would be weird."

"Max, I'm a professional, this is what I do daily. I also pierce, so I could give you a Prince Albert."

"I don't want a piercing thank you very much."

"But you haven't said no to the waxing," I laugh.

"Come on babe, it would look amazing, I'd be right up in all of that," Nicole says smiling.

"I can't believe I'm going to say this. Ok, let's do it." Max sighs.

"Fantastic, I'll show you were to park and then I can take you right in before my first client, before you chicken out."

Max parks the car and then the three of us make our way to my room in the salon.

"Come on, get your gear off."

"Carly, I'm not sure about this."

"Max, it won't take long and I know Nicole will be happy with the results."

"Yeah, don't be a sook. I get mine all waxed off, if I can do it then so can you. Man up," Nicole giggles.

"I'll go out of the room for a few minutes while you get yourself organised," I say and go to put my bag in my locker. After a few minutes I knock on the door. Max is laying there with a towel over his groin. I look at Max. "Are you ready?"

"Just do it," growls Max.

I move the towel, prep the area and apply the wax. Nicole grabs his hand as I start to remove the wax. "Ahhhhhhh fuck me!" Max yells. This makes Nicole laugh. "Not helping, Nic."

"It won't take long, then I can do the rest."

"What do you mean the rest?"

"I need to tidy up the back too."

"No fuckin' way, Carly, just the front and hurry up." I go to work and Max cries out every time I remove the wax. "I would prefer to be back in Iraq."

"Stop being such a baby, it's just hair removal, women do it all the time," Nicole says.

"Again Nicole, not helping."

I finish up and give Max a mirror so he can see how it looks. "Not bad," he concedes.

"So now the shock has gone how about you let Carly finish the job properly?"

"Nic really?"

"Babe if you do this I promise I will do that thing you want to do."

Max's head swings around to Nicole like she has just told him he has won lotto. "Where do you want me?"

I laugh "Sexual blackmail, I love it. Ok Max I need you to lie on your stomach and part your legs a bit." Max does as I ask. "Ready?"

"Just get on with it."

"Your arse isn't that hairy, it's light soft hair. But it has to go," I say as I rip the first strip off. Max tenses and bites down on his arm. I go as quickly as I can. "Max, this is the very last bit and then we are done."

"Just hurry the fuck up will you." I put the wax in between his cheeks and wipe on the strip to remove the wax and hair and without warning I rip it off. "You fuckin' Mother fucker."

"All done," I say laughing. "Nicole, I will leave you alone with Max so you can clean the area with this solution to remove any wax left on the skin. And then put this lotion on the areas because it'll sooth the skin. I will wait for you both out there."

After a while they come out of the room and Max is walking like he's been riding a horse. "You must be kidding me, harden up soldier boy," I laugh.   Nicole hugs and kisses me goodbye and Max gives me the middle finger.   "Don't be like that Maxy boy, you know you love me," I say as I blow him a kiss.

That night Ben picks me up from work and I tell him what happened today with Max. "I can't wait til I see him tomorrow, I am really going to give him shit about being a pussy. It's not pleasant but you get used to it. I have no problem with it now. Besides, you have very gentle hands, sweetheart," Ben laughs as he kisses the back of my hand.

On Friday Georgie comes up to me and offers to swap a shift so that I can spend the whole weekend with Max and Nicole. "Georgie thank you so much. I didn't want to ask for any more time off, you're a gem, I really appreciate this," I say as I hug her.

"You're welcome, I know how close you are with Nicole and how much you miss her."

"I won't forget this Georgie," I smile.

As the bus pulls up to my stop I notice Nicole and Roger there waiting for me. "Hey hun, thanks for meeting me," I say as I hug Nicole and pat Roger.

As we walk home I tell Nicole that I don't have to work this weekend and she squeals and hugs me. "How do you feel about meeting Max's family this weekend? They have invited you and Ben over for a BBQ on Saturday."

"Sounds good to me."

Max is sitting on the lounge drinking a beer. "How's it hanging Max?" I ask.

"I'm not sure if I'm talking to you or not, my junk feels weird and it's breezy down there." I fall on the other lounge laughing so hard that I snort, which makes Nicole laugh, and all too soon we are in hysterics.

"I'm thrilled I have given you both a good laugh," Max says.

"Stop being a pussy, Carly does mine all the time and you don't see me acting like this," laughs Ben.

"I feel violated and I couldn't have sex yesterday because I was too tender," sulks Max. Nicole and I laugh even harder.

"Get over yourself, Princess, have a few more beers and you'll be good to go. Ben says. Just then Ben's mobile rings. "Hey Darcy how's it goin?" he says as he makes his way to the kitchen.

"So guys, do you want a night in?" I ask. "Max, do you want to see if any or all of your sisters and their boyfriends want to come over for a few drinks? They can stay the night but will have to bring their own bedding."

"You sure? They're really full on, Carly."

"I like the sound of that. I'll just go and interrupt Ben's call and see if his lot would like to come too, I'll be right back." I get Ben to ask Darcy about tonight and get the thumbs up. I call Kelsey and Damon and they are up for it too. I walk back into the lounge and find that all of Max's sisters and boyfriends are coming, I'm so excited. Nicole and I go to the supermarket and get snacks, soft drinks, breakfast food, and alcohol, and we also pick up fish and chips for dinner.

Max's sisters and their boyfriend's all arrive at the same time and all of a sudden the place is alive and the noise is deafening. I love it. We put everyone's bedding in our room and then Max makes the introductions. Max's sister Alice has brought her best friend Emery with her because she was already at the house when Max made the call, the more the merrier. About an hour later Damon, Lily, Darcy, Kelsey and Ethan arrive. Ben makes the introductions as Nicole and I get the drinks.

"Before everyone gets too drunk there is only one rule, don't give my dog alcohol," I say.

"Is it ok if I dance with him?" Damon asks.

"If that's what floats your boat Damon," I laugh as I turn up the music.

The drinks are flowing, people are dancing and everyone is having a good time. Ben goes next door to see if Matt and Amber would like to come over and they arrive about half an hour later. I'm talking to Max's sister Claire and her boyfriend Parker when I notice Damon watching Emery.

"Claire does Emery have a boyfriend?" I ask.

"Ummm not anymore, she dumped her boyfriend because he was doing drugs and he wouldn't get help."

"That's one thing I have never been interested in, I enjoy a drink but drugs don't do it for me. By the way, I'm cool with the both of you drinking because there are a lot of family here to watch out for you, I know Max checked with your folks before you came over and they were ok as long as you don't get trolleyed," I smile.

I walk over to Nicole. "Hey bitch," she says as she wraps her arm around my shoulder.

"I want you to look at something for me. Look at everyone around the room and tell me what you see," I say.

"Ooooohhhhhh I love people watching." Nicole sips her drink as she scans the room. Max walks up and whispers something in her ear. "Babe, just give me a minute, I'm concentrating." Max gives me a puzzled look. "Ooh ooh I've got it, Damon is checking out Emery."

"Really? How can you tell?" Max asks.

"Damon is standing across the room from her and when she moves from his sight he moves with her. He will be talking to people but positions himself so he can look at her when he is talking. Also he isn't drinking much, he is still drinking the same beer that Ben gave him two hours ago," Nicole says.

"How do you know that it's the same beer?"

"Because he ripped the corner of the label off when he started drinking it. Hey Benny boy, come here," shouts Nicole.

Ben comes over. "How long has it been since Damon has had a girlfriend or has been seeing someone?"

"Shit I don't know, Damon pretty much keeps his private life private. Let me check with Darcy, he sees more of him than I do." Ben calls Darcy and Lily over. "Hey guys when was the last time Damon had a girlfriend?" Ben asks.

Darcy and Lily look at each other. "I don't think he really does the girlfriend thing, he's more into the hook-up. He has girls hitting on him all the time at the pub so I don't think he runs short of female attention. Why do you ask?" asks Darcy.

"Carly noticed him checking out Emery," says Nicole, and everyone turns to watch Damon watching Emery. "Guys don't be so obvious," she says. We all laugh and then look away. "Watch this space."

Why'd You Only Call Me when you're high by Arctic Monkeys starts playing and everyone goes wild, our lounge is packed with bodies dancing and singing. I look towards Damon and I notice he's the only one not dancing. I make my way over to him, take his hand and drag him into the sea of bodies.

"I don't dance, Carly," he says.

"You do tonight, now move your feet in time with the music."

"I told you I don't dance."

"Well you must be shit in bed then."

"WHAT THE FUCK CARLY, I'm fuckin' awesome in bed," states Damon.

"Is that so? Well you don't have the moves on the dance floor so I'm assuming you don't have the moves in the bedroom. You see Ben, look at how he's moving, he's a phenomenal lover."

Damon puts his fingers in his ears. "CARLY..fuck me...stop talking, I don't want to hear how my brother operates."

"Start dancing and I'll stop talking," I laugh. Damon starts to move with the music and sends me a pissed off smile. "Thata boy," I say as I tap his arm. While we dance I notice Damon watching Emery. I grab Damon's hand and move us towards Alice, Mitch and Emery. I wink at Alice and move next to Emery. "Hi, I'm Carly," I say to her.

"I'm Emery, thank you for letting me come tonight."

"You're very welcome. This is Damon, Ben's brother," I say as I step aside so they are dancing next to each other. They say hello and continue dancing. I move closer to Alice. "He has been watching Emery all night," I whisper in Alice's ear.

Alice smiles. "He is certainly her type, but she was really burnt by her ex-boyfriend so I'm not sure if she will be interested."

"Well we have brought them together so it's up to them," I say as I feel Ben's arms wrap around my stomach. He presses his body into my back as he moves with me.

"What's up to who?" he asks, and I explain what is going on. He looks at Damon and then at Emery, puts my arms around his neck as he kisses me.

"Jesus Christ bro put her down," says Damon.

"I can't keep my hands off her, she is beautiful and sexy and I love her to bits."

"That's adorable," Emery says.

"Thank you Emery, that's very kind of you to say so. Carly is the woman I am going to marry and have children with."

"Babe, how much have you had to drink?" I ask Ben.

"Why?"

"Because you only tell people that you're going to marry me and have children with me when you have been drinking quite a bit. I'm not angry, it's so cute," I say as I snuggle into his chest.

"I started drinking when Max and Nicole arrived this afternoon, so you could say I've had a few beers," he laughs. Just then One Republic's *Something I Need* comes on, and Ben pulls me closer and starts singing to me. I love it when he does this because I know in this particular moment in time I am the most important person in his world. *"I had a dream the other night, about how we only get one life, woke me up right after two, stayed awake and stared at you, so I wouldn't lose my mind."*

When the chorus starts everyone sings and jumps around It's such a wonderful moment, I get my phone out and take video of everyone. This is not bad for the first party I have ever thrown.

MUSE *Supremacy* comes on and a few of the guys start to head bang, which makes me laugh. I notice Damon and Emery haven't left each other's sides since they started dancing together. The music is loud, the drinks are flowing and everyone is really drunk. Luckily everyone is in a great mood and the atmosphere is electric.

Kelsey and Ethan let me know they are tired and we set their bedding up on the floor in our bedroom. Darcy and Lily will be sleeping on the floor too so none of us will be getting any tonight, but then I have to say that with the amount of beer Ben is drinking I doubt he could get it up. Max and Nicole are the only ones that won't be sharing because the bed in their room takes up all the space. Lucky bitch.

Matt and Amber go home around 3 am and they offer a bed to Helen and Will plus Sara and Oliver. Molly, Cory, Alice, Mitch, Claire, Parker, Emery and Damon sleep in the lounge room. We move the coffee table out of the way and push the lounges up against the wall. Everyone puts their bedding down and I notice Damon puts his next to Emery. I smile and wink at Nicole.

I wake mid-morning to noise coming from the lounge room and the smell of bacon cooking. I sit up and realise that I am the only one in the room. I grab my robe and walk into the lounge. "Good morning Chica," calls Nicole.

"Seriously bitch, since when do you wake up earlier than me?"

"I had a wonderful wake up this morning." Max's sisters throw cushions at Nicole and tell her to stop talking. "What?" she laughs.

Max, Cory, Mitch and Damon are cooking breakfast for everyone. Roger is panting heavily on his bed and it looks like Max took him for another run this morning. When the breakfast is ready the guys put the food in large trays and place them on the counter for everyone to help themselves. I go next door to Matt and Amber's to see if anyone is awake and if they want to join us for breakfast. I'm surprised when I find them up awake and sitting at the kitchen table drinking coffee, I invite everyone over for breakfast and we head back to my place.

Damon and Emery are sitting on the lounge next to each other deep in conversation. I notice he grabs her plate when she has finished, takes it to the bench and gets her a drink. How cute, I will have to keep an eye on these two.

We drive Max and Nicole to the BBQ because they are staying with us again tonight. I had enough to drink last night and I am happy being the skipper tonight. We stop off at the Cheesecake Shop to pick up a French Vanilla Cheesecake, Black Forrest Torte and Marble Mud Cake.

Max's parents are great even though his dad doesn't say much, he's not rude but I think he is just taking it all in. I can see he is very proud of his children and is fond of their partners, and truly loves his wife Louise.

When I go to get a drink Alice follows me. "Hey Carly, Emery and Damon are going out tonight."

"That's great Alice, he's a good guy and will treat her well. Do you know where they're going?"

"Dinner and a movie I think."

"That's so cool, I hope everything goes well because they had a good time together at the party and they look good together. I'll let you know if he says anything to Ben."

"Same here, I know I will get the goss from her sometime this weekend and if there is anything juicy I will let you know," laughs Alice.

We rejoin the BBQ and I really enjoy the banter that whips around the table. After a fantastic night we thank Louise and Bobby for their hospitality and leave just after midnight.

Ben and I fall into bed without showering and I fall asleep as Ben cuddles me from behind. I wake about 4 am because I'm thirsty, I take a mouthful of water from the glass on my bedside table then roll into the middle to cuddle with Ben. He's lying on his back with one of his arms above his head and the other by his side. I lay my left hand across his stomach and my head on his shoulder. I move my hand in slow circles and after a while Ben starts to let out soft moans, I move my hand lower and run my fingers through his snail trail, I can feel Ben's stomach muscles start to twitch. I move my hand lower and I can feel his cock start to harden with my touch, I move my hand even lower and massage his balls. Ben starts to move with my hand and moan my name, I increase the pressure and kiss my way down his stomach, his cock is rock hard as I flick the tip with my tongue. He arches his back and thrusts his cock into my mouth. I suck and lick and gently run my teeth over the tip, his moans become louder and he calls out my name as he places a hand on my head.   "Ohhhh god babe…don't stop," moans Ben as he wakes and realises that he's not dreaming. I speed up and increase the pressure as I use my hand to pump his cock in time with my mouth. "Fuuuc-cccckkkk Carly..I'm gunna come," cries Ben as he comes in my mouth.

"WOW you had a lot to say for yourself," I laugh as I lay down next to him wiping my mouth.

"That's because I haven't been able to touch you for two days, I thought I was going to get blue balls."

"Seriously, after two days? How did you go before you met me? Because you said it had been six months since you last had sex."

"My hand and I are very good friends," Ben laughs. "Now lay back and let me have my way with your body."

"If you insist," I squeal as Ben spreads my legs and dives between my legs, licking and sucking until I come in his mouth. "Holy shit..you are a very talented man, Ben Richardson," I sigh as my heart rate slows down.

We go back to sleep and wake mid-morning to Nicole and Max having VERY loud sex.

"Ohhhh Nic…your pussy is soooo wet…made just for me."

"MAX, shut up!" I yell, but it makes no difference.

"That's it Nic..squeeze harder…fuck you're tight…mmmmmm amazing."

"Max you fuckwit shut up, we can hear you," I laugh as I yell at him again. This time I think they hear me because they have gone quiet. I start laughing and all too soon I'm in hysterics.

"Shut up bitch, you ruined our moment," yells Nicole from the hallway before our bedroom door swings open.

"You girls really need to learn how to knock," Ben says as he scrambles to grab the sheet. Nicole walks in and gets into bed next to me. "Nic, what did I just say?"

"Benny boy, Carly and I have seen each other naked so many

times. We have showered together and slept naked in the same bed before so this is no big deal."

"Nicole I'm naked, in the bed, with Carly, and now you, this is not a porno. Do you mind leaving the room so we can get dressed?" Ben says through gritted teeth.

"Keep your hair on stud, I won't take a sneaky look at your junk," laughs Nicole as she gets out of our bed and heads towards Max who is leaning against the door frame.

"Dude, at least my girl didn't get a full view of your junk like yours did with mine the other night," smiles Max as he holds his hand out for Nicole.

"Seriously," Ben huffs as he grabs his boxers from the floor and walks over to shut our door.

"Why are you in such a bad mood?"

"I'm used to people knocking and being respectful of my privacy. I like Nicole but she really needs to learn how to knock."

I cuddle into Ben as he sits on the bed. "I'll have a word with her. We have always been very open with each other so it's hard now that things have changed." I kiss his shoulder. "Come and shower with me, I promise to really lather you up and pay a lot of attention to your amazing cock." Ben can't get to his feet quick enough. We spend a lot of time in the shower, taking our time with each other. Ben has calmed down and is very relaxed as we enter the lounge room.

34 | CARLY

"What time is your flight tomorrow?" I ask Nicole.

"We fly out at 1.45 pm," Nicole sighs as she pulls me in for a cuddle. "Gunna miss you Chica, but I'll be back just after Christmas."

"Yeah, I am looking forward to spending New Years Eve with you and Max watching the fireworks in Sydney, it's going to be amazing," I laugh. "Do you fancy going to Bondi beach today?"

"Sounds good to me. Max do you fancy a day at Bondi Beach?"

"Yeah, why not? And because it's our last day, is it ok if I invite the girls?"

"Hell yeah," Nicole and I say at the same time. I really enjoy the company of Max's sisters and their boyfriends. Max makes the calls as we get our stuff together. We take Ben's car and Nicole and Max go in his hire car because they are staying at his parents' home tonight. Bondi is very busy as it's a beautiful summer's day but we manage to find a spot big enough for everyone and Max sends his sisters a text to let them know where we are. I make sure that I put on a lot of sunscreen as I generally burn easily. I put some on Ben's back before he takes the tube from me and puts some on the rest of his body.

Max's lot walks over to us and I start to smile because Damon is holding hands with Emery. I get to my feet and give everyone a hug hello, I'm so happy to see them, they are all so close and it's nice to be a small part of that. I hope that when Max and Nicole go back to WA I will stay in contact with the girls.

A few of them decide to go for a swim while the rest sit on the beach chatting. I walk in the water up to the top of my thighs and I am happy standing there watching everyone when all of a sudden I'm knocked from behind and go under. I try to get up but something is on top of me and I can't get to my feet, I start to panic and swallow a lot of water. I'm not in deep water so I can't understand why I'm unable to get to my feet. I feel bodies all around me but I still can't stand, I'm running out of air fast and I need to get to the surface. I'm about to try one last time when I feel someone grab my foot and pull it to the surface while another pair of hands grab my shoulders and lift them above the surf. I cough and splutter as I gasp for air. As I'm carried to the shore I realise it's two lifeguards who are carrying me. They lay me on the sand and roll me into the recovery position where I cough up water and vomit.

"What's your name?" one of the lifeguards ask.

"Carly," I splutter.

"How are you feeling?"

"I feel si..sick and my th..throat is sore, wha..what happened?"

"A bunch of guys were playing footy near the water and they went in for a tackle and looks like you got caught up in it. I saw you go down and expected to see you come back up and when you didn't we rushed over to where you were."

"I could feel l..l..legs all around me b..but I was unable to get u..up," I stutter.

"That's because the tackle started a fight and it looks like no one noticed you."

"Thank god yo..you, thank you so mu..much. What's your n..name?"

"I'm Billy and this is Cooper."

"Thank you," I say as I sit up. "Am I ok t..to go back to m..my friends now?"

"Yeah, that's ok but I would like you to take it easy this afternoon, hopefully you have gotten all the sea water out but if your breathing changes in any way you have to promise me you will go to the hospital," states Billy.

"I prom..promise," I smile.

Nicole pushes through the crowd. "What the fuck, Chica, you ok?"

I take a deep breath. "Yeah, th..thanks to these two I a..am."

"Carly, I am so sorry. I was too busy talking to see what happened to you. I looked up to see where you were and noticed a crowd around someone. I never thought in a million years it would have been you."

I take a breath. "I'm ok now. Do you know where Ben is?"

"Yeah, he's out deeper with the boys, do you want me to get

him?"

"No, it's fine, I think I just want to lie on my towel for a while and catch my breath."

I lie down, take a deep breath and cough out a little more water and then relax and start to fall asleep. My eyes spring open when I hear Ben's voice yelling at someone.

"She could have fuckin' drowned, why were you playing so close to the water anyway?" yells Ben.

"Richo, we are so sorry, it got out of hand. I checked with the lifeguards and they said she is ok."

I sit up and see Ben right up in some guy's face. I get to my feet and make my way over to them. I put my hand on Ben's arm and he snatches it away from me not even looking in my direction. "Ben, it's me, what's going on?" I say as I try to get him to listen to me, still nothing "BEN!" I yell as I place my hand on his lower back.

It all happens so fast. Ben spins around with his fist clenched aimed at my head. I see the anger and blind fury in his eyes as I cover my face with my arms trying to protect myself, waiting for the punch to connect with my face. I hear *omph* and see Damon tackle Ben to the ground and hear a lot of yelling. My knees give out from underneath me and I fall to the ground shaking. I feel arms around me, I look up and see Nicole, she has tears running down her face, she's speaking to me but I can only hear noise, not words. I realise I'm having a panic attack. I feel my body being lifted up and placed onto something hard, and something light being placed over the top of me. We start to move and the next thing I know I'm inside laying on a bed with Nicole sitting next to me holding my hand.

I'm numb, I can't believe Ben nearly hit me. The reality of the situation catches up with me and I start to shake and cry uncontrollably. "I'm gunna be sick," I cry as I try to get up. Nicole hands me a bucket and grabs my hair before I begin to throw up everything that's in my stomach, including sea water. I continue to dry reach even though there is nothing left. When I finally finish Nicole takes the bucket from me and hands me a glass of water to rinse out my mouth. I lay back down with my arm over my head, how did a great day end up so fucked up?

There are footsteps and a familiar voice, which gets louder. All of a sudden Nicole jumps up and yells, "GET THE FUCK OUT OF HERE! YOU NEARLY HIT HER YOU ARSEHOLE. HASN'T SHE BEEN THOUGH ENOUGH ALREADY? YOU WERE IN A BAD MOOD

THIS MORNING AND NOW THIS."

"I didn't know it was you, Carly," Ben says, ignoring Nicole as he walks slowly towards me. "Babe, I'm so sorry, I had just heard what happened to you, I was making my way over to see if you were alright when one of the guys from the base stopped me and apologised for hurting you. I'm so sorry I scared you. I would never hit you, I'm not like him," Ben cries.

As Ben reaches me he slowly puts his hand out to touch my face.   "Ge..get him out o..of here," I whisper unable to look at him.

"No Carly, please don't do this," Ben pleads.

"YOU HEARD HER, GET THE FUCK OUT!" yells Nicole.

Ben moves towards me and I recoil up the bed avoiding eye contact with everyone. There's an almighty crack, I look up to see Nicole's hand on Ben's face and I realise Nicole has slapped him. Just then Max and Damon enter the room. They take one look at the situation and race to Ben to take him outside. Ben doesn't go willingly because he has to be restrained.

There is a lot of yelling and swearing from outside. Billy comes over and asks if I want to press charges. I shake my head because Ben hadn't touched me, he had just scared me.

Damon enters the room. "Carly, are you ok with me being here?" I don't look at him but I nod and he takes a seat at the bottom of my bed. "Do you mind if I speak to you in private?" Damon asks.

Nicole is about to say something when I look at her and say, "It's ok."

"I'll be right outside. You say or do anything to upset her I will cut your balls off and feed them to the fish. Do you understand?" Nicole snarls as she points her finger at Damon.

"Yeah, I understand, Nicole. I know Carly's your family but what I need you to understand is that Carly is my family too and I can see she is hurting. The last thing I want to do is add to that pain."

When Nicole leaves the room Damon sits closer to me. "How are you feeling?"

"I'm ok," I say.

"Carly, I'm not here to fight Ben's corner, I'm here to make sure you're ok. If you don't want him near you then I will make sure he stays away."

"Thank you," I whisper.

Damon takes my hand in his. "What do you remember?"

"I was just standing there watching everyone have a good time when all of a sudden I was under the water and I couldn't understand why I couldn't get up. I swallowed a lot of water, I was panicking and fighting for breath when the lifeguards Billy and Cooper pulled me out of the water. They realised I was ok and they let me go back to everyone. After a while I heard Ben yelling and that's when I went over and things got really crazy."

"That must have been really scary for you. Are you sure you're ok?"

"I have a sore throat and my stomach hurts because I threw up everything and then some." I smile.

"Have you thought about what you want to do now?"

"What do you mean?"

"Do you want to go home or do you want to go with Nicole?"

"I haven't thought that far. Where's Ben?"

"He's outside with Max."

"Is he ok?" I ask.

"No, he's not. He's worried about you and he's ashamed that he nearly hit you. Carly, I can say with hand on heart he didn't know it was you, he was so angry that you were hurt he just lashed out and unfortunately you were in the thick of it."

"I know he didn't know it was me and that he wouldn't hit me. I was scared and all I saw was a fist coming towards me and it freaked me out."

"That's totally understandable," Damon sighs.
We sit there in silence for a while. "Can you please ask Ben to come in?" I ask Damon.

"Of course I can." Damon stands, kisses me on the forehead and walks outside.

After a while Ben slowly walks into the room and just stands there looking at the ground. I can see he's in so much pain so I walk over to him, place my hands on either side of his face and lift it up so he is looking at me. I lean in and place a gentle kiss on his lips. "It's ok, I know you didn't know it was me, I was just scared that's all," I whisper.

"I would never hit you Carly. Please believe me," he says as tears fall from his eyes.

I wrap my arms around his neck. "I do believe you," I say as I melt into his arms.

Ben pulls me closer and hugs me hard. "I love you so much,

Carly," he says over and over as he holds me.

"Can we please go home?" I ask.

"Nothing would make me happier," he smiles.

Nicole glares at Ben as she walks up to us. "You ok?" Nicole asks.

"Yeah, I'm ok. Can I have a word with you in private please?" Nicole and I walk away from everyone else. "Nic, I know you were scared but please don't be angry with Ben."

"Are you fuckin' kidding me, he nearly hit you." Nicole gasps.

"He didn't know it was me, Nicole. You know that was so out of character for him and he would never lay a hand on me that way. He was so angry that I had been hurt that he lashed out and I got in the way. Please cut him some slack."

Nicole rolls her eyes and sighs, "Chica if that's what you want then I can do that for you. But if he steps one more foot out of line I will cut loose."

"I love you for loving me so much, you have always been there for me and you're my family. In this situation Ben overreacted but he didn't hit me and he certainly didn't know it was me, so please, for me, just drop it," I say as I hug Nicole.

Ben turns to Nicole "We ok?"

Nicole takes a minute. "Yeah, we're ok, but I have to say, Ben, you scared me and our girl today. I know you love and adore her but today you were out of control."

"I know, and I'm not proud of myself," Ben says as he hangs his head.

I take Ben's hand in mine. "Come on, let's go home. Are you lot coming round ours for a bit?"

Damon looks at Emery and she nods so they drive with us while Max and Nicole go in his car. We drive in silence, I reach over and rest my hand on Ben's thigh as he drives. I turn to look at Damon. "Thank you for today, I saw a side to you that I have never seen before, you're a good guy."

"No need to get all girlie on me, Carly," Damon says, looking embarrassed.

At home I walk into the bathroom and lean my hands on the vanity and look at myself in the mirror, I look tired and haggard, I think I've aged ten years today. I turn on the hot and cold taps in the shower and start to take my clothes off when there is a knock. "Hang on a sec," I call out as I grab a towel and wrap it around myself. "Come in," I say and the bathroom door slowly opens. I see Ben standing there. I give him a confused look "Why did you knock?"

"I wasn't sure you would want me in here," he says softly.

I slowly walk to Ben, shut the bathroom door behind him, take his hand in mine and walk him towards the shower. I drop my towel and start to undress him as he stands there silently. When I finish I take his hand in mine and walk us both under the water. Ben washes my hair and then we take our time washing each other, it's such a tender moment, nothing sexual; we are just being with each other, looking deep into one another's eyes.

Afterwards Ben grabs us all a drink and we sit in the lounge chatting to Max and Nicole. We go to the local pub for a meal and have a great time. Nicole relaxes a bit with Ben and even jokes around with him.

All too soon it's time to say goodbye to Nicole, this is so hard, I hate saying goodbye. We hug, cry and hold onto each other for dear life. "I wish you lived here," I say to Nicole.

"Hopefully one day we will live near each other again, I hold onto that and it gets me through life," cries Nicole.

BEN | 35

On Friday I pick Carly up from work because we were going to the MUSE concert. We take the train to the Allphones Arena, it's a great venue and we have amazing seats. The supporting act is Perth band Birds of Tokyo and they blow me away, they are fantastic and when they play Lanterns everyone gets their phones out and switch on the light and it looks amazing. We have a short interval before MUSE come on. Carly is jumping out of her skin with excitement as they put on an amazing show both with their music and visually. By the end of the night neither of us has much of a voice and my body aches from dancing the whole way through. The best part is that my girl is happy. My ears are buzzing when we leave to catch the train home. We've bought a few t-shirts, two with MUSE on them and one with Birds of Tokyo. The train is packed and we stand huddled close against one of the walls.

"I love watching you during a concert, you get so absorbed in the experience and you're like a kid at Christmas," I whisper in Carly's ear.

"You know how special and important music is to me, I feel very honoured to be at a concert and witness the band's talent and passion. I just loose myself, it's fantastic." She smiles up at me.

I hug her closer. "It's very contagious, Beautiful."

We get off at our stop and it's a nice night so we walk the short distance to our home. "I got a call from Mum today and she wants to know if we would like to stay there Christmas Eve and Christmas night?"

"I'm cool with that. We have to leave earlyish on Boxing Day because I have to be at work at noon."

"Yeah, no worries. We can take Roger with us too. It'll be our first Christmas as a family," I smile.

"I'm really excited, but nervous. Christmas has always been a non-event in my life so it'll be really different experiencing it with your family, especially with young children. Does your family go all out?"

"Yeah, Dad covers the outside of the house with lights and Mum decorates the inside. It slowed down a bit as we got older but when Chelsea was born they ramped it up again," Ben laughs as he shakes his head. "With us kids we all have our names in a hat and we pull one out and that's the only kid you buy for. Justin's name was added when he and Piper got together and this year yours has been added. The rules are that the gift cannot be over $50.00 and you cannot buy for your partner, so if I got your name I would have to put it back and take another. Because we aren't going there until Christmas Eve Mum will text us the name of the person we are to buy a present for. We still buy for Mum and Dad and for Chelsea, and now Noah."

"That's a great idea. I hope you don't mind but I have ordered a photo of the whole family that was taken on my twenty-first as a present for your Mum. I also got one of you, me and my dad for him for Christmas."

"That's fantastic, they will be over the moon. I have to give you the heads up: your present will be delivered to our house and you are not to open it until Christmas day, so no cheating," I smile.

"Well I can do one better, I have already got your gift and it's in the house, so no looking for it."

We arrive home, shower and go to bed because Carly has work in the morning. The lead up to Christmas is uneventful We buy Chelsea a new doona cover with Barbie on it and for Noah we get a storybook projection that projects a children's story on the ceiling, it should settle him down if he becomes restless. Carly and I get a text from Lucy to tell us I'm buying for Justin and Carly's buying for Damon.

The Sunday before Christmas Carly and I do the last of our Christmas shopping. Carly gets a box of chocolates for all the girls at the salon, I get Justin a pair of Billabong boardies and Carly gets Damon a game for his Play Station. The city is full of families with little kids excited about seeing Father Christmas and people looking for gifts, there is a real buzz and it's infectious. After we finish shopping we go to a pub for a few drinks and a meal. The pub is packed but we find a table in the corner. Out the corner of my eye I notice Hayley making her way to us. I see her first, and I place my hand on Carly's thigh and gently squeeze. I lean forward, kiss her and whisper, "Sorry." I move the bags of shopping off the chairs so Hayley and Sophie can sit across from us. It's a very awkward situation and you could cut the atmosphere with a knife.

"Carly, this is Hayley's girlfriend Sophie."

Carly reaches her hand across the table and shakes Sophie's hand and says hello. She just nods at Hayley. Hayley and I make small talk but Sophie and Carly stay silent. It feels very awkward.

After a while Hayley leans forward and asks, "Carly, can we talk in private please?"

"Anything you have to say to me you can say in front of Ben."

I can tell Hayley is not happy Carly's answer and shuffles uncomfortably in her seat. After a while she takes a deep breath. "Carly, I owe you an apology, the last time we spoke I was rude and condescending to you and that was very wrong of me. You were right on the money with what you said to me, I have had a thing for Ben since Recruit School, I am bi-sexual and I was hoping Ben would join Sophie and me in a threesome." I nearly choke on my beer. "But there was something you said that really hit home with me, you said that if Ben was interested in me he would have already made his move and I had two choices — either tell him how I feel or get over it and continue the friendship. So I made my choice. I have chosen friendship, if that's ok with you?"

"Hayley, I don't tell Ben who to be friends with, he's a big boy and can make that decision on his own. So if Ben wants to continue his friendship with you, that's his decision not mine."

"Ok, so the next question is, can we start over and hopefully be friends?"

"We can start over, but let's not force the friendship issue. If we are meant to be friends it will happen naturally, that's all I can give you at the moment," Carly says honestly.

"Ok I can handle that," says Hayley with a slight smile.

Sophie and Hayley make small talk but when our meal is ready they leave us to it. I go to the bar to get us another drink each and when I return I say, "Am I in the twilight zone? what the fuck just happened?"

"When we saw Hayley at the bar after our big fight I called her out on a few things and she confirmed today that I was right."

"So that's why you wouldn't tell me what happened." I didn't let on that I already knew.

"I didn't want to influence your friendship with her so that's the reason I didn't tell you what I thought. I wanted Hayley to know I was onto her and for her to figure it out on her own. If your friendship was that important to her she had to sort out her feelings and it looks like she has done that. I don't trust her but I am willing to be in her company and give her the chance to gain my trust, time will tell."

"Babe, you have such a unique way of looking at things. I can't believe you didn't tell me," I smile.

"I didn't want to inflate your ego, hot stuff, it's not every day two women are grooming you for a threesome."

"It sounds sorta creepy when you say it like that. I had no clue she felt that way about me."

"Yeah, well I picked it up within the first five seconds that night in the nightclub. Guys are so fuckin' clueless," Carly laughs as she rolls her eyes.

CARLY | 36

Before I leave for work on Christmas Eve a courier drops a package off for Ben, I sign for it and get excited because it must be my Christmas present from him. It's about the size of a shoe box. I shake and squeeze it but I have no idea what it is so I leave it on the kitchen table for Ben to find when he gets home from work.

The day goes fast and we work back a little later than normal to fit everyone in because everyone deserves to look their best at Christmas. Before leaving the salon the girls and I exchange our gifts, wish each other a happy and safe Christmas. Ben is leaning against the passenger side door of his car waiting for me. He pulls me in for a kiss and cuddle and then we make our way to Wollongong, the traffic is crazy. Our bags and presents are in the boot and Roger is on the back seat with his bedding and toys.

Chelsea comes running to the car as soon as we pull up at Lucy and James's, she must have been looking out the front window. Ben puts his arms out for her but she runs straight past him to the back to get Roger.

"I think you have been replaced," I laugh. Ben's very quiet as we get everything out of the car. "You ok?" I ask.

"Yeah, I'm fine." I look at him with my eyebrows raised. "She isn't excited to see me anymore, it's all about Roger."

"Honey she has fun with Roger and can have him all to herself, but she loves you, please don't doubt that. When she has played with Roger for a while I bet she will come up for a cuddle. Come on, let's get all of this inside and get ready for my first Richardson Christmas," I smile. I pull him in for a kiss and cuddle and then we make our way inside. "Holy shit," I say as Ben opens the front door, "you weren't kidding when you said they go all out, this is amazing." The foyer has been transformed into a winter wonderland. There is garland wrapped around the balustrade all the way from the bottom of the stairs to the top and there are led lanterns on each step giving off a beautiful glow. There is a massive real Christmas tree next to the staircase and the smell of pine is wonderful, I have never had a real Christmas tree before. I have a closer look and amongst the decorations there are some homemade ones. "Did you guys make these?"

"Yeah, they are what we made at school. Mum insists on putting them on the tree every year, it's a bit embarrassing," Ben laughs.

"No, I think it's wonderful to have something that you made all those years ago, it's priceless."

The mirrors have been made to look like the windows of homes, and it looks amazing, so inviting.

"It's about time you got here, we are starving!" exclaims Damon as we enter the lounge.

"Sorry guys, that's my fault. I ran over time at work and the traffic was crazy," I say as I hug and kiss them all hello. The whole family is here, even Ethan.

We sit down at the table and I notice Chelsea has placed herself between Ben and I and she snuggles into him. I look at them and I see he is in heaven, he really loves this little girl. He looks up, smiles and mouths *'I love you,' then goes back to talking to Chelsea.*

Justin is heating up Noah's bottle. I lean over to Piper. "Can I feed him, please?" The whole room stops what they are doing and look at me. "What?"

"Carly, you nearly drowned my son last time you fed him. Do you think you can do a better job this time?" laughs Piper.

"Shut up you, just give me the baby," I laugh as I make my way over to Piper. I take Noah from her and notice he has grown a lot in the last month. He is more aware and he has great head control. Justin hands me the bottle after he has checked the temperature. Lucy and Kelsey dish up the meal but everyone is waiting for me. "Guys please start eating, I will eat while I feed this little man."

"Are you sure you can handle that? I know multitasking is not your strong point," smiles Damon.

"I can't reply to you how I would like to because I would have to put a lot of money in the swear jar," I say sarcastically. "Ben, would you mind cutting my meat up for me?" I manage to feed both Noah and myself with the minimum of mess. I look down at Noah and notice he is smiling at me. "Awww how cute, he's smiling at me," I announce excitedly.

"I hate to burst your bubble but I think he has wind," explains Darcy.

"Really? That sucks. I have no clue how to burp him," I say as I look at Ben for some help.

"Give him here and I'll do it," says Ben. I pass Noah to Ben and mouth 'thank you'. Darcy was right, Noah has wind. I love watching Ben with Chelsea and Noah, he is so confident and loving in everything he does with them.

After we clean-up and are all in the lounge chatting, I turn to Damon and ask, "How's Emery?"

"Yeah, she's good. She's with her family tonight but she's coming here for Christmas dinner."

"So things going well for the two of you?"

"You're very nosey, Carly," laughs Damon.

"And that's a surprise how? I like her and you look happy when you're with her."

"I like her too, she's different from the other girls I have been out with, she puts me in my place and I find that sexy as fuck. She's got a great sense of humour and is really feisty, she keeps me on my toes."

"You, my friend, have it bad. When Richardson men fall they fall hard and fast," I laugh. I'm happy things are going well for him, he's a good guy.

When it goes dark we all go out the front to see if we can spot Santa and his reindeers in the sky and we go for a walk up the street to see the Christmas lights. There are a lot of families doing the same thing. Chelsea and Ben hold onto Roger's lead while we all take it in turns pushing Noah in his pram.

Ben and I head up to bed just after midnight. It's a warm night so we have the window and curtains open and there is a nice breeze coming off the ocean. We get changed and lay there looking at each other, talking.

"Do you want to exchange our gifts in private or with all the family?" I ask Ben.

"I think for our first Christmas together I would like to do it in private, if that's ok with you?"

"Of course, when do you want to do it?"

Ben looks at his watch. "It's technically Christmas Day, so we can do it now or wait until the morning."

"I vote for now," I squeal, then jump up out of bed and get Ben's present from my bag as Ben grabs mine from his bag. "You first," I say as I hand him my gift and card. It seems to take Ben forever to read the card I get him, I made sure it had beautiful words in it telling him how much he means to me and how much I love him.

"Babe, that's beautiful," he says as he leans in to kiss me. Then he opens the shark dive voucher and his eyes are as wide as saucers. "Carly, this is wonderful, I have wanted to do a shark dive for ages. Thank you so much, babe, I love it." He engulfs me in a hug and kisses the shit out of me.

Ben finally lets me go and then hands me my present and card. I squeeze and shake it. "Carly, really? I am pretty sure you did that yesterday when it arrived so don't try that with me, just open them."

"Yeah, ok, you got me," I giggle. I open and read the card, it has beautiful words in it just like the one I bought for Ben. "That's perfect, thank you. You know how important cards are to me and you did good," I say as I kiss him. I slowly pull the paper off the present and Ben is jumping out of his skin.

"Are you doing that on purpose? Just rip the bloody paper will you."

"Is this your present or mine?" I ask.

"Yours but you're killing me here."

"Ok, ok," I say as I rip off the paper. I open the box and there is a note inside: *Merry Christmas Carly, I hope you get everything you deserve in life xx.* I lift up the note and there is a thumb drive underneath it. I hold it up and look at Ben with a puzzled look.

"What's that, babe?" asks Ben.

"The present you got me."

"No it's not, why would I get you a thumb drive?"

"It could be the photos from my birthday," I say.

"It could be, but where's the present I got you?"

"I thought this was it. To my knowledge this is the only thing that has been delivered to our home. I'm confused," I say with a worried look.

"Let's see what's on it," Ben says as he gets off the bed to get his lap top. We settle down on the bed waiting for the lap top to come to life, then Ben puts in the thumb drive and presses play. The screen is blank for a couple of seconds before it comes to life with one of my baby photos then one when I was a toddler and photos right up until I was about sixteen. "You were a cute baby," he says as he snuggles into my neck.

As Ben is kissing my neck, the photos stop and there is a grainy vision of a bedroom. I'm not really paying it too much attention because I think it's another photo, and plus Ben is making it hard to concentrate. After a while I look back at the screen and notice there is a person moving on the lap top, I focus my eyes to look harder and I stop in my tracks. I'm frozen and I feel sick.   "Ben stop it." I say

"Mmmmhmmmmm," says Ben as he ignores me and continues to kiss my neck and shoulder.

"Ben please stop it!" I shriek.

He pulls away from me and looks at me with a confused look. "What?"

I can't move "Tu..turn it o..off."

Ben looks at the screen "WHAT THE FUCK!" he yells as he rips the thumb drive out of the lap top and looks back at me with disgust. TO BE CONTINUED...

ACKNOWLEDGEMENTS

Besides having my children, writing Ben and Carly's story has been the scariest and most exciting thing I have ever done. It was a secret I was able to keep from everyone for six months and then I had to talk to someone. Tracey, I will be forever grateful that you kept my secret and always found time to listen to me when I needed to talk about my characters.

Donz, my west coast best friend. We've known each other for over thirty years and in that time we have cried together, laughter a lot together and danced our way through countless concerts. I know my life would be empty without you, Craig and the kids in it. Thank you for encouraging me in this new chapter. I have always considered you my sister from another mother.

Sue, my east coast best friend. The day we were introduced I knew you would play a major part in my life and I have enjoyed our journey especially when we go travelling. My life would be empty without you and the kids in it. Thank you for your support and encouragement.

Thank you Rocky Hudson for accepting the job of editing my first book and making my words make sense. You're a very brave woman.

A big thank you to Liz Atherton of Conscious Care Publishing for encouraging me and being there to answer any question I had. Especially walking me through the basic use of a computer. I really need to catch up with the twenty first century.

To Teresa, Laura, Gill and Carolyn. Even though you didn't realise it you all contributed to this book through conversations, all the good times and laughs we shared.

Throughout my life my parents have always encouraged me to try my best and enjoy what I do. There is nothing greater than a parent telling you that they are proud of you. I am very lucky to have the parents I have.

To my daughters, you are my biggest pride and joy. Thank you for choosing me to be your mother.

My models, Chris and Tahlia. Thank you, thank you, thank you for agreeing to be on the front cover.

To my Husband. You have been my greatest support throughout this journey. You haven't complained when I've dropped everything and hide away in the bedroom writing or when I come to bed in the early hours of the morning because I was onto a great idea. I am so lucky you found me and I love you more than words can say.

Last but not least to my readers. I hope you enjoyed the beginning of Ben and Carly's story as much as I enjoyed writing it. I promise part two is in the works.

Thanks
Amanda